Praise for

DOROTHY CLARK

and her novels

"Clark's novel is a dynamic story of two
lonely people in a desperate search for love.
The conflict is riveting and the plot fast-paced.
Throw in a troubled hero, and innocent but
determined heroine and a truly nasty bad guy,
and you have a fabulous story."
—*Romantic Times BOOKclub* on *Beauty for Ashes*

"Clark's fabulous characterization
brings the story to life."
—*Romantic Times BOOKclub* on
Joy for Mourning

"Dorothy Clark is an astounding author! In a word,
Joy For Mourning is brilliant. Ms. Clark has combined
elements of inspirational and historical romance to
create a superb and supremely satisfying novel.
Joy for Mourning is a definite keeper."
—*Cataromance*

DOROTHY CLARK

Beauty for Ashes

Steeple
Hill®

Published by Steeple Hill Books™

STEEPLE HILL BOOKS

**Steeple
Hill®**

ISBN 0-373-47069-X

BEAUTY FOR ASHES

Copyright © 2004 by Dorothy Clark

www.SteepleHill.com

Printed in U.S.A.

This book is dedicated to my husband,
Ralph—because he's my Justin.
Thanks, honey, for being my hero, now and always.

Chapter One

New York
March, 1820

Elizabeth stopped outside the door of her father's study to gather her courage. She was certain his summons was about her refusal to accept Reginald Burton-Smythe's offer of marriage, and equally certain he would be very angry. There was simply no help for it. She couldn't abide Mr. Burton-Smythe. His mere presence made her skin crawl. And no one, not even her father, could force her to speak words of acceptance to him.

Elizabeth pressed her hands to her abdomen, drew a slow, deep breath to ease the sudden, painful spasm in her stomach and opened the door—delay would only increase her father's ire. She stepped inside, closing the door quietly behind her. The room smelled of smoke, after-dinner port and cigars. The combination did little to help the state of her stomach. "You wished to see me, Father?"

Ezra Frazier looked up, placed the paper he was reading on his desk and motioned her forward. "I understand from Burton-Smythe you refused his hand. Is that the right of it?"

His tone of voice did not bode well for her. Fear moistened her palms. Elizabeth pressed them to the soft velvet fabric of her long skirt. "Yes, Father, it is."

His features tightened. "Tomorrow when he comes calling, you will ask his forgiveness and tell him you accept." He lifted the paper from his desk and resumed reading.

She was dismissed. As easily as that her life was ruined—any hope for future happiness destroyed. Anger overrode the fear clamped around Elizabeth's chest. She squared her shoulders and forced words out of her constricted throat. "I'm sorry, Father, I cannot...I will not...accept Mr. Burton-Smythe's offer of marriage."

Shock spread across her father's face. The vein at his right temple pulsed. He rose to his feet. "You dare to defy me?"

The soft, icy tone of his voice made Elizabeth shiver in spite of the anger heating her blood. She searched for words to turn away his wrath. "It is not out of defiance I speak, Father. Rather, it is revulsion and fear of Mr. Burton-Smythe that gives me voice."

"Make me no puling excuses, Elizabeth!" The flames of the fire glittered in her father's cold, steel-gray eyes as he looked at her. "The betrothal agreement has been signed. When you wed Burton-Smythe the warehouse property he owns on South Street comes to me. My fortune will double—and more yet. I'll not lose my gain because of your mewling fear."

"But, Father, I—"

"Silence! I'll hear no more excuses. I've long sought that property and it *will* be mine. Now go to your room and prepare yourself to accept Mr. Burton-Smythe tomorrow. The banns will be read on Sunday."

Elizabeth's stomach churned. She took a deep breath. "I'm sorry to cause you distress, Father—but I will not wed Mr. Burton-Smythe."

The vein at her father's temple swelled. He placed his hands on his desk and leaned toward her. "Do not stand stubborn in this matter, Elizabeth—there are ways to ensure your compliance. It would be well if you yield gracefully—but yield you will."

Elizabeth stared into her father's eyes and knew further protest was useless. He would not listen to her. Greed was his master, and she nothing more than chattel to him. It had always been thus. She swallowed back the bile rising into her throat, lifted her long skirts and walked to the door.

"Elizabeth."

She paused. Took a breath. "Yes, Father?"

"I'll hear no complaints from Burton-Smythe. When you are wed—be as other wives and suffer your fate in silence."

Elizabeth shuddered and shook off the memory. She would not think of that meeting with her father two nights ago, or of the events that followed. Yesterday was a horror that must be forgotten. It robbed her of strength. She would think only of today. What would happen today?

Moisture filmed her eyes. Elizabeth blinked it away and

stared at the carriage waiting on the cobblestone street below. He was going to do it. *Oh, God, help me. Please help me!*

The front door of the house opened and her father stepped out onto the stoop. Elizabeth yanked open the double sashes of her bedroom window. "Father, stop! I *beg* you—please don't do this to me!"

Ezra Frazier halted.

Hope, born of desperation, trapped the breath in Elizabeth's lungs. She braced herself on the sill and leaned forward, willing her father to heed her plea. He removed his top hat and tilted his head back until their gazes met. "Close the window, Elizabeth."

Everything in her went still. The chill of displeasure in her father's eyes was colder than the March air blowing in around her. A shiver slithered down her spine. Cold knots formed in her stomach. That was it then. He was going to meet with Reginald Burton-Smythe to complete the wedding arrangements, and nothing she could say or do would change his mind. He had coveted that waterfront property for too long to let it slip through his grasping fingers now.

Elizabeth straightened, clenching her hands into fists at her sides as she watched her father walk down the marble steps, cross the sidewalk, and climb into the waiting carriage. Money was her father's god. His business properties all he cared about. He ruled over them and his household with an iron hand, showing no one love or mercy—and always he had his way. But not this time. No, not this time. *This* was about the rest of her life. And she would die before she would give herself to the man who had attacked her last night.

The driver cracked his whip.

Elizabeth flinched as if the lash had been laid against her own flesh. A sick emptiness replaced her vestige of last hope. She closed and latched the window sashes, then, lifted her chin and strode to her wardrobe. The sharp beat of the horse's hoofs against the cobblestone street rang in her ears as she fastened her cloak around her shoulders. The rumble of the carriage wheels spurred her resolve. She dragged the large drawstring bag she had made during her sleepless night from its hiding place, put the possessions she had chosen to take with her inside, then pulled from her pocket the note she had written.

Father and Mother,

I cannot marry Mr. Burton-Smythe. I could not endure it. As you intend to force that union upon me, you leave me no choice. I must go.

Elizabeth

Her stomach churned. She swallowed hard, drew another steadying breath, and placed the note on her bed. It was done. She was ready to go. All she needed now was her money, and the key.

Elizabeth snatched up the few coins hidden in her sewing box, dropped them into her reticule, then stepped to her dresser. Her hands trembled as she unscrewed the base of the pewter candlestick and dumped the key hidden there onto her upturned palm. She curled her fingers tightly around the small, cold metal shaft. *Thank God for Miss Essie. Oh, thank God her governess had hidden the key all those years ago!*

A rush of tears stung her swollen, burning eyes. She blinked them away, pulled on her kid gloves, then hurried to her bedroom door and pressed her ear against the flat center panel, listening for any sound of movement in the hallway beyond. She heard nothing.

Heartened by the silence, Elizabeth leaned down and fitted the key into the lock. The click of the bolt sliding back was loud in the silence. For a long moment she waited, then, grasping the knob firmly she turned it ever so slowly and eased the door open a crack.

There was no one in sight.

The air trapped in her lungs expelled in a burst of relief. She stepped into the hallway, locked her door, then tiptoed along the corridor to the top of the staircase. Footsteps sounded in the entrance hall below.

Elizabeth jolted to a stop. She whirled about and darted to the side of the stairs, pressing her body back against the wall where she would be hidden from view. *Whoever it is, don't let them come upstairs! Please, God, don't let them come upstairs!* Her heart hammered wildly against her ribs as the footsteps began to climb.

"Alice!"

Elizabeth gasped and squeezed more tightly against the wall at the sound of her mother's voice.

"I want no one upstairs until Mr. Frazier returns! Go tidy the drawing room."

The maid's footsteps retreated. Doors closed.

Elizabeth sagged against the wall, then immediately righted herself and moved to the banister to peek down into the room below. It was empty. *Thank heaven! If her mother should discover her*— She jerked her mind from the debilitating thought, took a firm grip on the handrail and started down the stairs.

There was a loud creak.

Elizabeth's heart leaped into her throat. She froze in place—waited. No one came to investigate. After a few moments, she tightened her grip on the railing and crept forward, her mouth dry as she tested each step, her long skirts sliding from tread to tread with a sibilant whisper that to her ears sounded like a roar. When she reached the solid floor of the entrance hall her heart was pounding so violently she felt giddy. She inched her way to the front door, eased it open and slid outside. The frigid air stung her face.

Elizabeth pulled her fur-lined hood in place, tucked the drawstring bag out of sight beneath her cloak, then rushed down the marble steps to the sidewalk and hurried away.

"Justin, do sit down! I hate it when you prowl about like a cat. Or should I say a nervous bridegroom?"

Justin Davidson Randolph turned and looked down into his sister's upturned face—into long, heavily lashed blue eyes so like his own. "If that was an attempt at levity, Laina, it failed miserably. I suggest you save your humor for a more appropriate time."

"But humor *is* appropriate at a farce."

The barb hit its mark. Justin frowned. "Be careful, Laina. You go too far."

"No, Justin, *you* go too far. 'Widower' and 'Interested' indeed! It's like a child's game."

The muscle along his jaw twitched. Justin took a calming breath. "Laina Brighton, marriage hasn't changed you at all. You can be a most provoking woman. I assure you it's no game. I called myself 'Widower' to protect my identity from the women who answered my Article of Intent."

"Which proves you know the character of the women you are dealing with! Including 'Interested.'"

"Laina—" He put a wealth of warning in the growled name.

"I'm sorry, Justin. I don't want to quarrel with you. But this plan of yours is ludicrous. I know you've been hurt. Terribly hurt. And I don't blame you for feeling bitter. But *please* don't do this to yourself. One rotten apple—"

His disgusted snort cut her off. "One?"

"All right, *two*. But Rebecca and Margaret were selfish, schem—"

"Laina, that's all past. Please—don't speak their names ever again!" The muscle at his jaw twitched again. Justin rubbed the spot, trying to ease the tightness away.

"Very well. I'll not mention them again—except to say they are not worth what you are doing to yourself."

He shouldn't have told her. Maybe if he didn't answer she'd give up. Justin shook his head and moved away to stare down into the fire. It didn't work. She followed him. His back muscles tensed at the light touch of her hand on his jacket.

"Justin, forget this plan. Give yourself another chance. Give those chil—"

She stopped as he pivoted about to face her. "No more arguments, Laina. Granted, Rebecca and Margaret were less than admirable women. Is that not all the more reason to do what I am doing?" He lifted his lips in a cynical smile. "You can't deny I've not done well choosing with my heart. It seems to have an abominable lack of good taste."

Tears welled into her eyes at his words. She glared up at him. "I *hate* this change in you, Justin. You've turned into this cold, remote, untouchable stranger. I want you to *stop* this foolishness! I want my warm, gentle, loving brother back. You're going to destroy your life."

"Don't cry, Lainy." The old childhood name slipped softly from Justin's lips. He drew his older sister into his arms and held her close. "I know a marriage of convenience is not ideal. But at least it will be an honest relationship."

He held up a hand to forestall her comment as she jerked backward out of his arms and drew breath to speak. "Yes, an *honest* relationship, even if it will be based purely on greed. At least this time the avarice will be out in the open."

Justin frowned, and turned away to put on his coat. Laina was right, he *had* changed—his voice sounded as cold and hard as his heart felt. He lifted her wool, fur-trimmed coat off the chair and held it for her. "We've talked enough. It's time to go."

He straightened the coat's overcape about her shoulders, handed her the matching coal-scuttle bonnet and opened the drawing room door, stepping back to let her precede him into the entrance hall. "The Haversham Coach House is some distance from here. Surely you'd not have me keep my bride waiting?" His attempt to ease the tension between them with the light remark failed. He winced inwardly as Laina's eyes flashed with anger. There was an audible snap from the bonnet's satin chin ribbons as she yanked them into place and tied them.

"She can wait till the stars fall from the sky for all I care! And don't call her your *bride* in my presence. I'll never accept her as such."

Justin's heart gave a painful wrench as Laina snatched her fur muff from the seat of the chair and swept past him. He didn't want to hurt her, but he couldn't let her dissuade him from the path he had chosen. He had been made a fool of twice. He didn't intend that it should ever happen again. But he needed a suitable wife—a mother for the children.

Justin set his jaw in grim determination, grabbed his felt top hat from the chair and followed Laina out her front door and down the brick steps to the waiting cabriolet he had hired.

Ora Scraggs gripped the sideboard of the wagon as it made its lumbering, lurching progress down the road toward New York. March 28, 1820—her wedding day. At least it would have been if it weren't for that addlebrained, dim-witted coach driver. The grip of her hand on the edge of the board seat tightened as she glared down at the long, jagged tear in the skirt of the red wool traveling outfit she had stolen from her mistress. A pox on him! A pox on the driver and his whole family! If he hadn't been going so fast he might have missed that deep hole, the wheel wouldn't have broken and—

Oh, what was the use? Why mull it over? The accident

had happened. She was beaten. And she had planned so carefully! From the moment she'd overheard her mistress and her friends reading and laughing about that Article of Intent, she'd been figuring her every move. Now, the splendid, genteel entrance she had planned for her arrival at the Haversham Coach House in the hired coach and fancy stolen clothes was ruined. The time of her marriage appointment with "Widower" long past. Now she had to think up a new scheme, find another rich man to diddle. And she would! Her plan to have "Widower's" money might be denied her by today's accident, but she was clever. She would think of something. There were a lot of rich gentlemen in New York. And meanwhile…

Ora cast a speculative glance at the farmer driving the wagon and her lips curved upward in a self-satisfied smirk. It was a bit of luck he had happened by and offered her a ride after the accident. She could cozy up to him until after he sold his grain in New York tonight—until he had all that lovely money she could steal. But she'd best get at it—it was already twilight. She smiled and slid closer to him.

Chapter Two

❧

"Oh!" Elizabeth stumbled over an exposed root, falling to her hands and knees on the hard-packed earth. The jar of her landing sent pain radiating throughout her bruised, exhausted body. She felt the jolt at every spot where Reginald's angry blows had landed.

She struggled to her feet, brushed the dry dirt from her cloak, then reached for the drawstring bag. Sharp pain shot through the tired muscles along her spine as her abused body protested. She eased herself erect and walked on, stinging darts prickling her cold, aching, satin-slipper-clad feet with every step. *If only her father hadn't taken her shoes and boots!*

Elizabeth pressed her lips together and set her mind against her discomfort. Ever since she ran away this morning she had been walking, searching for a way out of town, but soon she would be able to rest at the coach house that kind old man with the oyster barrow had told her of. It was only a little farther.

Rapid footsteps sounded behind her. Elizabeth started. Was that one of the servants Reginald had out searching for her? She'd managed to elude one of them earlier when she'd overheard him asking about her at The Black Horse Inn—but if she was caught out here in the open...

Panic seized her. She glanced toward the shadows at the side of the road but it was too late to hide. She swung the cloth bag in front of her, covered it with her cloak, then pulled her hood farther forward, ducking her head so her face would be fully hidden from view. Fear propelled her forward as the footsteps behind her grew louder; drew nearer. It took all of her inner strength not to look over her shoulder—not to drop the bag and run.

Please, God, don't let it be one of Reginald's lackeys! Please, God.

The footsteps picked up speed, then veered away down a narrow alley on her left. Elizabeth stopped. Dull fists of pain pounded at her temples. She set the bag on the ground at her feet and lifted her trembling hands to rub the pain away. A cat, prowling in the shadows, leaped to the top of a fence and yowled. Her frayed nerves jolted.

Oh, Lord, help me! I must find this Haversham Coach House, Lord. I must find a way out of town before—

What if she hadn't enough money to hire a carriage? Elizabeth drove her hand into her reticule, then stood staring at the few coins on her palm as the throbbing in her temples increased. She'd had no time to plan—to think of anything beyond escape—and now it was too late.

She frowned, then drew her weary body fully erect. She had no time for such discouraging thoughts. The coins clinked together dully as she dropped them back into her reticule. She was free of Reginald Burton-Smythe, that was what mattered. She would simply go as far as her funds would take her.

"But first, I must find this Haversham Coach House."

The sound of her voice startled her. Elizabeth glanced quickly up and down the street, but there was no one to overhear. She was all alone in the fading twilight. The thought brought a feeling of desolation so unexpected and powerful she gasped. She swallowed past the sudden lump in her throat, picked up the cloth bag, and walked on.

Justin pushed aside the remains of his half-eaten meal and looked up at "Judge," the man who had been a surrogate father to Laina and him since their own father's death in 1812. "Well, Judge, it seems I owe you an apology for wasting your time. Considering the lateness of the hour I can only surmise that 'Interested' lost her interest, and has changed her mind about marrying 'Widower.' It seems I cannot even *buy* loyalty from a woman."

"Justin!"

"Don't sound so shocked, Laina." He slid his gaze to his sister's face. "I'm simply stating the truth." He flung his napkin down on the scarred wood table and surged to his feet. "I'll have the carriages brought round."

"Not so fast, my boy."

Justin glanced down at the age-spotted hand gripping his arm, then lifted his gaze to the judge's face. "What is it?"

The elderly man dipped his head in the direction of the

entrance. "As much as I wish it were not so—I believe that may be your intended bride."

Justin turned. A woman in a blue wool, fur-trimmed cloak stood just inside the door looking about.

"Are you still determined to go through with this ridiculous marriage?"

The judge sounded less than enthusiastic. Justin nodded. "I am. As long as my conditions are met."

The judge sighed. "Very well. I have said all that I can say." He rose slowly to his feet.

Justin moved to join him.

The older man shook his gray head in negation. "You wait here. I want to talk privately with this woman to assure myself she fully understands the conditions of this preposterous union. Unless I do, I will have no part of it."

Justin frowned. "You leave me no choice."

"As was my intent." The judge gave him a fatherly pat on the shoulder and walked away.

"How may I serve you, madam?"

Elizabeth fastened a wary gaze on the proprietor. "You may tell me if a gentleman has been making inquiries about—that is, if *anyone* has inquired—"

"I believe I'm the one to answer that question."

Elizabeth jumped and spun about. A portly, prosperous-looking older man of medium height gave her a brief nod. "I am here on behalf of the gentleman you were asking about. I am Judge William Braden."

Judge? *The law!* Reginald had set the law on her to force her to honor the betrothal contract her father had signed! Elizabeth darted a panicked glance at the door beyond the judge, gauging the distance to freedom. It was too close to him. She'd never get the door open before he seized her. She looked back at the elderly man, who was still talking.

"The gentleman you were asking after has engaged my services to handle the legalities of this...er...situation. And, as the matter is of a delicate nature, we have arranged use of a private room. If you will come with me?"

Elizabeth cringed as the man picked up the bag that had fallen from her suddenly nerveless fingers, then grasped her elbow. Her stomach roiled. *He'd found her.* Reginald had hired a judge and—*Reginald.* She gazed frantically about as the judge ushered her into a small room. There was no one waiting there.

Relief stole the strength from her legs. She collapsed onto a hard wood chair, watching as the judge closed the door. There was no bolt. She might yet make good her escape. Oh, if only she weren't so weary! If only she could *think!*

Elizabeth straightened her shoulders and lifted her chin as the judge came to stand in front of her. One thing she knew. She would not go back. Jail would be better than marriage to Reginald Burton-Smythe.

"To begin, let me say that I do not approve of the action being taken by my client."

The judge's deep, authoritative voice cut across Elizabeth's dark thoughts. Her heart leaped with hope. If he didn't approve, would he help her escape?

"However, such actions are perfectly legal."

The abrupt words plunged her back into despair.

"As for you, I want to be certain, in my own mind, that you fully understand the seriousness of what you are doing before this...this *escapade* goes any further. In light of that, I feel it best if I review the circumstances of your position. After I have done so we can discuss any consequences that might depend from it."

Consequences? Shock streaked along Elizabeth's nerves. Perhaps she *would* go to jail. She clasped her hands tightly in her lap to hide their trembling.

"Shall I proceed?"

She gave a polite nod.

"Very well." The judge clasped his hands behind his back and cleared his throat. "As you know, my client stands ready to marry the woman that meets the qualifications set forth in his published Article of Intent." His voice sharpened. "*My* purpose, is to make certain those qualifications are understood and met. The first being, of course, that you agree to a marriage of convenience only."

Elizabeth lifted her head and stared at the man standing before her. Whatever could he be talking about?

"*Well?* You do understand what is meant by a marriage of convenience, do you not?"

The words cracked through the air. Elizabeth jumped. "I believe I do." Her cheeks warmed. "However, I'm not certain—"

"A marriage of convenience is one in which both parties agree to fulfill all the duties and responsibilities of a marriage except those of an intimate nature. It is a marriage that is never consummated." The judge scowled down at her. "Now, do you understand?"

"Yes." Elizabeth's cheeks burned. She could not force herself to meet the judge's direct gaze. She took a deep breath and focused her attention on his chin. Her pulse quickened as he reached for a chair, then sat facing her.

"You would agree to such a marriage? A marriage of convenience?"

"Yes, I would." Elizabeth made her voice very firm. She didn't understand why he should be asking her opinion, but after last night that sort of marriage sounded wonderful to her.

"Very well. My client has signed a legal document outlining such a stipulation. If all other particulars are met, his bride will be required to sign also."

It was a mistake! The thought sizzled through Elizabeth's mind, stiffening her back. It *had* to be a mistake. Reginald Burton-Smythe would never countenance such a situation or put his signature on something she'd see before a wedding. Last night proved that. Clearly, this matter had nothing to do with him—or her.

Elizabeth drew in a deep breath as the tightness in her chest released. She had only to explain the misunderstanding and she would be free to flee the city. "Sir, I believe you have made an— Oh!"

The judge reached out and pushed the hood back from her face. Elizabeth recoiled, turning her head so the bruising on her left cheek wouldn't show.

The old man's expression softened as her hood fell away. "How old are you, child?"

"E-eighteen."

"*Eighteen.* And you would be willing to enter into a relationship without intimacy for the rest of your life?"

"I would." Elizabeth winced at the soreness in her shoulder as she reached up and pushed at the curls that had popped free of her hair combs. *How unkempt she must look.* She pulled her hood back in place. "I don't care about intimacy. And I don't want to...to be consummated. Ever! But I—"

"That is sufficient answer. I do not wish to hear intimate details."

"But, sir, you don't understan—"

"Not another word! We shall proceed."

Elizabeth stared at him, taken aback by the sharp, censorial tone in his voice.

"What of children?"

"Children?"

"Yes, my client has young children. Babes really. Do you get on with them?"

"Of course. I love children. But, sir, truly I must explain—"

"No need. That is sufficient answer. And the last condition that must be met." The judge locked his gaze on her eyes. "That leaves only the settlement to be arranged before I call in my client and perform the ceremony."

"*Ceremony!*" Elizabeth leaped to her feet.

"Of course, ceremony. I told you this is to be a legally binding union." The judge leaned back in his chair, studying her. "This will be a true marriage in all but intimacy." His voice emphasized the point quietly. "I thought you understood that. If you did not—it's not too late to refuse my client's offer."

Elizabeth's mind reeled. He was offering *her* this strange marriage proposal from a man she had never met. Had never even seen! Why, such a deed was out of the question. And yet—he'd said it would be a legal marriage without consummation. She would be protected from Reginald and her parents by— No! She couldn't possibly. *Could she?*

Elizabeth sank back down onto the chair. If she accepted this strange offer of a marriage of convenience she would be safe. She would be legally protected from Reginald Burton-Smythe by marriage. *Safe!* Her mind locked on the word.

"Do you wish to refuse my client's offer?"

Elizabeth stared down at her trembling hands, then, aghast at what she was about to do, lifted her gaze to the judge's face and shook her head. "No."

"Very well. Then let us get on with the matter. There is still the settlement to discuss."

"The settlement?"

"Yes. The generous provision my client agreed to bestow on the woman that met his qualifications. He wishes the matter settled before the ceremony, and has empowered me to discuss it with you to decide upon an amount that is mutually acceptable."

Elizabeth gaped at him. This situation was becoming more and more confusing. She had heard of a bride's dowry, but she had never heard of a groom's settlement. She went very still as a glimmer of suspicion flickered through her mind. "Tell me, sir, is this 'groom's settlement' customary?"

A look of disgust passed fleetingly across the judge's distinguished features. "No, it is not. My client is making the settlement as a token of his good faith."

"I see." A sick, sinking feeling hit the pit of Elizabeth's stomach. It all made sense now. The judge's client—whoever he was—was *buying* a wife. And they thought she was that woman.

Elizabeth swallowed hard, bowing her head and fighting back tears of shame. She would have to allow the misconception to continue, but at least she could refuse the man's money. She lifted her head. "If this is not customary, sir, but is merely a gesture of your client's good faith, then I shall accept it as such—as a gesture."

"Of course. And the amount?"

She shook her head. "You mistake me, Judge Braden. There will be no amount. Your client has made a gesture which I have accepted. The money is not necessary. The offer of it is sufficient to establish good faith."

The judge's features went slack with shock. Elizabeth sat up a little straighter. "I understand that your client had no knowledge of the manner of person with whom he would be dealing. But—" Her voice broke. Tears of humiliation flooded her eyes. She lifted her chin and spoke with quiet dignity. "But I do not wish to feel purchased."

Her words faded away. There was dead silence in the room. It was broken by the sound of the judge's chair scraping backward on the floor as he rose to his feet. He inclined his head.

"My dear, I pray you will accept my apology on behalf of my client and myself. It was not our intent to insult you." He straightened and smiled down at her. "You are correct in your assumption. We had no idea of the manner of person with whom we would be dealing. You are a very pleasant surprise."

Elizabeth managed a shaky smile. "I pray your client may find me so."

The judge smiled and crossed to a small writing desk by the window. Elizabeth watched with trepidation as he removed some papers from his waistcoat pocket, spread them out, then selected a quill and dipped it into the ink pot. "Your full name, my dear?"

She took a deep breath. "Elizabeth Shannon Frazier."

The judge's hand froze in midair. He swivelled his head around, giving her a piercing look. "Did you say Frazier?"

Did he know her father? A spasm of fear closed Elizabeth's throat. She gave him a tremulous smile and nodded. For a long moment he studied her, then, to her immense relief, he turned, inscribed her name on one of the papers and reached for another.

She began to breathe again.

"What is he *doing* in there?" Justin drummed his long fingers on the table. "If he thinks he is going to keep me from—"

"Oh, hush!" Laina threw him a withering look and banged the teapot down onto the table. "I'm weary of hearing about this. What you're doing is wrong! You are a coward, my brother. You're willing to risk your money, but not your heart. Well, you're welcome to do so. But remember—if you can buy her, she will not be worth the price!"

She slammed his cup down in front of him. Tea sloshed over the rim into the saucer and splashed onto the table.

Justin grimaced and reached for his napkin to mop it up. "Laina, I know you feel strongly about what I am doing, but—"

"But you are determined to ruin your life. I know that, Justin. I know, also, that you are far too stubborn to listen to me." Laina's face tightened. Her gaze shifted to a point somewhere over his right shoulder. "The judge is beckoning."

"Finally!" Justin dropped his napkin onto the table and rose, stepping over to assist his sister from her chair. She laid her hand on his arm.

"Justin, I'm asking you one last time—I'm *begging* you—for your own sake, do not do this! It's not too late to change your mind. Give this woman whatever amount of money she and the judge have agreed upon and send her on her way. You can well afford to—"

"Buy an open, honest relationship based on greed." Justin heard the cold harshness in his voice and made an effort to soften it. "We've discussed this already, Laina."

"So we have." She drew herself up to her full height. "Very well, since you are determined to play the fool, Justin, do it quickly. I'm at the end of my patience!"

With a swish of her long skirts, Laina whirled about. Her boot heels clicked angrily against the wide plank floor as she walked across the common room.

Justin took a deep breath and followed her. He hesitated for a moment in the doorway of the little room as he caught sight of the hooded, cloak-draped figure of his intended bride standing in front of the judge, then, squaring his shoulders, he stepped into the dimly lit room and walked forward to take his place at her side.

Chapter Three

Elizabeth sat alone in the cabriolet absently twirling the gold band upon her finger. What had she done? She was *married!* To a total stranger! There had been no introduction, no exchange of pleasantries, nothing but the speaking of the vows.

A nervous giggle escaped her as she looked down at the ring. He had certainly been prepared. A careful man, her husband. *Husband! Oh, my!* She clamped her teeth down firmly on her lower lip as it started to tremble. Crying would help nothing; the deed was done.

The thought made her ill. Elizabeth took a deep breath and closed her eyes, leaning her head back against the padded seat. Had she lost her wits placing her life in the hands of a complete stranger? She didn't even know what the man looked like! She had been so nervous, frightened and ashamed during the brief ceremony, she had not once dared lift her head to look at him. Another nervous giggle burst forth. Perhaps that was just as well. Perhaps he was homely as a toad! Oh, what did it matter? She didn't care if he was the ugliest man in the world if he would take her away from here—if he would take her to a place where her parents or Reginald Burton-Smythe would never find her.

Approaching footsteps startled Elizabeth to attention. The *why* didn't matter, as long as he was honorable and kept his word. But if—

"Oh, God, this thing that I've done... There was no other way. I *have* to escape Reginald Burton-Smythe. Please, don't let this man be like him. Oh, God, *please* don't let him be like Reginald Burton-Smythe!"

The carriage leaned to one side, then quickly righted itself as the driver climbed aboard. Elizabeth's heart leaped into her throat choking off her whispered words. With horrified fascination she stared at the door handle as it dipped downward.

The door opened.

Her new husband tossed in a pile of lap robes, then climbed inside. For a moment, in the confined space, he loomed over her. Elizabeth shrank back against the seat, biting down hard on her lower lip to stop the scream clawing at her throat as her heart pumped wildly and her lungs forgot to breathe. From somewhere beyond the edge of a swirling darkness she heard him speak to her, and then there was nothing—nothing at all.

The horses' hooves clattered against the frost-hardened ground. The cabriolet lurched and rolled ahead. His bride jerked and sagged forward. "Madam?" No answer. Justin raised his voice. "Madam, I brought lap robes for your comfort." Still no answer. The woman was a sound sleeper. An unexpected blessing—there'd be no need for small talk on the journey to their night's lodging place.

Justin leaned forward to ease the slumped form of his new wife into the corner where she would have more protection from the bumps and jolts of the ride. The papers in his waistcoat pocket crackled. He curved his lips into a tight smile and gave his pocket a satisfied pat. There it was, his future, all safely planned out and committed to parchment. The marriage certificate, the bonded marriage agreement, and the financial settlement.

He frowned and reached for a lap rug. There had been no time to read the papers. What had he paid for her? Whatever the amount—and he had no doubt it was considerable—it was worth it. There would be no unpleasant surprises for him this time. He tucked the fur rug around his new wife. "If you were thinking of playing games with my money, madam, you would be wise not to try. I'm more than a match for a scheming female now."

Laina could not bear to watch the departure of her brother and the woman he had married. She turned her back on the hired cabriolet and faced the judge. "Well, he did it." She made no attempt to hide her angry astonishment. "He actually carried out that foolish plan and married a woman that would—would—" She bit off the rest of the irate words, curled her hands into fists and buried her face against the old man's shoulder.

"There, there, my dear." Judge Braden absently patted Laina's back as he stared after the departing cabriolet. "Don't despair, matters may well work out for the best." He chuckled softly. "Yes, indeed, matters may well turn out for the best."

"Judge!" Laina jerked her head back to look up at him. "I thought you loved Justin. How can you stand here and...and... Oh, words fail me!" She gave the elderly man a look that would have shriveled a lesser man and headed for his carriage.

"Laina, wait!" With a last, quick glance at the departing cabriolet, the judge hurried after her. "Let me explain, Laina. I— Here, let me do that." He removed her fingers from the handle and pulled open the carriage door. She refused his hand and climbed inside. The judge sighed and got in beside her.

The carriage lurched forward, then dipped and swayed as it crossed the courtyard and entered the rutted road. Laina jerked to one side, then held herself stiff and aloof, refusing to allow the motion to cause her body to come into contact with the judge.

"Laina, my dear, you are going to be terribly weary by the time you reach home if you do not relax. Besides, anger does not become you. Some women may look beautiful when they are angry—though I, personally, have never met one—but you..." The judge's infectious chuckle floated through the darkness to her. "You just turn red!"

Laina laughed in spite of herself. "Trying to get back into my good graces with flattery, Judge?" She relaxed back against the cushioned seat and glanced toward his dark form. "Very well, I forgive you. But all the same, I am hurt by your laughter."

"I know, my dear. But if you will permit me to explain, you will understand." The judge shook out a lap robe, spread it over her legs, then shook out another for himself. "Tell me, Laina, why did Justin devise this plan for a marriage of convenience?"

"Why? You know why. Or perhaps— Oh, Judge. Surely you weren't bamboozled by all those reasonable excuses Justin offered. Surely you knew…" She dismissed the excuses with one disparaging flick of her hand. "He was looking for a way to protect himself from further hurt and disappointment."

"Precisely! Your summation is correct, my dear. Justin needed a mother for those two children—but his main motive is to be safe from emotional entanglement. And, my dear Laina, your brother has never been farther removed from safety!"

Laina stiffened, and stared toward the judge. He was actually chortling with glee! "Have you taken leave of your senses?"

"No." The judge choked back his laughter. "It's only that I've been holding that back since the ceremony. Oh, Laina! That young lady—and I do mean *lady,* for there is breeding in every inch of her—is lovely. Absolutely lovely."

"*No!*"

"Yes." The judge wiped at his watering eyes. "Didn't you think it strange there was so little light in the room for the ceremony? I snuffed all but one candle! I was afraid if Justin had a good look at her he would refuse to marry her and try again with someone less appealing. The boy's only human after all."

"Why you wily, old— Is *that* why you had Thomas spirit her from the room so quickly? I thought you simply could not bear the sight of her any longer. I know I couldn't."

"No, no. Believe me, I found her lovely of face *and* character."

"Character?" Laina all but snorted. "I expected better of you, Judge." She threw a cool look his direction. "You are far too experienced to have your head turned by a pretty face. A woman of character does not blatantly sell herself."

"She refused the money."

"Refused it?" Laina gaped through the darkness at the judge's dark form. "She refused the settlement?"

"Indeed she did. And with such dignity and grace I felt the worst sort of bounder for having offered it!"

Laina burst into laughter.

"You find that amusing?"

"Amusing? No, not really." Laina yanked her hand out of her muff and grabbed for the hold strap as the carriage bounced over a deep rut in the road. "It's only that, for all your age and experience, you are still a man."

"And what does that mean?"

He sounded a little huffy. She smiled. The judge did not take kindly to truth he perceived as criticism. "It means you are sweet...and protective...and, *sometimes,* manipulated by cunning women with pretty faces." She put a teasing note in her voice. "I should know."

"That is different!"

Now he sounded defensive. "It may be." Laina made her tone placating.

The judge crossed his arms and leaned back against the seat. "She refused the money."

He obviously thought that was a strong point in the woman's favor. Laina sighed and leaned down to tuck the lap robe more closely about her boots. "That was quite clever of her. What better way to get into Justin's good graces? Any fool would know the generous settlement he offered is but a small portion of his wealth. And if she can make him trust her..." Laina straightened up and tucked her hands back into her muff. "Well—we both know what can happen." There was bitterness, fear and undeniable logic in her words.

The judge sighed heavily. "We must pray, Laina. We must continue to pray for Justin."

She shot a look his direction, then turned and stared straight ahead. "You pray if you wish, Judge, but I will not." Her voice was sharp with hurt and anger. "I prayed that God would keep Justin from ruining his life by marrying another low, greedy, scheming female and look what has happened. He's married to that—that *strumpet!*" She withdrew her hand from the muff and wiped sudden tears from her eyes. "God does not answer prayer. And I won't waste my time again!"

Chapter Four

❧

The cabriolet swept smartly into the courtyard of the Wetherstone Inn and rolled to a halt opposite the entrance. *At last!* Justin stretched the travel stiffness from his body, tossed his lap robe aside, and glanced at his bride—she was still sleeping. "Madam, wake up—we have arrived at our destination." The carriage swayed as the driver climbed from his seat. The horses snorted. "Madam?" There was no response.

Justin grasped his wife's shoulder and shook her lightly. Her head, hidden by the fur-lined hood, lolled forward onto her chest. A scowl creased his forehead. No one slept that soundly. The woman must be ill. Footsteps signaled the driver's approach. A blast of cold air hit him as the door was opened.

Justin scooped his new wife's limp body into his arms, climbed from the carriage and hurried toward the inn. With one booted foot he gave the door a solid, satisfying kick.

"Breams? *Josiah Breams!* Open the door!"

There was a protesting squeak of cold hinges. The door opened.

"Good evening, sir. We've been expecting you and your— Good heavens, sir!" The proprietor of the inn stared down at the cloak-draped body hanging across Justin's arms. "Has there been an accident, sir? Is your wife injured?"

"No, there's been no accident—she's taken ill." Justin pushed past the portly proprietor and headed for the stairs. "Have you prepared the room?"

"Oh, yes, sir." The little man closed the door and scurried forward, hurrying to get ahead of Justin's long-legged strides. "It's all exactly as you asked." He puffed his way up the long flight of stairs, using the banister to pull himself upward. "I'm sure you'll be pleased. I laid the fire and—"

"Save your air. You'll have an apoplectic fit." Justin followed the puffing, panting little man down the hall to a small, corner room.

"Yes, sir." The corpulent proprietor gasped out the words and opened the bedroom door. Justin brushed past the little man's protruding paunch and headed for the bed.

"There!" He deposited Elizabeth on the quilt-covered mattress and turned toward the proprietor who was busily poking up the fire. "I'll do that. You go get your wife to— What is it?" His eyes narrowed as he peered down at Josiah's face. "What's wrong?"

"My wife's not here."

"Not here? Then who is going to tend my wife?"

"Perhaps I might be of some assistance."

Justin pivoted. A tall, thin man with dark, penetrating eyes and brown hair stood in the open doorway. There was a black leather bag in his hand. "And who might you be?"

"Thaddeous Allen...at your service." The man gave a small, polite bow of his head. "I am a physician with the Pennsylvania Hospital."

"Come in, Dr. Allen, come in!" Justin crossed the room in three long strides and waved the doctor inside. "I would be most grateful if you would tend my wife. She has collapsed, and I am at a loss as to what to do for her."

"Yes. I witnessed your arrival. You seemed in need of aid, so I went for my bag."

"In need of aid?" Justin's left brow lifted. "You are a man of great tact, Doctor. I freely admit my helpless state."

"Then, if you will permit me?" The doctor's gaze slid past Justin to Elizabeth's still form as Josiah Breams left the room. At Justin's answering nod he crossed to the bed and placed his black bag on the nightstand. "Tell me, Mr. Randolph, when did your wife collapse?"

"You know me, Doctor?"

"Indeed. All of Philadelphia knows of Justin Randolph—especially those of us who have occasion to visit the waterfront."

Justin dipped his head. "You're too kind, Doctor. Now, about my wife..." He scowled at the inert form on the bed. "Perhaps *collapse* was too strong a word. She fell asleep while traveling and I was unable to rouse her upon our arrival."

"I see. I have one more question before I proceed. Is your wife with child?"

"With *child?* Of course not. We—" He stopped, staring at the doctor in sudden, stunned silence. How could he know? It was certainly possible. *With child!* Justin gave a short bark of laughter. So much for his clever plan. He had been tricked again. Made a fool of by a...a—

By sheer dint of will, Justin forced down the anger surging through him. "I cannot answer that question, Doctor. But, if you should find that to be the cause of her collapse, I would be most grateful if you would inform me at once. You see, we were married this evening."

There was a knock on the door. Justin whipped around and yanked it open. "What is it?"

"I've returned, sir. Josiah sent me. He said your bride's taken ill and you had need of me." The proprietor's wife glanced toward the bed.

"I do indeed." Justin stepped to one side allowing the woman entrance. His gaze swept to Thaddeous Allen. "Daisy will assist you in anything you require, Doctor. I shall be downstairs, awaiting your diagnosis." With a curt bow of his head he left the room.

The doctor whistled softly as the door clicked shut. "That is one angry man."

"He has a right. Likely he didn't plan on a weddin' night like this." Daisy Breams trudged to the bed and began to undo the fastenings on Elizabeth's cloak. "Likely she didn't either." She pushed the cloak off the young woman's shoulders and the hood fell away. "Here now, what's this?"

The doctor stepped closer. There was a large purple bruise swelling the left side of Justin Randolph's bride's face. He grabbed a spill from the box on the mantel, lit the candle on the nightstand, then slid it closer to the bed, studying the discoloration. He frowned and stepped back out of the way. "Remove her gown, Daisy. But proceed carefully—I expect she has other injuries."

Justin sat alone at a table in the common room of the inn. His face felt as if it were carved of stone. Every few seconds he lifted the fingers of his right hand slightly, then dropped them back. The measured thumps were the only sound in the room, save for the crackle of the fire and an occasional snore from one of the patrons that had disdained the use of a bed upstairs and fallen asleep sprawled in his chair, or across a table.

The fire belched a puff of smoke into the quiet room that spread itself across the low, beamed ceiling adding its acrid smell to that of hot candle wax, potent libations, stale food and unwashed bodies.

Justin frowned and waved the smoke away. How had such an obvious thing escaped his attention? His offer was the perfect answer for a woman who had gotten herself into a compromising situation and had no way out. And he—fool that he was—not only had he offered such a woman the perfect solution to her dilemma, he had paid her to accept it! What an idiot he was, thinking he could buy honesty. He had put his trust in the larcenous streak he had fallen prey to with the other women in his life, and now this!

Women are not even honorable in their dishonor. The incongruous thought brought a bitter smile to Justin's lips. One thing was certain. There would be no friendship with this lying, scheming woman. He wasn't *that* big a fool.

He lifted his hand, raked his fingers through his hair, then resumed his intermittent thudding. He had acquaintances who used their money to purchase love—or what passed for love in their eyes—from both wife and mistress. And with his wealth he had any number of women eager to marry or serve him in that manner, but something inside him shriveled at the thought. He wanted no part of it. He'd had his fill of phony affection turned on to coax a gift, or money, from him. A marriage of convenience had seemed the perfect answer.

A wry smile tugged at the corners of Justin's mouth. At least in that he was right. This woman didn't have to pretend to love him. All he required of her was that she sign a paper, take her settlement, and follow the rules of the agreement. But to do so while carrying another man's child! A scowl knit his brows together. This was worse than Margaret. At least Margaret had told him about the baby she carried *before* their marriage. Of course he had already been well and fairly caught, playing knight in shining armor to her helpless maiden.

Helpless maiden? "Hah!" The bark of scornful laughter burst from Justin's throat. He grasped the glass beside his hand and drank the contents swiftly, hoping to rid himself of the flat, metallic taste of bitterness in his mouth. He stared down at the glass, wanting to smash it. It was empty—like his life. His hand tightened.

"Mr. Randolph? I have finished my examination of your wife."

Justin set the glass on the table and looked up at the doctor. "And?"

"Let me begin by saying that I spoke in haste earlier, not knowing of your very recent marriage. I had no wish to malign your wife's character. It is a simple fact of my profession that most often when I am confronted by a married woman in a swoon, the diagnosis is that she is with child."

"I see. And am I to understand by this explanation, Doctor, that you have eliminated that possibility as far as my wife is concerned?"

"Not entirely. But, in light of the situation, I believe my assumption was wrong."

"Ah!" Justin's left brow raised. "I am astonished at your naiveté, Doctor. I would not expect a man of your profession to rule out the possibility of a woman carrying a child on the basis of her marital status."

"Your wife's marital state has nothing to do with my diagnosis, Mr. Randolph. I am hardly naive, sir." The doctor's voice hardened. "Neither am I easily fooled."

"Fooled?" Justin's eyes narrowed. "You mean she was *shamming?*"

"No. Her unconscious state is real enough. I meant your...confusion...as to its cause may not be."

Justin rose to his feet. "Would you care to explain that statement, Doctor?"

Thaddeous Allen glanced quickly around the room—everyone was sleeping. "Your wife's unconscious state is the result of extreme physical and emotional fatigue brought on by very rough handling."

Justin's brows shot skyward. *"Rough handling?"*

The man slumped over the table next to them snorted,

lifted his head, gave them a bleary-eyed look and dropped his head back down onto his arms. His heavy snoring resumed. Justin lowered his voice. "What 'rough handling,' Doctor? What are you talking about?"

"I'm talking about your wife's condition. Someone has handled her very roughly indeed. She is considerably bruised. I'm certain her collapse is a mental, physical and emotional result of the mistreatment she—"

Justin didn't wait for him to finish. He strode across the room and started upstairs, taking the steps two at a time.

Justin shoved open the bedroom door, crossed the room and grasped the bedcovers, flinging them back from his bride's prostrate form. His brows lowered in a dark scowl as he swept his gaze over her. The evidence of the claimed mistreatment was there—dark, ugly bruises marred the flesh of her upper arms, and a raw, jagged scratch ran from the slender column of her throat to the top of her shift. The vivid red color of the wound stood out in startling contrast to the creamy perfection of her skin.

Justin's jaw tightened. He flicked his gaze upward to his wife's face and, though it was turned away into the shadows, a discolored swelling along the clean, firm line of her jaw was visible to him.

"Those bruises were made by a man's hands, Mr. Randolph. A large man's hands."

Justin glanced at the doctor who had followed him into the room, then leaned forward and pulled the covers back over Elizabeth's slender form. "I am a large man, Doctor."

He turned and faced the physician. "Be done with innuendo—do you accuse me?"

For a moment the two men studied each other and then the doctor shook his head. "No, Mr. Randolph, I do not." His voice was noticeably warmer. "I confess that was my first thought, but, having witnessed your reactions, I am now convinced it was not you that harmed your wife." He stepped forward and nodded toward the still figure on the bed. "There is further evidence of mistreatment. Her right wrist is swollen and discolored, and there is a nasty lump on the back of her head."

He picked up his black bag and started for the door. "Her right knee is badly bruised also, but I do not believe the injury is serious." He reached for the doorknob.

"Doctor, wait!"

Thaddeous Allen stopped and turned to look at Justin.

"You haven't told me what is to be done for her."

"Only that." The physician gestured toward the bed. "She needs rest. In these situations of cruel treatment I have often found there is great stress placed on the nerves and emotions. Unfortunately, we know little about such things." He glanced over at his patient and then returned his gaze to Justin's hard, set face.

"It has been my experience, Mr. Randolph, that when a person is subjected to treatment such as your wife has obviously suffered, it leaves a bruise on the soul that takes much longer to heal than the physical ones. You may need to give her a good deal of love and understanding to bring that healing about."

The doctor shifted his black bag to his other hand and

pulled the door open. "Good evening, Mr. Randolph. May God grant your wife a speedy recovery." The door closed with a soft click behind him.

Justin stared at the closed door. *Love and understanding, indeed!* He turned and looked down at the slight rise in the coverlet that was caused by Elizabeth's body. One bruised, creamy-white shoulder was exposed to the cool night air. He walked to the bed, pulled the coverlet over her shoulder and gently tucked it under her swollen jaw. *What had happened to her? Why had—?* Abruptly, he chopped off the thought, spun on his heel and strode to the door. He had been ensnared by compassion once—he would not allow it to happen again. Never again!

The fire flared brightly in the draft as Justin yanked the door open and stepped into the hallway. It flickered wildly as he slammed the door closed again, then settled to a steady burn that warmed the room with soft golden light and lent radiance to the pale face of the young woman lying comatose on the bed as his angry footsteps faded away.

Chapter Five

❖

Elizabeth awakened to the sound of raindrops against the windowpane. A dull ache permeated her whole being, and the thought came to her that she was ill—that she had some dreadful disease. Tears pooled at the corners of her eyes and rolled down her face, making damp spots on the pillow. She lifted her hands to wipe the tears away and a sudden, sharp pain stung her left jaw as something solid bumped against it. There was a gold band on her finger. Her brow furrowed. She had no gold ring. She— *Reginald!*

Elizabeth jolted fully awake. *Was she married to Reginald?* A wave of sickening fear drove her lethargy away. She threw the covers aside and lunged to her feet, then halted as pain streaked through her body and the room started to spin. She groped wildly in the air for support and her hands closed on soft, warm flesh. A startled scream rose in her throat.

"Here now—you got up too quick-like." Small, work-roughened hands eased her gently back down onto the bed and smoothed her petticoats around her legs. "There. You'll soon feel better. The dizziness will pass. It's only 'cause you stood so fast." The softness of a blanket brushed her chin as it was tucked around her shoulders. Elizabeth's eyes prickled with hot tears. How could she escape with someone watching her? She drew a deep breath to quell the nausea that had accompanied the dizziness, and opened her eyes. They focused on a round face topped by gray hair. She'd never seen the woman before. "Where am I?"

"You're at the Wetherstone Inn. My husband owns it." The woman smiled. "An' a proper fright you gave him last night when Mr. Randolph come carryin' you in. He thought there'd been an accident."

Wetherstone Inn? Mr. Randolph? Who—? Oh! Elizabeth bolted to a sitting position. The judge! And that strange marriage proposal. Yes. *Yes!* She had married a man named Randolph last night to escape Reginald and—and what? Her heart fluttered wildly. She shut her eyes trying to remember. What had happened after the ceremony? Why was she here? And where was this Mr. Randolph now? She could vaguely remember him climbing into the carriage and then...then nothing. "Ooooh!"

"What is it, dear? Are you feelin' poorly?" The woman gently brushed a clinging tendril of hair from Elizabeth's temple. "You lay back an' rest. I'll go fetch Mr. Randolph an'—"

"No!" The woman glanced at her sharply and Elizabeth made a valiant effort to control her sudden panic. "I—I mean, that won't be necessary. I'm fine. Truly I am. The dizziness has passed. It's only that I can't seem to remember..."

"Remember?" The woman snorted the word. "My stars, child, how would you remember? You were fainted dead away! Josiah said when he opened the door you were hangin' across your husband's arms like a limp rag doll. An' your Mr. Randolph, well—" the woman's lips twitched with amusement "—Josiah says he was shoutin' an' stormin' an' hollerin' for Josiah to help him. Hah!" The snort was louder this time, and filled with lofty disdain. "As if Josiah ever knew what to do about a woman." The woman chuckled gleefully. "Oh, I wished I'd a been there! Josiah says Mr. Randolph was in a proper broil. There ain't nothin' so helpless as a man with a sick woman on his hands."

"Oh, my! Whatever must Mr. Randolph think of me?" With a flurry of arms, legs and ruffled petticoats, Elizabeth jumped from the bed. "I must see him immediately! I have to explain. I—" She stopped dead still. What would she say? What *could* she say?

"Now, now. There's no need to work yourself to a dither about last night." The woman retrieved Elizabeth's soft, satin slippers from under the bed and held them out to her. "You'd best put your shoes on, lest you catch a chill. There's no need to sicken yourself over the matter. Your husband ain't the first man to be disappointed on his weddin' night, an' he ain't likely to be the last."

Oh! Oh, my! She hadn't even *thought* about that! Hot blood surged into Elizabeth's cheeks. She looked away from the woman's knowing gaze, accepted the offered shoes, then grabbed her dress from off the back of a chair where someone had tossed it. Had it been this woman who had removed it from her unconscious body—or Mr. Randolph? The thought made the nausea worse. Elizabeth clasped the dress and shoes to her chest like a shield and forced herself to concentrate. Why was she here with the proprietor's wife? Where was her...her husband? And what was going to happen to her?

She closed her eyes for a moment to gain composure, then opened them and smiled at the short, stout woman who was watching her closely. Her eyes widened and she gave a startled little yelp as pain darted along her facial muscles. She lifted her hand to cup her throbbing jaw and her gaze fell on her upper arm. It was covered with ugly purple marks. "Well, I look a sight. I—I had a fall." A tremor slid through her body at the memory of crashing to the floor when Reginald struck her.

Disbelief flashed in the woman's eyes, her face softened. "I'll bring you the tub I have tucked away in the kitchen an' you can have yourself a proper soak. It will help with the soreness." She headed for the door.

"Wait!" Panic overrode Elizabeth's embarrassment. She took a deep breath as the woman looked her way. "Why was I left here alone? Where is Mr. Randolph?"

"Alone? Well bless my soul, child! You wasn't left here alone. Your husband set me to watchin' over you 'cause you was took ill, is all. He's waitin' on you down in the common room. You're to join him there as soon as you're able." She pulled the door open and stepped into the hallway. "He'll be at the table in front of the fire. He *always* sits starin' at the fire." The door closed behind her.

An odd sort of quivering began in Elizabeth's knees and spread throughout her body. She dropped into the chair behind her and stared at the door. What had she done? How could she explain to this Mr. Randolph that she had been forced by circumstances to accept his offer of marriage? She couldn't tell him about the betrothal agreement her father had signed—or about Reginald Burton-Smythe's attack—or running away. He might send her back.

Elizabeth's stomach roiled. She took a deep breath, but it didn't help. This time the nausea wouldn't be denied. She dropped the dress and shoes she still clutched in her hands and leaped for the washbowl. She reached it just in time.

She felt better—at least physically. The proprietor's wife had been right; the warm bathwater had taken a little of the stiffness and soreness away. Elizabeth dropped her hairbrush into her open bag, leaned closer to the mirror and pushed her ivory hair comb into the piled-up mass of her still-damp hair. A few rebellious curls popped free and fell onto her smooth forehead. Why, just this once, couldn't her hair behave? Elizabeth scowled, tucked the offending curls back under the confined tresses, then pulled a creamy length of lace from her bag and draped it around her throat to hide the ragged scratch left by Reginald's attack. With the sleeves of her dress hiding the bruises on her arms, that took care of everything but her face. There was nothing she could do to hide that reminder of Reginald's cruelty.

Elizabeth shuddered, closed her bag and stared down

at the large gold ring resting on the table beside it. When she put that ring on her finger she would be ready—there would be no further reason to delay her meeting with Mr. Randolph. A fit of trembling seized her. Before she lost all courage, she snatched up the ring, slid it onto her finger and hurried from the small bedroom.

Dear heaven! She could not identify her own husband! Elizabeth bit back a nervous giggle and gripped the banister for support as she skimmed her gaze over the men in the common room. One of them, seated at a table in front of the fireplace at the far end of the room with his back toward her, seemed to be staring into the flames. *Was that he?*

Any inclination toward laughter, nervous or otherwise, left Elizabeth in a rush. The man's long legs, crossed at the ankles, stretched out toward the fire, and one broad, long-fingered hand rested on the table. Her heart fluttered as she noted the powerful look of that hand. She suppressed a sudden, intense desire to turn and run away, descended the last step, and crossed the room.

"Mr. Randolph?"

"Dearest!"

Elizabeth froze as, with one fluid motion, the man leaped to his feet, spun about, grasped her upper arms and drew her close. Shock held her motionless. But only for an instant. She began to struggle. "Unhand me, sir!"

The grip on her arms tightened. "Stop fighting! Breams is watching."

The words were snarled under the man's breath as he

pinioned her to his broad chest. Elizabeth struggled harder, the feel of the man's powerful hands upon her driving all coherent thought from her mind. Fear writhed like a living thing in the pit of her stomach. Her pulse roared in her ears. Her head began to spin and she felt herself falling toward the deep, dark vortex of a whirling darkness. Terror gripped her. She forgot the man and fought the smothering darkness. When it receded, there was the firm, hard, security of a wooden chair beneath her. She drew a long, shuddering breath.

"Are you all right?"

The words were curt, abrupt, and full of distaste—but there was an underlying note of concern in Mr. Randolph's deep voice that made Elizabeth nod her head. It wasn't much of a nod, for her head was still spinning, but apparently it satisfied him for he removed his hand from her shoulder and moved away to seat himself on the other side of the table. Her breath came more easily when he had gone.

"You're certain you're all right?" His voice now held an impatient note of inquisition. "You look quite pale."

"I—I'm fine. If I might have a moment..." Elizabeth closed her lips firmly to prevent the sobs that were clawing at her throat from breaking free. She had nearly swooned again! What was *wrong* with her? Tears welled up behind her closed eyes. She swallowed painfully, fighting them back.

"It seems I startled you. I apologize for that, but I had to keep you from ruining my plan. You see, I am known here. And, as these people know only that we are newly married—not that we are newly met—they would naturally expect our meeting, after the disaster of last night, to be a loving one."

Elizabeth clamped her jaws tightly together, using the pain it caused to stifle a sudden, strong impulse to laugh. Their meeting had certainly fallen far short of such expectations! Her lips twitched.

"You find our situation amusing?"

A shiver of fear slithered down her spine at his cold tone. "No, I do not, Mr. Randolph. I only—" The laughter bubbled up and burst from Elizabeth's throat. She couldn't stop it. Horrified, she buried her face in her hands while the uncontrollable hilarity poured from her.

The table jerked and her new husband's chair scraped against the floor. "Your nerves are overwrought. I'll give you a moment to compose yourself."

The whispered words hit Elizabeth like a splash of cold water. The laughter died. She jerked her head up and stared at Mr. Randolph's rapidly retreating back. Of course she was overwrought! Who wouldn't be, in her situation? Still... Elizabeth's spurt of anger dissolved into worry. Why had she swooned? Was she ill? *Something* was wrong with her. She blinked away tears, leaned back against the turned wood spindles of the chair she occupied and stared down at the fire on the hearth. So much had happened so quickly. So much had changed! Surely it was natural that she should be—

"The arrangements are made. Mary will be bringing our meal promptly. Please comport yourself as a loving bride while she is near." The whispered order startled Elizabeth as much as Mr. Randolph's quiet return. She jumped and looked up at him. An expression of extreme distaste crossed his features as their gazes met for the first time. "You're beautiful!"

The words were an accusation, not a compliment. Elizabeth stiffened with shock at his rudeness. "Thank you, Mr. Randolph. You make a pleasing appearance yourself."

A small, mocking bow of her husband's dark, handsome head acknowledged her cool, impeccably correct response. "No doubt others will comment on what a lovely couple we make."

Elizabeth's chin lifted at the undertone of dislike in his voice. She stared fully into his acrimonious gaze, then sighed heavily and clasped her hands on top of the table. She'd been nothing but trouble to the man—how else should he feel about her? "Mr. Randolph, I realize I have made a very poor beginning in our...er...relationship. And I offer you my sincere apology for all of the embarrassment and trouble I have caused you." Her cheeks warmed. She looked down at the scarred tabletop. "I understand that I swooned last evening, and I am mortified, sir, that you were forced to carry me into the inn."

She looked back up at him. "I wish you to know that I have never swooned before, and that I am not weak or sickly. Also, I want to apologize for my actions upon our meeting earlier. They were out of character for me. And, last, permit me to say that you were most gracious and kind to provide such thoughtful care for me last evening. I am truly grateful."

"You are telling me that your fainting spell last evening was an unusual occurrence?"

He had completely ignored her apology! Elizabeth lifted her chin a notch higher. "Yes. Most unusual."

"I see. And to what do you attribute this...unusual... swoon?"

His dark, penetrating gaze made her want to squirm—and his cold, arrogant tone made her want to rise to her feet and walk away. She did neither. "I am without an explanation, Mr. Randolph. However, as I said earlier, I do not wish you to think me weak or sickly, for I am neither."

He made an abrupt gesture of dismissal with his hand and Elizabeth had the distinct impression he did not believe a word she had said. She drew breath to emphasize her point just as the door to the common room opened and a tall, thin man in a long, black great coat entered. The words she had been about to utter flew from her mind. The man slammed the door shut, stomped mud from his feet and swept his hat from his head. *Bald!* He was bald. It wasn't Reginald. Elizabeth sagged back against the chair.

"...your gratitude is unnecessary."

Mr. Randolph's cool voice caught her attention. She turned her gaze back to the stranger she had married.

"Our agreement states that I will provide for your needs—as my wife, that is due you. I am both willing, and able, to live up to the responsibilities placed upon me by this marriage. However, we shall delay discussion of these things until we are in the privacy of the carriage. For now, it is enough for you to know we must play the part of love-smitten newlyweds." His gaze hardened. "As I said earlier, I am known here. And I will have no doubt, or stigma, attached to this marriage." The coldness in his low-pitched

voice belied the attitude of adoration her new husband ex-
hibited as he leaned across the table toward her. "Do I
make myself clear?"

"Oh, yes. Quite clear. You wish me to portray a loving
bride so our relationship will appear to be as other marriages."

"Precisely!" He leaned back in his chair. "You do understand, however, that you are to perform so only when we
are in the company of others. When we are alone, there
will be *no* intimacy between us." He studied her closely.
"You do understand that?"

"Oh, yes. That is the basis of our...arrangement."

"Excellent! I'm pleased to learn you are not an empty-
headed piece of froth." He ignored her startled gasp and
continued. "Now, I dislike formality. Please call me by my
given name—Justin."

"Very well."

"And, of course, I shall call you Elizabeth. That is your
name, is it not?"

"Yes."

Suddenly he leaned toward her and smiled. Elizabeth
blinked, taken aback by the transformation in his face. A
warning look leaped into his eyes. "Here is Mary, with our
meal, dearest. I hope the food will strengthen you. You so
frightened me last night."

So that was what had brought about the sudden
change. What an actor! The man's voice was fairly throbbing with emotion. Well, Mr. Justin Randolph would not
find her performance wanting! Elizabeth glanced at him
from beneath lowered lashes as a young woman set plates

of hot stew before them. "There's no need for alarm, dearest, I'm quite recovered."

Her voice could have melted butter. She smiled with satisfaction, then grimaced at the hunger pang that cramped her stomach as the delicious aroma of the stew wafted upward. It had been more than a full day since her last meal.

"Pray begin, beloved. You had no meal last evening, and you are too slight to go so long without sustenance."

Now *that* had sounded almost sincere! The thoughtfulness surprised her. Elizabeth smiled and reached for her fork.

Justin stared. She had incredible eyes. They were the deepest, darkest blue he had ever seen. Something stirred at the fringe of his mind as he gazed into their depths, but when he grasped for the thought it disappeared into nothingness, as insubstantial as the wisps of steam rising from their food. He frowned and shifted his weight in his chair, uncomfortably aware that his emotions as well as his mind were stirring. Firmly he forced them to stillness. He was no longer a young, romantic fool to lose his head over a beautiful face. And she *was* beautiful—there was no denying that. His gaze swept over her finely molded nose, across her lovely high cheekbones, and down to her full, rose-colored lips. They were still curved in that warm, grateful smile and exposed small, even, white teeth to his view. Only the discolored, swollen jaw marred her features' perfection. The sight of the bruise jarred him back to his senses. He scowled, picked up his fork and began to eat.

Chapter Six

❧

It was raining when they left the inn. A howling wind whipped around the far corner of the building and tugged at Elizabeth's cloak. She staggered beneath the force of it.

Justin stepped between her and the frigid, buffeting gusts. "Nasty day."

"Yes." The word was snatched from her mouth and carried away.

Justin opened the door of the hired cabriolet, braced it with his shoulder and handed her inside. A sudden blast of icy air slammed the door shut as he climbed in after her. At once the throaty roar of the wind was reduced to a muffled, moaning sigh. A curious sense of intimacy pervaded the inside of the shuddering carriage as the elements were closed out. He settled himself on the seat beside her as the carriage gave a lurch and rolled forward. "Well, we are on our way."

"Yes." Elizabeth arranged her cloak, and, under cover

of the movement, slid closer to the outside of the carriage. "If I may ask, sir, what is our destination?"

"Philadelphia." Justin lifted a rug from the pile he'd placed on his lap and unfolded it. "Have you been to our fair city?" He leaned over and spread the fur robe across Elizabeth's lap.

"N-no. I haven't had the p-pleasure."

Justin frowned and looked up from covering his own lap. "Your face is pale and you're shivering. Are you taking a chill?"

"No. I'm f-fine." Elizabeth stared down at her hands trying to will them to stillness. It didn't work. She gave up and tucked them out of sight under the rug. *Philadelphia.* Reginald would never find her there. She was safe! She glanced up to find Justin Randolph looking expectantly at her. "I beg your pardon, sir. I fear I was wool-gathering. Did you say something?"

"I said—I dislike having my bride address me as sir." He gave her a level look. "You *did* agree to call me by my given name."

"So I did." She managed a shaky smile. "Please forgive me. I forgot."

"Forgot what? My name? That you agreed? Or that we are married?"

"That I agreed." Elizabeth couldn't keep the touch of asperity out of her voice. Justin Randolph had an irritating habit of ignoring small politenesses, such as apologies. "I could hardly forget about our...our..."

"Marriage?"

"Yes." Why couldn't she say the word? Embarrassed color warmed Elizabeth's cheeks. She stopped shivering.

"Perhaps, under the circumstances, Elizabeth, it would not be outside the realm of propriety for me to tell you that your blush is most becoming."

"Thank you." Fear coiled in her stomach. Maybe she *wasn't* safe! She stared at Justin, taken aback by the personal remark, then leaned forward to tuck the lap robe more closely around her cold feet. Tears stung her eyes at the memory of her father taking her boots and shoes with him when he left her room. She blinked the tears away, straightened, and leaned her head back against the padded seat. That was in the past—it was the present she must concern herself with now. She stared at a small, repaired rent in the fabric of the carriage wall opposite her as she considered the circumstances that had been thrust upon her. Everything was so strange and troublesome. On the one hand, every mile they traveled brought tremendous relief for it was a mile farther away from the danger and painful memories she desired to leave behind. But it was also a mile closer to the new life she was beginning as wife to this man—as his partner in this marriage of convenience.

Elizabeth sighed. What would her role be? What would he expect of her? And what of the children the judge had mentioned? Would she be responsible for their care? *Oh, dear Lord, help! I have no experience at rearing children. I—*

"Elizabeth?"

She started and glanced over at Justin. "Yes?"

"If I may intrude upon your thoughts—we have many matters to discuss concerning our relationship."

"Yes, of course." The implied rebuke stung. Elizabeth

lifted her chin. "But I assure you, Mr. Randolph, it is no intrusion. It is the very thing I was pondering."

"How fortunate. Please be more specific."

"Very well." Elizabeth ignored his sarcastic, disbelieving tone. "I was wondering—as I am unfamiliar with relationships of this nature—what my position will be."

"I suspect it will be as you expected."

The coldness in his voice could have frozen a pond. There was open dislike in his eyes. Elizabeth relaxed a little.

"I am a wealthy man. And, as such, I hold positions of importance in the social and business communities. As my wife you will, of course, share in those positions."

"I understand." Elizabeth struggled to maintain her poise in the face of Justin Randolph's seeming animosity. "I shall endeavor to be a credit to you—in society, and with your business associates." She fingered the ring making a bulge in her kid glove. "And as to my position and duties in your home?"

"In my home, it will be as the paper you signed stated. You will perform as my wife, caring for my home and the children, fulfilling social obligations, seeing to my needs as any wife is expected to do, *except*—" the harshly spoken word made Elizabeth flinch "—for those of a personal nature. There will be *no* personal involvement between us. However—" He held up a hand as she started to speak. "I expect you to play to perfection the part of a loving bride and doting wife in front of others. The truth of our relationship is to remain confidential. *You are to tell no one!*" He gave her a cool, distant smile and Elizabeth cringed. It was not pleasant to be so completely and coldly rejected. "It will, of course, be to your advantage to play your role well. As the 'loving' and 'loved' wife of a wealthy man there is little that will be denied you. But—" his voice took on an ominous tone "—as the faithless wife of a wealthy and powerful man, there is little that could save you."

A flame of resentment kindled in Elizabeth. How dare he speak to her as if she were a harlot! Yet, what else would a man think of a woman that married someone under these conditions? What else *could* he think? Elizabeth's honesty smothered the flaring indignation as her thoughts raced on. She could not tell him what had happened—she could never tell anyone that—but she had to try to make him understand that she was not what he thought her to be. She drew a deep breath and plunged into speech.

"Mr. Randolph, I realize that you know nothing of me. You know nothing of my character, or of the—the circumstances that placed me here. I know, also, that you spoke out of that ignorance." She lifted her head and met Justin Randolph's shocked, angry gaze head-on. "I'm sorry I've made such a poor impression you felt it necessary to speak as you did. But I assure you, sir, you have no need to bribe—"

Justin's straight brown eyebrows shot skyward, then lowered in a deep scowl.

Elizabeth faltered, gathered her courage and finished. "Or to threaten me. I am aware of the seriousness of the vows I made to you before God, and I intend to fulfill them all—within the conditions set forth in our agreement, of course." She gave him a small, polite smile as cool and distant as the one he had given her. "It will be easier now that

I know exactly what you require of me. I am determined, sir, that you shall not be sorry for our...our...alliance."

A heavy silence descended when she finished speaking. Had she gone too far? She squared her shoulders and lifted her chin. Something flashed in the depths of Justin's eyes, but before she could identify it, he dipped his dark, handsome head in a small, mocking bow.

"A very pretty speech, madam." Sarcasm tainted his every word. His gaze locked on hers. "However, I put little faith in a woman's words."

"Nor I in a man's, sir!" Tears sprang into Elizabeth's eyes. She turned her head aside and blinked them away.

With child...with child...with child... The words rang through Justin's head in time with the steady, rhythmic clop of the horse's hoofs against the hard, cold earth. He raked his hand through his hair, then leaned back in his seat and studied the young woman he had married. So she had no faith in a man's words. Obviously, the doctor was wrong. It sounded as if some man had sweet-talked her into an immoral liaison and then reneged on his word. It happened. His facial muscles tightened as he lowered his gaze to Elizabeth's swollen, discolored jaw. Probably her father had lost his temper when he learned of her dishonor. Yes, that would explain the bruises. It would also explain why someone of her obvious breeding would be forced to marry under the conditions he had offered. He slid his gaze down the expensive cloak draping Elizabeth's shoulders and rested it on the fur robe that covered her lap. There would be the need for haste if she was not to be branded a loose woman—if the child she carried was to have a name. He knit his brows in a deep frown. And then there was the money. There would be no chance for a good marriage in her future.

Justin closed his eyes and leaned his head back against the seat. He had been prepared to accept a woman that openly married him for his money and the comforts he could provide—but he had wanted honesty in return. What he had received was this deception! She was the same as the others. And he had made it so easy for her. He curved his lips in a small, cynical smile. Only a few little lies in the letter she had written in reply to his article and—

Justin jerked upright and stared hard at Elizabeth. That's what had been nagging at him—her letter! There was something about her letter. But what?

Silence prevailed. The weather continued to deteriorate until the fur robe that covered Elizabeth's lap could not keep out the biting, frigid air. Every lurch or jolt of the carriage caused shivers to run down her spine. Small gray clouds of warmth burst from her nostrils into the confined space of the carriage as she breathed. Her teeth began to chatter. Her feet burned with the cold. She wiggled her toes, biting back a moan at the prickles that shot through them. Thank heaven she was not still walking!

Justin pulled up the collar of his great coat, rubbed his hands together, and glanced over at Elizabeth. "I'm sorry for the discomfort. These hired carriages leave much to be desired. I hope you are not too uncomfortable."

Elizabeth shook her head, then quickly readjusted her hood as the cold nipped at her ears. "In truth, I was thinking how fortunate I am to be in this carriage protected from the freezing rain and howling wind." She gave him a small, grateful smile. If not for him she might well be out in the cold, wet storm. "You have provided everything possible for comfort, Mr. Ran—Justin." She looked down at the smooth, dark fur that covered her lap to avoid his suddenly intent gaze. "And, of course, you are not responsible for the weather."

"That's true. Yet, I know some who would hold me accountable nonetheless. And they would feel no reluctance in telling me so—especially now." He reached over and pulled aside the curtain covering the window at her side. "It's beginning to snow."

Elizabeth glanced out the window, then over at the dark, closed face of the man she had married. Would he ever relax that air of wary suspicion with which he regarded her? "I like snow."

"As do I." Justin let the curtain fall back in place, sacrificing the dim, gray light of the late afternoon to its scant protection from the cold air. "But not when I am traveling in the company of a young woman. Red noses are very unattractive."

"Oh!" Elizabeth clapped a cold hand over her nose.

Justin laughed. "Not your nose, Elizabeth—mine! You have a most attractive nose—red, or otherwise."

Elizabeth looked at him over the top of the covering hand. He had a nice laugh. It made him seem almost human! "I'm certain there is more gallantry than truth in that statement, sir. However, under the circumstances, I shall accept it at face value."

"Face value?" Justin stared at her a moment, then, again, burst into laughter. "An excellent pun, Elizabeth—excellent!" He leaned back in his seat and studied her. "So, you have a sense of humor." The laughter lent warmth to his voice. "A quick mind, and a sense of humor. I find that a pleasing combination."

"Thank you." The sudden praise was disconcerting—she did not want any personal observations from this man. Still...it pleased her that she had made him laugh when he seemed so cold and somber. Elizabeth pushed the window curtain open a tiny crack and watched the large, fluffy, white snowflakes dance their way to the ground. Perhaps she had something to offer this strange relationship after all. The thought was comforting to dwell on.

Chapter Seven

❦

The hour was late when they arrived at their lodging place for the evening. Large, fluffy snowflakes fell from the dark night sky, each one touched by the shimmering radiance of silver moonlight that caused them to sparkle like diamonds. With careless largesse they piled their lustrous splendor against fences and walls, clustered in glittering brilliance on trees, buildings, and bushes. Elizabeth gave a soft exclamation of pleasure at the beauty of it all as Justin opened the door and stepped down from the carriage. Steeling herself against his touch, she took his politely offered hand, stretched her foot forward and ducked through the door.

"What is *that?*"

Elizabeth jerked to a stop on the carriage step and dropped her gaze from the beauty of the snow-covered landscape to Justin's dark, scowling face. He was staring at the cream-colored satin slipper no longer hidden by her long skirts. "My shoe?"

"That may be a shoe in a ballroom—in this snow it is a piece of nonsense!"

Elizabeth winced at the disgust in his voice and pulled her foot back to hide the offending shoe under her skirt.

"Put your arms around my neck."

"Wh-what?"

"Put your arms around my neck! You cannot walk through this snow in those shoes. I shall have to carry you."

"No!"

Justin's brows shot skyward.

"I—I mean—please don't bother." Elizabeth shrank back against the carriage as he stepped closer. His grip tightened on her hand. "Please. You mustn't..." She tried, frantically, to pull her hand free from his grasp. "I can walk. I don't mind. I— Oh!" She gasped as Justin scooped her into his arms. "Put me down!" She pushed against his chest, twisting her body away and kicking her legs trying to get free. His arms tightened.

"Are you mad? Stop struggling! You'll make me drop you."

The snarled words penetrated Elizabeth's fear and she became suddenly aware of her actions. A new, terrible fright assailed her. *Was* she mad? Was that why she was acting this way? She forced herself to relax in his arms.

"That's better." He adjusted his grip and headed for the inn. "I'll thank you to remember you are supposed to be my loving bride—and to conduct yourself accordingly. I do not appreciate being made to look a fool."

Elizabeth bit her lip and nodded.

The snow crunched under Justin's feet. Fleecy piles of

it formed on his broad shoulders and filled the pocket made by her folded body. Its beauty was lost to Elizabeth. She concentrated all her attention on fighting the terror that was building in intensity at the feel of Justin's arms holding her. Just when she thought she could bear it no longer his foot thudded against the door. She glanced up, and drew breath to ask him to put her down just as the door opened. His arms tightened, pulling her more closely against his hard chest. She bit back a scream.

"Hey, Mr. Randolph!" A young towheaded boy pushed the door wide and stepped aside for them to enter. "We was beginnin' to wonder would you make it, what with the storm an' all." He slammed the door shut, then turned a frankly curious gaze on Elizabeth as the candlelight, flickering from the draft, steadied and poured its warm light over her. "That your bride?"

Justin glanced at her and his face went taut. "Yes, Lem. This is my bride. Is the room ready?"

"Yes, sir! She's all cleaned up an' fit to shine—just like you asked." The boy turned and headed toward a door on the other side of the smoky, patron-filled room. "Dan'l brung your carriage, Mr. Randolph." The towhead looked over his shoulder with pleading eyes. "Can I ride on the box when you're fixin' to leave?"

Justin nodded. "As far as the lightning-blasted oak. Now, go tell your father I want some hot mulled cider and tea brought to the room immediately." He shouldered open the door in front of them, stepped into a tiny room and gave a swift, backward kick that closed the door with a loud bang. Elizabeth jerked. He gave her a disgusted glance and headed for the bed. "This is getting to be a habit. Tell me, Elizabeth, do you ever *walk* into an inn, or is this a pleasure I may look forward to from now on?"

"Oh!" Elizabeth pushed uselessly against his chest to free herself. "I asked you not to carry me! I told you I—" She bit off the words as a sharp rap sounded on the door. "Put me down!"

"As you wish." Justin released his grip.

Elizabeth let out a startled squeal as she dropped to the center of the bed.

"Come in!"

She struggled to a sitting position as the door opened. The sweet odor of clean, fresh hay from the newly filled mattress rose in a cloud around her. It did little to reduce her vexation over Justin's cavalier treatment—nor did his amused glance. She lifted her chin and glared at him.

Justin grinned and stepped to the end of the bed to take the hot cider the innkeeper was carrying. "Ah! Just the thing to chase away the chill."

"Yeah." The man slid his gaze to Elizabeth's flushed face and his thick lips split his beard in a sly smirk. "Along with other things."

Justin stiffened. "You forget yourself, Johnson—and to whom you are speaking."

The innkeeper flushed a dull red and lifted an angry gaze to Justin's face. "An' you—" He stopped abruptly as he met Justin's steady, icy gaze. He uncurled the fingers he had tightened into fists and looked away. "I meant no disrespect to you, or your wife." The sullen words had barely left his mouth when there was a soft tap on the door and an Indian woman entered the room. He spun about. "You standin' outside that door listenin' to your betters?" He pointed toward a small table. "Set that down 'n' git outta here!" He turned back to Justin as the woman moved to obey.

"Little Fawn's brung your tea. Is there anythin' else you'll be wantin'?" He slid his gaze toward the bed.

"A meal." Justin moved forward to block Elizabeth from the man's view. "Venison stew will do."

The innkeeper's face tightened. "I'll fetch it."

"Little Fawn will bring the food." Justin's low voice was frigid. "You stay out of this room."

The man opened his mouth to speak, looked into Justin's cold, still eyes, and closed it again. With a muttered oath, he spun on his heel, gave the Indian woman a sharp shove toward the door, and stomped out of the room after her. Justin watched until the door latch clicked into place, then lifted the cider to his lips and took a swallow. "I'm sorry for that unpleasantness, Elizabeth. The man's a lout." He turned to face her, and frowned. She was shivering.

"You *have* taken a chill." His voice held both disgust and sympathy. "I'll get you some tea."

"No! I mean...certainly not." Elizabeth scrambled for the side of the bed, ready to fight, or flee, should he come near. "I'm perfectly capable of pouring for myself. It was only a—a temporary aberration." She brushed a curl back behind her ear. "I repeat, sir, I am neither weak nor sickly. And I do not take a chill easily."

Justin quirked his left eyebrow.

It was clear he did not believe her. Anger surged through Elizabeth, steadying her, driving away the fear engendered by Justin's arms and the leering glances of the innkeeper. With what she hoped was a haughty glance, she turned her back on Justin, removed her cloak and walked to the table to pour herself a cup of tea.

Justin leaned against the mantel and watched Elizabeth. She seemed fascinated by the Indian woman, who was shuffling about placing steaming plates of stew upon the table. For the first time she seemed unaware of him and he took advantage of the opportunity to study her closely. There was *something* about her—something that gnawed at the edge of his mind whenever he looked at her. *What was it?*

The thought eluded him. Justin turned away in disgust, then, abruptly, turned back again. He searched her face, taking note of the delicate bone structure, the exquisitely arched brows, the long, curling lashes that threw sooty shadows across her pink tinged cheeks. An ache began deep inside him and spread throughout his whole being. How lovely she was. How—

The door closed behind Little Fawn interrupting his thoughts. *Just as well.* The thought was a sour one. Justin looked down at the glass in his hand—the cider tasted sour, too. Everything was sour lately! He scowled and set the glass on the mantel. Silence filled the room.

Elizabeth took a sip of her tea and risked a quick glance at Justin from under her lowered lashes. He looked as grouchy as a bear with a sore tooth! Why didn't he say something? With a hand that was not quite steady she placed her empty cup back on its saucer. Maybe he was waiting for *her* to say something. But what? She groped around for a suitable topic of conversation but her mind seemed to have turned to mush. "Thank you, Miss Pettigrew." She muttered the disgusted words under her breath and reached for the pewter pot to pour herself another cup of tea.

"I beg your pardon."

Elizabeth jerked her gaze to Justin's face.

"Did I hear correctly? Did you say, 'Thank you, Miss Pettigrew'?"

"No." There went that eyebrow again. The man must have the hearing of a cat! Elizabeth felt her face flush. "That is—yes. But not really."

"Well, which is it?" Justin gave her a cool look. "It can't be both."

Elizabeth put the teapot down. "I did make the remark. I suddenly thought of Miss Pettigrew, and her name... slipped out." She gave him look for look, though her cheeks were burning. "I said, no, because the remark was not meant for your ears." *There! That should put Mr. Justin Randolph in his place.*

Elizabeth rose to her feet and made a small business of brushing at some imaginary lint on her skirt while she composed herself. She had no intention of telling him *why* she had suddenly thought of— A deep-throated chuckle froze her in midmotion.

"Miss Pettigrew. Yes, of course—Miss Pettigrew! I understand now." Justin's chuckle turned to full-blown laughter.

Elizabeth gaped at him. "You know of her?"

"Oh, yes indeed." He grinned down at her. "Miss Pettigrew was the bane of my sister Laina's school years. Let me see now...how did that go? Oh, yes." He squared his shoulders and held his hands rigidly at his sides. "'Miss Pettigrew's Academy for Young Ladies. Proper deportment and appropriate conversation for all occasions.'" He relaxed his stance and chuckled. "Did I get it right?"

"Yes!" Elizabeth fairly snapped the answer. It wasn't that amusing!

"And you feel that Miss Pettigrew was somewhat... er...*lax* in covering this particular situation in her teaching. Is that it?"

Elizabeth stuck her chin into the air at his teasing tone and turned to the table. "I think *remiss* would be a better word! *I* certainly could not recall one gambit from her 'Appropriate Conversation' class...though I tried."

Justin laughed and walked over to hold her chair. "Do not judge Miss Pettigrew too harshly, Elizabeth. After all, this is an unusual occasion. And she did come to your conversational rescue in the end."

The starch went out of Elizabeth. Her lips twitched, then curved into a smile. "She truly did—though certainly not in the way that she intended." She tilted her head back and looked up at Justin. He turned away and seated himself.

"No, not in the way that she intended." Justin picked up his fork, stabbed a piece of venison and lifted it in mock salute. "Nonetheless...to Miss Pettigrew." He looked across the table at Elizabeth. "May she forgive us for the black eye."

Elizabeth laughed, picked up her fork and joined him in the foolish toast. "To Miss Pettigrew...may she never know!"

The meal was a simple one, the room rough, but their conversation, once the ice had been broken, was interesting and lively. Justin suddenly realized, halfway through the meal, that he was enjoying himself. He found Elizabeth intelligent and sensitive, with a quick humor that caught him off guard and made him burst into laughter. It felt good. It had been a long time since he had laughed. And he liked her demeanor—liked! The word exploded through his mind. Liked! How could he so forget himself? He knew better than to allow Elizabeth's personal charm to blind him to her true nature. He knew—

The knock at the door interrupted his dark thoughts. He laid down his fork, grateful for the intrusion. "Yes?"

"Your bags, sir."

"A moment." Justin walked to the door and slid back the bolt. His groom stood just outside, outlined by the smoky candlelight of the common room.

"Good evening, sir."

"Good evening, Daniel." Justin's gaze dropped to the bags the man was holding. "Put the bags there—against the wall." He waved his hand to indicate a spot on the floor. "And fetch the carriage robes, we'll have need of them." The groom nodded and turned away. "And, Daniel—" The groom looked back. "See that the carriage is ready to go at first light. We have a great distance to travel tomorrow and I want no delays."

"Yes, sir."

Elizabeth laid down her fork and rose to her feet with words of protest frozen in her throat as the groom walked away. She stared at the bags the man had brought and her heart started an erratic beating that left her breathless. *Two* bags. But she had only one. She lifted her gaze to Justin and her mother's words surged into her mind— *"They are all alike...they are all alike...they are all alike."* Reginald Burton-Smythe's leering face swam toward her out of an approaching darkness. She tugged at the lace around her throat, trying to get more air, then clutched blindly for the table as her knees began to buckle.

"Well, Elizabeth, you'll by pleased to know—" Justin latched the door and turned back toward the table "—tomorrow's ride will be— *Elizabeth!*" He leaped forward and caught her in his arms as her limp body slid toward the floor.

"Let me go!" The darkness receded as quickly as it had come and Elizabeth fought furiously against the grip of Justin's powerful arms. Terror lent her strength. "I said, let me *go!*"

He lowered her onto the bed.

"No!" The anguished cry burst from Elizabeth's mouth. She wrenched herself free of Justin's relaxed grip, threw herself across the bed from him, and scrambled to her feet. "No!" She leaned against the wall behind her, quivering with fear.

"No?" Justin stared at her as if she'd lost her mind. "No, what?"

"Th-this." Elizabeth waved her trembling hand in a sweeping motion through the air over the bed.

"What are you—?" Justin's eyes narrowed. "You think I have *designs* on you?"

"Yes."

"Well you are mistaken, madam! Nothing could be farther from my mind!"

The roared words were full of contempt. Elizabeth flinched, but held her ground. "I am *not* mistaken, sir!" Anger replaced her fear. She lifted her hand and pointed toward the door. "That is *your* bag with mine!"

"Of course it is!" Justin glowered at her. "Is that the evidence on which you judge me guilty?" His voice lowered ominously. "Would you have me sleep in the carriage? Or perhaps the barn? Or common room?"

Elizabeth's outrage left her in a rush. She eyed him suspiciously. "I—I don't understand."

"*That* is because one must think before one can understand. And you, madam, are not thinking! If you will do so for a moment, you will recall that this marriage is one of *convenience*. That we have both signed a legally binding document to that effect at *my* insistence. And that *you,* madam, have recourse to the law should I ever touch you."

Cold dislike frosted his every word. Elizabeth swallowed hard. Everything he said was true. She cringed inwardly as he continued.

"You will also, no doubt recall—should you take a moment to *think*—that I told you earlier I have no desire for intimate contact with you when we are alone. This is, however, a public place, and again, I am known here. It is expected that newly married couples will share a conjugal bed. I have explained that I wish no stigma to attach itself to this marriage—that the truth of our relationship is to be our own private knowledge. With that in mind, perhaps you will be able to understand the necessity of my remaining in this room, *not* in your bed, for the night hours."

"Oh."

"*Oh,* madam? Is that all you have to say? *Oh!*"

Justin's frigid glare made icicles seem like cozy flames. Elizabeth's stomach started churning like a river in spate. She drew a deep breath to quell the nausea. "I—I beg your pardon." She stared in horror at his furious face. "Please forgive me. I did not mean to impugn your honor. I forgot—"

"Forgot? *Forgot!*" Justin's voice cracked through the air. "Then perhaps you will be able to remember this. After having known my former wife, I have no desire to be emotionally entangled, or romantically involved, with another woman. *Any* woman! You have my word as a gentleman that I will never—*never*—touch you, or try to bed you. You are—and you will remain—my wife *in name only.* I cannot say it more plainly than that!"

Before she could respond, he turned on his heel and stormed from the room.

Elizabeth lay on the bed with her cloak pulled closely around her for warmth and watched the firelight playing with the shadows on the rough wood ceiling above. What had she done? He was so angry! And rightfully so. All that he had said was true. Oh, if only she *had* thought, instead of reacting so violently to the sight of those bags. Yet, when she had remembered—

Elizabeth shuddered and closed her mind to the

thought. She climbed from the bed and walked over to stand with her ear pressed to the door. For some minutes she stood listening to the indistinguishable murmur of voices from the other room, but she could not tell if Justin Randolph was there. What if he had gone? What if she had made him so angry he had left her? What would she do?

The memory of the proprietor's leering face caused the trembling to begin again. Elizabeth backed away from the door and went to sit on the edge of the bed. A burst of muffled laughter reached her through the door and, suddenly, the crushing weight of all she had been through pressed down upon her. Uncontrollable sobs shook her slender frame and hot tears poured from her eyes as she grieved for the mother and father she had never had. Always, they had kept her at a distance, treated her as an unwelcome intrusion in their lives. Yet, through it all she had clung to the hope that someday—

Elizabeth wrenched her mind from the thought and sank back onto the mattress. Not even to herself would she admit how desperately she had hoped that one day her parents might love her in return. That hope was dead. And so was the dream. Her "someday" dream. She sighed, pulled her cloak around her shivering body, and stared at the ceiling. The "someday" dream had been her comfort when the loneliness and pain of her parents' rejection were too intense to be borne. It had given her hope. She had conceived it out of the unarticulated yearnings of innocence and youth, and fed it with her need for tenderness and laughter, gentleness and love. She had shared it with no one, carrying it deep inside where it could be nurtured and kept safe. Now it was gone—destroyed before it had been birthed—aborted by her mother's words. All that was left was emptiness. Her dream would never have a face or a voice. Now she knew there was no one like her "someone."

"They are all alike...they are all alike...they are all alike." Sobs racked Elizabeth's body as her mother's voice chanted the litany of death in her mind and Reginald's cruel face, distorted by lust, leered at her out of the darkness. With her last bit of strength she reached up and clutched the brooch that was fastened to the bodice of her gown, then, too exhausted to fight any longer, she closed her eyes, breathed a long tremulous sigh of surrender, and yielded to the oblivion of sleep.

A trace of tears was on Elizabeth's face when Justin returned. His anger dissolved as he stood looking down at her. She was so young...so helpless...so...vulnerable. Compassion tugged at his heart. He spun on his heel and stalked to the fireplace. Sparks flew up the chimney as he added logs to the fire. He watched until the logs started to flame, then dusted his hands, picked up the bundle of lap rugs and spread them on the floor. He pulled a chair close, sat down and began removing his boots.

Elizabeth gave a small moan and turned over—her cloak fell open. Justin scowled, removed his other boot, then rose and strode to the bed. He lifted Elizabeth into his arms, tossed her cloak aside, pulled back the covers, laid her down and removed the cream-colored satin shoes from her feet. With a snort of disgust at their inadequacy, he tossed them to the floor, then pulled the covers over her and tucked them beneath her chin.

Elizabeth sighed, and lifted her hand to rest on the pillow beside her cheek. The too large, gold ring she wore almost slipped from her finger. Justin stared at it for a moment, then slid it back in place. A sudden acute sense of loss stabbed him. He had made a mockery of everything he most desired. This woman was his wife. *His wife!* And he didn't even know her. He reached out and traced the path of tears on her face. Why had she been so frightened earlier? How had someone as lovely as she come to be in her present plight?

Elizabeth stirred. Her lips curved upward in a wistful smile and she turned her head toward his touch—her lips brushed softly against his hand. Justin inhaled sharply and jerked away. The muscle along his jaw twitched as his hands curled into fists. He'd almost fallen into the trap again! A dull throbbing pain took up residence in his head as he turned and stalked back to the fireplace. There would be no more questions. To wonder about someone was to be involved—and that road led to disappointment and pain. It was a road he'd sworn he would never travel again.

The fire snapped and crackled, its dancing fingers of light probing the darkness and highlighting Justin's long, muscular legs, his lean hips, broad chest and powerful shoulders. He turned away from its warmth, pulled a robe over himself and stared into the shadows. The loneliness was on him again. He didn't want to face the light.

Chapter Eight

❖

Dawn was beginning to lighten the sky. Justin stared at the dull gray outside the window for a moment, then sat up and yanked on his boots. He was tired and ill-humored. He had spent most of the night wrestling with emotions and dreams he had thought dead and buried, and, in the end, was forced to acknowledge he had made a grave mistake. The longings were still there. They had simply been buried under the debris of his disastrous marriage to Margaret. He still wanted someone to love, to share his life with, to love him. Now, through his own machinations, he had a sterile relationship with a greedy little liar. How much of a fool could one man be! He gave a snort of disgust and brushed viciously at his clothes.

Elizabeth awoke at the sound of Justin's movement. Immediately, the events of yesterday flooded her mind—especially last night's angry scene. The memory made her feel ill. She took a deep, quiet breath and lay perfectly still watching him from under lowered lashes. Her conscience pricked her when he stooped and began to roll the carriage rugs spread on the floor at his feet. *So that was where he had slept.* She winced inwardly and drew breath to speak, but before she could begin her apology he made a sound of disgust and straightened. Her shoes were in his hand. He was scowling. Suddenly, he lifted his head and looked her way.

Elizabeth closed her already slitted eyes. The apology could wait! She held her breath and strained her ears to detect his slightest movement over the pounding of her heart. Fabric rustled...footsteps crossed the floor...the door opened and closed.

Elizabeth popped her eyes open, threw off the covers, and ran to slide the bolt into place. Justin Randolph was still angry. And he had every right to be—she had treated him dreadfully. She sagged against the door and let her breath out in a long sigh. Yesterday had been a disaster and— And that was yesterday! This was today.

Elizabeth straightened her shoulders and pushed away from the door. She would make a new beginning starting right now. She picked up her bag and reached inside for her soap and towel as she hurried to the washstand. There would be no foolish incidents today!

The weather had turned bitterly cold. Justin lowered his head into the wind and hurried from the "necessary" toward the inn to wake Elizabeth. It was a miserable day to travel, but he had no desire to spend an entire day with her in that tiny room. At least at home he would not be forced to spend every moment in her company. He blew on his hands, rubbed them together and glanced over at the sudden activity in the barn. Daniel was leading the horses out to be harnessed. Good! Now, if Little Fawn had finished altering those moccasins they could be on their way before full light.

Justin blew on his hands again, tucked his chin into his collar and sprinted the remaining distance to the inn. *Miserable weather! It was cold enough to freeze a hog's squeal!* With a last disgusted look at the leaden sky, he stomped the snow from his boots and went inside.

She was finished. Elizabeth pushed the ivory comb deep into the pile of curls on her head, dropped her hairbrush into her bag, then ran to the door and slid the bolt free. Now, she had only to don her cloak and shoes. When Mr. Justin Randolph returned he would find her calmly seated in a chair, ready and waiting. Oh, it was good to feel in control again!

Elizabeth smiled, dropped her bag on the floor beside the door and walked briskly to the end of the bed to get her shoes. They were not there. She checked the floor on first one side of the bed, and then the other—her shoes were nowhere in sight. How odd! She had seen Justin Randolph with them in his hands at this very spot. She stood for a moment nibbling thoughtfully at her soft lower lip, then bent and lifted one end of the neatly rolled bundle of carriage rugs at her feet. No shoes. She straightened and gave the rugs a vigorous shake. Nothing. *Where were her shoes?*

Elizabeth's shoulders sagged. Justin Randolph was already annoyed with her, and if she delayed their departure again...well...she didn't even want to contemplate that! She shook her head and quickly rolled the rugs, then turned to the chair and snatched up her cloak to search beneath it. Nothing. *Where could her shoes be?*

Elizabeth curled her hands into fists and rested them on her hips while she scanned the little room. There was simply no place else to look unless— *"Aha!"* With the cry of triumph, she dropped to her hands and knees and bent her elbows to peer into the area under the bed. It was too dark to see. She wrinkled her nose in disgust, ducked her head under the side rail and slid forward to grope around in the inky blackness for her shoes.

The latch clicked.

Elizabeth froze as the door opened, then shoved quickly backward as someone stepped inside. She couldn't be caught under— Her head knocked sharply against the side rail. *"Ouch!"*

"Elizabeth!" Justin rushed forward.

She gave a nervous little gasp as he grasped her elbow and hauled her to her feet. "You startled me."

"You surprised me, also. I hardly expected to find you crawling around under the bed."

Elizabeth pulled her elbow out of his hold. "I was *not* crawling around." Her cheeks turned warm as she realized the picture she must have presented to him. "I was only—" She stopped, stared up at him for a moment, then quickly looked down and brushed at the dust on her long skirt.

"Yes? You were only…?"

"Nothing. It's unimportant." Elizabeth turned on her heel and walked over to the chair. Determination stiffened her spine as she picked up her cloak and swirled it about her shoulders. She would *not* delay their departure. She absolutely refused to give Justin Randolph any more fuel with which to feed his flaming dislike of her! She would leave without her shoes.

"What are you doing?"

Elizabeth pulled her hood into place and gave him a cool smile. Here was her opportunity to salvage something of her pride—to repair her tattered dignity and make amends at the same time. "I should think my actions clear enough, sir. I'm preparing to leave." She fastened the braided loops over the buttons on her cloak, adjusted the hood, then swept grandly toward the door.

"Elizabeth?"

"Yes?" Oh, how satisfyingly cool and aristocratic her voice sounded. *That* should favorably impress the arrogant Mr. Randolph!

"Have you forgotten something?"

"I don't believe so." She reached for the latch. "I assume your groom will fetch my bag."

"Indeed. But what of these?"

Elizabeth's heart sank into the pit of her stomach with a sickening thud at his tone of voice. *He knew. Somehow, he knew.* Her assumed dignity crumpled into a useless pile at her stocking-clad feet. Slowly—reluctantly—she turned to face Justin. Her shoes dangled from the first two fingers of his right hand.

"*You* had them!" Hot blood surged into Elizabeth's cheeks. "You had them all the time, while I—I—" She clamped her lips together and glared at him. She would say no more.

"While you were leaving in your stocking feet?"

The scorn in Justin's voice and eyes brought forth a surge of indignation. Elizabeth bit down on her bottom lip and remained silent.

"Have you no sense?"

She bit down harder.

In three quick steps Justin crossed the room to stand in front of her. The look in his eyes made her shiver. She squeezed back against the door to put as much space as possible between them.

"Why, Elizabeth?" He stepped closer. "Why would you do such a foolish thing?"

Fear knotted her stomach—her heart thundered in her ears.

"Answer me!"

"I didn't want to displease you." The words came out in a whisper.

"Displease me?"

Elizabeth flinched. "Yes. By delaying our departure." She lifted her chin and looked him square in the eyes. She would not give in to the fear, not this time. "You told your groom you wanted to leave at first light. That you wanted no delays. I heard you."

"Well, I certainly didn't mean stocking footed!" His hand lifted.

Elizabeth gasped.

Justin froze with his long fingers buried in his hair.

"What is it?" His eyes narrowed as he stared down at her. "You've gone white as a ghost. Are you ill? By heaven! Are you going to swoon again?"

Elizabeth rolled her head from side to side against the door.

Justin's mouth tightened. He gave an angry snort and turned away.

Elizabeth closed her eyes and sagged against the door. She drew great drafts of air into her lungs until the trembling that had manifested itself throughout her body began to abate. She opened her eyes. Justin was standing by the washstand watching her. His face was as cold and still as a stone.

"Would you like some water?"

She shook her head.

He stared hard at her for a moment, then released his grip on the water pitcher and walked over to lean against the mantel. "Come away from the door, Elizabeth. We are not leaving this room until you tell me why you were going out in the snow without shoes."

His voice made her shiver—and that made her angry. In spite of the weakness in her limbs, Elizabeth pushed away from the door and straightened to her full height. "I *have* told you. I did not want to displease you. I was unjust in my accusations last evening and I wanted to make amends."

"By leaving without shoes."

The cynicism in his voice brought the blood surging back into her face. "Yes, Mr. Randolph, by leaving without my shoes! I have caused you a great deal of trouble and embarrassment, and I am determined that I shall not do so again." She sighed. "I knew you wanted to leave this morning without delay, so, when my shoes came up missing, I decided to leave without them." She looked at the cold, disbelieving look in his eyes and wondered why she was bothering to explain. "You were already angry with me!"

His left eyebrow shot up.

Elizabeth swallowed her own irritation along with the little pride she had left. "Rightfully angry. And, as you said, the shoes were of little use in the snow." She looked down at the satin slippers he still held in his hand. How could she blame him for not believing her? It *did* sound foolish when she put it into words.

Justin snorted. He threw her shoes to the floor, scooped something up off the bed and stalked back to her. "Put these on, Elizabeth. You should find them a comfortable fit—Little Fawn used your shoes to alter the size."

He thrust a pair of moccasins into her trembling hands. His gaze dropped to the stocking-clad toes peeking out from under her long skirts, then lifted back to her face. "I don't know what sort of game you're playing, Elizabeth, but be warned—it'll not work with me!"

He reached for the door latch. She jumped aside. He frowned, and yanked open the door. "Be ready when Daniel comes for the bags."

The door slammed shut behind him. Elizabeth cringed. *So much for a day without foolish incidents!* She stared hard at the closed door and compressed her lips into a thin line. She would never apologize to Justin Randolph again. *Never!*

Elizabeth clenched her hands—the moccasins squashed. Her tirade stopped short as she looked down at them. Justin Randolph was a most unpleasant man, yet he was surprisingly thoughtful. Suddenly, she giggled. *Would that be unpleasantly thoughtful... or thoughtfully unpleasant?* Her amusement died. Either way it was incongruous. The two simply didn't go together—except in her new husband.

Elizabeth sighed, pushed the hood off her head and walked over to sit down in one of the two, crudely made slat-back chairs at the table. What could cause a person to have such divergent characteristics? She glanced down at the leather moccasins and shook her head. What did it matter? Whatever the reason, Justin Randolph *was* both—she would simply have to make the best of it.

She glanced over at her shoes on the floor in front of the fireplace where Justin had thrown them, gave another sigh, and went to retrieve them. She put them in her bag, then resumed her seat. Her lips twitched, then twitched again. *What a picture she must have made crawling out from under the bed and striding haughtily toward the door in her stocking feet!*

Elizabeth convulsed with laughter, then, suddenly, began to cry. He hated her. *He hated her!* She straightened and swiped at the tears on her cheeks. *Serves you right for trying to play the grande dame! You looked like a big fool. Let that be a lesson to you!*

She blinked rapidly, picked up the moccasins and ran the long, leather thongs that trailed from them through her fingers. What did Justin Randolph's opinion of her matter? She didn't *want* him to like her. Still, it would be nice if they could at least be pleasant to one another. She shook her head at the improbability of that ever occurring and leaned forward to pull the fur-lined moccasins onto her cold feet.

Chapter Nine

✧

The carriage ride seemed endless. Time dragged. Elizabeth glanced over at Justin, then turned and pulled the window curtain back to stare out at the snow-covered landscape. All of her efforts at polite conversation had met with cold, curt answers and she was not eager to be rebuffed again. The carriage shuddered as a gust of wind hit it. Hail began to pound the roof with icy fists, demanding entrance. The sound was a steady drumming that emphasized the silence.

Elizabeth dropped the curtain, wiggled her toes and smiled to herself at the warm, luxuriant feel of the soft fur that molded itself to her foot. Moccasins. Justin was right—they *were* comfortable. Yesterday her feet had been painfully cold, but now they were encased in a lovely warmth. Did he ever wear them? Is that why he had thought to provide them for her?

Elizabeth studied this stranger she had married from

under her lowered lashes. Try as she would, she couldn't imagine him in moccasins. His clothes were the latest fashion, the material and cut quietly stating wealth and good taste. Even in the matter of clothing his self-assurance was obvious—he disdained the popular use of breeches and wore trousers instead. Her gaze swept from his Hessian boots to the top of his dark head. His hair was cut so that it just brushed the top of his collar and fell in thick, springy waves about his temples and forehead. The style suited him.

Elizabeth lowered her gaze to Justin's face and bit back a giggle. He was certainly no toad! He had thick, straight, dark brows and blue eyes that would be truly lovely if they weren't so cold and unfriendly looking. And his lashes were extraordinary—long and thick and very black. She leaned back against the padded seat, entertaining herself by continuing her covert assessment of his appearance. His nose was long, straight and masculine. It held its own well against the high, prominent cheekbones that framed it. And when combined with his firm, square jaw, it gave his face a strong, rugged look that was softened only by his mouth.

Elizabeth tipped her head to one side and studied his mouth. It didn't seem to belong to the man. The bottom lip was soft and full, with corners that turned up slightly— as if he were in constant good humor. It added a touch of gentleness that made his face intriguing, and exceedingly pleasant to look upon. In truth, Justin Randolph was a very handsome man—and most definitely not what she had pictured when that judge had been talking with her.

Elizabeth choked back another giggle. "I'm certainly glad he's not old and ugly!" She gasped as Justin's eyebrows shot skyward. "Oh! I'm sorry. I didn't mean to—"

Justin burst into laughter. "You look absolutely appalled, Elizabeth! But there's no need to be embarrassed—or, to apologize. I, too, am glad I'm not old and ugly." Her face flamed at his teasing and she turned away. Disappointment smote him. His laughter died. It was just as well.

The thought sobered him. Justin arranged his features into the cool, aloof look he had schooled them to, and turned his gaze back to the snow-covered landscape outside the window. It would not do for Elizabeth to learn of the sudden hunger in his heart, brought to life by the enticing warmth of her personality. That knowledge was a weapon—and he did not intend to place the instrument of his destruction in this greedy woman's hand.

Night covered the land like a thick velvet blanket as they entered the city of Philadelphia. The darkness was relieved only by the candlelight pouring from the windows of the homes and shops they passed, and the glowing circles of light cast by the lampposts that stood guard on the street corners.

Elizabeth peered out the window as the carriage rolled down the unfamiliar street. She noted with interest the teeming night, the sounds of merriment that poured from the taverns and inns. A group of young blades, walking toward a swinging sign bearing the picture of a large blue anchor, swept off their hats and bowed low as they spotted her. Elizabeth jerked back and let the curtain fall into place. She pulled it aside again as they moved on.

The carriage turned a corner where a small group of fashionably dressed people was gathered around a chestnut vendor, then rolled down a street lined with tall, narrow, three-story houses standing side by side like soldiers standing at attention. The sounds of Philadelphia's lively nightlife faded away. They turned another corner. Here, the brick houses sat back from the street in stately splendor, guarded by low brick walls or black iron fences. Tall, majestic trees towered in their lawns.

The carriage swayed and lurched. Elizabeth caught a glimpse of large brick pillars topped by gleaming lamps as they swept into a circular way. Her stomach contracted in a spasm of nervous apprehension—her new life was about to begin. She clasped her trembling hands tightly on her lap, closed her eyes. *Most gracious, Heavenly Father, please help me to be equal to the tasks ahead of me as mistress of Justin Randolph's home. I—*

"Nervous?"

"Yes." Elizabeth opened her eyes.

The carriage slowed, then rolled to a stop. The horses snorted and stomped their hoofs on the brick paving.

Elizabeth removed the rug from her lap and placed it on the seat beside her. Her hands shook as she reached to smooth back the wayward curls that fell forward on her face. She drew her breath in sharply at the sound of approaching footsteps.

"You've no cause for concern, Elizabeth. Only remember the part you are to play." Justin's voice took on a warning note. "You are my loving bride."

"I'll remember." Elizabeth whispered the answer as

the carriage steps were pulled into place. "I'll not disappoint you."

"You will not be permitted to do so." Justin fastened his gaze on Elizabeth's, and suddenly, it was there again, that vague stirring at the fringe of his mind—that feeling that there was something he should remember. It was blown away by a blast of cold, damp air that hit him when the door was pulled open.

"Welcome home, sir."

Justin shifted his gaze to his butler. "Thank you, Owen. It's good to be back." He climbed from the carriage, then turned and held his hand out.

Elizabeth drew a deep breath and placed her cold, trembling hand in Justin's. His hand was warm and steady. The strength in his grip made her stomach flop. She ducked her head, extended her foot to the step, then immediately drew it back again. She had forgotten the moccasins. She darted her gaze to the impeccably garbed butler waiting in quiet dignity for her to descend and smiled.

The butler's staid visage creased into an answering smile. He bowed low. "Welcome home, Madam Randolph."

"Thank you." She exited the carriage before he straightened.

Justin clamped his hands firmly around her waist and lifted her to the ground. "Nicely done—but unnecessary." Amusement warmed his whisper. "Owen would never question the appearance of my bride."

"I didn't know." Elizabeth took a quick backward step as he released her. "And I didn't want—"

"To embarrasses me." Justin finished the sentence as Owen took their bags from Daniel.

"Yes." Elizabeth tensed at his sarcastic tone. "Are you always so observant?"

"I've learned to be where women are concerned." He gave her a look that sent a shiver racing up her spine, then abruptly changed his expression as Owen approached. "Welcome home, my darling. Welcome to Randolph Court."

Justin's voice was so soft and tender Elizabeth could hardly credit it as belonging to him. The metamorphosis in him was so swift, so complete, she was too stunned to struggle when he placed his hands lightly on her shoulders and turned her toward the house. And then she simply forgot everything and stared at her new home.

Soft, golden candlelight emanated from the mansion's large, small-paned windows, warming its bricks to a rosy hue, and adding a gentle sheen to the frost-covered leaves of the evergreen plants that graced its facade. A fanlight above the centered entrance door was graced by a white dove holding an olive branch in its beak. Below the soaring bird were waves of rippling blue-green water, and above it, forming the arch of the fanlight, was a glorious stained-glass rainbow. The beautiful colors seemed to melt and flow around Elizabeth as the light from inside poured through them. "The symbols of peace and promise. What a lovely way to welcome guests to your home, Justin."

He made a noncommittal grunt, tucked her hand through his arm and started toward the door. Elizabeth gave him a cool look. Even if he didn't like her, he could at least be polite!

She gripped her skirt in her free hand as they started up the steps to the portico. The colored light flooded over them. She looked up at the window again. "The fanlight is truly lovely, Justin. Did an English craftsman design it? Or is it the work of a local artist?" She was almost jerked from her feet as Justin came to an abrupt halt.

"The fanlight was designed by a young fool that had a head full of ideals—and a heart full of romantic nonsense. He's dead now. He was murdered. And I have no desire to discuss either the window, or the man responsible for it. Is that clear, Elizabeth?"

There was pain deep in his eyes. Elizabeth bit back the angry retort that sprang to her lips at Justin's unwarranted rebuke. Apparently, the young man had been someone he cared deeply about. "Yes. That's clear. Please forgive me. I didn't know."

"Nor could you have. We'll not speak of it again."

The words were cold and brusque, and the compassion Elizabeth felt for Justin disappeared like smoke before a hard-driving wind. He started forward again, his long strides forcing her to hurry her steps as they crossed the portico. She was musing on how effectively he managed to squelch every kindly emotion she felt toward him as she crossed the threshold of her new home.

Chapter Ten

✤

Elizabeth put on her shift, stepped into her petticoats, shook out their long folds and walked through the dressing room doorway into the bedroom. A blazing fire chased the chill from the room. She crossed quickly to the hearth, absorbed the warmth of the fire for a moment, then turned and swept the large room with her gaze. The sight of the four-poster bed that dominated it made her shiver. Justin Randolph had, thus far, lived up to their marriage of convenience agreement, but she was still apprehensive. She had learned the hard way that it was unwise to trust anyone.

Elizabeth frowned and turned her back on the unsettling sight of the large bed. Her abundant, unruly curls bobbed up and down as she bent forward from the waist to dry her hair before the fire. She fluffed her hair with her hands to speed the process.

"Beggin' your pardon, mum?"

"Oh!" Elizabeth gasped, jerked upright and spun about. A young maid stood before her with a garment draped across her outstretched arms. She bobbed an awkward curtsy.

"I'm sorry if I frightened you, mum. Mizz Jeffers told me to bring your dress up an—"

"It's all right...er..."

"Trudy, mum."

"Trudy." Elizabeth smiled to put the young English woman at ease. "You've done nothing wrong, Trudy. I'm just a little ner—" She bit off her words. What on earth was she doing discussing her state of mind with one of Justin Randolph's servants! "Put the dress on the bed, please. I'll put it on when I've finished drying my hair."

"Yes, mum."

The maid crossed to the bed, laid the dress out on its surface and gently smoothed out the generous folds of the long skirt.

"Will there be anythin' else, mum?"

"No, Trudy. That will be all."

"Yes, mum."

Again, the maid bobbed an awkward curtsy. She hurried to the door, then turned and smiled at Elizabeth. "Welcome to Randolph Court, mum." She stepped into the hall and closed the door softly behind her.

"Phew!" Elizabeth let her breath out in a long, shaky sigh and dropped into the chair beside her. This would never do! She had to stop being so nervous and frightened. This was her home now and—

Her home.

Elizabeth rose to her feet and finished fluffing and drying her hair while the words repeated themselves in her mind. Her home. What did she know of a home? She had never had a home. A house, yes. But never a home. She crossed to the bed, picked up the freshly pressed dress and pulled it over her head. A home meant love, warmth, protection, and— "And you are feeling sorry for yourself, Elizabeth Shannon. Stop it!"

Elizabeth fastened the gown, smoothed the cream-colored fabric of the skirt over her petticoats and fluffed the ecru lace at the neck and sleeves. It felt good to be neat and clean again. She started back toward the fire, then lifted her head and looked slowly about the room. Ivory-and-red-patterned silk covered the walls, and red silk trimmed with ivory braid draped elegantly around the windows and bed. The luxurious oriental carpet picked up the red and carried it across the floor to a black marble hearth where ornate bronze tools reflected the leaping flames.

Elizabeth sighed. Perfection. Rich...beautiful...cold...perfection. It was all too familiar to her. There was no feeling of warmth or welcome. It was only a room. A *red* room.

"I hate red!" Her words fell like stones into a pool of silence. She made a face at her reflection in the window, walked over to the large wardrobe and pulled open the ornately carved double doors. There, in the vast interior hung her blue wool gown, and her dark-blue cloak. Beneath them, side by side on the highly polished floor of the wardrobe, were her cream-colored satin shoes and the leather moccasins. That was all. One gown, one cloak, one pair of water-stained shoes and the moccasins.

The sight of her scant belongings jarred her. With everything that had happened, she had completely forgotten about her wardrobe—or more accurately, her lack of one. Elizabeth chewed at her soft bottom lip. There would be gossip in the servants' quarters about this! What possible explana—

"Is there something you need?"

Elizabeth jumped, slammed the doors of the wardrobe shut, and whirled about. Justin was standing at the door. She shook her head. She couldn't find her voice—it was cowering somewhere behind the suddenly throbbing pulse at the base of her throat.

Justin glanced at the wardrobe behind her, closed the bedroom door, then advanced slowly into the room. "I hope you like red." Color bloomed on her cheeks.

"It's a lovely room. I'm certain I shall be very comfortable in it."

It was a polite evasion. Judging from the blush, she didn't like red any more than he did. Justin dipped his head slightly. "How fortunate. I detest the color myself." He lifted his gaze from Elizabeth's pink cheeks to her deep-blue eyes. "Please keep that in mind while conferring with Madame Duval tomorrow."

"Madame Duval?"

"Yes. She's a modiste. I believe her to be the one most highly favored by the ladies of society in Philadelphia." Justin walked over to a chair and removed his frock coat. "I took the liberty of sending her a message requesting her attendance upon you tomorrow. Of course, if she does not please you, you are free to choose another."

"But I have no funds for gowns!"

Justin stiffened. How dare she cry poverty to his face when she had just received a generous settlement from him! He'd a good mind to go and retrieve the papers he had locked in his desk and face her down with them. He threw his coat over the back of the chair, then turned and stared at her. Her face paled.

"I'm not— You couldn't have known...." She turned toward the writing desk against the far wall. "There's no harm been done. I shall send Madame Duval my apologies, and—"

"You'll do no such thing!" What game was she playing now? Justin stalked over to the wardrobe, yanked open the doors and gestured at the two forlorn garments hanging inside. "The wife of a man of my position must have a suitable wardrobe. It's obvious you did not bring one along." He gave her a cold, hard look and shut the doors. "My purse will provide what is needed."

"That's very kind of you, but I prefer to— What are you doing?"

Justin glanced at her. She'd gone stiff as a board. He pulled off the silk cravat he had loosened and walked over to toss it atop his coat on the chair. "I should think it would be obvious." He began to undo the silver buttons on his waistcoat. "I am preparing for bed."

"*Bed!*" Elizabeth's voice squeaked. "*Here?* But, you have your own room!"

"I do." Justin threw her a disgusted look. "And how many newly married men do you know that spend their nights alone in their own rooms?"

"I don't know *any* newly married men! And I am certainly not familiar with their actions!"

"Another area in which Miss Pettigrew's teachings are woefully lacking?"

Elizabeth gasped.

Justin ignored it. He peeled off his waistcoat and added it to the pile on the chair. "You had better make up the lack, Elizabeth—and soon. Because *this* newly married man is growing weary of explaining his actions to you."

He dropped down onto the chair, bent over and tugged viciously at his boot. He was tired of her pretending to an innocent virginity with him when she was carrying another man's child. And he was heartily sick of her lies! He would confront her with the truth right now, but it would serve no good purpose—she would only lie again. "For your information..." Justin grunted as the boot came free "...newly married men..." he threw the boot to the floor with a thud "...spend every possible moment..." he tugged at the other boot "...in bed with their brides. And the rest of their time thinking about it. Ugh!"

The second boot came free in his hand. He leaned back in the chair and looked with satisfaction at Elizabeth's scarlet face. He had been abnormally coarse in his choice of language, but he was tired of pandering to a delicacy that was nonexistent in her. "That is, until their blood cools—which usually takes a few weeks." He gave her a cool smile. "And *that* is the picture I must portray to others—including the servants of this household, if our marriage is to be believed to be a normal one—no matter how distasteful or inconvenient it may be for us. Is that clear?"

"Very."

Justin studied Elizabeth closely. Her embarrassment was obvious—so was her anger. But for some reason she seemed more at ease than she had been since he entered the room. He tucked the knowledge away for later contemplation and rose to his feet. "Good. Then I shall not have to explain myself again." He tossed the second boot down beside the first and walked over to the fire. "I'll not disturb your rest. I'll be sleeping on the chaise."

"No."

"No?" Justin whipped around to face her. She flinched. "You are refusing me access to your bedroom?"

"No, I am not. You mistake me. I meant only that it is I that will sleep on the chaise."

He flicked a contemptuous gaze over her. "That will not be necessary."

"As you say. But, I believe it to be the more reasonable solution to the situation. You are much larger than I and would hardly fit comfortably on the chaise."

Elizabeth's full, lower lip quivered ever so slightly as he stared at her, and suddenly he felt tired. He was weary to his very soul of beautiful, selfish women who played cruel games with a man's emotions in order to satisfy their own greedy desires. Bitterness rose like bile within him—he could look at her no longer. "As you wish." He turned back to the fire.

Elizabeth stared at Justin's back. Why the sudden capitulation? This was a Justin Randolph she had not seen before. She studied his bowed head and slumped shoulders, the hands he braced against the mantel—he was the picture of dejection. The memory of his eyes as he had spoken of the fanlight flashed into her mind, and Elizabeth's heart seemed to swell. She had left the source of her pain behind. It seemed Justin Randolph had come home to his.

Elizabeth lifted her hand toward him, then let it fall back to her side, and turned away. Justin Randolph wanted nothing from her—and she had no comfort to offer him. She sighed, picked up the folded coverlet from the foot of the bed and walked to the chaise. It had been a long, wearying day, emotionally and physically. She was exhausted. She shook out the coverlet and spread it over the chaise.

"Are you going to sleep in your gown again? I appreciate your modesty—but I assure you it is not necessary."

Elizabeth caught her breath at Justin's innuendo. Evidently, her wild accusations of the night before still rankled. She stopped smoothing the coverlet and looked up. He was leaning against the mantel watching her. "I do not require your assurance, Mr. Randolph. I know, after last night, that you are a gentleman and a man of your word. I—I have no nightclothes."

The admission was made at no small cost to her pride, but Elizabeth refused to look away from Justin's cold gaze. She refused to yield to shame. This man did not like her. Her position would become intolerable if he should pity her as well. She lifted her chin and something flickered in the depths of Justin's eyes—the blue ice changed to flame. He lunged away from the mantel, strode rapidly to the door and left the room.

* * *

Elizabeth clenched her hands into fists and stared at the closed door. *What a horrible, impossible man! What a horrible, impossible situation!* Tears of humiliation spilled from her eyes. "Stop it! Stop crying this instant, Elizabeth Shannon! You will *not* feel sorry for yourself. You wanted to be safe, and you are. Be thankful!"

Bolstered by her own words, Elizabeth wiped her eyes and walked around the room snuffing the candles. The red was not half as overpowering in the gentle, flickering light of the fire. She placed her hands on her hips and stared into the darkness. "I *will* make this relationship work. I *will* make a home here. I *will.*"

There was no one to hear her, but she felt better for having made the declaration. She shook her head at her foolishness, and turned back toward the chaise. The door opened. She took an involuntary step backward as Justin entered and came across the room toward her.

"I believe this will serve." He thrust a dark-blue silk dressing gown at her. "Take it! Sleep in it until you can have proper garments made."

"But I can't take your—" He scowled. Elizabeth swallowed hard and took the garment into her hands. "Thank you."

His head dipped. "You'd best go put it on. The hour is late, and you've had a wearying day." He turned and walked over to the fire.

Elizabeth stared at him for a moment, then walked into the dressing room and closed the door behind her. What a perplexing man! She would never understand Justin Randolph or his moods. She dropped the dressing gown onto the seat of the chair, removed her dress, then draped it carefully over the chair back. He was like two different people—one moment he was thoughtful and kind, and the next he was cold and arrogant. She stepped out of her petticoats, laid them on top of her dress, then pulled the smooth blue silk over her shoulders and knotted the long sash around her small waist. Absentmindedly, she rolled the too long sleeves to free her hands. She could be friends with the one—but the other...

Elizabeth shuddered, pulled open the door and padded into the bedroom. She was too weary to think about it now.

Justin tensed when he heard the door open. He tossed the log he was holding onto the fire, brushed his hands free of tiny, clinging particles of bark, and turned to bid Elizabeth a polite good-night. "Dear heaven!"

Elizabeth froze. "Is something wrong?" She glanced down and tugged at the deep folds of fabric caused by the sash around her tiny waist. "I know the gown is far too large, but—"

"It will do." He scowled at the raspy sound of his voice and cleared his throat.

Elizabeth lifted her head and gave him an uneasy smile. "I rolled the sleeves to shorten them." She extended her arms for his examination. "But there is nothing I can do about the length." Her golden curls tumbled forward as she tilted her head down to look at the small pile of fabric at her feet.

Justin followed her gaze downward. It was a mistake.

He quickly lifted his gaze back to the top of Elizabeth's golden curls. He clenched his hands into fists at his sides. "Elizabeth?" *He sounded as if he were strangling!* He cleared his throat again.

Elizabeth tilted her head back to peer up at him. "Your voice sounds hoarse. Have you taken a chill? You look a little flushed."

Justin stared down into her beautiful, upturned face. By heaven, the little strumpet was playing games with him! No one was *that* innocent. Anger cooled his ardor. "I'm perfectly well—merely curious. Do you always sleep with your hair falling loose in that fashion? Or is it that you have no nightcap?"

Elizabeth gaped at him. "My hair! I—I must look—I mean, I have no nightcap." She lifted her hands to gather up the curly mass. "I forgot to put it up after drying it. I'll do so immediately." She whirled about and headed for the dressing table.

"No!" Justin's barked command halted her dead in her tracks. He softened his voice. "Leave it. You have beautiful hair."

"As you wish." Elizabeth lowered her hands to her sides. *Why did she sound so shaky?* Justin frowned, and headed for the bed. "I have instructed Owen to begin searching for a lady's maid to serve you." He reached up and undid the neck of his shirt. "Of course, the final choice will be yours." He turned to look at Elizabeth and his pulse began to thud. It was going to be a long night—a long, sleepless night. Disgusted by the betrayal of his flesh, he sank down onto the mattress.

"That's very generous of you." Elizabeth crossed to the chaise and climbed under the coverlet, pulling it up. "*Very* generous, but..."

"But what?" Justin leaned back against the pillows and stretched out his long legs.

Elizabeth took a deep breath. "But I would like Trudy to be my lady's maid."

"*Trudy?*" Justin lifted himself on his elbows to look at her. Her hair was fanned out on the pillow and the firelight was playing hide-and-seek among the valleys and crests of her golden curls. He lay back down on the pillows—it was easier to concentrate if he didn't look at her. "Trudy is an upstairs maid. She is not trained to serve a lady."

"I understand."

She sounded disappointed. Justin frowned. "Do you wish to try her in spite of her lack of training?"

Elizabeth caught her breath. "Yes."

"Very well. I will inform Owen of the change tomorrow. But, if Trudy does not work out satisfactorily, you are to have Owen seek a suitable replacement."

"I shall."

Justin cast a quick glance her direction. "That's settled then. Good night, Elizabeth."

"Good night...Justin. And thank you."

An intimate silence settled into the room.

Justin scowled. He folded his hands under his head and stared up at the tester overhead concentrating on the crackling of the fire, trying, unsuccessfully, to block out of his mind the soft, shy way she had spoken his name, the rustling whisper of silk as she settled herself for sleep.

Weary from the long hours of travel, Justin closed his eyes, then quickly opened them again as a vision of Elizabeth, dressed in the blue silk gown, slid into his mind. He took a deep breath, expelled it slowly, then repeated the process. It didn't help. Tired, but unable to sleep, he lay rigid and uncomfortable in the big, lonely bed cursing himself for ever having thought of such a thing as a marriage of convenience.

Chapter Eleven

✣

At the first hint of dawn, Justin stretched the stiffness from his muscles, scrubbed his hands through his thick hair, and tried, unsuccessfully, to knuckle the gritty feeling from his eyes. He'd been right. It *had* been a long, sleepless night.

He rose to his feet, shot a quick look in Elizabeth's direction, then moved quietly to the fireplace and squatted down to place a few small chunks of wood on top of the glowing embers. He could not discern, with that one quick glimpse, if Elizabeth was sleeping or awake, but he refused to look at her again. The memory of that clinging blue silk was enough to make him keep his gaze firmly fixed on the fire. Hungry tongues of flame began to lick up the sides of the kindling. He laid a few large logs on the greedily feeding fire and quietly left the room.

After getting dressed, Justin hurried back to the red bedroom. Elizabeth continued to sleep soundly. He crossed to the bed, pulled back the covers, and mussed the sheets and pillows. Satisfied his handiwork would fool the servants, he walked over to the chaise.

It was a shame to wake her. She, too, had slept little through the long hours of the night, though for different reasons, *very* different reasons. Justin's face tightened. He could carry her, but dare not risk a repeat of that scene last night within hearing distance of his servants. He lowered his gaze from the long, thick lashes that lay like a black smudge on Elizabeth's creamy skin, to her full, rose-colored lips. His breath shortened. They looked so soft...so sweet... so...tempting.

Justin scowled and moved away. The situation was rapidly assuming all the characteristics of a very bad comedy, with himself in the role of the dupe. It did not help that the role was one of his own making. Never, *never,* had he imagined he would be drawn to someone like Elizabeth.

The thought brought a surge of anger. He turned and gazed down at Elizabeth. She was a beautiful young woman, and he was a healthy young man. He was attracted to her. That's all that it was—a normal, healthy, *physical* attraction. Nothing more. He settled the thought firmly in his mind and moved back to the chaise.

"Elizabeth?"

"Ummm." She snuggled more deeply under the coverlet.

He bent forward and gently shook her shoulder. "Elizabeth? Wake up."

Her long, sooty lashes fluttered and swept upward. Her sleepy, dark-blue eyes gazed up at him. Justin's body responded with a flood of warmth. He jerked upright and stepped back. "I'm sorry to have to wake you."

Awareness hit. Elizabeth gasped, shrank back into the corner of the chaise longue and pulled the coverlet up to her chin. "Wh-what do you want?"

"Not what you seem to think!" Anger cooled the heat from Justin's blood. He was doing his best to squelch his baser emotions—the least she could do was give him credit for it! "I'm going down to my breakfast, and I want you to move into the bed. If this charade is going to work the servants mustn't find you sleeping there on the chaise— nor any evidence of your having done so." He scowled down at her. "Stop clutching that blanket as if it were a shield! There's no need. I've given my word not to touch you."

He stormed to the door, grabbed the knob and turned to face her. "And—so you will know, Elizabeth—I am a man of my word. You are secure in my honor. Do not abase it further!" He yanked open the door and stalked off down the hall.

Elizabeth slowly descended the stairs. She dreaded facing Justin's anger again—hated the prospect of conducting this interview with Madame Duval in his presence. If only she was not forced by circumstances to accept these clothes from him! She felt like a kept woman.

Elizabeth sighed, curled her fingers tightly around the slip of paper in her hand and followed the gray-haired butler across the wide entrance hall to the salon. At least this time she would do nothing to provoke Justin's anger or foster his dislike of her. She had prepared a very careful list.

The butler rapped his knuckles softly on the wood panel

of the door in front of him and Elizabeth drew her breath in sharply. This would be her first test as Justin's bride, and she was determined she would not fail. She lifted her head high and swept gracefully across the threshold as the butler thrust open the door and announced her.

"Dearest!"

Elizabeth froze in her tracks, her determination dissolving in fear as Justin swooped down upon her, clasped her hands in his and lifted them to his lips. She stiffened and pulled back. At least, she tried to pull back—Justin's hands held hers like a vise. He pulled her close. "Remember our agreement—loving newlyweds. Act like it!" The harsh whisper steadied her. She nodded and forced a smile.

"Step aside, monsieur!"

A small, brunette woman rushed toward them. Justin gave Elizabeth a warning look, released her hands and moved to one side.

"But *non!* This cannot be." The woman's black eyes glittered. She slapped her hands to her cheeks, tipped her small head, birdlike, to one side and studied Elizabeth.

"Monsieur!" The modiste whirled toward Justin and stretched her arms forward in an ecstasy of joy. "She is exquisite! She is perfection, *non!*" She darted forward, placed her hands on Elizabeth's cheeks and turned her head gently from side to side.

"Zat face! Ah, *monsieur!* Have you ever seen such beauty!" For an instant the modiste glared at Justin as if daring him to disagree, then she stepped back, placed her hands on her hips, and smiled archly at him. "And the blush, *monsieur?* A touch of innocence that makes your 'eart beat faster, *non?*"

Justin smiled and inclined his head in acknowledgment.

Elizabeth cringed inwardly. She wanted nothing more than to leave the room and the excessively flattering woman with the phony French accent—but, of course, that was impossible. She stood with clenched hands and burning cheeks, as the designer gave Justin a smart, saucy little wink, then turned her attention back to her.

"Ahhh!" Elizabeth restrained herself from jerking back as the little woman reached up and lifted a tendril of her hair. "I 'ave not before seen such a glorious color! You wear the sunshine upon your head, *madame.*"

It was too much. Elizabeth took a step backward. "Please, Madame Duval—I do not wish to seem ungracious, but—"

"Non!" The woman gestured wildly with her hands. "Later we talk, *oui?* For now, turn. Turn!" The modiste stepped back, narrowed her eyes in concentration, and made little, tight circles in the air with her small hand.

Elizabeth glanced at Justin for help. That warning look was in his eyes again. She took a deep breath and obeyed.

"Oui." The designer gave Justin a delighted smile. "Observe the height, *monsieur.*" She flashed her hand toward Elizabeth in a quick, darting movement. "And the slenderness of her!" Elizabeth looked his way. His gaze was fastened on her. The heat rose in her cheeks again.

"Ah, amour!" Madame Duval smiled, clapped her small hands and spun to face Justin. "I 'ave seen enough!"

Elizabeth expelled her breath in relief. *Thank goodness that was over!*

"It will be an honor to dress your bride, Monsieur Randolph. What is it you wish?"

The modiste's voice had changed. She was suddenly all business. Elizabeth hurried forward. "I've made a list, Madame Duval. My husband is being most generous." She forced a smile and offered the piece of paper she held in her hand to the designer.

Justin reached between them. Elizabeth started as he seized the paper, then watched with satisfaction as he scanned the items requested. There was nothing there to anger him. She had kept the list to the bare minimum of essentials.

Justin frowned. He read the scant list again, then looked up at Elizabeth. She smiled.

Justin's frown deepened. Why was she looking so pleased with herself when— Of course! The answer hit him like a bolt of lightning. She had no need to make an extensive list of garments—indeed, she had no need to ask for a single article of clothing. She knew the social embarrassment to him if his wife was inadequately garbed.

Justin lowered his gaze to the list in his hand to hide his anger. How sly! She had adroitly maneuvered things so he would be forced to provide an extensive wardrobe for her without her even having to ask for it. She was playing him for a fool! Well, two could play these games. She would not have complete victory—he would keep control. He crushed the list in his hand and tossed the paper into the fire. "Ladies, if you will be seated, we shall settle this matter."

Madame Duval perched herself on the edge of a shield-back Hepplewhite chair and looked eagerly at him. Elizabeth stared at the wadded piece of paper as it burst into flame.

"Elizabeth?" Justin smiled when she looked up at him. He

indicated a chair. "I understand your reluctance, as a new bride, to test my generosity too far—but your list was far too modest. We shall handle this matter my way." The words almost choked him. He cleared his throat and turned to smile down into the alert, heart-shaped face of the modiste.

"Madame Duval, it is my desire that my bride have an entire new wardrobe. I do not wish her to wear a single garment now in her possession—lovely though that garment may be. That means any garment, Madame, from the... er...necessary, to the frivolous. Do you understand?"

"Oui, monsieur." The designer smiled. "I understand."

"Good." Justin ignored the gasp of surprised protest that had come from Elizabeth. "Shall we discuss terms?"

"Very wise, *monsieur*." The designer's smile faded. "You have the, uh, conditions, hein?"

"Five of them, madame." Justin smiled inwardly at the sudden, wary look in the little woman's eyes. "The first is—you must begin work immediately and set aside all other commissions until my wife's wardrobe is completed."

A tiny frown formed on the designer's forehead. "Very well, *monsieur*. We can arrange that. An' your second condition?"

"You must use only the finest of materials—and the designs must be originals that will not be duplicated by you for any other client. Also, the final designs must be approved by me."

The designer's eyes widened in surprise, but she nodded her agreement. "Next, *monsieur?*"

Justin shifted his gaze briefly to Elizabeth. "My wife

seems reluctant to lighten my purse, but you, Madame Duval, I feel certain would have no such qualms." He gave the designer his most charming smile to take any insult from his words. "Therefore, *you* are to decide what is appropriate for a new bride's complete wardrobe—taking into consideration my position in the community. You will, of course, submit the list to me for final approval."

Madame Duval's eyes glittered with excitement. She slipped the tip of her tongue through her lips and swept it from side to side to moisten them. "But of course, *monsieur.* I will be happy to comply." She gazed up at Justin. *"La quatrième?"*

"No red."

The designer's eyes flashed. "Monsieur, you insult me!" She leaped to her feet, darted to Elizabeth and clasped her chin in her small hand. "Do you think that I, Maurelle Duval, the greatest designer in all of America, would put red next to that skin!"

Justin dipped his head. "I take it you will abide by my wishes in the matter, madame. In which case—if my wife concurs—the commission is yours." He stepped forward, bowed smoothly to the irate designer, captured one of Elizabeth's hands in his, brushed his lips lightly across its back and stepped back. "Ladies, I leave you to your discussion of fashion." He headed for the door.

"Justin?"

He turned around. Elizabeth was standing and staring at him. She did not look pleased. What could she possibly want that he had not made provision for? He frowned. "Yes, what is it?"

"You said there were five conditions Madame Duval must meet, yet you have given only four. If she is to fulfill all that you require, you must tell her the last one also."

Was that all she wanted? Justin studied her face for a moment, then swept his gaze to the pile of golden curls on top of her head. "No nightcaps, Madame Duval." He scowled at the betraying husky note in his voice and lowered his gaze to lock on Elizabeth's startled eyes. "Not one." He pivoted on his heel and left the room.

Elizabeth clenched her hands into fists and stared at the closed door. *How dare he humiliate—*

"Ooh-la-la!" The breathy sigh floated over her shoulder. "To have such a man look at you with such love!" Elizabeth spun about.

"Ah, Madame Randolph, do not be so surprise', *non?*" The designer tipped her head to one side and fastened a bright, knowing gaze on her. "I, too, have known the blessing of a loving husband's strong arms." Her voice dissolved into a throaty chuckle. "I have not always been so old, and unattractive, *chérie.*" The designer winked, then laughed with delight as embarrassed color heated Elizabeth's cheeks.

"Ah, the innocence of youth." Maurelle Duval's laughter died. Tears sprang into her eyes. She reached up and touched Elizabeth's cheek with her small, soft hand. "Enjoy your husband's love, *chérie.* The years, they are too quickly gone. Now—" She clapped her hands together briskly. "We must begin. Shall we repair to your boudoir? I have need to take your measurements."

"What? Oh. Yes. Yes, of course. Follow me, Madame Duval." Elizabeth led the way across the entrance hall to the staircase and began to climb. Why had Madame Duval said such a thing? It couldn't be true. There was no married love such as the designer described. Why her own mother had told her there was only what Reginald—

Elizabeth shuddered, wrenched her thoughts from the dark pathway they had started down, and hurried along the upstairs hall toward the red bedroom with the modiste close on her heels.

Elizabeth rubbed at her aching temples and stepped into the dressing room. She had spent the last two hours being measured, studied, exclaimed over and made to walk slowly about the bedroom while Madame Duval made hurried sketches and prodigious lists. Being honor-bound not to expose the truth of her relationship with Justin Randolph, she'd had no plausible reason for refusing his generosity, or curtailing the designer's excesses, and the nervous tension that stress created had translated itself into a fierce headache.

She poured cold water into the washbasin, dipped in the cloth, then wrung it out and held it to her head as she walked toward the bed. The wardrobe Justin had commissioned would cost a small fortune. How would she ever repay—?

A soft tap on the door made her jump. She frowned at her foolish behavior. Would she never get her nerves under control?

"Yes?" She sighed and removed the cool, damp cloth from her forehead as the door opened.

"Beggin' your pardon, mum. You— Are you not feelin' well, mum?" Trudy's brow creased with concern as she eyed the cloth.

"I'm fine, Trudy. Only a bit of headache. What is it?"

The maid's eyes narrowed as she studied Elizabeth. "Your husband wishes you t' join him in the salon. But you look pale, mum. And if you're feelin' poorly...I can send word you need rest."

"No. I'll go." Elizabeth handed Trudy the cool, moist rag, walked to the mirror to pinch some color into her cheeks, then headed for the salon to join Justin. The last thing in the world she wanted was to displease him again.

Chapter Twelve

✧

His children! Elizabeth's stomach fluttered nervously as she walked beside Justin down the long hallway that led to the nursery. She had little experience of children—certainly nothing to prepare her for dealing with a three-year-old toddler who puzzled doctors because she did not speak. Her stomach fluttered again. She pressed her hand against it and took a deep breath. Was there to be nothing *normal* in her new life?

Elizabeth glanced up at Justin from under her lowered lashes. He was staring down at her hand and frowning. She was beginning to dread those frowns. She lifted her hand to touch the brooch on her gown and Justin's gaze followed the movement, then continued to raise. She looked down at the floor, but she could feel his gaze on her face. After a moment the sensation faded away. She took a chance and glanced up. His own face, again viewed through the concealing fringe of her long, thick lashes, revealed nothing, but she could sense anger in him.

Elizabeth sighed. That same anger had been present when he had told her of the child's condition, and that the doctors he had consulted felt there was no physical reason for her silence. Was he angry because the toddler was less than perfect? Was that what made him sound so distant when he spoke of the little girl and her baby sister?

She frowned and looked down at the carpet runner disappearing beneath her long skirts as she hurried her steps to keep pace with Justin's long strides. Did he not love them? A sudden rush of anger toward him on his children's behalf swept over her. She knew what it was like to have parents that didn't love you—that were cold and indifferent to you. *Oh, God, help me to love these children. To be a good mother to them. And please give me wisdom to help—*

"Elizabeth?" Justin grasped her arm. "This is the nursery."

Why was she lying down? Elizabeth opened her eyes, took one look at the dark, scowling visage looming over her, and promptly closed them again. "Wh-what happened?"

"You swooned—*again.*"

The word was pointedly emphasized.

"Oh." Elizabeth opened her eyes and, careful to avoid Justin's irate gaze, glanced around the strange room. "Where are we?"

"The third-floor sitting room. I didn't want the nursery thrown into an upheaval."

"No, of course not." She could feel him glaring at her. She stirred uneasily, wishing he would move away. He didn't. "How did I get here?"

"I carried you—*again.*"

The words were spit out as if he couldn't stand the taste of them in his mouth. Elizabeth pushed herself to a sitting position while Justin stood and watched. He made no offer of help. She bit her lower lip and looked down at the floor. He was *very* angry. "I'm sorry, Justin. I—"

"Don't apologize, Elizabeth, I don't want your apology. I want the truth! I *demand* the truth." He clasped his hands behind his back and stared down at her. "Why did you swoon?"

"I don't know. I—" A sudden image of Justin's hand on her arm, every pore of his skin, every crisply curling hair clearly visible, halted her words. A deep shudder passed through her. She had swooned when he had gripped her arm. But why? *Why?* What was *wrong* with her?

"*Well?*"

The word exploded from Justin. Elizabeth flinched. How could she explain to him what she didn't understand herself? She blinked back hot tears. "I don't know why I swooned. But I am fine now, and—"

"How fortunate." His voice dripped sarcasm. His eyes narrowed. "And how untrue."

"I beg your pardon!"

"And well you might!" Justin glowered at her. "I am tired of your lies, Elizabeth. You are not *fine.* Nor will you be for several months. Admit the truth! I know you are with child!"

"With *child!*" Elizabeth jumped to her feet and almost fell. Her legs were wobbly. She braced them against the Chippendale sofa she had been lying on and gaped up at

Justin. *"With child?"* She couldn't even grasp the idea. "How did you ever—? I'm not with child."

"You are certain of that?" Justin's tone was scathing. He held up his hand when she started to speak. "Before you answer, Elizabeth, it's only fair for me to warn you I will no longer tolerate your lying to me!"

"Lying to— *I do not lie, sir!*" Elizabeth drew herself up with regal dignity. "Nor am I with child. And I am *very* certain of that. It's quite impossible!"

"Impossible? Hah!" Justin snorted. "The only way it would be impossible is if you have never—" He stopped short and stared down at her. "Are you telling me that you have never—"

"I believe my meaning is quite clear, sir. And I do *not* discuss such things with a gentleman!" Elizabeth's cheeks felt as if they were on fire. She grasped her long skirt in both hands, lifted her chin into the air and sailed out of the room.

Justin stood rooted to the floor by shock. Why would Elizabeth lie about carrying a child now? He was already ensnared—and such a lie would become apparent in a few weeks' time.

He lifted his hands, raked his fingers through his hair, and shook his head in disgust. There was only one answer. He had made a colossal error in judgment! But if she wasn't with child, why would she—?

Greed. The word slid smoothly into Justin's mind. Yes...of course...greed. *Money!* Always money. He twisted his lips into a bitter smile. *What did you expect? Wasn't your plan based on a woman's greed? And didn't you vow to accept that?*

Justin swallowed back the bile that rose in his throat, gave a snort of disgust and strode out into the hall. "Elizabeth?" His call ended her headlong flight. She turned to face him. "We have an appointment with the children and their nurse. If you are feeling well enough I should like to keep it."

She stiffened as if her dress were suddenly made of armor. "I am feeling quite well, sir. There is no reason why I should not."

"Very well." Justin conceded the point. He led the way to a closed door on the opposite side of the wide hall and placed his hand on the knob. "Remember—we are loving newlyweds." He pushed open the door.

"You need have no fear, sir." Elizabeth's voice was a frosty whisper that chilled him as she swept by. "I shall play my part."

"Then stop calling me sir!"

Justin hissed the words. Elizabeth gave him a cool nod, stepped over the threshold and swept her gaze around the room. The walls were covered with gaily patterned paper above painted wood paneling lined with shelves of toys and books. A child's table and chairs held place in front of the shelves. On the wall to the right a brick fireplace threw warmth into the room. An extremely thin woman sat in a Boston rocker on the hearth. A small child sat in a scaled-down version of the same rocker beside her. Elizabeth's breath caught in her throat—the child looked so forlorn!

The woman rose to her feet and Elizabeth shifted her gaze to her face. There was a tight little smile on the woman's thin straight lips. She dipped her head in their direction.

"Good afternoon, sir...madam."

Justin closed the door and stepped to Elizabeth's side. "Good afternoon, Miss Brown. I've brought my wife to meet the children."

"Yes. We've been awaiting your arrival." The nanny placed the book she was holding on one of the shelves built into an alcove formed by the brick fireplace, then snapped her thin, bony fingers at the child. "Quickly, Sarah! Where are your manners? Greet your father and your new mother."

The little girl slipped from the rocker and curtsied in their direction.

Elizabeth's heart melted. She glanced at Justin, saw his dark head incline toward the toddler in polite acknowledgment, and felt again that surge of anger on his children's behalf. Why such formality between father and daughter? Was it because *she* was here for the first time? Or were they always so distant? She looked back at the toddler and her heart gave a painful jolt. The child had a rag doll clutched to her narrow, little chest.

There was a sudden sharp hiss from the nanny. "Where did you find that filthy thing, Sarah? I thought I'd gotten rid of it!" The woman's talonlike fingers snatched it out of the child's hands, then gripped her small shoulder and propelled her forward. "Go and give your new mother a kiss!"

The toddler winced. Tears sprang into her round, brown eyes, but she didn't make a sound. She looked down at the floor and walked forward.

Elizabeth clenched her hands into fists and dropped to her knees to keep from grabbing the nurse by her skinny shoulders and shaking her. The toddler's gaze darted to her face at the movement. Elizabeth's heart swelled. Poor little tyke—she was frightened to death!

"Hello, Sarah. I've been looking forward to meeting you." Elizabeth smiled and took hold of the toddler's tiny hands. They were trembling. "I hope you and I will become good friends. However, I must tell you that I feel very uncomfortable kissing strangers. And as you and I are not yet friends...well...I hope you won't mind if we leave the kissing until we know each other better." The toddler's round, brown eyes widened. Elizabeth smiled reassurance. She was rewarded by a lessening of the trembling in the child's hands. She released her hold on them, sat back on her heels, and clasped her own hands in her lap.

"I see you have a doll, Sarah. And I would guess she's your favorite. I had a favorite doll when I was a little girl." Elizabeth leaned forward and lowered her voice to a confidential whisper. "Would you like to know my dolly's name?" She waited for a moment, hoping for a response, something beyond the unnatural silence of the toddler, but there was nothing except a deepened intensity in her gaze. "I called him Mr. Buffy."

There was an audible sniff from the nurse.

Elizabeth's anger flared. She looked up and extended her hand. "Give me the doll, Miss Brown." The woman compressed her lips into a thin line and handed it to her.

Elizabeth looked at the doll's face and smiled. One button eye was missing. "Well, I must say, Sarah, Mr. Buffy was not as pretty as your doll. But, I loved him anyway." She smoothed the doll's well-worn dress over its soiled legs, tucked some loose stuffing back into its torn arm, and looked up. The toddler was staring at her. She smiled and gave her the doll.

"When I come to see you tomorrow, I'll tell you more about Mr. Buffy if you would like." She reached out and touched the exposed stuffing on the doll's arm with her finger. "And I'll bring my sewing kit and mend your dolly's arm. For now though, I think she's tired and would like to rest. If you'll rock her, I think she'll go to sleep."

The toddler stared at Elizabeth for a moment, then turned and climbed into the rocker hugging the doll tightly all the while.

"There's no need to mend the doll, madam. The child has a new one. I don't know how she came to have that dirty old rag one today. I threw it out some time ago."

The nanny's cold, heartless words, increased Elizabeth's anger. She watched Sarah curl herself protectively around the doll in her arms, and for an instant she saw herself as a toddler clinging desperately to Mr. Buffy and sobbing because her mother had ordered the doll destroyed. As quickly as it had come the vision vanished, but it was enough. She looked up at the nanny. "Do not do so again, Miss Brown. Sarah is to have her doll."

The nurse's eyes glittered—her nostrils flared. "Mr. Randolph is the one that ordered me to throw that old rag away and buy Sarah a new doll."

Elizabeth's heart sank. She looked at her husband. "Is that true, Justin?"

"It is."

The words made her sick. Sarah was his child. She had no authority. "Very well." She turned back to the toddler. "I'm sorry, Sarah. I spoke rashly. I—" Tears flooded the toddler's eyes and Elizabeth's throat closed on her words. She looked at the thin little arms clutching the old, bedraggled doll and something inside her snapped. She looked up at her husband. "I'm sorry to go against your wishes, Justin, but dolls are very important to little girls. Please, allow Sarah to keep this one. I will repair and clean it." She was trembling. She drew a deep, steadying breath and waited for whatever was to come.

Justin stepped forward and made the silent child a polite bow. "I did not realize how much your doll meant to you, Sarah. You may keep her for as long as you wish. Do you understand?"

The toddler stared at him for a long moment, then nodded.

"Good. And you, Miss Brown..." Justin turned to the nurse. "Do you understand?"

"Perfectly, sir. It will be as you wish."

"As my *wife* wishes." Justin made the correction firmly, then turned to offer Elizabeth his hand. He frowned and helped her to her feet. "You needn't look so astonished, Elizabeth. I'm not an ogre."

"No. Of course not." *Sarah was to have her doll!* Elizabeth gave Justin a delighted smile. "That was very kind of you, Justin—and ogres are never kind."

"They're not?"

"What?" She looked her puzzlement into his eyes. He gave a barely perceptible nod of his head in Sarah's direction. Elizabeth sneaked a peek her way out of the corner of her eye—the toddler had stopped rocking her doll and was staring at them. *Ogres! Of course!* Elizabeth flashed Justin a look of understanding and followed his lead. "Why, no. Didn't you know that ogres are never, *never* kind?" She glanced furtively around the room, leaned toward Justin and whispered loudly. "If they are ever kind they are thrown out of the ogre kingdom."

"No!" Justin recoiled in dramatic shock. "I shall have to remember that." His voice took on a dire tone. "I would not want to falsely accuse one of kindness."

"Oh, no! Never!" Elizabeth gasped and clutched at her heart with both hands. "That would be insulting to an ogre. And ogres never forgive!"

"Never?"

"Never!" Elizabeth sneaked another peek at Sarah. Her little mouth was hanging open and her round, brown eyes were big as saucers.

"I see. And you, Elizabeth? If you were insulted by being wrongly accused, would you forgive?"

Elizabeth darted her gaze back to Justin. What was he doing? What had that to do with ogres? "I don't—I mean— Yes. I suppose I would—as I'm not an ogress."

"I'm pleased to hear that." Justin's gaze locked on hers. "I hope it means you will forgive me for the rash words I spoke earlier."

Elizabeth stared at him. Was he still acting? What did he expect of her? "I—of course."

"Good! Now..." Justin turned to the nanny. "Where is the baby, Miss Brown? Is she sleeping?"

"No, sir—here she is!"

The jolly voice came from behind them. Elizabeth turned. A solid looking woman with a merry face walked into the room carrying a squirming baby in her arms. She gave Elizabeth a warm smile. "Good day, madam." Her gaze shifted to Justin. "Good day, sir. Blessings on you and your bride. May this nursery always be filled with your little ones."

"Thank you, Delia." Justin shot Elizabeth a warning look. She smiled at the wet nurse. "How very kind of you."

The woman returned Elizabeth's smile and plodded into the room on slippered feet. "So, Sarah love—" She turned her merry brown gaze on the toddler quietly rocking her doll and gave her a cheerful smile. "Your new mama understands about dolls, eh?"

Elizabeth glanced at the wet nurse in surprise. So it was *she* who had rescued and returned Sarah's doll to her. She could have hugged the woman!

A sharp, irate, squeal split the momentary silence and Elizabeth snapped her gaze to the infant in the woman's arms. The baby had grabbed the ribbon tie on the front of her gown in one chubby little fist and was trying to raise it to her mouth. She gave another squeal of frustration and tugged harder, her apple cheeks turning pink with the effort. She kicked her little feet, opened her mouth wide to again express her displeasure when, suddenly, the connection between chubby fist and tiny mouth was made and she began, instead, to suck contentedly.

"Justin, she's adorable!" Elizabeth laughed as the baby stopped squirming in the woman's arms and gave her a wide, toothless smile. She glanced up at the wet nurse.

"May I hold her? Or is she shy of strangers? I wouldn't want to frighten her."

"Well bless my soul, madam. You couldn't frighten this little termagant if you tried!" The woman chuckled and pulled the now soggy ribbon from the baby's little mouth causing a howl of protest. "Here now—that's enough of that crying. What's your new mama gonna think of such carryin's on." She glanced over at Elizabeth. "This one hasn't learned yet that she can't have it all her own way." She padded across the room to place the baby in Elizabeth's willing arms. "But she will. Won't you, lovey?" She chucked the baby under her round little chin. The baby stopped crying, gave a small hiccough, and stared up at Elizabeth with her big, brown eyes.

For the second time in the space of a few minutes, Elizabeth's heart melted. She lifted the infant to her shoulder, breathed in the soft, sweet, baby smell of her, and laughed with pure joy as the baby turned its face to hers and, planting her moist little mouth on her cheek, searched for a source of nourishment or comfort. She pulled away, but the baby only squirmed closer and intensified her search.

"What a determined little thing you are! But, alas, my small darling, you will find determination is not always the answer." Elizabeth lowered the baby from her shoulder and smiled down at her as she brushed her fingertip lightly over her tiny, button nose and across one soft, rosy cheek. The infant opened her mouth and tried to follow and capture her trailing finger. Elizabeth laughed and hugged her. "I'm afraid I have nothing for you, precious. This is the one you seek." Reluctantly, she handed the baby back to the wet nurse.

"Oh, Justin, she's beautiful!" Elizabeth spun toward him. "Your children are both beautiful!" Her throat tightened. *There was such sadness in his eyes!* Quickly, she looked down at the floor. How thoughtless she was. She had not given a thought to how painful it must be for him to see her here with the children of his true wife—the woman that was lost to him forever. Her vision blurred with sudden tears. She was so distracted by the sudden, unexpected, glimpse of his pain she barely flinched when he took her arm and led her to the door.

"Your children are lovely." Elizabeth glanced at Justin, then looked down at the pattern in the carpet runner. "I shall do my best to care for them and...and love them."

"I'm certain you will." Justin gave her a sidelong glance. "It was very astute of you to recognize Sarah's deep attachment for her old doll."

Elizabeth shook her head. "It was not astuteness on my part, it was—" She clamped her mouth closed on her words.

"Mr. Buffy?"

Elizabeth jerked her head up and gaped at him. "Yes...Mr. Buffy." She turned her face away from his searching gaze. "My! What an interesting piece." She gathered her skirts in her hands and moved quickly down the hall to admire a carved chest that stood between two windows. Anything to change the subject! She wanted no questions about Mr. Buffy, or her childhood.

Chapter Thirteen

❦

"Shall I announce you, madam?"

"That won't be necessary, Owen." Elizabeth smiled at the elderly butler. "Thank you for showing me the way."

"You're welcome, madam." The old man returned Elizabeth's smile, gave her a polite bow, and walked off down the hall.

Elizabeth watched him out of sight, then stepped to the gilt-framed mirror hanging on the wall and checked her appearance one last time. The swelling on her jaw was gone, and the bruise had faded considerably. She poked at a curl that had popped free to hang in front of her ear and succeeded only in dislodging another—two more lay against her temple. She sighed, turned from the mirror and stepped through the open door of the drawing room. Her immediate impression was one of beauty. The room was perfectly proportioned, perfectly furnished, perfectly decorated in hues of blue, gold and cream. But its atmosphere was cold. Or maybe the chill came from the man that stood waiting by the fire.

"I hope I haven't kept you waiting long."

Justin lifted his dark head and turned toward her. "Not long. A matter of minutes only." He fastened his gaze on hers.

Elizabeth fought down a sudden intense desire to turn and flee the room. There was an aura about him, an energy, that made her clench her hands into fists at her sides. She lifted her chin, unclenched one hand and raised it to touch the brooch she had fastened to the bodice of her gown. "Is the fire so interesting?" She smiled, pleased at the calm, polite tone of her voice. "Or is it what you see in the fire that holds your attention?"

"It is always what one sees in the fire that is most interesting." Justin drifted his gaze over her. He gave her a cool smile. "You look especially lovely this evening, Elizabeth. The flower in your hair is quite attractive."

"Thank you." She resisted the urge to reach up and touch the pink flower nestled among her golden curls. "The flower was Trudy's idea."

"A most resourceful young lady it seems. Are you pleased with her?"

"Yes. Very pleased."

Justin acknowledged her words with a small nod, then stepped forward and extended his hand. "Perhaps you would like to come in and sit down." He nodded toward a settee covered in gold damask.

Elizabeth felt her face flush—why had she stood frozen in the doorway like an ill-bred dolt! She moved forward and, reluctantly, placed her hand in his. "This is a lovely room. Did your wife decorate it?"

"No." He gave her a sharp look. "I prefer not to talk about my first wife, Elizabeth."

She nodded her acquiescence of his wishes—and of the rebuke. *So much for her attempt at small talk.* Her long skirt swished softly across the carpet as Justin walked her to the settee.

"Tell me—" he released her hand and stepped back to let her seat herself "—did you find Madame Duval satisfactory? Or would you prefer to interview another designer? I believe there are several the good ladies of Philadelphia patronize."

"Madame Duval is more than satisfactory." Elizabeth placed herself in the center of the settee and spread her long skirts so there was no room for him to sit beside her. "The design sketches she drew were lovely." She looked up at Justin and smiled. "I want to thank you for your generosity and thoughtfulness. I was at a loss as to how to explain my lack of wardrobe to Madame Duval. And I'm still concerned about the servants. They will surely notice the lack."

"The servants have been told it was my wish that you bring nothing from your old life with you."

"I see. Again, I must thank—"

"No need." Justin waved away her gratitude. "As your husband it is my duty to care for you—and to provide for you. You will find me capable of doing so."

"I'm certain I shall. That was not my concern." Elizabeth looked down at her hands. "I did not want to prove an embarrassment to you."

"Nor shall you."

His tone of voice made her shiver.

"You are chilly. We shall have to make certain Madame Duval does not forget to include several wraps for these cool evenings."

"I believe there is little danger of that."

Justin quirked his eyebrow. "I take it from your comment you have discovered the avaricious side of Madame Duval's nature." He moved back to his place by the fire.

Elizabeth gave him a wry look. "I shouldn't call it a discovery. It is hardly hidden." She hunched her shoulders forward and rubbed her hands together in the age-old gesture of greed. "'Of course, *monsieur!*'" Her voice was a perfect imitation of Madame Duval's throaty tones and phony accent. "'I will be happy to comply!'"

Justin burst into laughter. "You do that very well, Elizabeth. But you are not laughing. You do not find Madame Duval amusing?"

"I do not find the *situation* amusing." Elizabeth smoothed a wrinkle from her skirt and folded her hands in her lap. "I do not feel that one should take advantage."

Justin stared at her. "That's an interesting observation under the circumstances, Elizabeth." He gave her a cool look. "Am I to understand your concern is that Madame Duval will take advantage of me?"

There was an undercurrent of anger in his voice. Elizabeth glanced at his furrowed brow. Did he think she was belittling him? "Yes. But only because, in your generosity, you placed so few restraints upon her."

"I see. Well...your concern for my purse does you credit."

Elizabeth blanched at the mockery in his voice.

"However, it changes nothing. We both know the bride of a man in my position must have a suitable wardrobe. As you do not, one must be provided. Since you inform me you are without funds for such necessities, I shall have to provide them. I am willing to do so, even to the extent of paying for Madame Duval's little extras in order to accomplish a quick and satisfactory solution to the problem—for until your wardrobe is complete, all social occasions must be avoided." Justin leaned his arm on the mantel and crossed one ankle over the other. His blue eyes glinted with anger. "I do not, however, wish to give you the wrong impression, Elizabeth. Therefore, I must caution you, do not rely too heavily upon my generosity in the future. You may be sorely disappointed."

Tears of humiliation sprang to Elizabeth's eyes. She lowered her head and blinked them away. Clearly, he blamed her for the circumstances forcing him to spend such a large sum of money upon her. Oh, if only she could explain she was as much a victim of the circumstances as he! But she dare not. He was a man of honor. And if he knew she had been promised to another—

"...about that."

Elizabeth started, and looked up. "I beg your pardon?"

"The ring." Justin dipped his head.

Elizabeth glanced down. She was absentmindedly twisting the wedding band around on her finger. She stopped.

Justin frowned. "The ring is too large for you, Elizabeth. Give it to me. I'll have it made smaller." He crossed to the settee and extended his hand.

Elizabeth's breath caught. Quickly, she removed the plain gold band and dropped it onto his upturned palm. His fingers curled into a fist over it. She shivered.

"You've gone pale again."

Elizabeth jerked her head up and their gazes met. Justin stiffened. Shock registered in his eyes.

"Elizabeth, what—?"

"Dinner is served, sir."

Justin spun toward the door.

Elizabeth rose quickly. She steeled herself to take the arm she knew he would offer, and forced a smile onto her face as she looked up at him. "Shall we go in?" Justin stared down at her for a long moment, then, to her immense relief, he stepped back and bowed her through the open door. She escaped into the hallway.

The room was elegant.

Elizabeth lowered herself to the seat of the chair Owen held for her and let her gaze touch lightly on the graceful cherry furniture, the lovely pearl-blue-paneled walls and the silver-gray fabric that hung in deep, elegant swags over the large, small-paned windows. The flames of the candles in the silver candelabra, reflected in the small panes of glass that held at bay the cold, dark night, gleamed back at her. Mindful of her wifely duties, she lowered her gaze to check the table.

Justin studied Elizabeth as she looked about the room. She was *afraid* of him! There had been naked fear in her eyes in the drawing room. But why? What had he done? He frowned and shook out his napkin. Whatever it was, he would have to rectify it. No one would believe their marriage to be a normal one if they witnessed her reaction to him. He laid the napkin on his lap, then looked back across the table at Elizabeth. His heart thudded. Madame Duval was right—she *was* exquisite. But it was more than her delicately formed features that made her so lovely. It was her humor and intelligence, her warmth and charm that drew him like a magnet.

Justin stirred uneasily in his chair. He was finding it increasingly difficult to believe Elizabeth's beauty was only on the surface—that the innocence and purity she professed to were lies. He was also unhappily aware his determination to remain uninvolved with a member of the female sex was being undermined by the young lady he had made his wife.

Elizabeth glanced up, caught his eyes on her and smiled. A warm, natural smile. It paralyzed Justin's lungs and knocked the air from his body. He tore his gaze away from her soft, full lips and focused on the floral bouquet in the center of the table. There was a hole in it. "So this is where the resourceful Trudy came up with your hair adornment." He glared at the flowers. "Very clever of her."

Elizabeth glanced at the bouquet. There *was* a definite hole where a flower should have been. She glanced up at Justin. He did not look pleased. "I'm sorry. I didn't realize. I'll make certain it doesn't happen again."

"You'll do no such thing! Flowers become your delicate beauty. You must wear them often."

"I— But, I thought you—" Elizabeth sighed. "Very well. If it will please you."

"It will." Justin picked up his knife and fork and vented

his frustration on the roast beef Owen placed before him. "Simply tell Trudy that from now on she is to take the flowers *before* they are arranged."

"I shall." Elizabeth picked up her fork. "I'll tell her immediately after dinner."

Justin lifted his dark head and looked at her. "That will not be possible, Elizabeth. Immediately after dinner you will accompany me to my study."

Justin placed his hand at the small of Elizabeth's back and guided her to a chair. He could feel her trembling. That she was frightened of him, there was no doubt. It was so obvious, now that he had realized it, he couldn't believe it had escaped his attention for even a moment. The question was—what was he to do about it? And how should he best approach the subject? "I think you will find this chair comfortable." He left Elizabeth to seat herself and walked over to the French doors to stare out into the darkness and gather his thoughts. His brow furrowed in concentration. *First, he must find out what he had done to so terrify her....*

Elizabeth lowered herself into the chair Justin had indicated and stared at his back. The all but overpowering fear had ebbed as he walked away but she still couldn't relax. It was impossible. Questions assailed her relentlessly. What was happening to her? Why did she feel this sense of panic every time he came near her? And why had he suddenly asked her to accompany him to his study? Her stomach flopped. She didn't want to ponder that. With this man it could be anything!

Elizabeth took a deep breath and looked around the room for a source of distraction. She skimmed her gaze over the large, mahogany desk and the bookshelves lining the wall behind it. So this was Justin Randolph's private place. Did he conduct his business, whatever it was, from here? Did he even have a business? Elizabeth frowned. How little she knew about Justin Randolph! Her frown dissolved into a tiny smile. She had just found the distraction from her troubles she craved.

Elizabeth turned her full attention to studying the room, to seeking clues to Justin's character and actions, to ferreting out bits of knowledge that would help her understand him. The books told her nothing—she had already discovered he was well-read. The neat desk and other attractive and comfortable furnishings revealed no secrets. She looked down at the floor and smiled. There was not a trace of red to be found in the rich, oriental carpet—or anywhere else for that matter. She lifted her gaze and again glanced around the room. He liked natural colors, like brown, green and blue, if this room reflected his personal choices. And ships.

Ah! Now here was a discovery about Justin Randolph's likes and dislikes. Elizabeth focused her attention on the large oil painting centered above the graceful brick arch of the fireplace. It depicted a storm-racked ship being tossed about by an angry sea. There was something so compellingly gallant about the little ship locked in battle with the superior force of the raging sea she rose from her chair and stepped over to study it more closely.

"That's the *Barbara*." Elizabeth started, and looked at

Justin. He nodded toward the painting. "She was a fine ship, named for a fine woman—my mother."

There was such gentleness, such love in Justin's eyes Elizabeth's heart did a funny little skip. *How different he looked!* Suddenly, she realized she hadn't even considered that he might have family. More information gained! She smiled. "Your mother's name is Barbara?"

Justin's gaze dropped to meet hers. "Was. She died when I was eight years old."

There was old pain, remembered loss, in his voice and eyes. Elizabeth felt a rush of sympathy. "You sound as if you miss her still."

"Surprisingly enough I do. Though it's been almost twenty years." Justin's face tightened. He looked away.

"So this ship is real." Elizabeth, tactfully, turned the conversation from his personal loss. "This incident really happened." She looked at the picture with new interest, then suddenly gasped and turned toward Justin. "This is *your* ship." A jolt of shock zinged from her head to her toes. *A ship owner would know her father and Reginald at least by name!*

"No. She was my father's."

Elizabeth went weak with relief. She gripped the mantel to steady herself.

"But, the rest of your surmise is accurate. It really happened."

He sounded odd. Had he noticed her shock? She risked a quick glance at Justin from beneath her lashes. He was looking at the painting, not her. She released her held breath, then quickly drew another as he started toward her.

"The *Barbara* was caught in a hurricane while crossing the Atlantic. There was no time to make a safe port. We had to ride out the storm."

"We? You were there?" Elizabeth forgot her fear and looked at him in horror. "You and your father were on board?"

Justin glanced at her and shook his head. "*I* was on board. Father was ill at the time and I went to London to handle some business in his stead. We were overtaken by the storm on the return voyage."

"Oh." Elizabeth returned her gaze to the painting and mentally placed Justin on board. What a horrendous experience! "Were you frightened?"

Justin stopped just behind her. He glanced down at the golden curls piled helter-skelter on top of Elizabeth's well-formed head. They looked soft and silky. His fingers twitched. He frowned, and looked back at the painting. "Yes. I was very frightened. And very tired. The storm lasted three days."

"Three days!" Elizabeth stared at the painting imagining the howl of the wind, the feel of the driving rain, the sound of the waves crashing on the deck. "It must have been terrible."

"It was. The second day was the worst. That's the day the mast broke. When it fell it crushed Captain Dunsten, and swept two of the crew overboard." Justin stepped up beside her and touched the spot on the picture where a tangle of rope and sheeting trailed over the side of the boat into the water. "I was fortunate. I managed to catch on to some downed rigging and it held."

"You might have been drowned!" Elizabeth shivered and looked away from the painting. It had lost its charm. "Do you travel to England often?"

"No. I haven't been since Father died. I have a factor who handles my London affairs."

"I see." *Did that mean he was a ship owner?* The fear came back full-blown. Elizabeth glanced up at him. "You said the *Barbara* was a fine ship. What happened to her?"

"She was lost to the British in 1812."

"How unfortunate. Did your father—?"

Justin shook his head stopping her query. "Father died a few weeks before it happened. He never knew she was lost."

Elizabeth's heart pounded. Perhaps Justin had inherited a shipping business when his father died. Had he lost it in the war as many had, or did he own it still? Her pulse throbbed in the hollow of her throat and her head began to pound. If he owned a shipping line... *Oh, dear God, help me! I have to know!*

Elizabeth stared hard at the painting. What more could she ask? What further comment could she make to gain her the information she needed? She studied the downed rigging that trailed in the water and thought about Justin's description of that harrowing time. "It's certainly realistic. The artist did an excellent job. It must be difficult to capture such a moment."

"Not when you have experienced it."

Elizabeth jerked her head toward him. "*You're* the artist? *You* painted it?"

Justin dipped his dark head in acknowledgment.

"But why? Oh!" Elizabeth's cheeks warmed. "I'm

sorry, that was rude. I only meant that I should think you would want to forget such an unpleasant and frightening experience."

"On the contrary." Justin looked back at the painting. "I painted it to serve as a constant reminder of the dangers that threaten the lives of the men I employ on my ships. I believe it makes me a more approachable, more...tractable...employer."

He *was* a ship owner! Elizabeth's heart pumped furiously. She clutched at the mantel for support as a fit of trembling seized her. *What should she do?*

"But, I did not bring you here to discuss my philosophies or business practices, Elizabeth. I brought you here to discuss us." Justin looked down at her. "Why are you so frightened of me?"

"Wh-what?" The change of subject was too sudden, too abrupt. Elizabeth's mind went blank.

"Why are you so frightened of me?"

"Frightened?" Elizabeth yielded to her trembling knees and sat back down in the chair she had vacated. "I don't know what— I can't think—"

"Do not play games with me, Elizabeth!" Justin started toward the chair opposite her. "You know exactly what I mean. And I intend that we shall sit here and discuss this problem until we find a solution."

Elizabeth looked up, saw him coming toward her and fear squeezed the breath from her body. She lunged from the chair in headlong flight. Her legs gave way. She grabbed the back of a settee and used its strength to support her sagging weight while she gasped for air.

Justin lifted her into his arms and carried her to the front of the settee. "Sit down, Elizabeth, before you swoon." He released her.

She sank down onto the cushion, leaned back and closed her eyes, listening to him walk away.

Silence descended.

Elizabeth concentrated on breathing. Her panic ebbed. She drew a long, steady breath and opened her eyes. Justin was across the room by his desk, watching her.

"Are you feeling better?"

"Yes."

He nodded. "That being the case, perhaps you will be good enough to answer my question." He leaned against his desk and crossed his arms over his chest. "Why are you frightened of me, Elizabeth?"

She bit her lip and shook her head.

"Don't bother to deny it. We both know it's true. I have only to walk over there to prove it." He straightened. "Do you want me to come over there?" He took a step toward her.

"No!"

"I thought not." He relaxed back against the desk. "Don't ever lie to me again, Elizabeth. I'll not tolerate it!"

Her chin jutted into the air. "I told you, I do *not* lie. I was not denying the fear. Only that I have no explanation for it." The admission sapped the false strength supplied by her anger. She leaned back against the leather settee, too weary to protest further.

Justin studied her for a moment, then walked to the French doors and stared out into the inky darkness. "It is nothing I have done?"

"No. Nothing."

"Yet you nearly pass out from fright when I come near you." He raked his hands through his hair and began to pace the room.

Elizabeth kept silent. Poor man. He must think himself burdened with a mad woman. *Was* she? Oh, there was so much she didn't understand! Tears sprang to Elizabeth's eyes. She blinked them away and lifted her hand to touch the brooch fastened to her gown. Her taut nerves jumped when Justin suddenly stopped pacing and looked at her.

"This cannot continue, Elizabeth. We *must* appear to be a normal, loving couple—in our home as well as in public. If this fear continues, it will not be long before the servants begin to notice and then——" He left the sentence unfinished and frowned, raking his hands through his hair again.

"I'll do better. Truly I will. Look, I'll show you!" She rose and rushed across the room to him. "Take my hands." She held them out in front of her. They were shaking.

"Elizabeth, this is not—"

"Please?" She fought back tears. What if he cast her out? What if he had their strange marriage set aside? *Oh, dear God—what if he knows Father and Reginald!* "Please, Justin."

He lifted his hands and gently folded them around hers.

"There! You see?" She gave him a tremulous smile. "You are touching me, and I am fine."

"So you are." He looked down at their joined hands.

The fear of being cast out and adrift on her own should Reginald or her parents find her left Elizabeth in a rush.

"Thank you, Justin. Thank you. I give you my pledge you'll not be sorry for your kindness."

He nodded and released her hands. "Go sit down, Elizabeth. You're still pale and trembling, and your hands are like ice." He walked around the desk to the bell pull by the window, gave it a yank, then turned back to face her. "I'll have Owen escort you to your room. You may rest easy tonight. I will stay in my own chambers out of consideration for your health."

"But what of—" His raised hand stopped her.

There was a discreet knock. The door opened.

"You wished to see me, sir?"

"Yes." Justin looked over at his aged butler. "Escort Mrs. Randolph to her room, Owen. And see that Trudy attends her—she's not feeling well. She needs rest."

"Yes, sir. Will that be all, sir?"

"No. Bring my greatcoat when you return. I'll be going out this evening."

The muscle along Justin's jaw twitched as the door closed behind Elizabeth and Owen. He marched over to the French doors, flung them open and took in deep gulps of the cold, damp air. He shouldn't have agreed when Elizabeth said she was fine. But, she'd been shaking so hard, had looked so frightened and fragile, and was trying so hard to be courageous in the face of it all, he simply hadn't been able to do anything else. But, he'd wanted to...he'd wanted to. He'd wanted to take her in his arms and hold her until whatever was causing the fear that haunted her went away.

Justin shook his head and rubbed the tense muscles at the back of his neck. He must not allow compassion to ensnare him—to blind him to the truth of Elizabeth's character. He would find another way. He stepped back and closed the French doors. There had to be a reason, something more than his occasional brusqueness that caused Elizabeth's fear, and he intended to find out what it was.

The door clicked shut.

Elizabeth sat up and looked at the tray of biscuits and warm milk on her bedside table. How kind and thoughtful of her comfort everyone was. No, that wasn't right. They were thoughtful of Justin Randolph's wife's comfort. Justin Randolph's wife. That sounded so strange! Somehow, she had to grasp the reality of the fact that *she* was Justin Randolph's wife. But how? And for how long? What would happen to her if Justin found out about her father and Reginald?

Elizabeth sighed and threw back the covers. It was safe to get up now. Owen had told Trudy of Justin's order for her rest. She would not be disturbed again. She lapped the sides of the blue silk dressing gown more closely about her and tightened the sash. She *was* exhausted. She could not remember ever feeling so unutterably weary. She did need rest. That she would get any in her present agitated state was unlikely. She glanced at the biscuits and milk again. How lovely if troubles could be cured so simply.

Elizabeth shrugged her shoulders and padded on bare feet to the window. Where had Justin gone? And for what purpose? There were no answers written on the darkness.

She shivered from the cold radiating off the glass, and left the window for the comfort of the fire. The heat felt good. She turned slowly, letting the warmth embrace her while she watched the play of firelight reflected in the dark-blue silk of the dressing gown. *His* dressing gown.

She stared down at her toes peeking out from under the fabric she held off the floor, then smiled and walked to the wardrobe, picked up the moccasins Justin had given her and carried them back to the chair by the fire. They felt good on her cold feet, but the rough leather looked ridiculous against the smooth elegance of the blue silk. She lifted her legs straight out in front of her and giggled. "Charming, my dear. Utterly charming!"

Her laughter was lost in the vastness of the room.

Elizabeth sobered and lifted her head to stare into the dark, distant corners the light of the fire did not reach. The room had not seemed so large or lonely last night. She threw another piece of wood on the fire. Hot flames licked hungrily at the new fuel. There. That should brighten things up. She turned to face the room. It still felt lonely. She sighed and walked to the writing desk, extending a long, tapered finger to trace the delicate lines of a scrimshaw ship. The ivory was cool and smooth to her touch. The outline of the ship was similar to the one in the oil painting in Justin's study—except that this one had its mast and rigging in place. Elizabeth shuddered and moved away.

Why was she so frightened by Justin? He had been thoughtful and kind—in his cold, distant way. There was simply no reason for that horrible, smothering fear that came over her every time he came near.

Elizabeth crossed to the mantel and took down a porcelain figurine. Whatever was causing the violent emotions that had shaken her these last few days, she wanted it to stop. It was exhausting, and unnerving, and *enervating* to suffer such— She caught her breath and stared down at the figurine in her hands. The man's hand gently cupped the woman's face as they gazed deeply into each other's eyes. It was a moment of tender intimacy. Elizabeth's face tightened. Why did artists portray love as something tender and beautiful, when the reality of love was so sordid and ugly?

"You're a lier!" Elizabeth placed the figurine on the mantel before she gave in to the impulse to smash it on the black marble hearth. As she lowered her hands, the man's face seemed to change. It became Reginald's face, contorted with anger.

Elizabeth gasped and backed away. She turned and ran to the window. There was nothing to see but inky darkness.

Why didn't he come back? Elizabeth went perfectly still, startled by the sudden realization that she wanted Justin to come back. She wanted him here—with her. How ridiculous when he terrified her! Yet, in some way she didn't understand, she felt safe with him. Oh, that made no sense at all!

Elizabeth leaned against the window frame and rubbed at her temples. Why would she want to be around a man who was cold and aloof, disdainful and abrupt, angry and bitter? Was it because that wasn't the real Justin Randolph, any more than this tearful, frightened person she had become was the real Elizabeth Frazier? Were the anger and bitterness simply Justin's way of dealing with pain and grief and loss?

Elizabeth rested her head against the wood and closed her eyes. So many people Justin loved had died—his mother and father, the young man that was murdered, his wife. His *true* wife. Small wonder his anger and bitterness were directed at herself. The woman he loved was dead—and she stood in her place.

Elizabeth arched her neck and leaned her forehead against the cold windowpane. What would it be like to be loved by Justin Randolph? To truly be his wife?

No! She jerked her head back and opened her eyes. She could no longer allow herself to think such thoughts—to dream foolish fantasies. Reginald had shown her the truth about such things. And her mother had told her all men were alike about married love.

Elizabeth shuddered, and returned to the fire.

She pulled the dressing gown closer about her legs, then curled into the chair and huddled there staring at the dark, empty room—hating the lie her life had become, and knowing it had to continue. Above everything, for her sanity and her safety, she dare not tell Justin Randolph the truth. She could not bear it—would not survive it—if he made her go back.

"Thank you for your time, Dr. Allen. I appreciate you seeing me this evening. And I apologize again for intruding on your personal time."

"Not at all, Mr. Randolph. I'm only sorry there is nothing positive I can offer you in the way of assistance. Unfortunately, emotional disturbances are very nebulous things that my profession knows little about. I can only advise patience and love."

"Yes. Well, thank you again, Doctor. For your advice *and* your time. Good evening."

"Good evening, Mr. Randolph."

Chapter Fourteen

❧

Elizabeth followed in the wake of the plump house-keeper's swinging skirts as they descended the stairs to the second floor. They had been through the entire house and she had found nothing to fault in the up-keep—only in the cold, sterile atmosphere. There was no warmth, no laughter, no life. Not even in the nurs-ery. *Especially* in the nursery—except for the baby and her wet nurse.

Elizabeth's forehead furrowed. Miss Brown should def-initely be replaced. Her original unpleasant impression of the woman had been reinforced upon their second meeting a few minutes ago. She quailed inside at the thought of fac-ing Justin with such a request, particularly after last night, but for the children's sake she would do it. The memory of Sarah's pinched little face would haunt her until she did.

The housekeeper turned left at the bottom of the stairs and Elizabeth looked about to get her bearings. She needed to become familiar with the large house quickly if she was to perform her wifely duties well.

"Mrs. Jeffers?"

"Yes, madam?"

"I don't recall this room." Elizabeth paused in front of the door beside her. "Have I seen it?"

"No, madam."

Elizabeth gave the woman a look of gentle rebuke. "I asked to see the entire house, Mrs. Jeffers. That includes this room." She reached for the doorknob and twisted her wrist—her hand slid on the cool metal. "It's locked!"

"Yes, madam."

Elizabeth frowned at the stilted answer. "Unlock it, please." She stepped back to give the woman room.

"I cannot do that, madam."

Elizabeth stiffened. Was the woman defying her? Was this some sort of test of her authority in this house? She lifted her chin and held out her hand. "Give me the key, Mrs. Jeffers."

The woman's face flushed. "Mr. Randolph has the only key, madam."

"Mr. Randolph?"

"Yes, madam."

"I see." Elizabeth slid her gaze back to the door. Why should it be locked? What was in there? She squared her shoulders and turned back to the housekeeper. It was time to establish her position as mistress of this house. "I think an explanation is in order, Mrs. Jeffers. What exactly is this room? And why is it locked?"

The housekeeper's face tightened. "It's the bridal chamber, madam. And it's been locked since...well... since the first Mrs. Randolph died. Mr. Randolph himself locked the door and walked away. It's not been opened since."

Elizabeth focused on the mundane to hide her shock. "You do not clean the room?"

"No, madam."

"I see." The pain she had seen on Justin's face in the nursery flashed into Elizabeth's mind. "He must have loved her very much."

The housekeeper stiffened. "It's not for me to say, madam."

Elizabeth bit her lip and frowned—she hadn't meant to speak that thought aloud. "No, of course it's not, Mrs. Jeffers. I didn't mean to—"

"I've found you, mum!"

Elizabeth turned toward a breathless Trudy and smiled her gratitude for the opportune interruption. "What is it, Trudy?"

"Beggin' your pardon, mum." The panting maid halted in front of Elizabeth and bobbed her imitation of a curtsy. "Madame Duval is here for your fittin'. I showed her to your room."

"Oh, my! I'd completely forgotten." Elizabeth started down the hall, then stopped, and turned back toward the housekeeper. "Mrs. Jeffers, I'd like to continue with a thorough examination of the linen stores after luncheon."

"As you wish, madam."

Elizabeth hurried away.

Penelope Jeffers blew out a gust of relief and looked at the young maid. "You came in the nick o' time, Trudy! She was askin' about the locked door."

"The locked door?" Trudy watched Elizabeth disappear around the far corner of the hallway. "Do you suppose he ain't told her about—?"

"The less said about the likes of Margaret Randolph the better!" The housekeeper started off down the hall.

Trudy fell into step beside her. "Well she's goin' to hear about her someday. Someone is certain to gossip when they start socializin' an' then—"

"And then Mr. Randolph will explain. It has aught to do with you, Trudy." The housekeeper gave her a fierce look. "You keep your place, missy! And don't you be actin' like that uppity stick of a children's nurse *she* brought with her. What a one to put on airs! And *mean...*" Penelope Jeffers's voice shook with anger. "It's criminal the way she treats that poor little girl in her care. And Mr. Randolph too wrapped up in his own miseries to notice what's going on under his very own—"

"There you are, Mrs. Jeffers! I've been searching for you."

The housekeeper jerked to a dead stop. "Land o' Goshen, Owen, you needn't scare a body out of their wits!" She glared at the silver-haired butler standing in her path. "What is it?"

"It's Cook." Owen gave the housekeeper an apologetic little smile. "She's having one of her little moods."

Penelope Jeffers gave a disgusted snort and raised her hands into the air. "I knew there was trouble brewin' in the kitchen this morning! I could smell it in the air." She hurried off toward the back stairs with her wide skirts swishing violently back and forth, and Trudy and Owen close on her heels.

* * *

The food was delicious, but Elizabeth was only toying with it. Justin took a last bite and laid down his fork. "You seem distracted, Elizabeth. Is something troubling you?"

She gave up the pretense of eating. "I'm sorry, Justin. I didn't mean to be rude. I do have something I would like to discuss with you. When it's convenient of course." She glanced up at him.

There it was again! Justin stared into Elizabeth's dark-blue eyes while the elusive something hovered at the fringe of his mind. *What was it?* He frowned, and she looked down at her plate. The thought disappeared. It just dissolved away before he could grasp it.

Justin threw his napkin onto the table, and looked back over at Elizabeth. There were faint dark circles under her eyes—evidence that she had not rested well last night in spite of his absence from her bedroom. Perhaps she was ill. Perhaps that was what she wanted to discuss with him. He didn't like the worm of fear that wiggled through him at the thought. He reached for the silver bell on the table beside him. "I've time now, Elizabeth. I'll have Owen fetch our wraps, and we'll stroll through the gardens and discuss whatever is troubling you as we walk. The weather has warmed considerably and the outside air will do us both good."

Elizabeth did her best to hide the nervous fear that Justin's closeness caused—after her avowals of last evening she dare not let it show. She took a deep breath of the cool, fresh air and concentrated on the bricks in the path. That one was a darker red than the others. And that one had a small chip out of one corner...

A bird in the trees to the left of the path twittered softly. Elizabeth lifted her head and searched for it among the branches.

Justin pointed. "It's a robin. The first I've seen this year. Spring is on its way."

"Yes. The first robin makes it official. Oh, and look! It's a primrose." Elizabeth rushed forward. Her long skirts billowed out around her as she squatted down at the edge of the path and reached out to touch the petals of a flower pushing its way through a shadowed patch of snow. "Isn't it beautiful? It's like a promise."

"A promise?" Justin glanced down at the small patch of bright yellow in the snow. "In what way?"

Elizabeth's pleasure in the moment flew. When would she learn not to blurt out what she was thinking! She glanced up at Justin. "It was only a foolish thought. Nothing you would care to hear about."

"Oh, but I would. Please explain." He folded his arms across his chest, leaned back against the thick trunk of a maple tree and crossed one ankle over the other. His attitude said more clearly than words he was prepared to stay here until she complied.

Elizabeth held back a sigh. "Very well. I simply meant that this flower, blooming as it is in the midst of the cold, dark and dead things that are all around it, is like a promise from God. A promise that life and beauty and the lovely things of this world go on in spite of...well...in spite of the cold, dark things that happen to us." She looked away, then placed the fingers of one hand on her forehead and closed her eyes. Why hadn't she made up a different story? Now he would add foolish whimsical romantic to his other low opinions of her.

Elizabeth braced herself for a scornful comment, but there was only silence. She gathered her courage and looked up. There was an odd expression on Justin's face. He looked stunned. No, that was too strong a word. He looked... shaken. Why? What was wrong? What had she done now? She rose to her feet and leaned forward to brush at the bits of snow clinging to her cloak. "I had better go in now." She turned toward the house.

"Not yet, Elizabeth. You haven't told me what it is you wish to discuss with me."

She halted and swept her gaze up to meet his.

"Are you chilled?"

She shook her head. "No. It's only that I told Mrs. Jeffers I wanted to go over the linen stores. And I promised Sarah I would visit her this afternoon and mend her doll." She took a deep breath. "Actually, it's Sarah I wanted to discuss with you. I'm concerned about her."

"Oh?" Justin straightened away from the tree. "Because she is mute?"

"Certainly not!" She shot him a look of pure indignation. "It has nothing to do with her inability to speak."

"I see. But there is a problem?"

"I believe so."

He studied her for a moment, then nodded. "You're very solemn, Elizabeth. I think I must hear what you have to say. Mrs. Jeffers can wait." He waved his hand, indicating the path ahead. "Shall we continue our stroll while you tell me what is troubling you?" It wasn't a question. She nodded and started down the path away from the house.

Justin fell into step beside her. She glanced up at him, then looked back down at the ground. It was obvious she was nervous. He kept silent and walked along beside her, giving her time to relax—if she *could* relax when she was with him. He frowned at the thought, and clasped his hands behind his back.

"I don't know how to begin."

Her voice was soft, hesitant. He glanced over at her, and she rushed into speech.

"I don't want to be presumptuous, Justin. And, of course, I know that as Sarah's father *you* know—far better than I—what is best for her. And yet, I...well...I..."

"Elizabeth?"

"Yes?"

"Will it be easier for you if I tell you I am not Sarah's father?"

She jerked to a stop and gaped up at him. "But I— You're not?"

"No. The children are not mine." Justin looked down at her shocked face and cursed himself for a fool. He was not ready for this. He had not intended to tell her at all. This woman played havoc with all his plans!

"I don't understand."

She was looking at him as if he had suddenly turned into one of those ogres they had discussed yesterday. Justin raked his hands through his hair. "It's quite simple. I married the children's mother while she was carrying Mary." He could hear the bitterness creeping into his voice, feel his facial muscles stiffening as he spoke of Margaret. He started off down the path. "Sarah has been in my care for a little less than a year—and, of course, for the first seven months of that time her mother was alive." The anger was building in him. Justin cleared his throat and made a conscious effort to relax. "She...died...a few weeks after Mary was born."

"Oh, Justin, I'm so sorry." Elizabeth's eyes filled with tears. She stopped to wipe them away. "I don't know what to say. It must have hurt terribly to lose her after so little time."

"I prefer not to discuss it, Elizabeth." Justin pressed his handkerchief into her hand and moved on. He kicked a clump of dirty snow off the path so her skirts would not become soiled. The violence of the gesture relieved his anger a little. "Tell me what is troubling you about Sarah."

Elizabeth dabbed the tears from her eyes, crumpled Justin's handkerchief into a damp wad in the palm of her hand and followed after him. "It's Miss Brown. I'd like to replace her."

"Replace her?" He stopped so abruptly Elizabeth almost ran into him.

"Yes." She adjusted the hood that had slipped to her shoulders. "She's bad for Sarah."

He stared down at her, intrigued by the sudden change in her voice. "You sound very certain of that."

"I am."

Justin's left brow rose. This was a different Elizabeth. One he'd not seen before. He fought back a smile. "Perhaps you had better explain."

She nodded and lifted her skirts over a damp spot on the path. "The thing that most concerns me is that Miss Brown frightens Sarah."

Justin's eyebrows shot skyward. He gave Elizabeth another quick assessing glance. She was dead serious. "Go on." He clasped his hands behind his back and walked forward beside her as she explained.

Chapter Fifteen

She couldn't sleep—a storm was brewing. Elizabeth slid from the chaise and padded across the carpet to look out the window. The wind whistled around the house, plucking with angry fingers at the denuded branches of the trees in the gardens and sliding through the tiny cracks around the window. She pulled the blue silk dressing gown more closely about her and watched the increasing frenzy of the thrashing branches as they struggled to battle their unseen foe. A shutter came loose and banged against the house.

Elizabeth darted a gaze at the bed. Justin hadn't stirred. How could he sleep with the wind howling so? For a moment she studied his face. In slumber, the cool, aloof look of rigid self-control was gone. He looked younger, softer, more approachable. And had certainly proved himself to be so today. Elizabeth smiled. Miss Brown had been dismissed.

Justin stirred and Elizabeth averted her gaze. She turned

back to the window and watched the shadowy branches continue their tortured dance in the darkness. They were like her thoughts, rushing this way and that way, trying to grasp an unseen, unrecognizable foe.

Like fear.

Elizabeth stole another look at Justin. What a complicated man she had married. He wasn't really cold, distant and impervious to human feelings as she had first thought. His mask of cool disdain had slipped several times since their arrival at Randolph Court and she had seen the pain in his eyes. She had also witnessed the anger and bitterness with which he fought the pain.

How terrible. How *tragic* to have love snatched from you after so short a time. Seven months. Only seven months! Such a short time to know happiness. Elizabeth lifted her hands and wiped the sudden, unwelcome tears from her eyes. Tears would not help, and she did want to help Justin. He had suffered so much loss—his parents, his wife, the young man that had been murdered. Elizabeth shuddered. What a horrible way to lose someone you loved.

Lightning lit the distant sky. She looked up at the sudden flash of light. One's life could change just that quickly. Hers had. And Justin's? Well, one moment he'd had a family—and then there were only the children. She thought she understood, now, why he seemed distant with them. It must be difficult to learn to be a father in the midst of grief. No wonder he had decided to purchase a wife. No wonder he wanted no personal involvement or intimacy.

Elizabeth sighed. She felt the same. And while she could not give Justin back his love or happiness, she could give him friendship and understanding. She could do her best to replace the cold, sterile atmosphere that filled his house with one of warmth and comfort. She could, and would, love and care for his children. And she could do her best to take the pain from his eyes and make him smile.

The wind stopped. There was a sudden, dead silence—and then the first drops of rain fell. They came slowly, distinct and separate, and then ever more rapidly until tiny rivulets of water coursed down the window in front of her like tears down a grief-stricken face. Elizabeth lifted her hand and rested her fingertips lightly against the cool windowpane. "Dear God, are You crying for the pain of Your children?" Her soft whisper was lost in the mournful sigh of the rising wind.

For a long time Elizabeth stood in the darkness and watched the raindrops slide down the window while she thought about Justin and the children. The compassion in her heart grew. Determination blossomed in her spirit. She lifted her face toward heaven. "Dear God, please help us. Please make this house into a home, and Justin, Sarah, Mary and myself into a true family. And, God, please—help me not to be afraid."

There was another flash of lightning. Thunder crashed and rumbled. Elizabeth sighed and padded back to the chaise. What good would her prayer do? How could God even hear her over the storm?

"Good morning."

Justin glanced up, then rose to his feet as Elizabeth swept into the dining room. "Good morning." His voice echoed the surprise on his face. "You're up early."

"Yes, I know." She stopped just inside the door. "Would you prefer to breakfast alone? I don't wish to intrude."

"Not at all." Justin left his chair and came around the table to seat her. "I would be glad of your company."

"You mustn't say so unless you mean it." Elizabeth ignored the nervous fear that surged through her as he came near. "For I warn you, I intend to join you at breakfast every morning."

Justin stared.

"There now—I've done it again." Elizabeth smoothed out her skirts. "I have shocked you also."

"Also?"

"Yes." She nodded. "I'm afraid Trudy is scandalized by my unladylike behavior. She takes her position very seriously." She gave an exaggerated sigh and shook her head in mock despair. "No doubt the other servants will be shocked as well."

Justin chuckled. "That does not seem to concern you overmuch." He returned to his place. "I'm sure Trudy will recover. As will the others."

"Then you truly don't mind?" Elizabeth's lighthearted manner gave way to serious demeanor. "I honestly don't wish to intrude."

"And, I, honestly, don't mind."

"Oh, I *am* glad. I know it's fashionable for a lady to languish in bed mornings, but I enjoy getting up and watching the world come to life. Sunsets are beautiful, but a sunrise is...is..."

"Invigorating?"

"Yes! That's it exactly. Invigorating!" She smiled across the table at Justin. "You must feel the same for you knew the exact word to describe what I— Oh, Owen. Good morning."

"Good morning, madam. I hope this day finds you well."

Elizabeth smiled. The dignified butler hadn't turned a hair at her unexpected appearance. "Wonderfully well. And ravenous."

"We shall serve immediately, madam." The butler went to the server, collected the appropriate pieces of china and silver and placed them on the table before her. "I apologize, madam, that all was not in readiness for your appearance." He motioned the maid forward.

"The fault was mine, Owen." Elizabeth picked up her napkin and spread it over her lap. "I was remiss in not informing you that I would be joining my husband—" There! She had said *husband* quite naturally. "—for breakfast this morning. Ummm! This looks wonderful!" She turned her attention to the food.

Justin looked up at the butler. "It seems we will need two places at table in the future, Owen."

The old man inclined his head. "Very good, sir. Will there be anything else, sir?"

"Not at the moment. I'll ring if you're needed."

"Yes, sir." Owen bowed, motioned the maid out the door and followed after her.

"I thought you were ravenous?"

Elizabeth stopped pushing her food around on the plate and looked up at him. "The quote is correct, sir."

Justin looked down at her untouched plate. "If the food

is not to your liking you've only to tell Owen your preference." He reached for the bell beside his plate.

"Please, don't ring, Justin." Elizabeth sighed and looked up at him. "The food is fine. I'm a little nervous."

"You've no reason to be." Justin frowned. That niggling thought was hovering at the edge of his mind, again. If only he could pin it down!

"I know. Forgive me." She smiled and reached for her tea. "What do you find of interest in the paper?"

"I was reading about the new play that is coming to the Chestnut Street Theater. I have a box. We shall have to attend a performance when Madame Duval has made you a suitable gown."

"That sounds lovely. I'll look forward to it." Elizabeth removed the cover from a silver tray. The delicious aroma of hot scones wafted upward. She looked up at Justin. "Would you like—"

"By heaven that's it!" Justin slapped the table and surged to his feet. *"You have blue eyes!"*

Elizabeth jumped and dropped the tray. It clattered against the table. Scones spilled onto the spotless white cloth. "Yes. Yes, I—I do."

Fear leaped into her eyes. He suddenly realized he was bracing himself on the table and leaning toward her. "Lovely...blue...eyes." He relaxed his grip and lowered himself to his chair.

"Th-thank you."

Her voice was shaking. So was her hand. She lowered it to her lap.

Justin scowled. "Forgive me, Elizabeth, I didn't mean to

startle you. I just suddenly realized—" He stopped short. "I...er...suddenly realized I have some urgent business to attend to. If you will excuse me..." He tossed his napkin onto the table and hurried from the room.

Elizabeth stared at Justin's empty chair. What had caused that sudden, odd outburst? She reached out to pick up the spilled scones, then shivered, and clenched her trembling hands in her lap. Why had he mentioned the color of her eyes? And what, if anything, did it portend for her future?

Justin rushed down the hallway to his study. He knew now what had been nagging him all along—Elizabeth's blue eyes! In her letter "Interested" had described herself as having blond hair and *brown* eyes. He had married the wrong woman! He was sure of it. But how had it happened?

Justin entered his study, slammed the door shut behind him and rushed to his desk. There was a small click as he unlocked the top drawer. He stuffed the key back into his waistcoat pocket and began rummaging among the papers. Where was that letter? He tossed the marriage certificate, the marriage of convenience agreement and the financial settlement contract he and Elizabeth had signed to the top of the desk out of his way and continued to search for "Interested's" letter. Suddenly he straightened. He had given the woman's letter to the judge. Now what? He wanted to make absolutely sure before he— Before he what? Accused Elizabeth of being an impostor?

Justin scowled and sat down in his chair. Did he want to do that? What purpose would it serve? He scooped up the papers on the desktop to toss them back into the drawer and then stopped. He ought to read them. Especially the financial agreement. But did he want to know the extent of Elizabeth's greed?

Justin twisted his lips into a smile of contempt for his weakness. The papers he held in his hand contained all he knew of the woman he had married and—no. No! That wasn't true. He knew much more than these papers could ever tell him. He knew the warmth of her smile and the music of her laughter. He knew the shy way she spoke his name, and the delicate blush that tinted her cheeks when one hinted at intimacy. He knew the softness of her heart toward children, and the courage with which she tried to hide the fear that haunted her. He knew her candor, and her humor. And he had tasted of her indignation and spirit. He knew the gentleness that clothed her, and the innocence and vulnerability that looked out of her eyes. He knew she was everything he had ever wanted and had given up all hope of ever finding.

Justin surged to his feet and threw the documents down onto the desk. How had this happened? With all his careful planning, how had everything gotten so turned around?

He lifted his hands, raked them through his hair, and began to pace the room. It was impossible, that's all. Impossible! How had Elizabeth happened to arrive at the Haversham Coach House just at that time? And why had she married him? Only the woman that—

Justin jolted to a halt. What had happened to *her?* To the woman whose letter he had answered? Where was she? His features tightened. The woman. He didn't even know her name. She had signed all correspondence "Interested"— and he had signed his "Widower." He quirked his lips into a wry smile. What elaborate care he had paid to every detail of his plan. He had left nothing to chance. Yet the carefully thought out scheme had somehow become rearranged into something entirely different. Thank God it had! Thank God "Interested" had, for whatever reason, not kept their appointment. If she had...if he had left when he started to...if Elizabeth had arrived even a few minutes later...

Something very like panic seized Justin. He had a sudden, urgent desire to run and find Elizabeth—to hold her close. Only a few minutes either way, and he would never have met her. Never have married her. A knot the size of his fist tightened in Justin's stomach. Something as simple as a few minutes, and their lives would have been irrevocably altered. The thought set him pacing again.

How had it happened? The question went over and over in his mind as he sought an answer. No one had known he was going to be at the Haversham Coach House that evening, except the woman to whom he had written. Not even the judge and Laina had known until a few hours before the appointed time. It was an accident. A bizarre circumstance of fate. It *had* to be. There was no way Elizabeth could have known. No way she could have planned to—

Justin went dead still. If Elizabeth hadn't known...if she hadn't planned it...if she hadn't written the letter— *Then she had never lied to him!* Justin's heart thudded with excitement, then lurched painfully. Unless, of course, it was over the money.

The knot in the pit of his stomach grew. He turned back to the desk and stared down at the documents he had thrown there. Financial settlement contract—the words fairly leaped up at him. Elizabeth had told him she had no money. Justin picked up the contract and slapped it softly against his palm as he began to pace once more, the greed and deceptions of the women in his past rising in his mind.

Elizabeth was quick, intelligent. Even if her appearance at the Haversham Coach House *was* a quirk of fate, she must have realized immediately the golden opportunity being offered her as the judge explained about the marriage of convenience and the financial settlement. She must have decided, then and there, to marry him for the money. It was the only answer that made sense since she was not with child. It *had* to be the money. There was no other plausible explanation.

Justin looked down at the title of the paper he held in his hand: Financial Settlement Contract. Was Elizabeth what she claimed to be—or a greedy little liar? The answer was there. Should he give in to the mistrust caused by Rebecca and Margaret and read it? Or should he trust his heart?

Justin convulsed his hand into a fist, crushed the paper into a wadded mass and sent it flying into the fire. The paper flamed brightly, curled into black ash and disintegrated into small black flecks that fell through the grate to the red-hot coals pulsing beneath.

Stunned by what he had done, Justin sank down onto the leather settee, propped his elbows on his knees, and covered his face with his hands.

Chapter Sixteen

❖

Justin couldn't leave Christ Church fast enough. The pew that had been his family's since before he was born felt uncomfortable and alien to him. Not surprising since he felt the same way about God. The only reason he attended church at all was ingrained habit, and—if he was honest—to maintain an acceptable image among his peers. It had been that way for months now.

Justin held back a scowl, put on a smile and doffed his hat as friends bid them good day. He turned toward the carriage, relieved the after service amenities were over and they could go home. He had much to think about. There had to be a way to find out who Elizabeth was, and how she had come to marry him. He nodded a polite greeting to a passing Quaker family, handed Elizabeth into the carriage, then climbed in after her.

The horses' hoofs clattered against the cobblestones. The buggy lurched away from the raised brick walkway and fell into line with the other carriages heading south on Second Street. Justin relaxed back against the seat.

"Your friends are very kind." Elizabeth smoothed a fold in her skirt, then raised her gaze to him. "I hope you were pleased with my performance as your bride."

Performance. The word added to his foul mood. He gave a brief nod. "More than pleased."

Elizabeth waited, but he said nothing more. She held back a sigh. "Christ Church is beautiful. I've never seen such a tall steeple."

Justin glanced her way. "It's almost two hundred feet tall. It's the first thing one sees of the city when sailing up the Delaware. A welcome sight to those who have been months at sea."

Elizabeth tensed. It unnerved her to think of Justin's possible business connections to her father, or Reginald Burton-Smythe. She glanced out the window as the carriage turned right. A building stood in the middle of the street. A long row of adjoining one-story stalls stretched out behind it. "What is this place?"

"That's the Old Court House. It was built in William Penn's time. That building has seen a lot of history—as has the whole of Philadelphia."

His voice had warmed. Elizabeth smiled. "You sound proud of your city."

"I am. Justifiably so." He removed his hat and placed it on his knee. "America was born here. Philadelphia deserves pride from all her citizens. From all Americans."

"I'm afraid my knowledge of our country's history is woefully lacking. We weren't taught such things at Miss

Pettigrew's Academy." Elizabeth turned back to the window. "And what are the empty stalls?"

"A marketplace. The stalls are deserted now, but early tomorrow morning they will be teeming with farmers, butchers and craftsmen selling their produce and wares. The street will be so crowded with ladies and their maids, cooks and others seeking to purchase what is offered, it will be all but impassable for those in carriages."

"I see." Elizabeth felt a twinge of housewifely duty. She glanced back over at Justin. "I shall accompany Cook here one day and discover what is offered—though I've yet to learn what foods are to your liking." Her cheeks warmed. That had sounded too intimate.

Justin stared at her for a moment, then stirred in his seat and cleared his throat. "I'm easily pleased."

He sounded brusque. Elizabeth nodded and reached for the hold strap as the carriage swayed left. They rounded another corner. She stared out the window, taking in the sights of her new home town. At least the sun was shining on her first excursion beyond the walls of Randolph Court. "Those are lovely gardens, it must be beautiful when all the trees are leafed out and the flowers are in bloom." Another building cut off her view. "What is that building?"

"Philosophical Hall—where the American Philosophical Society meets."

Elizabeth leaned back and looked at Justin, intrigued by all she was learning. She had never been free to ask her father questions. "And what do they do?"

"They discuss ways to improve farm crops, new business practices—things that will improve the quality of life." His eyes lit with enthusiasm. "Right now we are discussing the possibility of a canal system to ease and increase trade with the west—" He stopped as the carriage came to a halt. "Ah, home again."

The door opened. Justin climbed out, then turned and offered her his hand. Elizabeth took a deep breath, put her hand in his and stepped out. The sun warmed her face as she walked beside him up the steps of the portico. *Things that will improve the quality of life.* That certainly didn't sound self-serving. She looked at her husband with new-found respect, then lifted her gaze to the lovely fanlight. Peace and promise. Perhaps she *would* find those here.

Elizabeth finished pouring their tea and handed Justin his cup. He lifted it to his mouth and studied her over the brim as he took a swallow of the hot, black brew. There were so many questions he wanted to ask her—so much he wanted to know. Plague that agreement! The thing was haunting him. "No personal contact"…"no probing into the past"…"each partner's life to remain separate and private." Hah! He was shackled by his own cleverness.

Justin scowled, took another swallow of tea and winced as the hot liquid burned his throat. He coughed, put the cup down, and leaned back in his chair. There had to be a way to find out about Elizabeth—who she was and how she had come to marry him. Of all his questions, that was the one he needed an answer for: *Why had she married him?* It was obvious she was well-born, and since she wasn't carrying a child she would have had every opportunity for a good marriage.

"Would you care for a biscuit? Or cake?"

The question jerked Justin out of his thoughts. Elizabeth gave him an uneasy smile, and he suddenly realized he'd been staring at her. Probably glowering, given his frame of mind. He shook his head and reached for his cup. "No. Tea is fine."

Elizabeth shifted in her chair. "I believe I'm making progress with Sarah."

"Oh?" Justin made a mental change of focus. "What sort of progress?"

She put down her cup and looked at him. "She smiled at me today. A big, *wide* smile. I was telling her about Mr. Buffy and I being stuck in the evergreen tree, and she—"

"You were stuck in an evergreen?" Justin leaned forward in his chair and gave Elizabeth his full attention. Here was an opportunity to learn something about her past—perhaps glean information that would lead to the answers to his questions. "How did that come about?"

"It was an accident. And very dull in the telling." Elizabeth reached up and tucked a curl that had fallen onto her forehead back where it belonged. "Now, as I was saying about Sarah, she—"

"I'd like to hear it."

"What?"

"The story of how you and Mr. Buffy got stuck in the evergreen. I'd like to hear it."

"Oh."

She looked decidedly uneasy. Would she remember their agreement and refuse?

"It happened a long time ago."

Justin relaxed. She hadn't remembered—or she was

too afraid of him to ignore his request? He ignored a faint twinge of guilt and leaned back in his chair. "Go on."

Elizabeth stared down at her empty cup. There was no point in refusing. There was an undercurrent of determination in Justin's voice that said he would not be diverted or dissuaded. And she needn't tell it all. She took a deep breath and folded her hands in her lap. "Every spring my mother gave a large party. The house was always full of guests, and the servants were kept busy attending them. On this particular day, Miss Essie—" She glanced up at Justin. "That was my nurse-governess—had been unexpectedly called away by a death in the family."

She lifted the teapot and looked over at him. "More tea?"

"I still have some. Please continue. You were saying your nurse-governess had been unexpectedly called away, and...?"

"And, I was not to be underfoot. So Barky—" Elizabeth poured herself more tea and added a bit of honey. "I mean, Barkley. The man was father's head groom and his name was Barkley." She stopped stirring the honey into her tea and glanced at Justin. "At three years old I couldn't pronounce his name correctly. I still think of him as Barky."

Justin grinned. "So you couldn't pronounce your l's when you were a toddler."

Elizabeth's cheeks prickled with heat. "That's correct. Anyway...Barkley took me to the grounds behind the stables to play. He had made a swing for me in a large oak tree that grows at the edge of the wooded area bordering Father's land. For a few minutes he pushed me on it, testing it I suppose, then he sat me at the base of the tree and told me to stay there until Billy—one of the stable boys—came to watch over me." She sighed and laid her spoon down.

"I obeyed for a few minutes, but soon grew impatient. I tried to climb onto the swing seat by myself but was too small to manage. And then it occurred to me that Mr. Buffy might like to swing. I laid him on the board seat and pushed as hard as I was able. The seat wobbled through the air, and Mr. Buffy flew off and landed in the top branches of a large, old laurel bush." Justin was grinning again. Elizabeth looked down and straightened her napkin.

"What did you do?"

She lifted her chin. "I tried to rescue him. I climbed into the laurel and had almost reached him when one of the branches broke and I fell. I tore my frock and grazed my face and arms on the branches, but the worst part was my hair became entangled with a branch and I couldn't move. Billy found me there, struggling and crying, frightened and furious, because I couldn't reach Mr. Buffy."

"He must have been very important to you."

Elizabeth nodded, wishing she had never opened the door for this conversation. "I have no brothers or sisters—or cousins. I do have an uncle that made an occasional, unexpected visit." She shuddered, drew a deep breath, and went on. "And, of course, Mother and Father. But they were busy with their social obligations." She could hear the loneliness of her childhood, the hurt of rejection, in her voice. She cleared her throat and tried for a lighter tone. "Mr. Buffy was more than a doll to me—he was my friend. My grandmother gave him to me." She stopped talking, and took a swallow of her tea. Maybe he would be satisfied—

"Is your grandmother still alive?"

Elizabeth stared at the pattern twining around the rim of her cup and shook her head. "No. My grandmother died when I was two years old. I never knew her. But Miss Essie said she loved me very much." Sudden tears filled her eyes. She blinked them away and raised her hand to touch the brooch on her dress.

"What happened after Billy found you in the laurel?"

Elizabeth smoothed a fold from her skirt and glanced over at Justin from under her lashes. He was watching her—waiting. She took another deep breath. "Billy was frightened when he found me. He was only a boy, and I was dirty, disheveled and bleeding—and crying, of course. And I was still struggling to reach Mr. Buffy. Billy retrieved him—to quiet me I suppose—and then untangled my hair. When he had freed me, he ran with me to the house and carried me directly to my mother."

Elizabeth's voice sounded strange and far away to her. She intended to stop the story there, but the words kept tumbling from her mouth. "Mother was terribly embarrassed. Her friends were there and my appearance was disgraceful. She demanded to know why Billy had disturbed them, and he blurted out the whole story. Her friends laughed. Mother—" Elizabeth's throat thickened. She swallowed convulsively. "Mother ordered Barkley to burn my doll, but I fought him. I held on to Mr. Buffy with all my strength, and begged Barkley not to hurt him. He let go of Mr. Buffy and lifted me into his arms. I cried and kicked and fought to get free, and then—and then Mother came and took Mr. Buffy from me. She threw him into the fire."

Something hot and wet fell on Elizabeth's hand. She looked down—another tear fell. She wiped it away. "I was banished to the nursery in disgrace, and then Father came and—and disciplined me." She shuddered and closed her eyes. "Billy and Barkley were let go. I never saw them again."

A heavy silence descended. The fire crackled. A glowing coal arced out into the room and fell on the floor at Justin's feet. He drew back his foot, kicked the ember back into the fire, then withdrew his handkerchief from his waistcoat pocket and pressed it into Elizabeth's hand.

She dabbed at her eyes. "Thank you. I seem to be very needful of your handkerchiefs." She tried to laugh, but only succeeded in causing an odd little catch in her voice.

Justin lunged to his feet. If he sat looking at Elizabeth a moment longer he would not be able to resist the temptation to hold her. He didn't know if he wanted most to comfort Elizabeth the child, or love Elizabeth the woman, but he knew he wanted her in his arms. *How he wanted her in his arms!* He moved to the fire and threw another log on the blaze.

"Forgive me, Elizabeth. I didn't realize the story would bring back painful memories, or I—"

"Please, don't." Elizabeth stared down at his handkerchief in her hand. "Please don't apologize, Justin. I'm embarrassed enough." She took a deep breath and let it out slowly. When she spoke again her voice was steadier. "I don't normally lose control like that, and I apologize for subjecting you to such a display. To cry over something that happened so long ago is foolish indeed."

"It's not foolish, Elizabeth. Time doesn't always help. Sometimes pain doesn't go away." Justin rubbed a hard knuckle across the throbbing nerve in his clenched jaw and made a determined effort to keep the bitterness out of his voice. "Sometimes pain only gets buried."

"I suppose that's true."

She lifted her gaze to his.

Justin cleared his throat. "I can see now why you understood about Sarah's rag doll. All I saw was its deplorable condition. That's why I ordered it replaced. I thought the child would be happy to have a new one." He was suddenly uncomfortably aware that he had been so caught up in his own pain, anger and wounded pride he had been as callously indifferent to little Sarah's need for love and security as Elizabeth's parents had been to hers. Margaret had never loved her daughter. She had been too busy playing her greedy little games to have any time for Sarah—but he had been just as neglectful. That she was not his daughter was no excuse—she was a child under his care. He stared down at the fire not liking the picture he saw of the man he had become. "That wasn't very sensitive of me, was it?"

He sounded...contrite. Elizabeth raised her head. "You mustn't blame yourself." Again, she strove for a light note. "After all, you didn't have Mr. Buffy to teach you."

"Perhaps he's teaching me now."

Elizabeth smiled. She'd never imagined Justin Randolph capable of such a whimsical thought. "Perhaps."

Justin turned and looked at her. "It seems unfair that Sarah and I should profit from an experience that was so painful for you."

Elizabeth raised her hand to the brooch on her bodice. "It would please me if you did."

Justin nodded and leaned back against the mantel. "That's a lovely brooch. It seems special to you."

"It is." Elizabeth smiled and looked down at the pin on her gown. "My grandmother left it to me—the one that gave me Mr. Buffy. It's all I have of her, now." She returned her gaze to him. "Sometimes when I think of her I have an impression of laughter and warmth—and sometimes I smell flowers. But it isn't even a memory. It's only an impression."

"It's an unusual piece." Justin looked away from the sadness in Elizabeth's eyes. "I've noticed it before."

Elizabeth nodded. "Grandfather had it made specially for Grandmother." She unfastened the brooch and held it out to him. "Would you care to examine it more closely?" He moved to the table and Elizabeth laid the brooch on his palm. It was a small tree, with a solid gold trunk and filigree branches dotted with tiny emerald leaves.

"It's beautiful. And, as I said, very unusual. The workmanship is exquisite."

"Grandfather gave it to Grandmother on their wedding day. He chose a tree design because he said it was an appropriate symbol of the strength of their love, the beauty it brought to their lives, and the fact that it would continue to grow as long as they lived. Grandmother left me a lovely note explaining it all. She wanted me to—" She came to a dead halt.

"To have the same kind of love in your marriage?"

She stared at him for a moment, then nodded. "Yes."

Guilt twisted deep within Justin. He laid the brooch on the table and walked back to the fire. Again, he was faced with a picture of himself that was ugly and unsettling. Not only had he consigned himself to a lonely, empty life—he had destined Elizabeth to the same fate. His bitterness and anger had reached out and engulfed her life also.

Justin gave a soft snort. How had he imagined himself so brilliantly clever when in truth he was the biggest fool he had ever known! He looked down at the gray ash at the edge of the fire and his face tightened. If he were to choose a symbol of their future life together that's what it would be—cold, gray, dead ashes. Ashes that would lay forever on the perimeter of the beautiful, flaming warmth of what might have been. He pushed the thought away. "Your grandparents were very fortunate to find a lasting love that grew with time, Elizabeth. It doesn't always happen that way."

"I don't believe it ever does."

Justin turned around. "That's an interesting observation—especially in the face of your grandmother's note. She clearly stated otherwise."

Elizabeth finished pinning the brooch back on her gown and looked up at him. "The note explained the *symbolism* of the brooch. It didn't say that it was true."

Justin stared at her, taken aback by the cynicism. "You don't believe that love between a husband and wife can grow?"

Elizabeth shook her head. "You mistake me. I don't believe that it *exists.*"

"I see." *And there was his answer.* "Is that why you married me?"

"I—" She took a deep breath and lifted her chin. "Yes. That was part of it."

Justin's questioning gaze bored down into hers but she did not explain further. She rose from her chair and began to move idly about the room. He watched her for a moment, then turned and stared down at the fire. The awful stillness in her voice as she answered had chilled him. What had *happened* to her? What was the other part she referred—?

"Is this your family Bible?"

Justin turned. Elizabeth's hand rested on the large Bible that occupied a place of honor on the rosewood table beside his favorite reading chair. Though he no longer read it, he had been unable to make himself put the Bible away—Nana would be extremely upset. He smiled at the thought. "Yes it is. It's *my* grandmother's legacy to me."

"How lovely." Elizabeth brushed her fingers lightly across the cover. "Did you know your grandmother?"

"Oh, yes." Justin smiled at a sudden rush of tender memories. "I knew her very well. She came to care for us—Father, my sister Laina, and me—when Mother died." He grinned. "I was her favorite."

Elizabeth laughed. "You seem very certain of that."

"I am. I can prove it."

Justin stepped to her side, reached down and flipped open the Bible. "There." He pointed at some handwriting on the inside of the front cover.

Elizabeth leaned over the Bible. Her blond curls fell forward and gently brushed against Justin's hand. She read the inscription aloud. "To Justin Davidson Randolph, the fourth greatest love of my life."

"That's me." Justin fought the urge to turn his hand over and run the silky softness of Elizabeth's hair through his fingers. "I'm Nana's 'fourth greatest love.'" His heart thudded when Elizabeth straightened and raised her gaze to meet his. For a moment he lost himself in the dark-blue depths of her eyes.

"And who were the three greatest loves that came before you?"

"God...Grandfather...and Mother." Being near her played havoc with his self-control. Justin walked away. He rested one arm on the mantel. "You're wrong, you know."

"Wrong?" Elizabeth gave him a quizzical look. "About what?"

"Love." Justin locked his gaze on hers. "It *does* exist between a husband and wife. And it *does* grow. I've lived in the warmth of it."

His words brought all his old, warm, wonderful memories surging to the fore. Justin fell silent. Somehow, all his memories of the goodness of love had gotten buried under the hurt and bitterness brought into his life by Rebecca and Margaret. But they were still there. They were all still there. He had just remembered them too late.

"Forgive me, Justin. I should not have spoken so. I should have remembered your wife."

Justin stared at Elizabeth. Should he explain that she had misunderstood—that he had not been speaking of

An Important Message from the Editors of Steeple Hill Books

Dear Reader,

Because you've chosen to read one of our fine novels, we'd like to say "thank you!" And, as a **special** way to thank you, we've selected <u>two more</u> of the books you love so well, **and** a surprise gift to send you — absolutely <u>FREE!</u>

Please enjoy them with our compliments...

Jean Gordon

Editor,
Love Inspired®

Peel off seal and place inside...

What's Your Reading Pleasure...
ROMANCE? _OR_ SUSPENSE?

Do you prefer heartwarming inspirational romance or riveting inspirational suspense? Tell us which books you enjoy – and you'll get **2 FREE "ROMANCE" BOOKS or 2 FREE "SUSPENSE" BOOKS with no obligation to purchase anything.**

Choose **"ROMANCE"** and get **2 FREE BOOKS**- contemporary, inspirational romances with Christian characters facing the challenges of life and love in today's world.

FREE!

Choose **"SUSPENSE"** and you'll get **2 FREE BOOKS**- contemporary tales of intrigue and romance featuring Christian characters facing challenges to their faith... and their lives!

FREE!

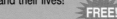

Whichever category you select, your 2 free books have a combined cover price of $9.98 or more in the U.S. and $11.98 or more in Canada.

And remember. . . just for accepting the Editor's Free Gift Offer, we'll send you 2 books and a gift, ABSOLUTELY FREE!

YOURS FREE!
We'll send you a fabulous surprise gift absolutely FREE, simply for accepting our no-risk offer!

® and ™ are trademarks owned and used by the trademark owner and/or its licensee.

THE EDITOR'S "THANK YOU" FREE GIFTS INCLUDE:

▶ 2 Romance OR 2 Suspense books

▶ An exciting surprise gift

YES! I have placed my Editor's "thank you" Free Gifts seal in the space provided at right. Please send me the 2 FREE books which I have selected, and my FREE Mystery Gift. I understand that I am under no obligation to purchase anything further, as explained on the back of this card.

PLACE FREE GIFTS SEAL HERE

Check one:

| ROMANCE |
| 113 IDL EEWU   313 IDL EFW6 |

| SUSPENSE |
| 123 IDL EFXJ 323 IDL EFXU |

FIRST NAME

LAST NAME

ADDRESS

APT.#

CITY

STATE/PROV.

ZIP/POSTAL CODE

▶ DETACH AND MAIL CARD TODAY! ▶

© 1997 STEEPLE HILL BOOKS

(LICOM-EC-06)

Steeple Hill Reader Service™ — Here's How It Works:

Accepting your 2 free books and gift places you under no obligation to buy anything. You may keep the books and gift and return the shipping statement marked "cancel." If you do not cancel, about a month later we will send you 4 additional books and bill you just $3.99 each in the U.S., or $4.74 each in Canada, plus 25¢ shipping & handling per book and applicable taxes if any.* That's the complete price, and — compared to cover prices of $4.99 each in the U.S. and $5.99 each in Canada — it's quite a bargain! You may cancel at any time, but if you choose to continue we'll send you 4 more Romance books every month or 4 more Suspense books every other month, depending on what you've chosen, which you may either purchase at the discount price…or return to us and cancel your subscription.

*Terms and prices subject to change without notice. Sales tax applicable in N.Y.
Canadian residents will be charged applicable provincial taxes and GST.

If offer card is missing write to: Steeple Hill Reader Service, 3010 Walden Ave., P.O. Box 1867, Buffalo, NY 14240-1867

BUSINESS REPLY MAIL
FIRST-CLASS MAIL   PERMIT NO. 717-003   BUFFALO, NY

POSTAGE WILL BE PAID BY ADDRESSEE

STEEPLE HILL READER SERVICE
3010 WALDEN AVE
PO BOX 1867
BUFFALO NY 14240-9952

NO POSTAGE
NECESSARY
IF MAILED
IN THE
UNITED STATES

himself, but of the love he had witnessed in his parents' and grandparents' marriages? Should he tell her the truth about his own marriage? He considered the idea, fleetingly—but only fleetingly. It would serve no purpose, and he did not care to admit to others what a fool he had been.

"There's nothing to forgive, Elizabeth." He nodded toward the Bible. "There is more writing inside." He made his voice cool and matter-of-fact, deliberately dispelling the tender emotions that filled him. "Nana was quite a one for underlining favorite passages and writing small comments in the books that she read. You'll find evidence of that in many of the books in this room. The Bible is no exception. It was her favorite reading material."

He pushed away from the mantel, moved to the table and thumbed idly through the pages of the Bible until he found what he sought. "There." He pointed to an inscription in the margin of a gilt-edged page.

Elizabeth leaned forward and read aloud the verse that was underlined. "For thus saith the high and lofty One that inhabiteth eternity, whose name is Holy; I dwell in the high and holy place, with him also that is of a contrite and humble spirit, to revive the spirit of the humble, and to revive the heart of the contrite ones." Her gaze shifted to the notation he'd indicated, and she read that also. "'Must have Laina memorize this. It will be good for her character.'" She straightened and gave him an inquiring look.

Justin chuckled. "Grandmother Davidson thought Laina a little too proud and haughty for her own good. Nana was always trying to undo the damage she said my father wreaked on Laina's character by his 'mindless doting.'" He grinned widely. "It was an old, rather comfortable, argument between them."

He reached down and tapped the underlined scripture. "This was Nana's favorite weapon. She loved to memorize and quote scripture. She firmly believed that God has an answer for every problem or circumstance of life." With a flick of his wrist he closed the Bible. His smile died.

"I take it you do not agree."

Justin looked from Elizabeth's deep-blue eyes, to the cold, gray ashes on the edge of the fire—there were a lot of empty years ahead. "You're right—I do not agree. Not anymore. For some things, there are no answers."

Elizabeth watched a bleak, bitter look settle on Justin's face. *He must be thinking of his wife again.* Her heart went out to him. She longed to offer some comfort, some word of hope, but she could find none within herself. She agreed with him. She, too, had been taught the hard lesson of hopelessness. She, too, had lost her dream, her hope of love. There was no answer for that.

She turned back to the Bible and leafed through its pages, leaving Justin to his private thoughts. At least he had this. It was almost as if his grandmother were still here. She paused at another verse that had been underlined and leaned forward to read the terse inscription beside it. "For Isaac." She looked up to ask Justin who Isaac was, but he was lost in thought. She left him to his memories and began to read, her soft voice accompanied by the crackling of the fire.

"'The spirit of the Lord God is upon me; because the Lord hath anointed me to preach good tidings unto the meek; he hath sent me to bind up the brokenhearted, to proclaim liberty to the captives, and the opening of the prison to them that are bound; To proclaim the acceptable year of the Lord, and the day of vengeance of our God; to comfort all that mourn—'"

Elizabeth's voice trembled. She lifted her gaze to Justin. He was staring intently at her, listening to her read. A feeling of awe swept over her. It was almost as if God was speaking directly to them. She lowered her gaze to the Bible and read on. "'...To appoint unto them that mourn in Zion, to give unto them beauty for ashes...'" Her throat tightened, tears filled her eyes and blurred the words—she could read no more.

Justin stared at Elizabeth. She stopped reading and silence settled around them. It was impossible. He couldn't have heard her right! He crossed to the table and looked down at the Bible, searching the page for the underlined scripture. It was there. Just as she had read it: "to give unto them beauty for ashes." He looked over at the fireplace, at the cold, gray ashes he had named the symbol of their future, then looked back to the words that seemed to leap off the page at him. *"To give unto them beauty for ashes."*

A brilliant, bright light of hope pierced Justin's soul. He looked back at Elizabeth. If only—

If!

Doubt flooded Justin's mind, and, as quickly as it had come, the hope disappeared, leaving a desolation that was worse than any he had previously known. Without a word he pivoted on his heel and left the room.

Chapter Seventeen

❖

Elizabeth flailed her arms out into the surrounding darkness to fight off her attacker. With a strangled cry she flung herself upward, then sat looking frantically about unable to accept that there was no one there. Trembling, afraid to close her eyes, she sank back against the fluffy feather pillows and stared up at the red silk tester overhead. "It was only the nightmare—only the nightmare. Reginald is not here. He cannot find you. He cannot hurt you. You're safe."

Elizabeth's voice shook as she spoke the words aloud to reassure herself. It didn't work. Fear engulfed her like a dark cloud. She shuddered and climbed wearily from the bed. There would be no sleep for her now. She resigned herself to another sleepless night, loosened the sash of Justin's dark-blue dressing gown, then knotted it more snugly about her small waist. A frown knit her brows together. She was losing weight—and she could ill-afford it.

She gave a long sigh and crossed to the window. Moonlight washed the landscape with silver, giving an ethereal beauty to the trees and plants in the gardens below. She ignored the lovely scene and focused her gaze on the golden candlelight that spilled across the brick walkway. *He was in his study again.*

Elizabeth shivered, wrapped her arms about herself and moved to the hearth. It seemed she was always cold lately. She placed more wood on the fire, sank into the chair behind her, and stared into the leaping flames. What had gone wrong? Why had Justin withdrawn himself so completely from her? She'd thought they were communicating well lately. That they'd become—well, not exactly friendly—but at least more than coldly polite.

Elizabeth rose to her feet and walked to the dressing table to pick up her grandmother's brooch. Touching it made her feel a little better—a little less alone. She fastened it haphazardly to the blue silk dressing gown. It didn't matter. No one would see her. She sighed and padded barefoot across the rich, Oriental carpet.

Had she done something to offend Justin? Was that why he no longer spent time in her company, or slept in this room? Or was the problem his grief over his wife? She knew he grieved. She had seen the look of hopeless despair that had swept over his face that afternoon in the library just before he walked out—and since that day he had not come near her. He left the house before dawn and returned long after the household was asleep. She, alone, was a silent witness to his comings and goings—to the long, lonely hours of solitude he spent in his study. She was distressed by his pain. She wanted to help him. But what could she do?

Elizabeth shivered again, then brushed her hands rapidly up and down her arms creating a false sense of warmth as she moved back to the window and gazed at the patch of light below. Didn't he notice that the candles burned in her room also? That she, too, was unable to sleep? Or had he noticed and simply didn't care?

Sudden tears blurred her vision. She turned from the window. What did she expect? Elizabeth blinked away the tears and swept the vastness in front of her with her weary gaze. She hated this room. It was so big...so lonely...so red!

So empty without him.

Unbidden, and unwelcome, the thought tumbled into her mind. Elizabeth frowned. It wasn't only the room that seemed empty without him—it was her life. Her days were full. She spent her mornings planning menus with Cook and consulting with Mrs. Jeffers and Owen about household matters. Her afternoons were occupied playing with the children, overseeing their care with the new nanny, discussing patterns and styles with Madame Duval and making herself available for fittings. She had never been so busy. Yet her life felt so empty. It was a contradiction of facts.

Elizabeth closed her eyes and leaned her head back against the window frame. Her entire relationship with Justin Randolph was a contradiction of facts. When he was with her—she wanted him gone. When he was gone—she wanted him with her. Without him she was lonely and afraid—and with him—

Elizabeth jerked her head upright. Afraid *without* him? Now, why had she thought that? It was Justin himself that terrified her to the point of swooning! Yet, if she was honest, she had to admit that somehow his presence in the room at night made her feel secure enough that it had kept away the nightmare of Reginald's attack. That horror had not started until after he had left her alone. Oh, that was ridiculous! How could a man that terrified her make her feel safe?

Elizabeth pushed the confusing thoughts away and went to curl up in the chair by the hearth. If only she had someone to talk to—someone to advise her, to help her through the morass of emotions and fears that beset her so she could find her way in this strange relationship. She sighed, leaned her head back against the soft, padded wing and stared into the flames feeling more rejected, more bereft and lonely than ever before.

Justin scrubbed at his tired eyes with the heels of his hands, stretched his arms, then pushed back from his desk. It was no use. He couldn't concentrate. He'd read the same bill of lading a dozen times and still couldn't remember the items listed.

He walked to the French doors and threw them open. The soft sounds of night rushed in on the cool, fresh air. He threw a disgusted glance at the pile of papers waiting on his desk, stepped out onto the porch and swept his gaze over the moonlit gardens. He knew what the problem was. The problem was, he'd been forced to make a decision he didn't want to make.

Decision. Hah! That word was only to salve his pride. He had made no decision. A decision was based on choices. He had none. He was well and fairly ensnared by his own clever plan—hoist with his own petard!

Justin scowled and leaned his shoulder against the pillar at the top of the steps. Why, in the name of all that was holy, had he ever given Elizabeth his word not to touch her? *I will never touch you... there will be no personal involvement between us... you are, and will remain, my wife in name only...* How those words haunted him, taunted him, these last few days. He was trapped by them. They gave him no peace. If he'd never spoken them he would at least be free to court Elizabeth, to woo her and try to win her heart. Instead, he must remain detached and distant.

Justin turned his back on the moonlit night and returned to his study. He had only himself to blame this time. He had tried to use his anger and bitterness as weapons against further hurt and disappointment, but, somehow, those weapons had been turned against him. He was now their victim, instead of their master.

Justin strode to the fireplace, kicked the burning logs apart with the heel of his boot and knelt down to bank the fire. Why did he bother with the reasons? The matter was clear. He must live by his word. *An honorable and upright man, Justin, is one that 'sweareth to his own hurt, and changeth not!' That man, Justin, shall dwell with the Lord.* His lips twisted into a grim smile at the memory of his grandmother's teachings. He scooped up ashes and spread them over the smoldering wood. *Ashes.*

Justin tossed down the shovel, rose to his feet, and

picked up his jacket, waistcoat and jabot from a chair. "Well, Nana, you will be pleased to know that I learned that lesson well. I will not go back on my word." He grimaced at the taste of bitterness in his mouth and threw a sour look at the ceiling. "But just the same, that promise rings hollow tonight. You see, Nana, what I want now—is to dwell with Elizabeth."

Admitting it out loud made it worse. Justin looked down at the gray ash smothering the fire from the logs hidden beneath, then glanced back up at the ceiling. He slanted his lips into a bittersweet smile. "And I wish you had made me memorize that 'beauty for ashes' verse, Nana— *before* it was too late."

Justin snuffed the candles, let himself out into the hall and closed the door softly behind him. Candles burned in the hallway to light his way. He grimaced and snuffed them out as he went. Owen knew. They all knew. Thought of the gossip that must be buzzing around the servants' quarters made him cringe. But that, too, was his own fault. Elizabeth had been playing her part well—he would have to do better. He smiled grimly, climbed the stairs and walked down the hallway to Elizabeth's room.

The click of the door latch startled her. Elizabeth dropped her hairbrush and spun about. Justin was standing in the doorway looking as surprised as she. For a moment they simply stared at one another, then, he nodded politely, pulled the door closed and advanced into the room. "I didn't expect to find you awake at this hour, Elizabeth. Is something wrong? Are you ill?"

"No. I'm quite well, thank you." She felt a little breathless—he must have frightened her more than she realized. Afraid her shaking knees might give way at any moment, Elizabeth reached out and gripped the back of a nearby chair.

Justin glanced down at her hand and stopped. "I'm sorry if I startled you. I would have knocked had I known you were awake." He scanned her face. "You *are* ill."

"No, I'm fine. Truly."

Her voice was shaking. Justin frowned. "You don't look fine. You're pale, and there are circles under your eyes." He slid his gaze down her slender form. "Are you losing weight?"

A tingling warmth spread across her cheeks at his close perusal. "A little."

"If you're not ill, why are you losing weight? Aren't you eating properly?"

Elizabeth bit her lip and bent to retrieve her hairbrush. She had no answer. She could not admit to him she'd had little appetite since he'd left her to dine alone. She was acutely aware of him standing behind her as she placed the brush on the dressing table.

"Elizabeth?"

His voice floated over her shoulder. Her stomach knotted. She was feeling far too weary and distressed to spar with him tonight. Her eyes filled with sudden, unwelcome tears of self-pity. She took a deep breath, blinked them away and turned toward him. "Yes?"

"You're not sleeping, are you?"

It was the unexpected tenderness in his voice that was

her undoing. Elizabeth's defenses collapsed. Tears sprang into her eyes and her lower lip began to quiver. She opened her mouth to answer and a sob burst from her throat.

"Elizabeth!" Justin reached for her, then dropped his hand to his side. "What is it, Elizabeth?" Emotion thickened his voice. "Tell me what's wrong. Perhaps I can help."

"No!" The very idea of Justin's knowing of Reginald's attack filled her with horror. Elizabeth spun away. "I can't talk about it, it's too—too— It's the nightmare!" She gasped as the words burst out of their own volition. She began to tremble. "It's horrible! And frightening! And it comes back every time I fall asleep."

The tears came in earnest then. She couldn't stop them. They poured down her cheeks. She buried her face in her hands and pressed her trembling fingers against her closed eyes, but still could not stem the flood. "Oh, dear God— oh, dear God—I'm so tired...and frightened...and *alone!*" She rocked back and forth in her misery, and then, suddenly, Justin's arms were around her.

"You're not alone, Elizabeth. I'm here."

His voice was soft and comforting. His arms strong and warm. Elizabeth sagged against him. Her hands buried themselves in the crisp, white front of his shirt. She clung to him, sobbing, and the hot moisture of her tears soaked the fabric beneath her face. He drew her closer—laid his cheek against her hair. "Don't cry, Elizabeth. Shhh...please don't cry. You're not alone. I'm here. I'm here, Elizabeth. Shhh...shhh..."

Justin slid his hand up and stroked her hair. He cupped her head and rocked her in his arms. Elizabeth sighed and relaxed against him. Her hands released their clutching hold on his shirt and slid slowly down his chest. His heart beat with heavy, rhythmic thuds beneath her ear. Her eyelids fluttered...stilled.

Justin glanced down as Elizabeth went limp in his arms. He skimmed his gaze over her long, damp lashes, pale cheeks, and soft rose-colored lips. They were parted ever so slightly in slumber. He tore his gaze away from her, lifted her into his arms and carried her to the bed. His face taut with the effort to withstand his feelings, he laid her down and drew the covers over her.

She was sleeping like a child. Justin brushed a curling, golden tendril of silky hair back from her temple, then turned away.

Elizabeth whimpered—stirred.

Justin turned back. He took her hand in his. She quieted. For a moment he stood looking down at her, then he reached behind him, pulled a chair over, sat and leaned back and closed his eyes.

"Good afternoon, mum."

"Good afternoon, Trudy." Elizabeth mumbled the words and swept her heavy eyelids back down over her tired eyes as she snuggled more deeply under the covers. *Good afternoon!*

Elizabeth jerked to a sitting position and stared at the maid sitting quietly in a chair beside her bed. "Trudy! Why are you here? What—" She stopped and gave her head a quick shake to try and clear her sleep-befuddled mind. "Is something wrong?"

"No, mum." Trudy set aside the apron she was hemming and rose to her feet. "That is, if you're feelin' better."

"If I'm *feeling* better?"

"Yes, mum." Trudy cocked her head to one side and studied her. "Mr. Randolph said you was feelin' poorly last evenin', an' I was to stay with—"

"Oh! *Oh, no!*" Elizabeth threw herself back against the pillows, rolled over and hid her face in their fluffy softness. Her cheeks burned. She burrowed deeper trying to blot out the image that had flashed into her mind. How *could* she have? Oh, how could she possibly have *snuggled* against Justin like that? What must he think? *"Ohhh!"*

"Mum? Mum! Are you all right?" Trudy's low-pitched voice rose in a wail of concern.

Elizabeth gave another muffled moan and shook her head as best she could with it buried in the pillows.

"Oh, you *are* feelin' poorly!"

Elizabeth felt Trudy's pats of comfort on her back.

"Don't worry, mum. I'll run fetch Mrs. Jeffers. She'll know what's proper to dose you with."

The pats stopped. There was the sound of rushing footsteps. Elizabeth bolted upright. "No!"

The sharp command halted Trudy's headlong rush. She spun about. "But, mum, I don't know what to do! An' Mr. Randolph said—"

"That will be enough, Trudy!" Elizabeth had no intention of listening to what Justin had said about her. "I'm not ill. And I do not need to be dosed with anything. What I need is a nice, soothing bath. Have Tobie bring the water immediately." She dropped back against the pillows.

"A bath. Yes, mum." Trudy bobbed a curtsy. "Do you want a tray then, mum? Some broth?"

"No. Only the bath. I'm not hungry." In truth, she didn't care if she ever ate again. What she wanted was to *hide*—to simply stay in bed forever. Elizabeth lifted a silk-clad arm to cover her eyes, and bit back another moan. How could she possibly face Justin?

"If you'll be all right alone, mum. I'll go an' fetch your bathwater."

"I'll be fine, Trudy, I—*you?*" Elizabeth lowered her arm and looked at her maid. "Where is Tobie?"

"He's helpin' with all the scrubbin' an' cleanin', mum." Trudy turned and headed for the door. "I'll be—"

"What scrubbing and cleaning?" Elizabeth pushed herself to a sitting position. "What are you talking about, Trudy? I've ordered no special scrubbing and cleaning done."

"No, mum. It's the bridal chamber." Trudy pulled the door open, then turned back and smiled. "Mr. Randolph ordered it ready for tonight." She stepped out into the hall.

"Trudy, wait!"

The maid paused. "Yes, mum?"

"Are—are we having guests?"

"Oh, no, mum. It's for you an' Mr. Randolph."

The door closed.

The bridal chamber! Elizabeth stared at the closed door while fear twisted and coiled in her stomach. *Justin had ordered the bridal chamber prepared!* She retched—then retched again. Bile rose into her throat. She threw back the covers, clapped a hand over her mouth and ran for the dressing room.

* * *

She was being cowardly—she knew that—but Elizabeth couldn't make herself leave the nursery. Justin had been gone all day, called away by some emergency at his waterfront warehouse, but now he had sent word of his return—along with a request that she join him at table. How could she? Oh, how could she?

Elizabeth laid her hand on her churning stomach and tried to ignore the tension thrumming along her nerves. Her embarrassment over her actions of the night before no longer troubled her. It had been swallowed up by this new terror she faced. She needed a solution before she faced Justin. But what? She'd wrestled with the problem all day and no answer had presented itself. She was so terrified by all that the move to the bridal chamber implied, she couldn't think straight. She couldn't think at all. She could only feel.

Elizabeth thrust all thought of the coming night away and focused her attention on the little girl looking up at her. Poor little girl, locked in her world of silence. She closed the book she held in her hands, placed it on the bedside table and looked down into Sarah's watchful brown eyes. "That's enough for tonight, Sarah. I'll read more tomorrow. Do you like the story?" She waited, hoping for a response. Her heart lifted when the toddler gave a brief nod. At least she was making some progress with the silent child.

"Good. I'm glad you like it. Now, it's time to say goodnight. I'm afraid it's past time for little girls to go to sleep." Elizabeth rose from her chair and tucked the covers closely around the toddler and the freshly washed, mended but still ragged doll she clutched tightly in her arms. "Sweet dreams, Sarah." She longed to hug and kiss the child good-night, but contented herself with brushing a stray wisp of hair back from her soft, smooth cheek. "Close your eyes now, while I pray."

The little girl shut her eyes. Elizabeth's throat tightened. Sarah was such a good little girl. But she was so sad and wary and distrustful. Had her mother's death caused her to become this silent, cautious creature that looked out at the world from some safe hiding place? It must have been a terrible, frightening experience for her. Elizabeth swallowed past the lump in her throat, bowed her head and closed her eyes.

"Dear God, in heaven, I pray that You will bless Sarah. That You will give her visions of Your holy angels watching over her to keep her safe. And that You will bless her father and her sister Mary. Keep them safe, dear God, and help Sarah not to be afraid. Help us *all* not to be afraid. Oh, God, please, take our separate, wounded souls and make them whole. Turn us into a family, God, and make this house a true home. Amen."

Well! Her heart had quite run away with her. Thank goodness Sarah was too young to understand what she had prayed! Elizabeth opened her eyes and gazed down at the toddler. She was already asleep.

"Good night, precious Sarah, sweet dreams."

She snuffed out the bedside candle and turned to leave the room.

"Good evening."

"Oh!" Elizabeth's hand flew to her throat. She stared, wide-eyed, at the tall, shadowy form in the doorway.

"I keep startling you. I'm sorry." Justin moved forward into the room.

Hot blood flooded Elizabeth's cheeks. How long had he been standing there? Had he heard her prayer? She had just called him a *wounded soul!* She stared up into Justin's dark, unfathomable gaze as he came toward her.

"I came to join you in saying good-night to the children." He smiled. "I thought Mr. Buffy might approve."

Elizabeth gave him a weak smile, took a step backward and clutched at the corner post of the bed for support as he stopped beside her. "I'm certain that he would. But, I'm afraid you're too late. The children are asleep."

"So I see." Justin looked down at the sleeping toddler. "She's awfully small, isn't she?" He lifted his gaze back to Elizabeth. "Does she always look that angelic when she's sleeping?"

There was something warm and wonderful in his eyes. Elizabeth nodded and gripped the bedpost harder. She had a sudden, all but overwhelming desire to step into Justin's arms—to find out if his embrace would be as gently comforting, as safe and secure, as it had seemed last night. Her cheeks burned at the thought. She glanced, thankfully, at the extinguished candle and turned away.

"Elizabeth?"

"Yes?"

"As I have failed to accomplish my first purpose in coming here, I wonder if perhaps you would be kind enough to grant me my second." She turned back to look at him. He smiled. "I dislike eating alone, Mrs. Randolph. I'd like you to join me at table."

Mrs. Randolph! Shock jolted Elizabeth to her very toes. Warning signals flashed in her mind. He had never before called her Mrs. Randolph! Was it his subtle way of telling her what was to come?

Everything inside Elizabeth screamed run—*run!* But there was no place to go. She would not escape this time. Her heart hammered against her ribs, and her mouth went dry. It took every ounce of courage and self-control she possessed to stay in his presence. "As you wish."

She stiffened with fear when Justin placed his hand in the small of her back and guided her toward the door. Her legs felt as if they were made of wood as she walked beside him.

"Oooh, mum!" Trudy crooned as she unwrapped the parcel and lifted the garment out for Elizabeth's inspection. "It's the perfect gown for you to wear on your first night in the bridal chamber! An' look!" She reached into the crumpled wrapping paper and pulled out a frothy mixture of white silk and lace. "A dressing gown that matches it! Oh, mum. You'll be a true picture you will!"

Elizabeth's face blanched—her stomach knotted. Thank heaven she hadn't been able to swallow a bite of food at dinner!

Trudy laid the beautiful garments carefully on the bed and reached into the wrappings again. "Oh!" The maid turned to Elizabeth. There was a pair of silk slippers trimmed with white fur on the palms of her outstretched hands. "Did you ever see the like?" Her words were an awed whisper.

"No, I never have. They're lovely." Elizabeth reached

out and brushed a trembling fingertip along the soft fur of the exquisitely feminine creations, then turned away, unable to bear the sight of them.

"Slip 'em on, mum, do!" Trudy thrust the slippers into Elizabeth's hands. "I'll get the gown...."

Elizabeth shook her head to clear her mind of the memory. She glanced down at the lovely nightwear created for her by Madame Duval and frowned. She hadn't wanted to wear it—but there had been no reasonable excuse she could think of for not doing so. She could not tell Trudy the truth of their marriage of convenience. What a sensation *that* would cause in the servants' quarters!

Elizabeth paced the length of the large room, the beautiful white-silk dressing gown floating about her like a cloud, her hands clenched in helpless anger. He couldn't do this to her. He couldn't change his mind. He had given her his word! But what else could explain his sudden orders to have them moved into a bridal chamber that had been locked since his first wife's death? What other motive could he have?

Elizabeth's anger dissolved before a rush of fear. Justin Randolph could do anything he wanted in his own home. Who was to deny him? She darted her gaze about the room. What should she do? What *could* she do? She was at Justin's mercy. "Oh, God, I'm so afraid! Help me. Please help me!"

What time I am afraid, I will trust in Thee.

The verse out of the book of Psalms slid into Elizabeth's mind. She stopped pacing. That's what Miss Essie had always said. Was that the answer—to trust God to protect her?

A soft knock on the door made her jump.

"I put my trust in Thee, God! I put my trust in Thee!" Elizabeth whispered the words into the emptiness of the room, then turned toward the door to face whatever was to come.

"Has Trudy gone, Elizabeth?" Justin stepped into the room and pulled the door shut behind him. "Or is she—?" His words stuck in his throat, choked him. Elizabeth stood before him in a chaste white dressing gown, her golden curls framing her lovely face, tumbling over her shoulders. His heart thudded. "I see Madame Duval has made another delivery." He frowned, and cleared the huskiness from his voice.

"Yes." Elizabeth stared at his frown. "You're not pleased?"

"Oh, I'm...pleased." Justin twisted his lips into a wry grimace at the anemic description of the emotion the sight of her produced in him. He kept his gaze locked on her face. Now that he knew it was no act her innocence amazed him—it also drew him like a magnet. "Madame Duval is to be commended on her work. It's lovely. And I'm certain she has achieved the very result she was hoping for." He started forward into the room, then paused as Elizabeth stiffened and raised her chin. "You give yourself away, you know."

"I beg your pardon?"

"When you lift your chin like that." Justin fastened his gaze on Elizabeth's small, rounded chin. "You give yourself away. It means you are either frightened, or ready to do battle." He lifted his gaze and locked it on her dark-blue eyes. "Which is it?"

She took a deep breath. "Both."

"I see." He took a few more steps into the room and stopped a short distance from her. "Would you care to explain?"

"We are in the bridal chamber."

The muscle along his jaw twitched. "So we are." He glanced at the ornately carved four-poster bed draped with beautifully worked needlepoint. "I swore I would never open these rooms again."

"Then why have you?"

He shifted his gaze to her face. She went as white as the gown.

"I—I mean if…if these rooms hold painful memories for you, then why open them?"

"It seemed the best solution."

"Solution?" She shuddered. "To what?"

There was a tremor in her voice. She didn't trust him and her courage was deserting her. Justin frowned. "To sleepless nights, loneliness…fear and nightmares."

Her eyes widened with shock. "You've opened these rooms for *my* sake?"

He shrugged his shoulders. "You can't sleep forever on a chaise, Elizabeth. And if I'm absent it seems you can't sleep at all. These rooms seemed the sensible solution." He inclined his head toward the far end of the room. "That door leads to the husband's dressing room. There's a bed there for when the wife is…in a delicate condition. That's where I'll sleep." He looked back at her. "I trust it will be both close enough—and far enough—to assure you of your safety, and permit you to rest."

"Oh."

It was a very small word, spoken in a very small voice, but it said volumes. Suddenly, Justin was weary. This business of coming to life again was painful. "If you've no further questions, Elizabeth, I'll bid you good evening." He made her an impeccably proper bow, then started for his sleeping quarters. "I trust you will find your room comfortable." He paused and gave her a wry smile. "At least it's not red." He reached for the door.

"Justin, wait. Please."

He turned to face her. "Yes?"

"I want to apologize." Her cheeks turned pink. "You see, I thought...well...I thought—"

He lifted his hand to halt her stumbling attempt to explain. "I know what you thought, Elizabeth. But you were wrong. Perhaps one day you'll learn to trust me." He dipped his head, stepped through the opened door into the room beyond, and pulled the door closed.

Shame washed over Elizabeth. How selfless of him to endure the pain of opening these rooms so she might not have to be afraid. It was the kindest, most generous thing anyone had ever done for her—and she had repaid him with nasty suspicion.

Perhaps one day you'll learn to trust me. Tears sprang to Elizabeth's eyes. A lump formed in her throat. *Could* she learn to trust him? Would she ever trust *anyone* again? She sighed, blinked away the tears that blurred her vision and turned toward the bed. The beautiful white dressing gown billowed out in a frothy mist around her at the movement.

Elizabeth stared at the image reflected against the darkness outside the window. Was that truly her face staring back at her? She stepped closer. Was that young bride really Elizabeth Shannon Frazier? An unrelenting pressure filled her chest, a sob burst from her throat. No! *That* bride was Justin Davidson Randolph's wife! And *that*, was a lie.

Elizabeth ran to the bed and buried her face in a pillow to muffle the sobs that shook her for the young bride in the window that would never truly be.

Chapter Eighteen
❧

"There, Sarah. What a splendid job you have done!"

Elizabeth held the uneven, ragged-edged lump of clay on the palm of her outstretched hand the better to admire it. "It's the perfect dish to hold biscuits when your dolly has tea." She smiled and lifted her gaze from the crudely formed plate to the toddler's beaming face. What a change from the little girl she had met when she first arrived! How thankful she was that Justin had agreed to employ a new nanny for the children. She had known immediately upon interviewing Mrs. Hammerfield she would be excellent with the children—and the past few weeks had proved her right. The nanny was working out wonderfully well.

"Shall we put it here on the bench with the others to dry?" At the toddler's answering nod, Elizabeth placed the dish on the bench beside her. "Now then, what more do we need?" She waited patiently while Sarah studied the display of wet clay dishes that marched down the bench in a staggered procession. She was determined to make the little girl communicate, and had fallen upon the strategy of asking her direct questions and then waiting silently until she made her answer known. Suddenly, Sarah smiled and pointed a tiny, clay-covered finger.

"Ah, another cup. How clever you are! That is exactly what we need." Elizabeth smiled her approval. "Shall you make this one? Or shall I?"

Sarah bent and scooped up a handful of wet clay from the bucketful the gardener had brought them at Elizabeth's request. She smiled and held it out to Elizabeth.

"Very well." Elizabeth accepted the clay. "I only hope I do as well as you." She molded the pliable earth with her fingers while the toddler crowded close to watch. "There." She held the small cup up for Sarah's inspection. "Will that do?"

Sarah nodded, smiled, and bobbed up and down on her toes and clapped her two small hands together.

"Oh! Oh my!" Elizabeth jerked back as wet clay spattered everywhere. "Oh, Sarah, look at you! You've bits of wet clay all over your dress and face and hair." She set down the cup and reached for her.

Sarah's eyes widened with fear. She backed away.

Elizabeth froze. The laughter that had begun to bubble up inside her died at the look in the little girl's eyes. Her hands began to shake with anger. She knew who was responsible for that fear. Miss Brown.

"What is it, Sarah?" Elizabeth slid off the bench onto her knees in front of the child. "What's wrong?"

The toddler lifted her small hand and pointed at Elizabeth's chest.

Elizabeth looked down. "Oh, I see." She brushed at the spatters of gray clay on the front of her bodice. They only smeared. Thankful that she had worn her old blue dress and not one of Madame Duval's lovely new creations on this dish-making excursion, Elizabeth lifted her gaze back to the frightened child.

"Well! We're quite a pair, Sarah—aren't we?" She smiled at the tense toddler. "I'm not angry, Sarah. Did you think I would be angry with you? Is that why you're afraid?"

The little girl backed up against the bench and nodded. Her eyes were bright with unshed tears. Elizabeth's heart ached for her. She wanted so much to hug her—to hold her close and tell her it was all right, no one would hurt her again—but it was too soon. Sarah was still wary of her. She had to earn her trust.

Elizabeth rose to her feet and made a great show of brushing at the dirt clinging to the skirt of her blue gown. "Well I'm not angry, Sarah. But that's not to say Mrs. Hammerfield isn't going to be put out with the pair of us." She looked down at the little girl and gave an exaggerated sigh. "We are a sight." She placed her fisted hands on her hips and studied the toddler.

"I must say, you look quite fetching with freckles, Miss Sarah." She tilted her head to one side, and smiled. "Especially with that rather large one on the tip of your nose." The little girl crossed her eyes in an effort to see the spot and Elizabeth burst into laughter. "It's right there!" She leaned forward and touched the end of Sarah's nose. "And there...and there...and there...and there..."

Sarah squealed and burst into giggles as Elizabeth poked and tickled her tiny body. Elizabeth couldn't resist—she dropped to the ground and gathered the toddler into her arms. How wonderful it was to hear her laugh! Surely if she could laugh she could—

"Well, my stars! What have we here?"

Elizabeth and Sarah both jumped and turned startled, clay-spattered faces toward the strange voice. A short, stout, richly garbed elderly woman stood at the bend of the brick pathway with her hands clasped on top of an elegant walking stick.

"Urchins." The woman lifted the stick and struck the brick in sharp emphasis of the word.

Sarah gave a startled cry. Elizabeth tightened her arms protectively about her. "I'll thank you not to frighten my daughter, madam!" She ignored the woman's shocked gasp and turned her attention to the toddler in her arms. "It's all right, darling." A surge of maternal love rose in her as Sarah twisted her tiny body in her arms and pressed her small face against her neck. "It's all right—"

"Well, of course it's all right. I wouldn't hurt the child. But *you*, young woman—you might be more careful in the way you speak to your betters! It's—"

"Abigail!"

The name rang joyously through the afternoon air. The woman broke off her scolding to turn and look down the brick path behind her. A smile deepened the creases at the edges of her mouth and wrinkled the corners of her eyes.

Justin! He wasn't supposed to return home until evening! Elizabeth freed one hand to brush at the dirty smudges on her gown.

"Owen just informed me of your visit, Abigail. How are you? When did you return?"

Justin's deep voice was accompanied by staccato footsteps as he hurried down the path toward the woman. "I'm sorry I wasn't here to introduce you to—" He stopped dead in his tracks when he rounded the bend. Shock spread across his features as he stared at Elizabeth.

Elizabeth's cheeks burned. "Good afternoon, Justin." She tried to rise, but her usually graceful movements were made awkward by the child clinging tightly to her neck. "I didn't expect— Oh!" Sarah suddenly shifted her position and Elizabeth fell sideways. Her shoulder banged against the wooden bench. "Ouch!"

"Elizabeth!"

Justin rushed forward, gripped her arms and lifted her to her feet. "Are you all right? What happened? Did you fall? Did Sarah fall?" He scanned them both with an anxious gaze. "Answer me!" He gave Elizabeth a little shake. "Are you all right?"

"Well, of course we're all right. Why shouldn't we be? We—"

"Why shouldn't you be? *Look* at you!"

"They've been making mud pies."

"*Mud pies?*" Justin's head swiveled toward the woman.

Elizabeth turned her head and glared at her. Amusement brightened the woman's faded blue eyes. She was clearly enjoying herself. "Madam, I—"

"You were making *mud pies?*"

Elizabeth forgot the woman and looked back at Justin. He was scowling at her. "There's no reason to be upset, Justin. I—"

"No reason? I thought you'd had an accident. Mud pies indeed!"

"They are *not* mud pies." Elizabeth drew herself up as straight as she was able within the confines of Justin's arms. "They are dishes. And you are hurting me."

"Dishes?" Justin's eyebrows shot skyward. He relaxed his grip.

"Yes, dishes. For Sarah's doll." Elizabeth nodded toward the display of ragged dishes on the bench. "It's a tea set."

"A tea set? *That!*" Justin's eyes flashed angrily. "I assure you, Elizabeth, my purse is sufficient to purchase dishes for Sarah's doll."

Elizabeth bit down on her lower lip and stared at his angry face. Had she embarrassed him? Oh, why had that woman come and spoiled everything? She'd been having such a lovely time with Sarah. And now everything was ruined.

"I'm sorry. I didn't mean to embarrass you, Justin. I only—" She stopped—that little muscle along his jaw was twitching. She seemed to have a definite talent for doing, and saying, the wrong thing where this man was concerned. Elizabeth sighed and looked over at the bench. "I thought making dishes together might help Sarah and I become closer." She lifted her chin, and shifted her gaze back to meet his. She refused to grovel when she had done nothing wrong! "It would not have been the same to purchase the dishes."

Justin stared down at her, then lowered his gaze to Sarah, who was clinging to her neck. "It seems to have worked."

Elizabeth relaxed. "It's because she was frightened." She smiled and lowered her cheek to rest against Sarah's soft brown hair. The child's small arms tightened in response.

"Well, Justin, since I don't believe you have taken to cavorting with your servants, I assume this must be your bride." The woman's voice was stringent. "If you would remember your manners and introduce me, I will offer the young lady an apology."

Justin released his grip on Elizabeth's arms and stepped back. "Forgive me, Abigail." He lifted his hand toward Elizabeth. "Allow me to present my bride, Elizabeth." He looked back at Elizabeth and waved his hand toward the elderly woman. "Elizabeth, our neighbor, and my dear friend, Abigail Twiggs."

Elizabeth stared at him. *His dear friend.* No wonder he was angry. If he knew she had— Oh, my! She gave the woman a nervous little smile. "I'm pleased to make your acquaintance. And I beg your pardon for my appearance, and the—the misunderstanding. I—"

"Nonsense, child. It's I who should beg your pardon. I certainly would not have called you an urchin had I known—"

"Urchin?" Justin stared at Abigail Twiggs. "What's this?"

The woman turned an autocratic gaze on him. "I thought your bride was a servant."

Justin grinned. He turned his head to look at Elizabeth. She ignored him and gave Abigail Twiggs a gracious, if somewhat rueful, smile. "You have no need to apologize. You couldn't have known. I certainly *look* like an urchin."

"An adorable one."

Blood surged into Elizabeth's cheeks. She snapped her gaze back to Justin. "You may find my discomfort amusing, but you needn't tease!"

"I wasn't teasing."

Elizabeth's breath caught in her throat. Her stomach gave a queer little flutter at the look in Justin's eyes, and her knees went weak. "Well—well, then..." She turned back to Abigail Twiggs whose alert gaze was taking in every nuance of the scene before her. "It seems we are all agreed as to my appearance. So, if you will excuse us, Sarah and I will go in now. We are both in need of a good wash."

"Of course." Abigail Twiggs's lips twitched. "Go have your wash, child. And forgive this old woman for interrupting. I should have sent my card and given proper notice." She smiled, leaned heavily on her ebony walking stick and moved toward the bench.

Elizabeth felt a sudden twinge of concern—the woman looked very tired. "Please don't feel you must stand on ceremony in this house—I am always happy to receive my...husband's friends." She frowned and hurried on hoping neither the woman nor Justin had noticed her hesitation over the word *husband*. "And I shall endeavor to make a better impression in the future." She turned back to Justin.

"Do you wish me to return?"

"Yes. Please, join us in the salon for tea as soon as you have changed. I...require...your presence."

That look was back in his eyes. Elizabeth suddenly felt shy. She nodded and swept her lashes down to hide from his unsettling gaze. What was wrong with her anyway? Why was she reacting so foolishly to his playacting? It was for his friend's benefit he was pretending to be enamored of her. But all the same, he needn't make such a masterful performance of it. It was unnerving.

Elizabeth lowered Sarah to the ground, retrieved the doll from the bench, then clasped the child's small hand in hers and started down the path matching her steps to the short legs of the toddler. It felt as if Justin's gaze was fastened on her the whole way. By sheer strength of will she held the sedate pace until she rounded the bend in the walkway, then, unable to stand it another moment, she scooped the child into her arms and raced toward the house. She needed a good wash and one of Madame Duval's gowns. There was nothing like a lovely gown to help build one's confidence—and hers was in sad need of repair. Urchin, indeed!

Chapter Nineteen

✤

Elizabeth turned Sarah over to the warm, capable ministrations of Anna Hammerfield and rushed down the hallway to her room. She had just reached for the doorknob when the realization that she was no longer afraid of Justin struck her. She stopped dead still. How had that happened? *When* had that happened? The fear was gone. Justin had held her in his arms and she had not been afraid. Nervous, yes. But not afraid. How extraordinary!

Elizabeth twisted the knob, stepped into the bridal chamber, and began undoing the bodice of her clay-spattered gown as she crossed to her dressing room. What had happened? Had God answered her prayer? She smiled at the foolish thought and called for Trudy. Saying a prayer was something one did to make oneself feel better in difficult circumstances. No one she knew actually expected God to *answer* their prayers.

A sudden image of herself, weary and desperate, standing on the street that led to the Haversham Coach House counting her coins and praying for the Lord to help her find a way out of town popped into Elizabeth's mind. Her hands stilled. Chills ran down her spine—her flesh prickled. Had God answered that prayer? Had *Justin* been the answer to her desperate plea?

"Did you call, mum?"

Elizabeth jumped and undid the last of the fastenings on her bodice. "Yes. I need a wash, Trudy. Have Tobie bring water immediately."

"Yes, mum." The maid bobbed her awkward curtsy and rushed from the room.

Elizabeth sank down onto the chair behind her. What about when Reginald had attacked her? Had God heard her prayer for help then? Was that why her Uncle Charles had appeared unexpectedly and saved her? Had the hidden key and the servants being ordered away from her room, Reginald's servant not seeing her at Carrington's Inn and the old gentleman with the oyster barrow directing her to the Haversham Coach House, the judge mistaking her for another woman and Justin's marrying her, *all* been God's answer to her frantic prayers for help?

The thoughts came faster and faster, and chill after chill chased down Elizabeth's spine and spread throughout her body. *Had* God heard her? *Was* He watching over her? Helping her? Protecting her? Elizabeth lifted an awed gaze to the ceiling. Could it be? Could it be that prayers *were* more than something you said to make yourself feel better?

The bedroom door opened. Elizabeth shoved her startling

thoughts aside, removed her soiled gown and walked to the wash basin as Trudy and Tobie filled it with hot water.

Abigail Twiggs switched from studying the dishes on the bench to studying Justin as he watched Elizabeth disappear down the path to the house. She smiled and nodded her satisfaction. "So, Justin, you forgot that nonsense you wrote me about a marriage of convenience and married for love after all."

"No, Abigail." Justin turned and walked over to stand looking down at the ragged, lopsided dishes. "My marriage to Elizabeth is one of convenience."

"I see." The man looked wretched. Abigail grinned and plopped down on the bench, barely missing the dishes. She was suddenly very tired. It came on her like that.

"No one is to know, Abigail. I know you do not approve, but the deed is done and I would appreciate your silence in the matter. If my plan is to work, our marriage must appear to be a normal one. My pride insists on that." Justin smiled at her. "And if we managed to fool you, we can fool anyone."

Abigail snorted. "Don't you be trying your charm on me, Justin Davidson Randolph. I'm too old, and I've known you too long, to be swayed by your winning ways. You didn't fool me for an instant—you love that girl!"

For a long moment Justin stared at her, then his shoulders sagged. "All right, I admit it. I love her. But that knowledge is for you alone, Abigail. No one else knows—not even Elizabeth. *Especially* not Elizabeth." He raked his hands through his hair. "I've told you the truth. The marriage is one of convenience only."

"Hmm." Abigail pursed her dry, wrinkled lips and fastened her gaze on Justin's young, miserable face. "Hoist with your own petard are you?"

He winced. "You might say that. In fact, the thought has occurred to me more than once."

"Well, what are you doing about it?"

"Doing?" He shot her a look of pure frustration. "Nothing."

"Nothing!"

"It's a marriage of *convenience*, Abigail." Justin jammed his hands into his pockets. "There's nothing I *can* do."

"Balderdash!" Abigail lifted her cane and struck the brick paving with a sharp crack. "That's the most ridiculous thing I've ever heard. Have you never heard of wooing a woman?"

"Of course I have." Justin glared at her from under lowered brows. "But I've given my word there will be no personal relationship between us."

"More fool, you!" Abigail gave a disgusted snort and glared right back.

Justin made her a mocking bow of acknowledgment. "Exactly. Nonetheless, my word stands."

"Hmm."

Justin quirked his left eyebrow and gave her a wary look. "I know you well, old friend—and that look in your eyes is alarming me. I'd like your promise not to interfere."

For a long moment the old woman stared up at Justin, then, abruptly, she looked away. "There's naught I can do if you've given your word." She peeked up at him.

Justin's eyes narrowed. "That was far too easy, Abigail."

The old woman looked up at the warning note in his voice and immediately realized her mistake. "That doesn't mean I don't still think you're a fool! I like her."

"But you *will* keep our secret?"

Abigail smiled inwardly. She had won. "Oh, yes. You've no cause to fret over that, Justin. Your secret will be safe with me."

"*And*...you will not interfere?"

So she hadn't sidetracked him after all. Abigail gave him a look of disgust. "Oh, very well! There's no need to belabor the point. I'll not interfere." There was a distinctly sour note in her voice.

Justin chuckled. "Thank you, Abigail." He leaned down and kissed her dry, wrinkled cheek. "I knew I could count on you."

The old woman scowled. "It's a waste of time talking to you, Justin Randolph. And I'm too old to waste time." She tightened her grip on her cane and rose slowly to her feet. "I'm going to go have tea."

She ignored his proffered arm and started down the path rapping her walking stick sharply against the bricks with every step. She was annoyed and wanted to make certain he knew it. She never had been a good loser.

"Did I do well?"

"Undeniably." Justin smiled. "You parried Abigail's questions very well, Elizabeth. And she can be formidable when she is after information."

Elizabeth laughed. "She was a little daunting, but I survived. And I'm glad you're pleased. I was concerned since her visit had a less than desirable beginning. But even so, I like Abigail Twiggs—she's lovely. So warm and caring under that crusty exterior."

Justin hooted. "Abigail would not thank you for seeing through her so quickly, Elizabeth. She prides herself on her irascibility."

"Well I think she's a dear." She gave him an amused look. "And she certainly thinks highly of you."

Justin nodded agreement. "She was Grandmother Davidson's best friend. I expect some of her fondness for me stems from their relationship."

"Only some of it?" Elizabeth couldn't resist teasing Justin a little—he was always so controlled. "You seem very sure of yourself."

"Why shouldn't I be?" He grinned at her. "Don't you find me a very likable fellow?"

Elizabeth cheeks prickled with sudden warmth. "We were discussing your relationship with Abigail Twiggs—not ours."

"So we were."

The woman was gone, so why was he looking at her that way? Probably he was paying her back for teasing him. Elizabeth looked down, flicked some imaginary lint from her new gown and directed their conversation onto a more comfortable path. "It must be lovely to have a good friend like Abigail."

"It is." Justin's lips twisted into a wry smile. "Of course there are times when it is decidedly uncomfortable."

"Such as when I embarrassed you in front of her this afternoon?" Elizabeth forced herself to meet his gaze. "I ask your forgiveness for that."

"For what? There's nothing to forgive."

Elizabeth looked down at her hands—the look in his eyes made her nervous. "That's very gracious of you. But I know better." She smoothed a fold in her skirt. "Abigail is your friend, and a lady of society."

"What of that?"

She glanced up at him. "I could hardly have made a less favorable impression. I looked...well...I looked like an urchin!"

"Yes, I know." Justin grinned. "An urchin with a smudge of clay on her proud little chin."

"You might have told me of that!"

"Why?" Justin's grin widened. "I found it rather charming."

"Charming?" Elizabeth stared at him. "I failed, Justin."

"Failed?" His grin disappeared. "In what way?"

"I did not live up to our agreement." Elizabeth rose to her feet. "Do you truly not understand? One of my responsibilities under our agreement is to help you fulfill your social obligations. I completely failed at that. Not only did I look uncomely for your guest, I acted it. I—I ordered her to stop frightening Sarah. And— Why are you laughing?" Elizabeth glared down at him. "Owen told me Abigail Twiggs is the undisputed leader of Philadelphia society and—"

"And so she is." Justin looked up at Elizabeth and made a valiant effort to choke back his laughter. "And she is certainly not accustomed to being ordered about—especially by someone she thought was a servant. But she—" He burst into laughter again.

Elizabeth stiffened. "I'm so glad you find my faux pas amusing!"

"It's not that, Elizabeth." Justin pulled his handkerchief from his waistcoat pocket and wiped at his tearing eyes. "It's only— I'd give the profit from my next ship to reach port to have seen her face!"

Elizabeth's lips twitched. "I must admit she did look a bit taken aback."

"Taken aback?" Justin howled. "A choice piece of understatement that. She must have been apoplectic!"

"Apoplectic? Oh, my!" Elizabeth's amusement died. She sank back down onto her chair and nibbled at her soft bottom lip.

Justin wiped his eyes, again, and tucked his handkerchief back in his pocket. "There's no need for concern, Elizabeth. Abigail has a wonderful sense of humor. She'll be laughing over this day for a long while."

She shot him a slanted look. "Are you being kind? Or do you truly believe so?"

"I know so."

Elizabeth noticed his gaze locked on her mouth and stopped nibbling. It was a bad habit, but he needn't be rude and stare.

Justin shifted in his seat. "Abigail is a very honest woman. She'll not blame you for her mistake. She probably admires you tremendously for standing up to her. And I know she admires your desire to become close to the children. As do I."

Elizabeth gave him a grateful smile. "Thank you."

Justin rose to his feet, walked to her chair and lifted her

hand to his mouth. "You are a beautiful woman, Elizabeth—and your blushes delight me." He pressed his lips lightly to the back of her fingers.

Elizabeth's breath left her in a rush. Her heart fluttered furiously and heat streaked along her arm as Justin's lips brushed against her skin. She gasped, snatched her hand from his grasp and pressed back against the chair.

Justin's jaw tightened. He snapped upright and dropped his hand to his side. "Forgive me, Elizabeth, I forgot your fear of me." He inclined his head in a tight little bow and left the room.

Elizabeth sat in the chair and stared at the closed door. "I'm *not* afraid anymore. I'm not." Her brave, defiant words were swallowed by the silence. She lifted her hand and brushed back the wayward curls that had fallen onto her forehead. Was that true? If she was no longer afraid of Justin why was she trembling? Why had she reacted so violently to his touch?

Elizabeth sighed and lowered her hand to the brooch pinned on her gown. If only her grandmother was here. If only she could talk to her perhaps she could tell her what was wrong with her, why she was acting this way. But, since she couldn't—what about Justin's grandmother?

Elizabeth smiled, rose to her feet and hurried from the room. If her own grandmother couldn't speak to her, perhaps Justin's could!

Elizabeth twisted the doorknob. If Justin's grandmother was right—if God *did* have an answer for every situation and problem of life, then maybe she would find her answer here. She smiled at her whimsy and pushed open the door to the library. Answer or not, reading was better than sitting around indulging in self-pity.

There were candles burning.

Elizabeth paused inside the door, but a quick sweeping glance told her the room was unoccupied. She crossed quickly to the rosewood table and gently trailed her finger across the gold lettering on the worn cover of the large Bible. The smell of old leather rose to her nostrils.

She sat in the tapestry-covered chair, lifted the heavy tome onto her lap, and, being careful not to touch the hot globe that protected the flame from drafts, pulled the candlestick closer. It was foolishness, but she was unable to stop the surge of hope that rose in her as she opened the cover to the list of names of the books the Bible contained. Her attention was caught by spidery handwriting in the margin. *My favorite story.* The inscription was written beside the book of Ruth. Elizabeth settled herself more comfortably in the chair, turned to the beginning page of the story, and began to read.

One by one the candles in the room guttered and died. Elizabeth closed the Bible. What a beautiful story. She could understand why Justin's grandmother had loved it, though it was sad in the beginning, when tragedy forced Ruth to leave her home and family and travel to a strange place to start a new life.

Elizabeth leaned her head back against the soft chair and closed her eyes. She could imagine how Ruth must have felt since the same thing had happened to her. Still, everything had started to come right for Ruth when she accidentally met Boaz and they married. She opened her eyes and glanced down at the Bible beneath her hands. How very strange! That also had happened to her. She had met Justin accidentally and *they* had married. She lifted the Bible and placed it back on the rosewood table. That, of course, was where the similarity in their stories ended. Ruth had fallen in love with Boaz and she—

Elizabeth stiffened with shock. Could it be that she had reacted so violently to Justin's touch because she— No. That was ridiculous. She didn't love— Elizabeth shook her head, and turned her thoughts back to the story. None of that mattered anyway. Boaz had fallen deeply in love with Ruth, also, and Justin certainly didn't love her. He had made that very clear.

Elizabeth walked over to the French doors and stood gazing out at the gardens that were washed in the silvery shimmer of moonlight. Why was she even thinking about love? Love did not exist. At least, not love as she defined it. Her mother's words had left no doubt about that. And she was definitely not interested in the sort of married love Reginald had—

Elizabeth shuddered and turned away from the doors. She walked over to the Bible and again traced the gold lettering with her finger. If God's word was true, then— She shivered. What if it was true? She hugged herself for warmth against a sudden chill that came from deep inside her. There was no way she could reconcile what her mother had told her—what Reginald had demonstrated to her—with the love she had read about in the Bible. She looked down at the large tome that was bathed in moonlight. What if her mother had lied? What if love, as it was written of in the Bible, *did* exist? What if there were men like Boaz who—

Tears stung Elizabeth's eyes. Her throat closed. She blinked the tears away and looked around the room. She suddenly felt hemmed in—trapped. If the Bible was true...if love was real...then...then she would never have a Boaz. She would never know love!

Elizabeth choked back the sobs rising in her constricted throat, gathered her long skirts into her hands and ran from the room.

Elizabeth's lips curved upward. Her "Someday" dream had returned. But this time it was different. This time, her someday was *now,* and her someone had a face, and a voice—Justin's face and Justin's voice. Elizabeth's eyelashes fluttered, she turned onto her side, tucked her hand under her pillow and gave a long, soft sigh. It was a wonderful dream.

Chapter Twenty

❧

Elizabeth awoke to the softness of a summer breeze blowing a rosy dawn in glorious streaks across the gray night sky, and to the knowledge that she—Elizabeth Shannon Frazier Randolph—was in love with her husband. She couldn't say how she knew, or when it had happened, but the knowledge of it was like a song inside her.

Elizabeth climbed from her bed, wrapped the beautiful white dressing gown around her and went to the window. Standing by the casement, with her arms clasped tightly across her chest as if she could physically hold on to this tender new emotion that had permeated her entire being, she deliberately shut out the doubts, the dark thoughts that were clamoring for her attention, and thought only of the beauty that filled her as she watched the dawn break. For this little while—for this tiny space of time—she was determined to listen only to the song her heart was singing. To think only of the incredible, beautiful, wonderful truth of love.

A soft tap, followed by the opening of her bedroom door ended her reverie.

"Mornin', mum."

"Good morning, Trudy."

Elizabeth continued to stare out the window, trying her best to ignore the familiar sounds of her maid's daily morning routine, but the harsh intrusion of reality defeated her. She sighed and turned from the window. She couldn't possibly face Justin the way she was feeling.

"I will not be going down to breakfast this morning, Trudy." Elizabeth smiled when the maid stopped bustling about and gave her a questioning look—it must be that odd, languorous tone in her voice. "And my bath can wait. Right now, I'd like to be alone. I'll ring when I'm ready for you." The question in Trudy's eyes sprang into full-blown curiosity at this sudden departure from their customary morning routine. Elizabeth turned her back and looked out the window.

"Yes, mum. I'll wait for your ring."

Elizabeth's shoulders slumped as the door closed behind her maid. Tears welled into her eyes and spilled down her cheeks. She lifted her hand and wiped them away. So this despair was the other side of love's joy. She drew a deep breath, squared her shoulders and lifted her head to stare up at the ever brightening sky. Even if she must hide her feelings...even if Justin did not return them...at least she now knew that love was real. It had to be. Nothing else could possibly make you so happy to feel so miserable.

Elizabeth laughed aloud at the incongruity of the thought. She looked up at the beautiful dawn sky through shimmering tears and whispered the words to the only one she could tell. "I'm in love, dear God. I'm in love with Justin!"

Joy coursed through her at the sheer magnitude of the miracle that had taken place in her heart. She laughed, threw her arms wide and whirled. The lovely white dressing gown billowed out around her. "I'm in love with my husba—"

The connecting door to the groom's dressing room opened. Elizabeth halted in midspin. *Justin!* Her dressing gown fluttered down to rest against her slender form.

"You didn't answer my knock, madam. Are you all right? I thought I heard—"

Owen! Elizabeth sagged with relief. "I'm fine." She turned toward the door.

"Very good. Forgive me, madam—I didn't mean to intrude." The elderly butler backed quickly out the door and closed it behind him.

The breath whooshed from Elizabeth's lungs. That was close! A fit of trembling seized her. She plopped down onto the edge of the bed. What if it had been Justin? Elizabeth bit her lip to stop a sudden rush of tears and stared at the closed door. She could not speak of her love for Justin even here in her own rooms. The bitter knowledge took the luster from the morning.

She rose on her still-trembling legs, walked over to the bell pull and gave it a sharp, frustrated yank to summon Trudy. She could not afford to indulge herself. This day must be as any other. She straightened her shoulders, lifted her head high and turned toward her dressing room as Trudy returned.

* * *

"No, no, no, little one!" Elizabeth gently freed Sarah's hair from Mary's tiny fist. "You mustn't hurt your sister. Here, you play with this." She picked up a wooden horse and held it out to Mary. The baby grasped it in her chubby little hands and promptly began to suck loudly on its ear.

"What a greedy little thing you are, Mary!" Elizabeth laughed and hugged the baby tightly for a moment, then settled her comfortably on her lap while she reached out to brush back the lock of hair dangling in front of Sarah's tear-filled eyes. "I'm sorry, Sarah." She smiled down at the toddler who had a wary gaze fastened on her baby sister. "Mary didn't mean to hurt you. She only wanted your pretty new hair ribbon. Are you all right?"

Sarah nodded and rubbed her head.

Elizabeth looked down into the round, brown eyes swimming with unshed tears and, careful of the baby on her lap, leaned forward to drop a kiss on top of the toddler's head. "You're a brave little girl. Shall we continue?" She was rewarded with a happy smile. She leaned back in the chair and resumed the gentle rocking that had been interrupted by the small crisis. "Turn the page."

Sarah settled herself on her little chair and reached out to carefully turn the page of the book that lay on the table in front of her. She looked up at Elizabeth.

"That's a kitten." Elizabeth glanced down at Mary's drooping eyelids and lowered her voice. "Isn't he cute, Sarah? Kittens are very soft and playful. They say meow, meow. Look." She reached down and tapped lightly on the picture. "He's chasing a butterfly. Isn't it pretty?"

Sarah nodded and studied the picture.

"Where is the kitten?"

Sarah pointed.

"Very good." Elizabeth smoothed the gown of the sleeping baby. "And where is the butterfly?"

Again, Sarah pointed.

"Yes. That's the butterfly." Elizabeth smiled as Sarah beamed up at her. "Shall we see what's on the next page?"

The toddler nodded, turned the page and looked expectantly at Elizabeth.

"Oh, Sarah, look—it's a puppy!"

The little girl stared down at the picture.

"Puppies are soft and playful, too, just like the kitten. And puppies are very loving. They give you kisses with their rough little tongues, and wag their tails. They jump around when they're happy and—" Elizabeth stopped and stared down at the picture with the glimmer of an idea forming in her mind. Surely a puppy would be good for Sarah. She could just imagine them playing together. But, would Justin agree? She looked up at an impatient tug on her skirt. Sarah pointed at the book.

"All right—I'm sorry." Elizabeth laughed softly. "Now let me see…what more can I— Oh, yes. Puppies say arf! arf! And you can teach them tricks. They can even learn to catch a ball."

Sarah clapped her small hands together, went to the shelves along the wall and took down a ball. She brought it back and held it out to Elizabeth.

"Yes. That's a ball." Elizabeth smiled at the toddler. "Would you like to play with it?"

Sarah nodded.

"Very well." Elizabeth removed the wooden horse from Mary's relaxed hand and placed it on the table. "Let me put Mary down for her nap and then we will roll the ball." She shifted the baby to her shoulder, got carefully to her feet, then paused at the sound of footsteps in the hall.

The door opened and Justin entered.

All the force of her newfound love rushed upon Elizabeth. Her heart fluttered. Her knees went weak. For one frightful moment she was afraid she would drop the baby. She stood trembling, afraid to move, certain her legs would give way should she try. She looked away, avoiding Justin's gaze until she could compose herself.

"So, I have found you." Justin walked toward her. "I missed you at breakfast."

Elizabeth moistened her dry lips. "I'm sorry. I found myself with little appetite. I should have sent word."

Justin frowned. "Are you taking ill?"

"No, I'm fine." Goodness! Was that *her* voice. Elizabeth smoothed the baby's gown as an excuse not to have to look at Justin. "Was there something you needed?" She flushed at the rudeness of the abrupt question.

"As a matter of fact there is. I need some advice about a certain matter and thought perhaps you might help me."

She glanced up at him. Her breath caught as their gazes met. She looked away again. "I shall be glad to render whatever assistance I am capable of, of course. But first, if you will excuse me, I was about to put Mary down for her nap." Elizabeth sent a short prayer that she wouldn't collapse into a graceless heap on the floor winging toward Heaven, and started for the baby's room.

"I'll wait." Justin's brow furrowed in thought as he called the words after Elizabeth. She was acting strangely. Was she angry with him for his lapse last evening? Self-disgust filled him. He never should have indulged his desire to touch her, to kiss her hand. He would have to do better. But how? So often he found himself unprepared for the force of the emotions she roused in him. Even his dislike of the greed that had led her to marry him was insufficient to quell his growing love for her. How was he to find the strength to abide by his word? He scowled and turned away from the sight of Elizabeth carrying the baby off to bed and almost stumbled over Sarah.

"Well, good morning." He stared down at the silent child wondering what to do or say next. She was such a timid little thing—always wary and fearful. How had Elizabeth penetrated that barrier of distrust and fear the toddler lived in? For that matter, how had she penetrated his own? The thought was disquieting. So was the child. He leaned down and retrieved the ball he had unwittingly knocked from her small hands.

"Do you like to play ball, Sarah?"

She nodded politely.

"And do you know how to catch?"

She stared up at him in steady, silent regard, and Justin was suddenly, uncomfortably aware that she knew he didn't really care—that he was only filling the unnatural silence with words. The tails of her pink hair ribbon fluttered as she shook her head.

"Well, we must remedy that." He squatted down in front of her. "Go stand over there—in front of the shelves." He pointed his finger to indicate the spot.

Sarah stared at him for a moment, then obediently turned and walked to the place he had indicated.

"Fine. Now...hold out your hands like this." He nodded with satisfaction as Sarah dutifully imitated him.

"Good. Now...here it comes!"

Justin tossed the ball gently into Sarah's outstretched arms.

The toddler's eyes widened in surprise. Her hands, instinctively, closed around the ball as it rolled down into them. She clasped it tightly and hugged it to her narrow little chest.

"Excellent!" Justin felt an unusual tightening in his chest as she smiled shyly at him. "Let's try it again. Throw the ball to me."

Sarah looked from Justin's face to his outstretched hands. Her eyes narrowed in concentration, the tip of her tongue came peeking out of the corner of her mouth, and she drew back her arm and let the ball fly.

"Splendid!" Justin shot to his feet and stretched out his arm to catch the wildly thrown ball. "Now it's your turn to catch it again. Arms together!"

Sarah immediately stretched her arms out in front as she had been shown. She locked her gaze on his face.

"No, no. Don't look at me, Sarah—you must watch the ball."

The little girl immediately shifted her gaze to the ball in Justin's hands.

"Good girl." Justin smiled at her intense look of concentration. "Are you ready?"

Sarah nodded. She never lifted her gaze from the ball.

"Very well. Here it comes."

Again, Justin tossed the ball gently into Sarah's small outstretched arms. The toddler squealed with delight and hopped up and down in excitement. Her eyes were shining. Justin chuckled, enjoying her pleasure.

"All right, then—" He clapped his hands together in front of him. "Toss it here."

Sarah drew back her arm as far as it would go and threw the ball with all her might.

"Whoops!" Justin lunged to the side and stretched his arm out to catch the ball that headed wide to his left. His shinbone met the low child's table with a sharp crack. "Ugh!" He grabbed for his leg. The ball flew by and landed with a crash against the candlestick sitting on the chest beside the connecting door to the children's bedroom.

"Sarah!" Elizabeth rushed into the room. "Sarah, sweetheart, are you—?"

"Sarah's fine."

Elizabeth stopped and stared at Justin who was hopping up and down on one foot while rubbing his shin. "What happened?"

Justin winced as he put his weight on the wounded leg. "Sarah and I were playing catch and I missed." He straightened and gave Elizabeth a sheepish smile. "I barked my shin on the table."

"I see." Elizabeth crossed over to him. "Are you hurt?"

"No. It's nothing really. But thank you for your concern." Justin glanced over at Sarah who was pressed back against the shelves staring up at him. There was naked fear in her eyes. Shame twisted his stomach.

"Well, Sarah, that was quite a throw." He grinned down at her. "But I think from now on we had better play outside—it's safer." He picked up the ball that had rolled to a stop at his feet and held it out to her. "Would you like to play catch again tomorrow?"

For a long moment she stared at him. The fear left her eyes. She gave him a timid smile, nodded, and ran over to take the ball from him.

"Good. I shall look forward to it." Justin gave her a reassuring smile, then turned back to Elizabeth. "Are you ready?"

"Ready?" Elizabeth struggled to keep the swell of love and admiration she felt for Justin at his treatment of the child from showing on her face. "Ready for what?"

"To give me your advice. My sister, Laina, will be celebrating a birthday soon and I thought you might help me select a gift for her."

"Oh. Yes, of course. I'm certain I could offer some suggestions." Elizabeth moved over to the chest and set the candlestick aright with trembling fingers.

Justin followed. "That would be helpful. But I had hoped you would come into town with me—to help me choose."

His deep voice came over her shoulder. An excited little shiver skittered down Elizabeth's spine. He was so close. She had only to turn and—

"Will you come?"

Her romantic daydream disappeared in a rush of apprehension. Leave Randolph Court on a weekday? She stopped fussing with the candlestick and folded her shaking hands in front of her while her mind searched for an acceptable reason to refuse. She could think of none. Reluctantly, she nodded.

"Good. I've ordered the chaise brought round."

It was a beautiful day. The bright, summer sun beamed down upon them as they drove down the cobblestone street in the smart, stone-colored rig. The golden rays glinted off the chaise's polished brass lamps, highlighted its green and black striping, and made dappled patterns on the rich, black leather upholstery as they rolled along under the leafy cover of overhanging branches. The heat made Elizabeth grateful for the shade and the gentle, cooling breeze that carried the sumptuous fragrance of lavish summer blooms on its breath.

She took a long, appreciative sniff, but not even the myriad pleasures of the gorgeous summer day could allay her trepidation. She was quite sure her parents had no dealings in this city, but she was uncertain about Reginald Burton-Smythe. Though several months had passed since her escape, her fear of discovery had not lessened. If anything it had grown. She was no longer concerned only with her own personal safety. Now, the thought of being separated from Justin and the children terrified her as well.

Elizabeth reached up and tucked the curl that was tickling her cheek as it fluttered in the breeze behind her ear and scanned the people on the street for a tall, thin, dark-haired man dressed in black. Reginald always wore black.

* * *

Justin stared at the spot just behind Elizabeth's ear where a golden curl now nestled, exhaled a long, slow breath, and forced his gaze back to the road ahead. Bringing her along had probably been a mistake—but he would do it again. He wanted to be alone with her. More and more of late he found himself inventing excuses to be in the same room with her—reasons to be close to her. He lifted his lips in a rueful smile. A rather exquisite form of self-torture judging by the havoc sitting beside her was raising with his emotions.

"Justin?"

His stomach muscles jerked taut. Every nerve in his body tingled with awareness as Elizabeth shifted her position on the seat beside him. Her arm brushed against his as she moved and heat raced along his arm, communicated itself to every part of his body. He tightened his hands on the reins and clenched his jaw. This woman would be his downfall if he was not careful! He arranged his features in the cool mask that hid his true feelings and turned to look at her. "Yes?"

"I was thinking about the gift for your sister. Though it's difficult to choose because I know only the little you have told me about her—and what I have gleaned from reading your grandmother's notations in the family Bible. I thought perhaps, an objet d'art?"

Justin nodded and looked back at the street—her mouth was far too enticing. "An excellent suggestion, Elizabeth. You have thought of the very thing—and I know where to find it, at Caleb's shop." He flexed his powerful wrists, the movement rippled along the reins and the black gelding stepped forward smartly.

The bell over the shop door tinkled merrily. Caleb frowned and lifted his head. "Ne'er fails." He muttered the words under his breath, put down his cutting tool, wiped his hands on a rag he tossed onto his workbench, and rose laboriously to his feet. His movements were hampered by the wooden leg he had never quite become accustomed to wearing.

Pain stabbed through the stump of his leg when it took his weight. Caleb mumbled an oath, grabbed up the crutch he had carved from a large tree branch and shoved it under his arm. It was at moments like these he wished he could get his hands around the throat of the pirate whose ball had struck his lower leg forcing the ship's doctor to amputate the shattered remains. It angered him still that the black-hearted, cowardly blighter was out of his reach on the ocean floor—that is if a shark hadn't eaten him. Caleb twisted his lips into a smile of grim satisfaction at the thought. He thumped his way across the room and shoved aside the curtain covering the connecting doorway.

"Eh! Mr. Randolph, sir!" Caleb's glad words exploded into the silence of the small room like the boom of a cannon.

Elizabeth gasped. She spun toward the voice, gave a squeak of shock at sight of the red-bearded giant descending on them and grabbed for Justin's arm.

Caleb stopped. The heavy thud of his uneven tread upon the bare floorboards faded away into silence. He swept his gaze from Elizabeth to Justin and nodded his massive head. "I heard you'd taken a new bride." His voice echoed from the walls of the shop. He glanced at Elizabeth. "I beg your pardon if I gave you a fright. I didn't see you standin' there in your man's shadow." His brows knit in a frown. "You've no need to be alarmed—I'd never harm you."

"I—I'm the one to beg pardon, Mr...."

"Caleb—if you please."

The words reverberated through the room. Elizabeth's hand tightened on Justin's arm. He grinned at the giant. "I forgot to warn Elizabeth of your great size, Caleb. And of that foghorn you call a voice."

The big man nodded. "It's a fearsome thing to some."

Justin looked down at Elizabeth. "I'm sorry you were frightened. I'm so accustomed to Caleb-I'd forgotten how overwhelming an experience it can be seeing him for the first time."

"I must admit he gave me a fright—but I'm quite recovered." She gave Justin a shaky smile.

"Your hand is still trembling."

Elizabeth looked down in surprise at her hand clinging possessively to Justin's arm. Her cheeks warmed. She lifted the betraying hand. "I'm sorry, I didn't mean to—"

"Leave it." He caught and imprisoned her hand in his, giving her no choice. "It's right that it should be there."

Elizabeth could think of no appropriate response. In truth, she could think of nothing at all. She was aware only of the soft warm glow spreading through her at Justin's touch. She looked down at the hand that encased hers in its strong, steady warmth and felt a sudden, intense desire to press her cheek against it. It *was* right that her hand should be there joined with his. Not as he had meant it—not simply because she was lawfully wed to him—but because she loved him. If only— No! Elizabeth put the dreamy thought from her mind. There *was* no *if only.* There was merely the truth: Justin did not love her. He still loved his true wife. She, herself, was only a convenience.

Elizabeth pretended interest in the items in the glass-topped display case beside her as she struggled to get her traitorous emotions under control. She must do nothing to cause Justin to suspect the truth. Should he ever guess she loved him— She shuddered inwardly at the thought of his scorn. He had made his position on the subject of their relationship abundantly clear. Her only recourse was to take refuge in a cool, distant politeness. She must treat him in a gracious but formal fashion, ignoring the strange sensations he brought to life within her. It was the only sensible solution to her problem. She settled that thought firmly in her mind and turned her attention back to the men's conversation.

"...the horse you were working on a few weeks ago?"

"Aye. It's finished."

Caleb thumped his way behind the display case, took an object from a small cupboard that hung on the wall and held it out to Justin.

"Give it to Elizabeth." Justin freed her hand.

Elizabeth stared down at the object Caleb placed on her palm. It was a small, alabaster statue of a horse with a delicate vine of small jade leaves and tiny coral flowers twined around its neck. "It's beautiful!"

Elizabeth looked from the delicate statue to the huge man towering over her. "You made this?" She could not keep the astonishment out of her voice.

"Aye." Caleb nodded his massive head.

"But it's so delicate, and you're so big! I don't see how— Oh! I'm sorry! That was terribly rude of me. Please—" She stopped and gaped up at Caleb. A sound not unlike the far-off rumblings of thunder was rolling from the giant's deep chest. She put the horse on top of the display case and inched backward.

Justin grinned. "Unbelievable, isn't it?" He clasped his hands behind his back and leaned forward until his lips were on a level with Elizabeth's ear. "The first time I heard him laugh I ran for cover."

"You never!" Elizabeth smiled.

"Oh, but I did. I dived under the nearest lifeboat. We were at sea and I was sure a storm was coming."

Elizabeth laughed in spite of her embarrassment. "Surely you do not expect me to believe such an outrageous tale?"

Justin shook his head. "No, I don't expect you to believe the tale, Elizabeth. I simply wanted to see your beautiful smile."

The words took her breath. Elizabeth gazed up into Justin's eyes and all of her fine resolve melted away in the warmth of the smoky blue flames flickering in their depths.

Chapter Twenty-One

⚜

The trip to town...supper...and now Justin's request for her company on a walk through the gardens. Would this day never end? Her nerves were stretched raw. Elizabeth stole a sidelong glance at her husband and held back a sigh. Being with him was wonderful, exciting and torturous all at the same time.

Justin glanced at her and smiled. "You're wondering why I asked you to come outside." His smile widened and he stopped walking. "I want to build a playhouse for the children, and I want your advice." He swept his hand forward. "I had thought, there—across from the pavilion—would be a good place." He looked down at her. "What do you think?"

Elizabeth looked at the graceful pavilion at the end of the brick path, then swept her gaze to the large grassy area Justin had pointed out. "I think it would be perfect. A playhouse is a wonderful idea, Justin. I'm sure Sarah will love it. And Mary, also, when she gets a little older."

She walked to the pavilion and rested her hands on the ornate railing that enclosed it while she surveyed its recently completed interior. A twinge of guilt tugged at her heart—work on it had been stopped at the time of Justin's first wife's death and he had ordered it finished at her request. She thrust the feeling from her. It was not good for Justin to keep these monuments to a dead woman. It was unhealthy.

Elizabeth examined the furnishings with a critical eye. Everything was just as she had suggested. There were benches and chairs cushioned in bright colors, hooked area rugs for comfort, and a table and chairs suitable for a light luncheon or tea. He had even added a lounge one could recline upon for a brief rest. It was lovely.

"This is the perfect place for Nanny Hammerfield to sit and relax while watching over the children, Justin. I'm so glad you had it finished." Elizabeth turned, smiled across the path at him and patted the railing. "And this will do very nicely to curtail Mary's adventurous forays. I'm afraid she's rather fond of putting things in her mouth just now, and she's not very selective. It wouldn't do to have her crawling about on the ground—there's no knowing what she would find to her liking." She gave a delicate shudder.

Justin grinned. "Well then, we must, by all means, keep Mistress Mary confined until her culinary habits improve." He chuckled and glanced up at the setting sun.

"I couldn't agree more." Elizabeth laughed, then gripped the railing tightly as Justin walked over to stand beside her. That queer, trembling weakness was overtaking her again. She took a deep breath.

"I don't believe Nanny Hammerfield will be the only one sitting in the pavilion watching over the children, Elizabeth." Justin smiled down at her. "I want you to know that I am aware of the time you spend with the children—especially Sarah—and I'm grateful."

Elizabeth stared hard at her hands on the railing and dipped her head in acknowledgment. She did not trust her voice to answer—tears were threatening. This was all she would ever have from him—gratitude for caring for his first wife's children.

She swallowed back the tears, released her grip on the railing and walked a few steps away in what she hoped would appear to be a casual fashion. She plucked a leaf from the boxwood hedge lining the brick path, tore it into tiny shreds with her trembling fingers, moved a few steps forward and reached for another. Putting distance between them helped, but it was not enough. She needed to be alone to think. She needed time to come to grips with these strange new emotions that were assaulting her senses. Most of all she needed to be away from Justin. He was so—so overwhelming.

Elizabeth brushed the clinging bits of leaf from her fingers, wrapped her arms about herself and stared up the path toward the safety of the house. "If there is nothing further you wish to discuss I believe I will go in now, Justin." She forced a false brightness into her voice that she hated. She started up the path toward the sanctuary of her room.

"Is there something wrong, Elizabeth?"

She jerked to a halt. "Wrong?" The word came out in a nervous squeak.

"Yes, wrong."

She heard him start up the path after her. She listened to his footsteps draw near, then stop behind her. *I'm in love with a man who is in love with a dead woman, that's what's wrong!* The words screamed in her mind and she longed to turn around and shout them at him, but of course that was impossible. She shivered and hugged herself tighter. "I suddenly felt chilled." It was the only explanation she could offer—and it was the truth. She felt chilled to her very bones.

"Perhaps this will help."

Justin's suit coat dropped about her shoulders. Elizabeth stiffened. The fabric, warm from his body, enveloped her. The sharp, manly scent of his cologne rose from its folds to her nostrils. Her senses reeled. She swayed, suddenly lightheaded. Justin clasped her upper arms in his strong hands to steady her.

"I'm sorry, Elizabeth. I should have realized it would be heavy for you."

His voice was as soft and warm as the sunset. Elizabeth didn't know whether to laugh, or cry. How could one person change so much? Such a short time ago, the thought of Justin's hands upon her had terrified her. Now, all she wanted to do was lean back into his arms and rest her head against his shoulder. She fought back an hysterical giggle at the thought of his reaction should she do so. He would most likely thrust her away so violently she would end up in the boxwood. She bit down on her lip, gathered all of her inner strength and stepped forward out of temptation's grip. She forced a cool politeness into her voice. "That's much better. Thank you." She could feel his gaze on her as she walked away from him.

"There is one other thing I wanted to discuss with you, Elizabeth." He called the words after her, his voice now as coolly remote as her own had been.

She turned toward him. His face wore no expression, but his long fingers flexed and unflexed at his sides. *Had she made him angry?*

"I have instructed Webber to put up a swing for Sarah. There—in that large oak." He pointed. "But I want your opinion. I will rescind the order if you feel Sarah is too young."

Elizabeth glanced at the tree he had indicated. There was a large branch parallel to the ground that was perfect for a swing. "She's not too young. And I'm certain Sarah would enjoy a swing." She forced a smile. "It's a lovely idea, Justin."

He shrugged. "The credit is yours."

"Mine?"

He nodded affirmation. "Yours, and Mr. Buffy's. I was inspired by your story."

Elizabeth stared at him, then pivoted away as tears welled into her eyes. "I see. Well, I'm pleased to have been of service." She bit her lip to stop its trembling, gripped her skirt in her hands and hurried up the path to escape Justin's presence before she broke down completely. *Please Lord, no more delays. Just let me reach my room and—*

"Elizabeth?"

"Don't *do* that!" Elizabeth jerked away from the detaining hand Justin had placed on her arm and spun to face him. "Don't ever do that again!" She stamped her foot. "Not *ever* again!" Her voice broke. She had been so close to escaping his presence! Only a few feet more and—

"I meant nothing personal, I assure you! I'm aware that you cannot abide my touch. I merely wanted to give you this." Justin grabbed her hand, dropped an object onto her palm, and strode up the stairs, across the porch, and into the house. The door slammed behind him.

Elizabeth felt ill. She had shouted at him. She had actually *shouted* at Justin. She turned and sank down onto the steps. The tails of Justin's suit coat bunched beneath her and the coat slid from her shoulders. She grabbed for the coat and lost her grip on the object in her hand. It rolled across the porch and came to rest under the wooden bench by the salon doors. Elizabeth stared after it and sighed. She wasn't even surprised. Her life had become a series of calamities both large and small. This was just one more which would, no doubt, result in Justin's further displeasure.

Elizabeth sighed again, rose to her feet and walked to the bench hoping that whatever it was had not been damaged. She knelt and peered underneath the seat. It was there. At least *something* was there—it was too dark in the shadows to see clearly. She reached out and gave the dark spot a quick, tentative poke, hoping that it was indeed the object she was seeking and not some small creeping creature. It scraped along the floor. *Metal.* Thank heaven it hadn't been a spider! She picked it up, and her fingers immediately identified the object as a ring. Her wedding ring! She had forgotten about it.

Elizabeth rose to her feet, held her hand in the circle of light thrown by the coach lamp beside the door and opened her fingers. Her eyes widened. She gave a small gasp and pressed her free hand against her chest at the base of her throat. *That wasn't her ring!* What if she had *lost* it? A feeling of nausea swept through her. She clasped her fingers tightly over the ring and rushed into the house. She must give it back to Justin immediately. She didn't want it in her possession a moment longer. She hurried down the hall to his study, rapped smartly on the door and pushed it open.

Elizabeth saw the shock that spread across Justin's face as she burst through his door. It was instantly replaced with a scowl. He rose to his feet.

"Was there something you wanted?"

"Yes! I'm sorry to disturb you, Justin, but I wanted to return this to you." The tails of his suit coat flopped against her skirts as she rushed toward him. She leaned across his desk and extended her hand.

He flicked his gaze down to the ring that lay on her open palm. His face went taut. "You do not wish to wear my ring?"

"That's not your ring, Justin—it's the wrong one! There's been an error made. Look." Elizabeth placed the ring in the circle of candlelight on the desktop. It glowed like green fire. "Those are *emeralds*. Beautiful, flawless *emeralds!*" She shook her head in awe. "That ring is worth a fortune. It must be returned to—"

"It's the right ring, Elizabeth."

She lifted her head and stared at him. "What did you say?"

"I said that is your ring."

"But it's not! It's—" Justin's brows lowered in a dark scowl. She broke off her protestations and glanced in confusion from him, to the ring, and back again. "I don't understand."

"There's nothing *to* understand, Elizabeth. It's your ring. I had it made for you."

"You had it made for *me!*" Shock stole her good manners. She gaped up at him, her heart swelling with hope. "Why?"

"Because you're my wife and I wanted you to have it!" Justin glowered at her. "I thought it would match the brooch your grandmother gave you."

Elizabeth stared at him. *And be suitable for Justin Randolph's wife?* The unspoken comment lingered in her mind and her hope died. Tears smarted the backs of her eyes. She blinked them away and cleared her throat. "Thank you, Justin. It was very thoughtful of you to consider my grandmother's brooch when you chose the design."

His face darkened at her polite words. The candlelight glinted in his stormy blue eyes. He snatched up the ring and headed around the desk, the muscle along his tightly clenched jaw twitching as he strode toward her. He looked angry, dangerous, and heart-stoppingly handsome. Elizabeth sucked her breath in sharply and began to back away.

Justin stopped. His gaze locked on hers. He advanced slowly. She started to tremble. She tried to look away, but could not. She tried to speak, and found herself powerless to do so. She went hot, then cold, then hot again. Her heart began an erratic pounding that thundered in her ears and she was suddenly, unbearably aware of Justin's proximity—and, more devastatingly, of her own womanhood. With sudden, startling clarity she understood that what she felt was the desire that was a natural, beautiful part of her love for Justin. She wanted to be his wife. She wanted to belong to him completely. She closed her eyes lest they betray her, and fixed her mind on one thought, and one thought alone—he must never know. His kindness would never be more than a part of his duty for her.

Justin stared at Elizabeth's face, at the sooty lashes that lay in startling contrast against the sudden pallor of her skin. Even paralyzed by the fear she felt for him, she was stunningly beautiful and devastatingly desirable. He had to get her out of there before his control broke. He moved forward, lifted her trembling hand and slipped the ring on her finger. There was no response. She didn't even open her eyes. He swallowed his disappointment, released her hand and went back to his desk.

"You'd better go now, Elizabeth. I've work to do."

He grabbed a paper from his desk drawer, laid it on the desk and sat staring down at it until he heard the click of the door closing. The title read: Certificate of Marriage. How appropriate that he should have grabbed that particular one.

With one angry, frustrated swipe of his hand, Justin shoved the paper back into the drawer and slammed it shut. He surged to his feet, then froze, staring at his suit coat. Elizabeth had taken it off and draped it over the back of the leather settee. He grabbed it up, yanked open the French doors and stormed out into the dark, lonely night.

* * *

Her mother had lied. She knew that now. Men were *not* all alike. Reginald Burton-Smythe was evil. But Justin— "Justin." Elizabeth smiled. Merely saying his name made her feel as if she were melting. How had it happened? She had been so frightened of him and now—

Her cheeks grew warm at the memory of those moments in his study when they had stood facing each other. Thank heaven he hadn't guessed, hadn't *suspected,* what she had been thinking and feeling. Thank heaven he still thought it was fear that made her tremble at his touch. How humiliating would be his scorn, how devastating his rejection, if he was to learn of her love for him—of her desire to truly be his wife.

Elizabeth stared at the door that led to Justin's quarters—the husband's chambers. It was closed, just like the door to his heart. Oh, how was she to hide the truth from him? How was she to prevent her hands, her lips, her eyes, from betraying her secret when she was with him? She could not hide forever in her room.

Elizabeth sighed, turned her back on the closed door and walked to the dressing table. Perhaps it was only that her love for Justin was so new—so overwhelming. Perhaps it would become easier as time passed. She reached up and pulled the pins and ivory combs from her hair. The silky mass tumbled down over her shoulders. She dropped the pins into a small silver box, picked up the brush, and glanced into the mirror. There was a flash as the light from the candles glinted off the emerald and gold ring Justin had placed on her finger. Tears sprang into her eyes.

Elizabeth tossed the brush down and jumped to her feet. She needed something to distract her—to absorb her mind with other thoughts until she was able to sleep. And she knew where to find it. She would read the Bible in the library.

Elizabeth read the underlined scripture one more time in the light of the flickering candle, placed the Bible back on the rosewood table and stepped out into the soft, warm night. A light breeze whispered softly through the trees and blew her curls into her eyes. She brushed them back from her face and crossed the brick porch, then paused at the top of the steps and looked up at the stars. So many stars. And God had hung them there.

Was such an enormously powerful and majestic God truly concerned about her? Did He see her standing here looking toward the heavens? Did He know how much she loved Justin? How much she wanted to be his wife? How much she wanted them all to become a family? She couldn't bear it if He didn't, because He was her only hope. She had to trust Him. Like the scripture she had just read said.

"'Delight thyself also in the Lord; and He shall give thee the desires of thine heart. Commit thy way unto the Lord; trust also in Him; and He shall bring it to pass'—" Elizabeth gasped and swallowed the rest of the beautiful words at the sound of footsteps on the path below her. Justin stepped out from under the deep shadows of a tree and looked up at her.

"Do you really believe the Lord knows the desires of your heart and will give them to you if you make Him your delight? Do you really think He cares?"

The scorn in his voice stung Elizabeth. She lifted her chin. "I was taught it was rude to eavesdrop. But, to answer your question, yes, I choose to believe that. I take it you do not?"

Justin started up the steps. She could see his eyes clearly as the starlight bathed his face in cool radiance. She had made him angry again. Or maybe he was angry still.

"I did once. There was a time when I believed in God." He stepped onto the porch and his eyes glittered with bitterness as he looked down at her. "There was a time when I believed He would give me what my heart desired, if only I served Him faithfully. When I believed in His promises. That was when I designed the fanlight you so admire." His lips curved into a thin, cool smile. "I see that surprises you."

"Only because you told me the young man who designed the window had died."

"And so he did. There are many ways to die, Elizabeth." Justin turned away to stare out over the silver-shadowed gardens. "Many ways."

He sounded so lost, so full of pain, Elizabeth's heart ached for him. She stepped toward him, then froze as her movement drew his frosty gaze. She saw him look down at the betraying hand she had reached out to comfort him, and quickly she lifted it to pluck a flower from the bush beside the railing. She held the blossom to her nose, sniffing delicately, and moved away into a deeper shadow. He did not want her comfort, or her love—she must remember that.

Justin turned back to face the gardens and cleared his throat. "I don't know what you desire, Elizabeth. But, my desire was for a marriage like that of my parents, and grandparents. And then I married my wife and she...died."

He turned to face her again, and Elizabeth saw the same pain and grief she had witnessed before in his eyes. "The trusting, believing Justin Randolph died with her. He was murdered just as surely as if a sword had been plunged through him." He spun back around and stared up at the sky. "He's gone forever—unless God chooses to resurrect him with a miracle."

There was a moment of absolute silence. Elizabeth did not trust her voice to speak—nor did she know what to say. She could only stand there loving Justin and sharing his pain. Slowly, the soft night sounds rose to fill the air around them. Justin drew a deep breath and brushed his fingers through his hair.

"Forgive me, Elizabeth. I did not intend to say all that— to let my bitterness spill over onto you. But when I heard you quoting that verse with such trust in your voice I wanted—I wanted to keep you from the same disappointment I have suffered. I don't want you to be hurt believing in something that will never happen." With a terse nod in her direction he walked into his study and pulled the door closed behind him.

I don't want you to be hurt believing in something that will never happen. The words stabbed like a knife into Elizabeth's heart. She lifted her head to stare dry-eyed at the star-strewn sky. She couldn't cry. Some things went beyond tears. Justin's bitterness sat like a stone upon her heart. Her own desires no longer mattered.

Elizabeth walked down the steps and strolled along the brick path that stretched out into the converging darkness. It seemed as if she was about to burst asunder with her love for Justin. It kept growing and growing—and there was no release for it. She wanted so much to help him, to comfort him, to make him happy...and she could do nothing.

She stopped walking and lifted her gaze to the starry night sky. God seemed so close out here in the gardens. She smiled at her foolishness. As if place mattered—God was everywhere. The thought brought her a measure of comfort.

She caught sight of movement out of the corner of her eye and turned her head in time to see the shadowy form of a small animal merge with the darkness of the bushes. An owl hooted somewhere off to her left, and some small creature made tiny rustling noises in the flower bed at her feet.

She stood very still, listening to the gentle sounds— sensing the teeming life in the quiet night. She felt very small and insignificant, awed by the force of life and the power and majesty of the Almighty God that spoke it into existence. She looked down at the flowers that were washed by the silver radiance of the stars and tears filled her eyes. What she had said to Justin was true. She *did* choose to believe. God was all she had. She would put her trust in Him.

"Dear God, You are the creator of life. Give Justin new life I pray. Give him his miracle." Her memory stirred and Elizabeth looked up toward the sky. "Give him beauty for ashes, Lord. Give him beauty for ashes that his heart might turn again to Thee."

Chapter Twenty-Two

✧

"Why, Sarah!" Abigail Twiggs leaned her walking stick against the railing and reached out to take the offered bouquet. "What lovely flowers." She fixed a stern look upon the smiling three-year-old. "Did Webber say you might pick them?"

The toddler nodded.

"Then, I thank you very much." Abigail's face creased into a delighted smile as Sarah bobbed a quick curtsy and skipped away.

Elizabeth's heart swelled with maternal pride. She watched for a moment as Sarah ran across the green lawn to join the gardener, then gave Abigail a rueful smile and went back to trying to extricate a crushed flower from Mary's clenched fist.

"You might rescue that one, Elizabeth, but I fear it's too late for the one in her mouth."

"Oh!" Elizabeth snatched hold of the bit of stem protruding from the baby's mouth and with her other hand tickled Mary's tummy. She pulled the flower free as the baby began to laugh, then tossed it over the railing and gave Mary a comforting hug as she began to howl her displeasure. "It's all right, precious."

Elizabeth settled the baby on her lap, moved her knees slightly so that the teacup on the table beside her was out of Mary's reach, and offered her a spoon. The baby grabbed for the shiny object with her pudgy hands. Elizabeth smiled and picked up the crushed flower that fell from Mary's opened fist.

"Very clever."

Elizabeth lifted her head and met Abigail's amused gaze. "Another crisis dealt with. Does it ever stop?" She laughed and tossed the flower away.

Abigail chuckled. "I'm afraid not. It changes—but it never stops."

"Oh, dear." Elizabeth dodged the wildly waving spoon. "I hope I prove adequate."

"There's no doubt of that. You're a wonderful mother to these little ones. And the Lord knows they needed one."

"I beg your pardon?" Elizabeth lifted the baby to her shoulder to stop her from drumming on the chair arm with the spoon. She gave the older woman a rueful smile. "I couldn't hear you above the noise."

"I shouldn't wonder. I said—" Abigail leaned forward, snatched the spoon from the baby's grasp and popped a bit of sugar into her mouth when Mary opened it to howl her protest "—you are a wonderful mother to these children. To Sarah especially." She leaned back in her chair and eyed the happily sucking baby with smug satisfaction. "There is an astonishing difference in her since you came."

"Do you truly believe so?"

"I truly do."

"Thank you, Abigail." Elizabeth smiled at the elderly woman, then shifted her gaze to Sarah. "I do *so* want to help her. But it's difficult to know what is best for her. She's such a...a delicate little girl." She sighed. "Anyway, you're very kind."

"Nonsense." Abigail gave an unladylike snort. "I haven't a kind bone in my body."

Elizabeth laughed. "You're a dear, and you know it." She sobered as she watched Sarah run toward them. "If only Sarah would talk, Abigail. I've tried everything I can think of to encourage her." She looked across the table at the elderly woman who had become a dear friend. "I'm certain she could, if she would only try."

"Perhaps she will in time, dear."

"Yes. Perhaps in time." Elizabeth repeated the words softly, then shrugged off the suddenly serious mood and smiled across the table. "Would you care for more tea, Abigail? Or perhaps— *Ouch!*" Elizabeth stared down at the ivory hair comb gripped tightly in Mary's tiny, pudgy hands.

"Oh, Mary. Look what you've done!" Elizabeth grasped one of the curls that had tumbled onto her shoulders when freed of the constraining comb and tickled the baby's cheek with it. "What a little troublemaker you are!" Mary gave her a semitoothless grin and waved her hands in the air. Elizabeth laughed, lifted the gurgling baby into the air, and covered her little face with kisses. An insistent tug on her skirt stopped the playful interlude. She looked down at Sarah.

"What is it, precious?"

Sarah pointed.

Elizabeth's heart skipped a beat—Justin was coming down the path to the pavilion. Her gaze met his over the distance and she forgot to breathe when he smiled at her. Would she ever get over this desire to rush into his arms every time she saw him? She sighed and turned her attention back to the problem at hand—her hair.

Thankful Justin was too far away to see her disheveled appearance, Elizabeth freed one hand and searched in her lap for her hair comb. It wasn't there. She bit her lower lip in consternation, then, almost cried aloud when she spotted the comb still clasped tightly in Mary's pudgy hand. Now, what was she to do? The sound of Justin's footsteps climbing the pavilion stairs gave Elizabeth her answer. She could do nothing—it was too late. She cast a last, longing look at the comb and smiled a greeting. "Good afternoon."

No answer. Justin simply looked at her. Elizabeth's cheeks warmed. "Forgive my appearance. Mary pulled the comb from my hair and—well—you know how she is at giving things up." She tried to balance the baby with one hand and gather her hair with the other.

"Leave it." Justin's voice came out husky and ragged. He cleared his throat, placed the basket he was carrying on the floor at his feet, then, looked back at Elizabeth. "It doesn't matter that your hair is down, Elizabeth. I don't mind." He scowled at the muffled snort that came from beside him and turned to glare at Abigail.

She gave him a sweet smile. A patently phony sweet smile.

Justin burst into laughter. He leaned down, kissed Abigail's dry, wrinkled cheek, then crouched down by the basket at his feet. He smiled at the toddler standing by Elizabeth's knee. "We have a present for you, Sarah. Would you like to see it?"

The little girl clapped her hands and nodded.

Justin gave Elizabeth a conspiratorial wink and lifted the lid off the basket. For a moment nothing happened, then, furious scrabbling sounds issued forth and the basket began to rock back and forth precariously. A round black ball of fur with a red tongue and a white tip on a fluffy upright tail scrambled over the basket rim and fell with a yelp to the floor at Sarah's feet. The puppy righted himself, shook himself vigorously—which made him lose his balance again—tipped his head to one side, gave two sharp yips and attacked Sarah's shoe.

The little girl stared wide-eyed as the puppy growled, lunged, backed away, and then repeated the process. She glanced up at Elizabeth and Justin, then dropped to her knees on the floor and giggled as the puppy, wagging his tail furiously, leaped up to bestow rough wet kisses on her face. He wiggled with joy when Justin scooped him up and placed him in Sarah's arms, and set at once to licking her small ear with his tiny tongue. Sarah giggled and hugged him tight.

Elizabeth's eyes blurred with happy tears, but she dared not wipe them away, for she, too, had a squealing, wiggling bundle on her lap. Clearly, Mary wanted the puppy.

"Let me have her." Justin's deep voice cut through the

squeals and giggles as he lifted the baby from Elizabeth's lap. "This one is getting to be quite a handful." He grinned and took a firmer hold on Mary as she twisted about to try and reach the puppy.

"I know—especially when she's excited." Elizabeth laughed as Mary tried to fling herself backward, only to find a large, strong hand waiting to catch her. For a moment the baby struggled against Justin's hold, then, acknowledging defeat, she contented herself with chewing on the snowy white cravat at her jailer's throat. Justin gave Elizabeth a rueful grin, and nodded toward Sarah and the puppy.

"She seems to like him." There was relief in his voice. "She's so timid, I thought perhaps he might frighten her."

Elizabeth nodded. "I was concerned about that, too." She looked down at Sarah who was giggling happily while the puppy licked her neck, and her heart swelled. How good it was to hear her laugh! Surely, if she could laugh, she could talk.

"I believe you're about to be rescued, Justin."

Elizabeth glanced over at Abigail who waved a hand forward directing her gaze to the sturdy figure of Nurse Hammerfield who was making her way toward the pavilion. A sudden squeal of joy from Sarah drew her attention back. Elizabeth smiled. It was wonderful to see the child running and playing—to hear her laughing and squealing. Surely she could talk. Surely she could. She blinked back a rush of tears and closed her eyes. *Dear God, please help Sarah talk.*

Mary gurgled. Elizabeth opened her eyes and watched

Justin hand the baby to the nurse, then squat to rescue Sarah's hem from the puppy's sharp little teeth. She smiled and stepped forward. "I think we might bend the rules and allow Sarah to play a little longer, Anna. She's having such a good time I hate to stop it. I'll bring her in a little later for her nap."

"Very good, madam." The nurse smiled as she looked down at Sarah's beaming face. "There are some things more important than rules, or sleep—but not for this one." She settled the baby more comfortably in her arms and started down the stairs. "This one needs her rest."

Elizabeth smiled as Mary snuggled contentedly against the nurse's ample bosom and closed her eyes. The baby would be asleep before they reached the house.

"Hold still!"

Elizabeth turned. Justin was attempting to free Sarah's dress from the wriggling, snarling puppy. "Do you need help?"

He glanced up and shook his head. "No, I think I've got it." He released the hem and watched with a crooked grin as Sarah ran around the pavilion with the puppy in hot pursuit. "At least for the moment." He dropped into the chair beside the one Elizabeth had taken and stretched his long legs out in front of him. "That little beast could prove costly. There's a tear in her dress."

"Trudy will mend— Oh, look!" Elizabeth laughed as the puppy gave up the chase, dropped to the floor and fell fast asleep. Sarah stopped running, looked at the sleeping puppy for a moment, then ran back, plopped down on the floor and tugged him onto her lap. Elizabeth's heart melted.

Sarah looked so sweet, so little, sitting there patting the puppy's soft fur with her small hand—

"Ummm, you're right, Abigail."

"Right?" Elizabeth came out of her reverie. "I seem to have missed something. What is Abigail right about?"

Justin glanced over at her. "Abigail was just saying that yon beasty requires a name." He nodded toward the sleeping puppy, then looked back at her. "Have you a suggestion?"

"Well..." Elizabeth pursed her lips and studied the puppy. "His appearance would suggest Blackie—or perhaps, Tippy."

Abigail nodded. "And his character suggests Scamp."

"Or Destroyer." Justin looked askance at the puppy who had awakened from his brief snooze and was now chewing contentedly on Sarah's sleeve.

Elizabeth laughed. Justin looked at her. Their gazes locked. Held. Heat climbed into her cheeks. She looked down at her hands. "Perhaps his name should be...Happy."

"Mithter Buffy."

Elizabeth's heart stopped. For that small space of time in which she, Justin and Abigail stared at each other in disbelief, her heart stopped beating. It started again when they each swiveled their heads and stared at the toddler in utter astonishment.

Sarah looked up at them with complete equanimity, and repeated the name carefully. "Mithter Buffy."

It took Justin a moment, but he was the first to recover. He cleared his throat, handed his handkerchief to Elizabeth, and rose from his chair to go and squat down in front of Sarah. "An excellent choice, Sarah. Mr. Buffy, it is." He cleared his throat again.

Sarah beamed at him and held up her arms.

Justin's chest tightened. It was the first time she had ever done more than smile timidly at him. He laid the puppy in the basket and lifted Sarah into his arms, totally unprepared for the rush of paternal love that filled him when her little arms circled his neck and squeezed. His child. Not his ward—*his child*. Dear heaven, he had missed so much!

Justin laid his cheek against Sarah's fine, soft, brown hair and tears stung his eyes. He tightened his arms protectively around her small body and swallowed hard when her head dropped down onto his shoulder. He held her gently, marveling at the incredible feel of her in his arms. Her soft, warm breath blew across his neck in a long, contented sigh and she went limp. He glanced down. She was fast asleep.

"I think she's had enough excitement for now, Justin. Will you take her in for her nap?" Elizabeth's voice was choked with emotion.

Justin nodded. He tightened his grip on Sarah, walked down the stairs and started up the brick path toward the house.

Elizabeth stood at the railing and watched the man she loved carrying the small child she considered her own. Her heart swelled until she was sure it would burst. The pain in her chest was so intense she couldn't breathe, but she couldn't succumb to the temptation to ease the pressure with tears. Abigail was watching her, and no one must know. *No one must know.* Elizabeth used the thought to battle the terrible ache in her heart.

"Are you all right, dear?"

"Why of course, Abigail. Why shouldn't I be?" Elizabeth fastened a bright smile on her face, turned, and met the sympathetic gaze of the older woman. Her throat closed. She blinked rapidly, walked over to the basket, lifted the sleeping puppy into her arms and stroked his smooth, soft fur. After a few moments she felt sufficiently in command of her emotions to turn and join Abigail at the table. She stooped to pick up the puppy's basket and gave a soft exclamation of surprise. Her hair comb was under the chair she had occupied earlier.

"Well, imagine that." She picked up the carved ivory hair comb, seated herself and laid it on the table. "Mary let go of my comb after all. It seems to be a day for miracles." She glanced over at Abigail and smiled, then buried her face in the puppy's soft, black fur and burst into tears.

Chapter Twenty-Three

❧

Laina smiled as her brother wrapped his arms around her in a warm embrace. All evening she had seen flashes of the old Justin—the Justin she knew and loved. That horrid cold mask he had worn for so long was slipping and there were cracks in the wall he had erected around himself. Large cracks. But there was still a shadow of unhappiness in his eyes and she could sense tension in him. He hid it well, but it was there. She tightened her arms around his hard, muscular body and stood on tiptoe to kiss his cheek.

Justin smiled. "What was that for? The horse?"

"Well, I do love it, Justin. It's exquisite. But, no." Laina returned his smile. "The kiss was for you. I've missed you." She studied his face. "I haven't had a chance to ask. Are things better?"

Justin twisted his mouth into a wry smile. "Yes, they're better—and worse. No!" He laughed and placed his finger gently across Laina's lips when she started to speak. "I am *not* going to explain. You're too curious by half."

"It's only because I love you."

Laina put on her prettiest pout and looked, hopefully, up at Justin. He merely grinned. She tossed her head and stepped back from his embrace. "Oh, very well. I suppose it isn't the best time, or circumstance, as I must return to my guests. Anyway, it doesn't matter." She linked her arm through the judge's and gave him a beguiling smile. "I'll wheedle everything out of Judge after you've gone back to Philadelphia."

Justin burst into laughter. "Laina, you have no shame. You haven't grown up a bit."

"Nor do I intend to." She wrinkled her nose at her brother and laid her head on the judge's shoulder. "I learn so much this way."

"No doubt." Justin chuckled and exchanged a look of loving male forbearance with the judge.

Laina flashed him a saucy smile. Things *were* better! She hadn't been able to laugh and exchange teasing banter with her brother in months. She lifted her head and cast a slanted glance up at the dignified old man smiling fondly at them.

"Judge?" She crooned the respectful endearment and lifted her hand to rest lightly against his chest. "I want you to be a darling and learn every little detail about every little thing." She tugged playfully at his cravat and gave him an exaggeratedly sweet smile. "Else, I'll give you no peace."

Justin hooted.

The judge dropped a fatherly kiss on Laina's smooth

forehead and shot Justin a look of indulgent resignation. Both men knew she spoke the truth.

Laina laughed, extricated herself from the judge's arms and threw her brother a blatant look of victory.

Justin shook his head in fond exasperation and bent down to kiss her cheek. "I know when I'm beaten. It's time to go." He straightened and glanced at their old friend. "If you're ready, Judge? Laina has guests to tend to, and I'm weary from my journey."

Laina reached out and laid a detaining hand on her brother's arm. "Justin, wait. I want you to carry a message to...to..."

"Elizabeth?"

"Yes. Elizabeth. Please tell her that I'm most eager for a chance to become acquainted with her. And that I hope we will become friends. All I remember of her is her soft husky voice as she spoke her vows. You whisked her away so quickly that day in March we didn't have an opportunity to speak." She gave him a wry look. "Not that I wanted to then. But now— Well, now, I feel badly about it."

Justin dropped a kiss on top of his sister's head. "You've no cause to feel badly, Laina. The circumstances of my marriage to Elizabeth were unusual at best."

"I know." Laina's gaze dropped to her brother's chest and she absently plucked a speck of lint from his coat. "But I did treat her, and you, shabbily that day, Justin. I've been waiting for an opportunity to ask your forgiveness."

"Laina! Is that why we've not heard from you? I wondered..." Justin lifted his hands to his sister's shoulders.

"You are welcome at Randolph Court anytime, you know that. My marriage to Elizabeth has not changed that. Why don't you come to Philadelphia for a visit?"

"A visit? Now? Hardly." Laina's voice reflected horror at the suggestion. "One does not visit a new bride and groom before a suitable time has passed, Justin."

He scowled and dropped his hands to his sides. "Laina, you know very well—" Her finger on his lips stopped the terse words.

"She is still a bride, Justin. And there is a time of adjustment necessary in any marriage. I meant only that. Nothing more." She scanned her brother's scowling face and gave him a roguish smile. "But it's interesting that you react with such fervor."

Justin made an inarticulate sound of frustrated male tolerance and headed for the door. Laina laughed. She grasped the judge's arm, halting him in midstride as he started after her departing brother, stood on tiptoes and whispered in his ear. "So, Judge, you are a prophet. You were right in your assessment of Elizabeth's character. And, best of all, my brother has fallen in love with his bride."

"So it would seem." The judge chuckled and placed his lips close to Laina's ear. "I know of nothing outside of love that can make a patient man as touchy as a she bear with cubs." He threw her a gleeful smile. "He's absolutely miserable!"

Laina burst into laughter.

The judge winked, gave her a quick, affectionate hug and hurried after Justin, who was about to step outside.

Happiness bubbled up inside Laina. Elizabeth *must* be a lovely person or Justin's mask would still be firmly in place. No one else had been able to dislodge it. She did a quick pirouette and turned to the mirror to check her appearance before returning to her guests. Her coiffure had become disarranged. She lifted her hand to smooth back a stray wisp of hair, then stopped and watched in the mirror as a man's head appeared out of the shadow created by the stairs. He gave a furtive glance in her direction and slipped back into the darkened area. Laina spun about and marched to the stairs.

"Come out of there immediately!"

A man stepped out into the light and a shiver slid down Laina's spine. She would have been hard put to explain why. There was simply something about him that made her skin crawl. "Is there something you require?"

"Yes. I was looking for your man." He inclined his head. "I regret I must leave your delightful birthday celebration and I need my hat."

"Well, you'll not find your hat, *or* my man, lurking in the shadows." Laina was unimpressed by the anger that flashed in the man's small, black eyes at her sharp retort. She gave him look for look. "I shall send Beaumont to you immediately—I would not want to delay your departure."

The insult was deliberate and the man's face flushed angrily.

Laina gave him a last icy look of disdain and turned her back on him. The long skirt of her elegant, red satin gown whispered against the gleaming floor as she walked down the hallway and entered the ballroom. She would have

Beaumont escort the man out the door himself. He looked sneaky. She didn't trust him a fig's worth! Who was he anyway? And what was he doing in her home?

Espying her butler carrying punch to an elderly widow, Laina lifted a lace-gloved hand and summoned him to her. She wanted that man out of her house—and she wanted him out now.

Reginald Burton-Smythe stared after Laina Brighton. How dare she speak to him as if he were some lowly flunky! No one talked to him that way. No one! He would— He would do nothing. Reginald took a firm hold on his temper. The insult was not of importance, now. Not in the light of his good fortune. He curled his straight, thin lips into a smile. He had been invited along tonight by Stanford Brighton to talk about an amalgamation of the warehouse properties they owned on South Street. Now it seemed he might need to maintain sole interest in his warehouse property after all. It was Ezra Frazier's price for his daughter.

"Elizabeth." Reginald's pulse quickened. Was it possible? Could it be she? Stanford Brighton's wife had said March— and it had been March when Elizabeth Frazier disappeared. What luck! All these months he had been searching without a clue. And now, because of a chance conversation... *"Her soft husky voice."*

Reginald shook his head in amazement. All the money, time and effort he had spent searching for her and it had all come down to chance. Chance, and his own cleverness. If he hadn't hidden himself away and eavesdropped on

Laina Brighton's conversation when he had heard her mention the name Elizabeth...

Reginald licked his lips and flexed his long, skinny fingers at the memory of Elizabeth's soft, slender form. His breath came in quick, shallow drafts. If it hadn't been for that uncle of hers he would have—

"Your hat, sir."

Reginald started, grabbed his hat and followed the Brighton's butler to the door. A thin film of moisture broke out on his face as he thought about the smooth, silky feel of Elizabeth's flesh. His hands twitched. He stepped out into the warm night and closed his eyes to better picture the flawless perfection of her beauty. His shallow breathing grew ragged. Reluctantly, he dragged his mind away from the memory of that night in her father's study, opened his eyes and walked down the marble steps. There would be another memory soon. And this time there would be no uncle to interfere.

"Ralston!" Reginald hurried toward his waiting carriage. "Take me home. And when we get there don't unharness the horses. I've only to pick up a valise and we'll be off to Philadelphia." He yanked open the carriage door and climbed inside, then leaned forward and stuck his head back out the door. "And get some speed out of these nags!" He pulled his head back inside and closed the door.

The driver's whip cracked. The carriage lurched forward. Reginald grabbed for the hold strap and lifted his thin lips in a smug smile. Ralston was afraid of him—he would waste no time. He knew he would be dismissed if he didn't please him.

Reginald settled back in his seat, glanced out at the night and nodded with satisfaction. Fortune was indeed smiling on him. There was a full moon. They would be able to travel all night, and haste was most important. Not only because he had waited so long to possess what had been promised to him—but because he needed to reach Philadelphia before Elizabeth's husband returned to complicate matters. It would be much easier to deal with the servants at— Where? A string of expletives poured from Reginald's mouth. *What was that name?*

Randolph Court.

The name popped into his mind. Reginald smiled. That was it—Randolph Court. When they arrived in Philadelphia he had only to inquire as to its location and then he would have her. If, indeed, it was *his* Elizabeth that Justin Randolph had married.

Reginald scowled and pushed that thought away. He was unwilling to entertain the possibility that he might be chasing after the wrong woman. There were too many coincidences—the name, the distinctive voice, the hasty marriage that coincided with the time of her disappearance. He clenched his hands into fists. So Elizabeth had married to escape him. Had given the treasure he had been promised to another! She would pay for that. They would *both* pay for that.

The carriage rolled to a stop in front of the Burton-Smythe mansion and Reginald threw open the door. He would have Justin Randolph killed. There were always cutthroats to be found in rough, waterfront grog shops who would do anything for a bit of gold. It wouldn't be the first time he had made use of their services. He smiled grimly, climbed out of the carriage and ran up the stairs to the entrance door. He would make arrangements for Justin Randolph's demise as soon as he had Elizabeth in his hands.

Reginald shouted orders concerning the packing of his valise to his butler, stalked to his library, slammed the door shut behind him, crossed to the fireplace and twisted a leaf in the ornate carving on the mantel. A small piece of paneling slid aside. He removed a locked box and carried it to his desk, then pulled a key from his waistcoat pocket and opened it. He gathered the small drawstring bags inside into his hands. They hit against one another with a muffled clunk. One of these would take care of Justin Randolph. As for Elizabeth...

Reginald closed his eyes and envisioned what he planned for Elizabeth. Lust surged and pulsed in him. For a moment he let it have its way, then, reluctantly, he forced the images aside and opened his eyes. He scribbled a note of instructions for his manager, snatched up the bank draft in the bottom of the box and started for the door shouting for his valise. His revenge upon Elizabeth would be personal—and it would not be quickly over. He intended to make her pay...and pay...and pay....

Reginald licked his lips, closed the library door, snatched his valise from his butler's hand and rushed to the front door. One word kept repeating itself over and over in his mind as he climbed back into the carriage. Soon...soon...soon... He settled himself comfortably on the seat, leaned his head back, closed his eyes and gave himself over to his imaginings.

* * *

"A glass of wine, Justin? It might help you to relax." The judge added the inducement as Justin turned from the window and shook his head.

Justin grimaced. "Am I that obvious?"

"I'm afraid so. At least to someone who knows you well."

"Humph."

The judge grinned at the disgusted sound that acknowledged the truth of his words. "What about the wine?"

"No. None for me, thank you." Justin dropped into a chair and stretched his long, muscular legs out in front of him. "I've made such a mess of things, I shudder to think what damage I could do if I dulled my senses with wine."

"You may be right." The judge grinned as Justin threw him a dark look. "Do you want to talk about it?"

"No. Yes!" Justin surged to his feet, rubbed the tense muscles at the back of his neck and began pacing the room. "I don't know, Judge. I doubt that talking about it will do any good. Words won't change anything. But I'm so…so…"

"In love with your wife?"

Justin's broad shoulders slumped in defeat. "Yes. That's why I came to New York. Laina's birthday was only a handy excuse. In truth—I simply had to get away."

"Tension?"

Justin twisted his lips into a grim smile. "You might say that." He walked over to the judge's large mahogany desk, picked up a stick of sealing wax and slapped it against his palm with a soft splat…splat…splat. "It's not only that, Judge. I'm not some callow youth. I can control my impulses." He slanted a rueful glance at him. "Not that it's easy." He tossed the stick of wax onto the desk, raked his fingers through his hair and walked over to stare out a window at the moonlit night. "She's everything I've ever wanted, Judge. But I can't trust her."

The judge winced at the raw agony in Justin's voice. "It's time you got over that, son. And I believe Elizabeth is the one that can help you to do just that. I see the hand of God in this marriage, Justin, and—"

"The hand of God!" Justin gave a short, hard bark of a laugh and spun about to face the elderly man. "*The hand of God?* You don't know how funny that is, Judge." He laughed bitterly. "I'm in love with a woman I have sworn not to touch. A woman to whom I have given my word that there will be no personal involvement between us. A woman that nearly *swoons* with fright every time I go near her. And you say you can see the hand of *God* in it!"

The judge fixed him with a level gaze. "I did not say I could not, also, see the hand of man in it, son."

Justin's scornful laughter died. For a moment he met the judge's steady gaze, then, he drew air deep into his lungs and shook his head. "I'm sorry, Judge. I guess I'm not quite myself. This whole situation has me going in circles! I feel like a dog chasing his own tail." He turned and pushed the casement open—he needed air. "Besides, you mistook my meaning. It's not because of my experiences with Rebecca and Margaret that I cannot trust Elizabeth—at least not wholly. It's because of her lies."

"Lies?" The judge sat up straighter in his chair. "What lies?"

"Lies about money. What else?" Justin walked over and slumped down into the chair he had vacated earlier. He was weary of talking. What good would talking do?

The judge frowned. "What lies has she told you about money?"

Justin snapped his head erect at the judge's tone. "She denies having any." His voice was bitter. "We both know that's impossible since the settlement was—"

"Settlement?"

"Yes, settlement. Financial agreement. Whatever you choose to call it. It's still—"

"By jove!" The judge gave his thigh a resounding slap and jumped to his feet. *"You haven't read it."* He pointed an accusing finger at Justin's chest. "Why not?"

"Because there was no need." Justin felt himself flush as the judge fixed him with a disbelieving gaze. "All right. I burned it." He muttered the admission under his breath.

"Burned it? *Burned it!* Without *reading* it?" The judge let out a hoot. "Oh, that's rich." He chortled with glee. "You *are* in a bad way, my boy."

Justin stared sourly at his mentor. "Thank you so much for that piece of wisdom."

The judge grinned. "Justin, my boy, you have tortured yourself needlessly." He crossed to his desk, unlocked a drawer, took out a piece of paper, walked back and dropped it into Justin's lap. "That's my copy. Read it, Justin. There *was* no settlement." He gazed down into Justin's astonished eyes and his voice softened. "Go on, look at it, son. She refused the money."

"Refused it?"

The judge nodded, then stood quietly by the chair and watched Justin scan the paper. He reached out and rested his hand on the young man's shoulder when he saw the disbelief and bewilderment spread across his face. "She said she didn't want to feel purchased, Justin. Said the gesture of good faith on your part was enough. She was never interested in your money."

"Then why did she marry me?"

The judge shook his head at the frustrated roar. "The only one that knows the answer to that is Elizabeth, son. Why don't you ask her?"

Justin stared up at him, then, suddenly, threw down the paper, surged to his feet and strode to the window. "I'm a fool."

The words were soft and bitter. The judge studied him for a moment, then shook his head. "You've been telling yourself that for quite some time now, Justin. It's time you stopped." His voice sharpened. "Get on with your life, son!"

"My *life. What life?*" Justin spun to face the quiet, dignified old gentleman. "Don't you see it's worse than ever now. At least before I could tell myself she was a greedy little liar like the others, but now..." He clenched his hands into fists and fought back the anguish in his voice. "Now, I have *no* weapon with which to fight my love for her."

"Then why fight it?"

Justin sucked in his breath. "Haven't you been *listening?* I gave my word not to touch her. Would you have me break my word?" He gave him a sour smile. "*You* wrote up the papers. She could have the law on me were I to do so."

The judge sat down and placed his elbows on the padded arms of his favorite chair. He folded his hands, made a steeple of his index fingers and looked up at Justin over the top of them. "A word of legal advice, my boy. You won't break your word, *or* the contract, if the decision to make the marriage a real one is mutual." He leaned forward in his chair. "Justin, lad, you don't need to *touch* the lady to make her fall in love with you."

A light of hope kindled in Justin—then quickly dimmed. His lips tightened. "You don't understand, Judge. For some reason Elizabeth is terrified of me. What I said before is the literal truth, she has swooned in fear at my most innocent touch."

"*Swooned?*"

"Yes."

Justin walked over and dropped into the chair opposite the judge.

"Why?"

Justin shrugged. "She denies knowing any reason for such a thing. And I certainly don't know, unless—"

The judge's gaze sharpened. "Unless what?"

"Oh, I don't know." Justin closed his eyes and rubbed the tension from his temples with the tips of his long fingers. "I can't think of anything I've done to provoke such a reaction, so I've wondered if perhaps it could be from something that happened to her before I knew her." He opened his eyes and looked across at the elderly man.

"She swooned in the carriage soon after we left the Haversham Coach House the night we were married. I thought she was simply tired and had fallen asleep, but when we arrived at the inn I couldn't rouse her." He leaned back in his chair and stared up at the plaster ceiling. "Dr. Allen was there simply by happenstance and he examined Elizabeth. She was badly bruised—by a man. The marks of his hands were on her arms."

Justin's voice shook with anger, the nerve along his jaw began to twitch. He looked down at his clenched fists and opened them. "The doctor said an experience like that could leave a bruise on one's soul. So, when she continued to swoon, and I could think of no other reason, I thought perhaps...I don't know...perhaps whatever had happened to her might have something to do with it."

The judge's eyes narrowed. Slowly, he nodded. "You may be right, son. I remember how frightened and tense Elizabeth was when I interviewed her. What did the doctor say?"

"That Elizabeth had been physically abused and was emotionally and mentally exhausted. He advised rest and patience." Justin closed his eyes. He was too tired to talk further.

The judge tapped his steepled fingers gently against his pursed lips and stared off into the distance. After a short time he dropped his hands and fixed his gaze on his young friend. "Do you want to end this sham of a marriage, Justin? Do you want Elizabeth as your true wife?"

Justin opened his eyes, tipped his head forward to give the judge a long look, then slumped back and closed them again. "More than anything in the world."

"Very well..." The judge rose to his feet and crossed to the table by the window. He picked up the well-worn Bible that rested there, walked back to Justin and placed it in his lap. "If you meant what you said, son, the answer is in there. First John, chapter four, verse eighteen." He laid his hand briefly on Justin's shoulder, then turned and left the room.

Justin stared after the judge for a long moment, then dropped his gaze to the Bible that rested in his lap. His face tightened. He picked up the Bible, placed it on the table beside the chair and walked to the window. The beauty of the moonlit night only served to heighten his misery. He closed the casement, snuffed the candles in the sconce on the wall, then moved to the candle on the table beside the chair and reached to do the same. His gaze fell on the Bible and he paused. He looked at his hand, poised to extinguish the light and scowled. What if the judge was right? What if the answer *was* there? What if God, by some miracle, *was* able to make something beautiful and real out of the hopeless mess he had created? God's hand—or man's hand? He had never thought of it in those terms before. Which did he want?

The stillness of the night seemed to close in around him as the bitter disappointments of the past warred with his longings for the future. He was achingly, acutely aware that he had a choice to make—and that the choice he made would affect not only *his* future, but the future of those he loved as well. Elizabeth, Sarah and little Mary would all be touched by it. He closed his eyes in an agony of indecision. He had believed once. But then Rebecca and Margaret—

Man's hand! Man's hand! Man's hand! The words rang in his spirit. Justin's eyes burned with tears as he faced the truth. He had blamed God for what had been done by man. For what he, himself, had a part in. And he had denied the truth in order to soothe his pride.

"Oh, God, forgive me!" Justin fell to his knees in front of the table and covered his face with his trembling hands. "Forgive me, Lord. Please, forgive me." His desperate words scraped their way out of his aching, constricted throat. "I was wrong. I know I was wrong. Please help me to find my way back to You, Lord. Please help me. I choose Your hand."

The terrible shame and sorrow that had flooded his heart was replaced by a sense of peace. For a long while Justin stayed on his knees receiving and basking in the forgiving, healing love of his Heavenly Father. When he finally rose to his feet, he reached for the Bible. For the truth he had rejected. His hand trembled as he turned the pages. "First John...First John, four..." He trailed his finger down the page until he found the verse he was seeking. "There is no fear in love; but perfect love casteth out fear...." He read it again, then straightened and closed the Bible. "There is no fear in love; but perfect love casteth out fear..."

Fear. Elizabeth's fear. *His* fear. For the first time, Justin admitted to himself that it had been fear, not anger, that had driven him to seek a marriage of convenience. Oh, the anger and bitterness had been real enough, but they were rooted in his fear of being hurt again. Suddenly everything seemed so clear. He sat down and thought about the past and the present in the light of that new knowledge. At last he rose, snuffed out the candle and made his way to the bedroom that was set aside for his use whenever he was in New York. He needed to sleep. It was a long, hard ride to Philadelphia and he would be leaving at first light. His heart gave a little skip of excitement—with God's help he was going home to win Elizabeth's heart.

Chapter Twenty-Four

❧

"What do you mean she's not here!" Abigail lifted her cane and struck the floor dangerously close to Owen's foot. "I was asked to come immediately. Where is she?"

"I don't know, madam. I am the one that sent for you."

"*You?*" Abigail folded her hands over the top of her cane and leaned forward to peer up at the butler through narrowed eyes. "Owen, we are both too old to play these little games." She lifted her cane and cracked it sharply against the floor. "Explain!"

"Yes, madam. It's because of the little miss that I summoned you. Mr. Randolph is in New York, and Mrs. Randolph has gone. She left with a...gentleman...that came calling a short while ago. Miss Sarah saw her leave from her window and is now inconsolable. She keeps calling for her mama and crying. Nurse Hammerfield is quite concerned that she will make herself ill, and I thought that perhaps you—"

"Enough!" Abigail glared up at the butler. "You're blathering. It's perfectly natural for Sarah to take on a bit under the circumstances. She and Elizabeth have become very close—and you know what the child has been through. It's not surprising she would be upset to see her mother go away. She'll be fine when Elizabeth returns and you know it." Abigail stared at Owen's carefully held, expressionless butler face and felt a sudden chill of apprehension. "Unless there is something you are not telling me. Who is this gentleman Elizabeth went off with? And when will she return? Why did you *really* call me?"

Owen met her suspicious gaze for a moment, then looked away. "Because I don't know what to do, madam. I don't know what to do about the little miss, *or* Mr. Randolph. You see...Madam Randolph will not be returning."

"Nonsense!" Abigail smacked her cane sharply against the floor and glared at Owen. "Of course she will return. Why would you think that? This is her home." The quick denial sprang from her heart, but even as it burst from her mouth Abigail was aware of a sense of dread spreading through her. She looked down at her hands clasped tightly on top of her cane and sighed. Her fingers were beginning to twist, her skin was thin, dry and blotchy. "I'm old, Owen. I'm much too old for this."

"Yes, madam."

The sympathy in his voice put the starch back in her spine. Abigail shoved the loathsome self-pity aside and looked up at the aged butler. He would never make such a statement without good and sufficient reason. Especially after— *Oh, dear Heavenly Father!* The silent plea rose as

Abigail's heart thumped erratically. Her knees began to wobble. He had to be wrong. He *had* to. Justin would— Justin would—

Oh, Lord, please. Lord, please! It was all she could think of to pray. Abigail closed her eyes and drew as deep a breath as she could manage before opening them again. Owen was watching her closely. "When will Justin return?" She frowned at his close perusal. Had he guessed? "How much time do we have?"

"A few days, madam. Three, possibly four."

Abigail sagged with relief. "Good. That's very good. Old or not, I'll have this whole…misunderstanding… straightened out by then." A squeezing pain came in her chest. Abigail closed her eyes and waited. She knew from experience the pain would fade. It was the weakness it left behind that so annoyed her. That, and the inability to breathe properly. Both irritated her. They made it difficult to concentrate. The pain abated and she opened her eyes. Owen was staring at her with concern written all over his face.

"Well?" She snapped the word out and glowered up at him. "Don't just *stand* there. If I'm to find Elizabeth I must know what happened. Tell me everything."

"Yes, madam. But, first…" Abigail stiffened as he moved to take her elbow. "If I might help you to a chair? Perhaps bring you some tea?"

She gave a derisive snort and snatched her elbow from his grasp. "I said I was old, Owen—not infirm. Now, get on with it! You're wasting valuable time."

"Yes, madam." Owen stepped back. "There's not much

I can tell you. Madam Randolph was in the library reading to Miss Sarah, as has become their custom, when a stranger came to the door and asked to see her. When I inquired as to his name, he replied that he wished to surprise Madam and asked that I announce him only as an old friend. I bade him enter and be seated while I went to the library to inquire as to Madam Elizabeth's wishes in the matter—but I had no opportunity to do so. As I opened the library door the gentleman rushed up from behind, pushed me aside, and burst into the room."

"My word!" Abigail ignored her shock, and the butler's obvious outrage over such rudeness and concentrated on the facts. "What happened then?"

"Madam Elizabeth leaped to her feet and cried out— 'Reginald!'"

The blood drained from Abigail's face. She swayed. Owen hesitated, but an imperious wave of her hand urged him on.

"The rogue bowed then, brazen as you please, and said, 'So, Elizabeth, it *is* you.' He was smiling like a cat that had found a dish of cream."

Abigail gave him a piercing look. "He said it exactly that way? As if he were uncertain of whom he was calling upon?"

Owen nodded.

"And how did Elizabeth respond?"

"She simply stared at him, looking startled...dazed."

Abigail pounced on the thread of hope. "So she was not expecting him?"

"No, madam." Owen's voice was cautious. "I don't believe she was."

Abigail stared at him. Her uneasiness returned—Owen

was too astute not to have noticed that for himself. "All right." She sighed deeply. "Tell me the rest of it. What happened next?"

"Miss Sarah became frightened and began to cry. She called out, 'Mama!' and tugged at Madam's skirt in that way she does when she wants her attention." The old man cleared his throat and blinked his eyes. "That seemed to bring Madam Randolph to herself and she knelt down to comfort Miss Sarah." Owen's voice shook. "That's when the stranger spoke again. 'Very touching, Elizabeth,' he said, 'I always thought you would make an excellent mother.'"

Abigail sagged.

"Madam Twiggs, please let me—"

"Continue!"

Owen sighed. "There's not much more to tell. Madam Randolph looked up at the stranger when he spoke and he suggested that it would be good if they were alone to talk. She agreed. She put Sarah in my arms and told me to take her to Nurse Hammerfield. She said she would ring if she needed me." He paused.

Abigail glared. *"And?"*

The old butler sighed again. "It was not long until she rang. When I answered her summons she told me to fetch Trudy. That was all, simply—fetch Trudy. She ordered the maid to pack some things for her and bring them to the library. Then, she left." Owen blinked away the sudden moisture in his eyes. "She walked out the door with the stranger, climbed into a waiting carriage and drove off. She never said a word—not even goodbye. Not to anyone."

Abigail's knees gave way. They began to wobble dreadfully. She accepted Owen's help to the settee at the side of the stairs and sank down heavily onto the blue brocade cushion feeling all the weight of her many years. She was too old. She was simply too old to cope with this. She didn't want to hear any more—didn't want to have to think about it. She wanted to go home and have Jeanne put her to bed. She wanted to close her eyes and sleep until the pain of this betrayal went away. *Elizabeth. Oh, Elizabeth. What have you done?*

Ignoring the leaden weight that settled in her chest, Abigail laid her walking stick on the seat beside her. Rest was out of the question. She would have to talk to the others—to Trudy. Perhaps Elizabeth had left an explanation with her maid. She grabbed firmly on to the thin, tenuous hope and looked up at Owen. "Don't stand there staring at me!" She snapped the words out. It was expected of her. "Fetch the maid. Fetch Trudy."

"Yes, madam."

Abigail leaned back and rested her head against the soft back of the settee as Owen hurried off to do her bidding. For a moment she simply sat there, staring off into space and thinking. What would this do to Justin? He was only now beginning to heal from— Pain ripped through her chest. She gasped and closed her eyes. *Oh, Katherine, I don't know if I have the strength to see him through this one. Forgive me, old friend, if I fail.*

Tears squeezed from under Abigail's closed eyelids and made damp paths down her dry, wrinkled cheeks. She lifted a trembling hand, wiped them away and set her mind against the viselike pain that was stealing her strength. She couldn't give in to it yet. She had to pray.

"Lord Jesus, I place Justin and Elizabeth in Your hands. Please help them, according to Your will." She looked toward the ceiling and curved her lips into an angelic smile reminiscent of the ones that had made numerous young men vie for the opportunity to do her bidding. "And I would be ever so grateful if You would give me enough time to see this thing through. Nevertheless, Lord, Thy will be done." Her strength was gone. Abigail closed her eyes and breathed carefully as the pain lessened.

Caleb lifted his head at the click of the back door latch. He paused momentarily in his task of tying up the package that lay on the counter before him to listen to the soft sounds of movement in his workroom, then frowned and turned again to the task at hand. He knotted the string quickly and competently with his sailor's expertise and handed the small bundle to the young servant boy that stood waiting.

"Here you are, Jeremiah." He curved his lips in a smile. "Tell your mistress the candlesticks will be ready in time for her musicale."

"Yes, sir." The young boy's hand shook when he accepted the package. He clutched the bundle tightly to his chest, dipped his head in farewell, and turned to leave. Caleb thumped around the counter. The boy rushed for the door of the shop, yanked it open, leaped down the steps and raced away into the warm evening as if dogs nipped at his heels.

Caleb shook his head. No matter what he did, the town's youngsters were still frightened by him. He sighed, bid the lady and gentleman strolling past a pleasant good evening, hung the Closed sign in the window and headed for his workroom.

"So, Shinny—" Caleb looked into the dark eyes of the small man that stood in the center of the room waiting for him, and frowned. Only the prospect of a fight made Shinny's eyes glitter that way. He thumped his way to his workbench and plunked down heavily on his stool. "There's trouble afoot?"

"Aye." Shinny almost bounced in his excitement. "For Justin Randolph."

Caleb jerked his head up. "What kind of trouble? If it is the dock—"

"No." Shinny shook his dark head. "The whole of Philadelphia's waterfront knows if they trouble Justin Randolph they deal with you." His gaze fastened on his old shipmate's eyes. "Some strange bloke has come to town. He wants Justin Randolph dead."

"Dead!"

The word echoed off the walls. Shinny nodded. "Aye. Dead."

Caleb's face tightened. "You'd best tell me the whole of it." His tone of voice did not bode well for the stranger.

Shinny grinned and moved closer to his giant friend. "Tommy an' some of the mates were at Gilly's a bit ago, when this strange man—one of the gentry—comes in. He walks to a table, tosses down a bag of coins and starts askin' for someone willin' to do some mischief for a price. Well, Tommy eyes the weight of the gent's purse and steps up to the table. 'I'm your man,' he says."

Caleb looked at him sharply.

Shinny's lips twitched. "So the man looks him up and down and asks him, real polite like, if he has any qualms about killin' a man." Shinny guffawed, then quickly sobered at the look in Caleb's eyes. "Tommy told him, all serious like, that a heavy weight of gold keeps his qualms down. And then the man upends the purse on the table."

Caleb's bushy red brows rose. "The whole purse?"

"Aye." Shinny nodded confirmation. "The whole purse. 'Is that heavy enough?' he asks, and Tommy laughs. He grabs up the gold eagles before the stranger can change his mind, and says to him, 'It'll do. Does this dead man have a name?' And the man nods. 'Justin Randolph', he says."

Shinny stared at the fierce light that flamed in Caleb's eyes. "Of course Tommy come and told me. He was all for stickin' the man, but I thought you might like that pleasure yourself, so I come to fetch you." He backed up a few steps to give Caleb room as the giant got to his feet and shoved his crutch under his arm. He stared in admiration at the tight little smile that lifted the corners of Caleb's mouth as the big man passed him on his way to the back door. He knew that look—knew exactly what his friend was thinking. Caleb owed his life to Justin Randolph.

Shinny furrowed his brow. It had been seven—no, eight years ago that Caleb had been lying unconscious and half-buried by a pile of rigging on one of the Randolph docks when Justin Randolph had stumbled over his protruding foot. Justin had called him out for drunkenness and thrown back the tarp. When he had seen the swollen, discolored stump that was all that remained of the big man's leg, he had ordered some nearby seamen to lift him into his carriage. He had taken Caleb to his own home, summoned his doctor and demanded that he treat the dying sailor. It had been a long, hard battle, but Caleb had survived. While he was recuperating he had made Justin a scrimshaw of the *Barbara*. Justin had recognized the seaman's talent, and when Caleb had fully recovered, he set him up in the small shop.

Shinny shook his head at the wonder of it. Justin Randolph had not only saved Caleb's life, he had made it one worth living. The big man had been waiting a long time for the opportunity to repay him. There were a *lot* of seamen waiting to repay a kindness from Justin Randolph. And tonight they would get their chance.

Smiling at what was ahead, Shinny hurried after Caleb who was thumping his way down the steps. He almost felt sorry for the stranger that had tried to buy Justin Randolph's death. Almost. His gaze fastened gleefully on the face of the huge man walking with grim determination toward Gilly's waterfront grog shop. This was no artisan, no pleasant shopkeeper. This was Caleb the seaman...the fighter...the captain of the boarding crew. This was the man he would follow anywhere.

Voices inside Gilly's hushed, heads turned, and eyes gleamed with excited expectancy as Caleb and Shinny entered. News travels fast along the waterfront and those present had heard the story of the threat to Justin Randolph's life. They knew, also, of Caleb's devotion to Justin. That Caleb would act was understood—it was the *how* they were waiting to see. They watched as Caleb moved slowly through the room, each thud of his wooden leg reverberating in the sudden silence.

The men seated at the table in the far corner rose, and, carrying their tankards of ale with them, moved to find places among the other tables. Without protest those already seated crowded together to make room. Everyone knew the corner table was Caleb's favored place, and no one challenged his right to it. A few foolhardy men, with more courage than sense, had tried over the years to usurp his place. None had. But it was not out of fear that those present yielded place to the giant—fearful, life-threatening circumstances were common occurrences for them. Rather, they yielded out of respect and admiration. Some of them had experienced, and all had heard, of Caleb's courageous and daring feats at sea. He was a mate that could be counted on when danger reared its familiar head, be it caused by man or nature, and these men did not take that lightly. He had earned his place.

A slight tremor traveled through the floor as Caleb lowered his bulk onto a bench and thrust his crutch into the corner. Shinny slid into place beside him. His dark gaze swept the room.

"He's not here."

"Aye. We'll wait. He'll come." The words rumbled out of Caleb with the sound of distant thunder. "Gilly, bring us an ale!" He roared the order—and the room came to life. A heavily muscled man with a wicked gleam in his remaining eye pushed away from a table and crossed the room to him on catlike feet. He dropped onto the bench.

"I have a name. Burton-Smythe."

Caleb drew his bushy red brows together. "You know him?"

"No." The gold hoop of an earring gleamed dully with reflected candlelight as the sailor leaned forward. "But I've seen him. He has some warehouses on the docks in New York. When I went with Tommy to follow him, the ensign on his carriage jogged my mind. It's the same as what's on the warehouse. It's him all right." He nodded emphatically. "I seen him clear when he climbed in the carriage." The seaman got slowly to his feet. "Tommy went on to follow him, and I come back here to wait for you." His lips split into a nasty grin. "When you go after him, Caleb, I'd admire to go along. I owe Justin Randolph, too."

Caleb nodded and the seaman walked away, calling for another ale.

"Name mean anything to you, Shinny?" Caleb shifted his bulk to a more comfortable position on the bench.

"Nah." Shinny shook his head, put his noggin down on the table, and wiped his mouth with the back of his hand. "Never heard it afore. I'll ask 'round though, some-one—"

"Here's Tommy!"

The head of every sailor in Gilly's raised as one when the voice cried out. Every expectant gaze fastened on the tall, lean seaman that had just entered. A low, excited murmur ran through the crowded tavern—things would begin to happen now. The waiting was over. The crowd of seamen watched eagerly as Tommy made his way to Caleb's table.

"He's aboard the *Cormorant.*"

"The *Cormorant!*"

"Aye." Tommy slid onto the bench and motioned for an ale.

Caleb's brow furrowed into a fierce scowl. "What's he doin' aboard the *Cormorant?*"

"He's bound for London, and she's the only one sailin' with the tide."

"In a hurry, is he?"

Tommy's gaze slid to Shinny and he nodded. "Aye." He looked back at Caleb. "He's booked passage for two—himself an' a lady." He darted his gaze around the room and leaned closer. "He's got Justin Randolph's bride with him."

Shinny's gaze flew to Caleb's face. His breath caught with excitement as the big man looked his way. They both knew Justin was out of town. Wordlessly, he handed Caleb his crutch, and rose to follow the giant from the tavern.

As one man the seamen present lifted their mugs, drained their contents, and fell in line. Gilly eyed the rapidly emptying room, finished his own quaff, wiped his mouth on the dirty bar rag, then opened the barricade and hurried after the seamen crowding out the door to form an ever widening wake behind the huge man they all admired. Nobody wanted to miss what was to come.

Chapter Twenty-Five

❧

"Madam?"

Abigail opened her eyes. Owen was bent over her. He looked worried.

"Are you all right, madam? Would a cup of tea help, or—"

"No, no." Abigail waved away the offer. "I'm fine." She *was* feeling better. The weight had lifted from her chest and she felt able to breathe again. She lifted her gaze to the maid that stood a short distance away watching them with red, puffy eyes and motioned the girl closer.

"Trudy, is it?"

"Yes, mum." The maid stepped forward and bobbed an awkward curtsy.

"Trudy, I'd like you to answer a few questions for me." Abigail smiled to put the girl at ease. "You are Elizabeth's lady's maid, are you not?"

"Yes, mum." The girl's lips quivered.

"And you get on well with your mistress?"

"Oh yes, mum!"

"Ah!" Abigail nodded her satisfaction. "I know how that is. My Jeanne is my best confidant. We share our most private thoughts, and exchange perfectly scandalous confidences." She arched her thinning brows coyly. "Of course there is not as much to share now, as when I was young, but still, we have our moments—as you and Elizabeth have your little moments and confidences. Now, I want—" Abigail stopped speaking as the young maid shook her head.

"If you mean secrets, mum, I don't know any. She kept her secrets to herself."

Abigail stared at the maid. She appeared to be telling the truth. "Did she tell you the name of the gentleman she went off with? Or where they were going?" Her voice was harsh with disappointment.

"No, mum." Trudy's eyes filled with tears. "She told me to put her two old dresses, Mr. Randolph's blue dressing gown, and her necessaries in the cloth bag she brung with her and bring it to the library." Her voice quavered. "She didn't say nothing else. Not even goodbye!" Trudy's voice broke and she burst into tears.

"Stop that crying this instant!" Abigail struck the floor with her cane. The sharp crack was satisfying. She struggled to her feet. "Crying is not going to help anyth—"

"Papa!"

Abigail snapped her head up. Sarah popped into view on the landing. She ran across it and headed down the stairs.

"Don't run, Sarah! You'll fall!"

Nanny Hammerfield came puffing onto the landing, cast an apologetic look at Abigail, and rushed after her charge. "She saw her papa through the window and—Sarah, slow down!" She grabbed for the toddler and missed.

Justin? Abigail twisted about as the sobbing child jumped from the bottom step and ran for the front door. *"Stop her!"* She jabbed her cane sharply into Owen's ribs. *"Stop her, I say!"*

Owen recovered his equilibrium and started after the toddler, but he was too late. The door opened, and with a broken sob Sarah hurled herself at Justin.

"Papa!"

"Well, well! What's this?" Justin bent and scooped his daughter into his arms. "This is quite a welcome." He smiled as Sarah flung her small arms around his neck and buried her face against his shoulder. Her tiny body shuddered. Justin's smile faded. He glanced down at Sarah, then looked at Owen.

"What's happening here? Why is Sarah crying?"

"I w-want my m-mama!"

Justin grinned at the plaintive wail. "Oh, I see. A childhood crisis." He kissed the top of Sarah's head and patted her back. "Don't cry, Sarah. If you want your mama, you shall have her." He glanced at his butler. "Owen go—"

The old man went rigid.

Justin scowled. What was wrong? Why was everyone gathered in the entrance hall? Everyone except the one he wanted most to see. He swept his gaze around the large room. Elizabeth was nowhere in sight. He looked back to the others and fear clutched his heart. They were frozen in place—like statues.

"Abigail?" He locked his gaze on his old friend's face. "What's wrong? Where is Elizabeth?"

"The b-bad mans t-tooked her a-w-way!"

"Out of the mouths of babes." Abigail muttered the words under her breath and turned and glared at Trudy as she burst into tears, again. "Leave us! Go!" She swept her gaze to the nurse who stood at the bottom of the stairs with her mouth gaping open, lifted her cane and snapped it forward. "Take Sarah to the nursery and—" Her gaze met Justin's. She sighed, lowered her hand and leaned heavily upon the cane.

"What man, Abigail?" Justin lifted a hand and halted Anna Hammerfield in her tracks. "What man took Elizabeth away? Where is she now?"

"I can answer that, sir." Shinny stepped through the open door. "She's aboard the *Cormorant*."

Abigail gave a snort of disgust and sank down on the settee.

Justin turned toward the man behind him. "My wife is on the *Cormorant*?"

Shinny bobbed his head. "Aye. Caleb's watchin' her."

"Watching her?" Justin's eyes narrowed. "Why is Caleb watching her?"

Shinny shifted his weight. "Well, when he heard you was back in town he decided it would be best if he stayed there and kept an eye on her while I come to fetch you."

An ugly suspicion popped into Justin's mind. He

stared hard at the seaman. "The *Cormorant* sails for London with the tide."

"Aye. That she does."

Shinny slid his gaze away to stare at the floor and Justin's suspicion turned into certainty. The hope that had warmed him on the way home turned into an icy fist that gripped his heart. His face stiffened. He turned back to Owen.

"Did my wife leave a message for me, Owen? Did she say where she was going—or why? Or when she would return?"

"No, sir."

The ice shattered, spreading its cold to every part of him. Justin loosed Sarah's grip from around his neck, placed her in her nanny's arms and walked out into the night. The numbing cold deadened his thoughts and feelings as he walked steadily toward the road, with Shinny at his side.

"Justin? Justin, wait! I've ordered my carriage brought round!"

He paid no heed to Abigail's frantic call.

The cold was still there. Justin sat in the carriage listening to Abigail relate what she had learned of Elizabeth's abrupt, unexplained departure with an unknown man and waited for anger to warm him, but the cold remained. Not even Shinny's tale of the threat to his life heated his blood. When the soft lap of water replaced the clop of the horses' hoofs and the rumble of the wheels, he climbed from the carriage, looked at the ship that held his wife and waited for the pain to hit him. There was only the cold. He could feel it in his flesh...in his eyes. He moved forward and stepped onto the wharf. His footsteps echoed hollowly over the water as he walked toward the *Cormorant*.

"Get Caleb."

"Aye, sir."

Zachariah Darby watched the seaman slip away, swore softly, then squared his shoulders as Justin Randolph stepped off the gangplank onto the deck.

"Good evening, Captain. I understand you have some passengers aboard."

The captain flicked his gaze to Shinny who gave a negative shake of his head and sidled past Justin to lose himself in the shadows.

"I have only one passenger aboard, sir—your wife."

Justin stepped closer. "I was told my wife came on board this vessel accompanied by a man, Captain—I want that man." Anger began to burn like a red-hot coal in the pit of his stomach. "Where is he?"

"He's gone." The words roared across the deck as Caleb thumped his way out of the shadows to join them.

"Gone!" The shimmering coal of anger burst into flames and melted the ice that had frozen Justin's feelings. He fastened a scorching gaze on the two men before him. "You let him get away."

"Not exactly, sir."

Justin stiffened. "Explain yourself, Captain."

"Yes, sir." Zachariah Darby glanced at Caleb. "Burton-Smythe had some difficulty on his way back to the ship from Gilly's. He's been impressed."

Caleb chuckled.

Justin shifted his gaze to his huge friend.

Caleb sobered. "He's aboard the *Samurai*. He didn't do too well in his struggle against them that set upon him." His lips drew back in a wicked grin of satisfaction. "Cap'n Snell owed me a favor."

Justin clenched his hands into fists. "An imaginative solution, but I have other plans for Burton-Smythe." He turned to leave.

"It won't do you no good to go lookin' for him. You won't find anything but an empty berth."

"The *Samurai*'s sailed?" Justin spun back. "With Burton-Smythe aboard?"

"Aye."

He stared hard at Caleb. "I had thought to have satisfaction of the man."

Caleb nodded. "It's your right. I'd not have denied you your satisfaction had you been in town." He lifted his massive shoulders in an apologetic shrug. "With you gone, I took matters in my own hands." His voice sharpened with anger. "He was London bound with your wife! A quick death was too good for him." The ex-seaman dropped his huge hand on Justin's shoulder. "Snell will feed what's left of him to the sharks. Still...I am sorry that the deed was already done when you returned. If I had known—"

"No matter." Justin swallowed back his choler and looked up at the huge artisan. "I'll not deny my disappointment, but it was a job well done in any case. I'm indebted to you, Caleb."

"And to you, Captain." Justin turned his attention to

Zachariah Darby. "I'll not forget your help in this matter. Now, since Burton-Smythe has been dealt with—" His voice hardened. "Where is my wife?"

"Right this way, sir. She's in their...*her* cabin." He turned to lead the way.

"One moment, Captain."

"Sir?" Zachariah halted and turned to face Justin.

"The cabin—is it locked?"

The captain's eyes darted to Caleb, then back to Justin. "No. The cabin has never been locked, Mr. Randolph."

"She has not been forcibly detained?"

"No, sir."

"And she has made no attempt to leave?"

The captain shook his head. "Not since boarding, though Burton-Smythe left her alone soon thereafter, and, of course, has not returned."

"I see." The ice returned and settled around Justin's heart. "Has she made any requests of you for aid, Captain? Or of any of your crew?"

"I have had no conversation with your wife, sir. And no one aboard has approached the cabin. Caleb made certain of that."

Justin shifted his gaze to his friend.

The big man nodded confirmation.

Justin's last tiny glimmer of hope died. Elizabeth was here because she chose to be. The cold spread through him. He swept his hand forward. "Proceed, Captain." The ship rocked gently under his feet as he followed Zachariah Darby toward the small passenger cabin that housed his wife.

* * *

Elizabeth stared out the porthole and watched the water lapping softly at the shoreline. *It was so close!* She slid her glance to the unlocked door and her hands clenched in helpless anger. Escape would be so easy—yet she dare not try. Reginald's threats of physical harm to Justin and Sarah made her his prisoner more surely than any locked door, and he knew it. She would do anything to keep them safe. Oh, the evil arrogance of the man! He was so certain she would do exactly as he wished—and so she would—until they were upon the high seas. When they were where he could no longer reach out and harm Justin and Sarah she would be free to act.

Elizabeth's gaze dropped to the beautiful emerald studded gold band upon her finger and she slipped it off and put it in her pocket where it would be hidden from Reginald's sight. It was the only thing of value she had, and it might buy her the captain's protection. The thought of parting with it brought tears to her eyes but she brushed them away. She could not afford the luxury of sentiment. Nor had she time for weakness. She must think—plan her every move before Reginald returned. She turned her thoughts from Justin and the children, for to think of them would be her undoing. Those thoughts held a pain she could not bear.

Elizabeth looked again at the dark water and clenched her hands in determination. If all else failed, she would bribe a seaman to fashion a raft for her and trust herself to the sea and the mercy of the Lord. One thing was certain—Reginald would not touch her. Not ever! That would be worse than—

Elizabeth's breath caught in her throat. She tipped her head to one side and listened. Footsteps! He had returned. Fear robbed her of the strength to stand. She sagged against the wall as a wave of nausea swept over her.

Father God, please be with me now.

Elizabeth's heart cried the prayer in silent entreaty when her lips refused to move. From somewhere deep inside she found the strength to push away from the wall and stand on her shaking legs. She drew a deep breath and lifted her chin proudly, knowing that above all else she must not exhibit fear. Reginald must never know how he terrified her. Her lips finally moved in a soft whisper as she stared with dread at the door. "What time I am afraid, I will trust in Thee."

The door opened and Justin stepped into the room.

Elizabeth stared. His appearance was so unexpected she could not comprehend what she was seeing. Was it a trick of her mind? Was he only a cruel figment of her imagination? She closed her eyes, then quickly opened them again. He was still there—strong, solid and real!

"Justin!" She stumbled forward, sobbing his name.

"Stop!"

The word snapped through the air. Elizabeth stopped so suddenly she grabbed for his arm to steady herself.

Justin jerked away. "Do not touch me, madam! You sicken me."

Elizabeth swayed.

"Do you intend to swoon now, madam?"

His voice was frigid. She looked up at him. Looked up into his cold, *cold* eyes.

"I can assure you it will do you no good. I am on to your tricks. I know of your lover, and your plot to have me murdered."

"Murdered!" Elizabeth's knees gave way. She dropped onto the edge of the cot. *"Murdered?* But that can't be, I—"

"Enough! I don't care to hear your lies." Justin waved his hand toward the door. "The carriage is waiting. Will you come along quietly? Or must I use force?"

Force? Elizabeth's mind reeled. She stared at Justin's cold, stony face and her emotions plunged to a depth she hadn't known existed. How could she have been so foolish as to think, for even a brief moment, that he had come to rescue her? That he cared what happened to her? He had merely come to take her back to—to what? Jail? Did it matter? Did anything matter now? She put her hand against the wall and rose slowly to her feet.

"I see it did not take you long to remove my ring." Justin lifted his gaze from the bare hand Elizabeth had braced against the wall and locked it on her face. "Did your lover pawn it to pay for your passage to London?"

The cold contempt in his eyes and voice pierced Elizabeth's heart. Pride gave her strength. She straightened her shoulders and lifted her chin. "No. Reginald didn't pawn it. I removed it myself." She reached into her pocket and pulled out her wedding ring. Her heart splintered into a million tiny pieces as she held it out to him. "You keep it, Justin. It's foolish of me to continue to wear the symbol of something that has never existed." She thrust it into his hand, held her head high and walked out the door.

* * *

The sound of the horses' hoofs ringing against the cobblestones was loud in the silent carriage. Too loud. They irritated Abigail. She glanced over at Elizabeth and frowned. The girl was so pale, so still, she might be dead. Except for that rigidly erect posture. Abigail sighed and looked down at her hands. She just couldn't make herself believe that Elizabeth had deliberately plotted Justin's murder. Run away with a lover, perhaps, but— No. *No!* She couldn't make herself believe even that. There had to be an explanation! A reasonable—

A knife-edged pain slashed across Abigail's chest. She winced and held her breath. Her misshapen fingers tightened on the cane she held. Slowly, the pain abated. She expelled her breath and cast a sidelong glance at Justin to see if he had noticed. She needn't have worried. He was as still as Elizabeth, but there was an anger—no, a *fury* emanating from him that frightened her. She sighed heavily and leaned back against the seat. They were beyond her abilities. Only God could help them now.

Feeling old and weak and helpless, Abigail closed her eyes. *Dear God in Heaven, have Your way in—* Pain exploded in her chest. Abigail gave a surprised, agonized cry. The pain came again, sharper, more intense. She slumped forward, aware that somewhere beyond the white heat that stabbed through her Justin and Elizabeth were calling her name. And then, suddenly, the pain stopped. She slid into darkness.

Chapter Twenty-Six

✧

The door opened quietly. Elizabeth turned from the window and watched Justin enter the room. Their gazes met briefly before she turned back to stare out into the night.

"She hasn't stirred?" Justin walked over and looked down at the still form on the bed.

"No. There's been no change." Elizabeth took a deep breath and concentrated on the contrast of silver moonlight and dark shadows in the gardens below. "What did Dr. Allen say?"

"It's her heart."

Elizabeth spun about. For a moment all that had happened disappeared in the face of their mutual fear. "Why did he leave? Is there nothing he can do?"

"Nothing." The answer was short and bitter. "We can only wait." Justin's voice was ragged. He rubbed his forehead, then lowered his hand to knead the tense muscles in the back of his neck. "I feel so helpless!"

Elizabeth bit down hard on her soft lower lip and steeled herself against the pain in his voice. How she longed to comfort him! She started for the door.

"Where are you going?"

The obvious distrust in his voice stopped her in mid-flight. She turned to look at him. "To my room. I thought you would prefer that I leave now that you have returned to sit with Abigail." His eyes flashed with—what? Anger? Disgust? She couldn't tell it happened so quickly.

Justin dropped into a chair beside the bed and wrapped his strong fingers gently around Abigail's old, misshapen hand. "There are times when personal desires must be set aside, Elizabeth. I want you here when Abigail awakens. She has grown fond of you."

Elizabeth sucked her breath in sharply. How he hated her! It was there in his voice and eyes. She turned and walked back to the window, angry with herself for the tears that caused the silver streaks of moonlight to shimmer and shift, the shadows to blur into formless areas of darkness. She clamped her lips together to hold back the sobs building to an unbearable pressure inside her and clenched her hands in grim determination. She would *not* cry! She would *not* reveal her anguish to him! The last few hours of horror and fear, rejection and hurt, had taken a terrible toll. She had faced his unjust accusations, and his anger with dignity, but she had no strength left with which to face his scorn. What fortitude remained she needed to fight the stultifying physical, mental and emotional weariness that threatened to overwhelm her.

* * *

Time passed slowly, dragged reluctantly forward by the hands of the clock that sat on the mantel. The night shadows deepened. Elizabeth sighed and glanced at Justin. Moonlight outlined his weary, drawn face. If only they could talk! It was hard waiting in silence. The only sounds that broke the oppressive quiet of the room were the ticking of the clock, and Abigail's heavy, labored breathing.

Elizabeth looked down at the woman who had become so dear to her and fear clawed at her heart. If Abigail died, she would lose everyone she loved tonight—and there was nothing she could do about it. Justin had made his position clear. He did not want to hear her explanation. And even if, by some miracle, she could make him listen, now was not the time. There would never be a time. They were separated by far more than the expanse of bed between them—they were separated by his love for his dead wife.

The darkness deepened. The cool, silver light in the room began to disappear. Elizabeth shivered as a sudden, strong apprehension gripped her. She lifted her head, looked into the thickening darkness above the bed and shivered again. Something was wrong. Something was very wrong! She looked down at Abigail's still form and watched the uneven rise and fall of the covers over her chest.

Justin stirred restlessly—the inactivity was wearing at his nerves. He released Abigail's hand, stretched his arms over his head and rose from his chair. It felt good to move. He walked around the room, rotating his shoulders, and lifting his hands to rub at the tight, thick muscles trying to relax them. He glanced at Elizabeth, met her sympathetic gaze, scowled and looked away. What an actress she was! The rush of anger made his muscles tense again. He reached up and massaged his temples, trying to rub away the dull, throbbing ache in his head.

What a night! It didn't seem possible that only a few hours ago he had been riding home from New York with a heart full of hope. What a fool he was! He'd been blithely planning to win Elizabeth's heart while she'd been planning his murder with her lover! The pain in Justin's head sharpened and settled behind his eyes. His stomach roiled. He thrust all thoughts of Elizabeth away, lowered his head and walked around the room.

Elizabeth watched Justin as he paced. The moonlight was fading quickly, but she could still see the weariness and fear on his face. How hard this must be for him. He had lost so many loved ones. The thought brought a surge of compassion so strong it threatened to choke her. If only she could help him! But he wanted nothing from her. Elizabeth fought back tears, and clasped her hands tightly in her lap. Through all that had happened, she had learned there was only one source of help and comfort in times of need and despair. *Father God in Heaven, I pray Your blessing on Justin and Abigail—*

"I've had enough of this gloom!"

Elizabeth jumped at the sound of Justin's voice. She held her breath as he spun about and yanked opened the door. He was leaving! She started to her feet, then sat back in her chair as he lifted the candle from the wall sconce in the hallway and headed for the bed, his long strides eating up the distance. Light surrounded him, bathed Abigail in its golden rays when he neared. Elizabeth blinked her eyes as the hovering shadows dissipated and darkness fled out the window into the safety of the night.

"I should have done this before." Justin lit the candle on the bedside table with the taper he held in his hand. "There's no reason to sit here in the dark." He replaced the glass globe that protected the flame from the breeze coming in the windows, then moved about the room lighting every candle he found. "That's better." When he finished, he returned the taper to its place in the sconce beside the door, glanced at Abigail and resumed his restless pacing.

It was hard for him to ignore Elizabeth. She was sitting as quiet and motionless as a statue in her chair beside the bed, but her very stillness drew his attention. Justin scowled and cast a covert glance at her as he passed by. She was not acting the way he expected her to act—but then, she seldom did. Certainly her behavior was nothing like Margaret's had been. Of course Abigail's collapse— No. That would not explain it. Margaret would not have cared if Abigail, or anyone else, had died—including her own children. The pain in Justin's temples increased. He sat in his chair, leaned back and closed his eyes, emptying his mind of all the disturbing thoughts. He was too exhausted, too angry, to think clearly now.

Someone was sitting on her chest! Abigail scowled. The pressure increased, and a wild fluttering occurred beneath her ribs. Fear pounced. She opened her eyes and stared up at the strange tester over her head. *Where was she?* She tried to lift her head to look around, but she was too weak. She slid her gaze to the right and the fluttering calmed. She was not alone—Elizabeth was with her. She studied the young woman for a moment, thinking her asleep, then noticed her lips moving slightly.

"Is that prayer for me?" Abigail frowned at the weakness in her voice. "I certainly feel as if I need one."

"Abigail!"

Elizabeth jumped to her feet and placed her cheek against Abigail's dry, wrinkled one. "How are you feeling?" She straightened and looked down at the elderly woman. "Are you in pain?"

"I'll be fine as soon as whoever is sitting on my chest moves!"

There was a chuckle and Justin suddenly appeared in Abigail's line of vision. "Gentle and sweet-natured as always I see." His tone was light. He bent down and kissed her cheek. "That's why I love you."

"And I love you because you're always so reverent!"

The words lacked her old snap.

Justin smiled. "Well, it's clear there's nothing wrong with your spirit, Abigail."

His voice was hearty, but he didn't fool her. The hand that held hers was trembling. She tried to squeeze it in reassurance, but the best she could manage was a gentle curling of her fingers.

Justin's gaze dropped to their joined hands and he swallowed hard.

Abigail's heart constricted. Did he know? Had he guessed? Surely he wouldn't be this upset if he thought this a simple attack of the vapors? She drew a shaky breath—there was one way to find out. "What happened, Justin?" Abigail pushed the words past her weakness. "Why am I here?" He lifted his gaze to meet hers, and she sighed—he knew.

"Don't play games, Abigail. Not about this." Justin cleared the huskiness from his voice. "You know perfectly well what happened. Dr. Allen has explained your condition to you every bit as carefully and precisely as he did to me." He held up a hand to stop her when she started to speak. "Yes, Dr. Allen. I sent for him when you collapsed."

Oh bother! Abigail closed her eyes. She had wanted to spare him—

"It won't do you any good to try to ignore me, Abigail." Justin's voice was quiet but firm. "When you are better, we're going to discuss the fact that you didn't tell me of your condition."

Abigail snorted and looked up at him.

Justin's control broke. "As God is my witness, Abigail, if you weren't ill I would shake you! What were you thinking of, chasing after me in that carriage in your condition! You could have—" He stopped, lifted his hands and raked them through his hair.

When he looked back down at her she smiled. "Feel better?"

Justin scowled. "This is not a matter for jest, Abigail! You will stay in this bed until Dr. Allen pronounces you fit enough to be up and about. And that is not debatable!" He took hold of her hand again. "I've sent the carriage for

Jeanne. She will stay here and care for you until Dr. Allen gives his permission for you to go home. Until then, you must rest and obey his instructions. Do it for my sake, Abigail. Please, do it for my sake."

The plea robbed her of all argument.

Justin smiled, bent down to kiss her cheek, then straightened and cleared his throat. "Owen's waiting downstairs. I have to go and give him the good news of your recovery. I'll not be long." He gave her hand a gentle squeeze, cast a cold glance in Elizabeth's direction and left the room.

Abigail watched him go. She watched the door close behind him, then waited for his footsteps to fade away. She didn't want him returning and interrupting her. When she could hear him no longer, she garnered her strength and turned her gaze on Elizabeth.

He was gone. What would happen to her when he returned? Elizabeth took a deep breath, turned her back toward the bed and pretended to plump a pillow in the chair beside her.

"Justin's a dear, dear boy, and I love him—but he is also a fool."

Abigail's voice was gruff. Elizabeth blinked her eyes and smoothed over a dented spot in the pillow. "I'm sure I don't know what you mean."

"You know." Abigail sighed. "Stop fiddling with that pillow and turn around, Elizabeth. I know you're crying."

"Crying?" Elizabeth wiped her face and turned to smile down at her friend. "Why ever would I be crying when I'm so happy you are all right?" She busied herself smoothing the already perfectly straight counterpane to avoid Abigail's eyes.

"Because you love Justin, and he's treating you in a perfectly beastly manner."

Elizabeth gasped. "Abigail! How—?"

The old woman gave her an exasperated look. "I may be old, weak and ill, Elizabeth—but there is nothing wrong with my eyes."

"Oh. Oh my." Elizabeth sank down onto the chair and pulled the pillow onto her lap. "You must tell no one, Abigail. No one! I—I couldn't bear it if Justin knew. I—" She stopped. *What was she saying!* She couldn't betray the secret of their marriage. "I mean now that he thinks— Oh, Abigail." Elizabeth covered her face with her hands. "What am I to do?"

"You might tell him."

Elizabeth snapped her head erect. "*Tell him.* That I love him? Never."

"Why not?"

"Because he hates me."

"Nonsense! He's simply—" Abigail closed her mouth tightly and glared up at the tester overhead. "He's simply a fool! And so am I for making him a promise that's almost choking me! Don't you be one, too." She locked her gaze on the young woman's. "You listen to me, Elizabeth Randolph. A man does not chase after a woman he hates—at least not to bring her back into his home."

"He does if she's a purchased possession and his pride is injured!" Elizabeth gasped and clamped her lips together.

She hadn't meant to reveal that. She was too upset and weary to think straight. She rose to her feet and moved away before she blurted out more secrets. Not that it mattered now. She would not be in Justin's home long. She would probably be sent to jail once this immediate crisis was over. Being innocent would avail her little against a man of Justin's wealth and power.

"Then you won't tell him?"

Elizabeth glanced back at Abigail and shook her head. "No, I won't tell him."

"Because of pride? Or because of that man you ran off with?"

Elizabeth stiffened with hurt and shock at Abigail's questions. "It has nothing to do with Reginald Burton-Smythe—I loathe him! As for pride? I suppose that is the reason. And you may think it a foolish one..." In spite of her best effort, her voice trembled. She turned away before her, all too ready, tears started flowing. "*I* think it a foolish one. But pride is all I have left."

Abigail's heart squeezed painfully at the depth of pain and despair in Elizabeth's voice and eyes. She sagged into her pillow, too weak, too weary, to think or talk further. Disappointment eroded her meager strength. She'd thought if she made Elizabeth angry she would blurt out the truth, but it hadn't worked.

Abigail closed her eyes, then snapped them open again, afraid to rest—afraid to sleep—lest she not awaken. She forced herself to concentrate. She *had* to try again. She might not have another chance, and these two young people she loved so much belonged together—*truly* together. If only they would talk to each other!

"Elizabeth, please!" Her voice came out weak and thready. "You must listen to me, dear." Abigail had never begged for anything in her life, but she begged now. "Elizabeth, you *must* talk to Justin. You must tell him how you feel. You must explain…what has…happened…and…"

Elizabeth spun around frightened by the increasing weakness in the elderly woman's voice. "No, Abigail." She made her voice firm. "I promise I will explain everything to you when you are better, but I will not talk to Justin. I have tried. He is not interested in my explanation. Now—not another word. You need to rest."

"But, Elizabeth…Justin—"

"Not another word." Elizabeth hurried to the bed. "You need to rest, Abigail. If you don't—I'll leave the room." She lifted Abigail's plump arm and tucked it under the covers, then arranged the blankets under the old woman's chin. "The doctor left some medicine for pain. Would you like some?"

"No."

"Water?"

"No."

Elizabeth smiled. Abigail sounded like a petulant child—she was not used to being thwarted. "Very well then." She made her voice soothing. "I'll stay with you while you sleep. And we'll talk again when you're stronger. I promise. But, for now, sweet dreams, Abigail." She leaned over and kissed the old woman's wrinkled cheek.

"They'd be sweeter if…you'd tell Justin…the truth!"

Elizabeth shook her head.

Abigail sighed and tried again. "You *have* to…hear me out. Jus—"

Elizabeth placed her finger on Abigail's lips and stopped her words. "After you've rested, Abigail. Or I leave."

The old woman's eyes closed. She muttered something about a broken vow and then she was breathing softly.

"Sleep well, Abigail." Elizabeth stood looking down at her aged friend praying with all her heart that she would be all right, that she would have a chance to talk with her again. She wanted Abigail to know the truth of all that had happened. She gave a last pat to the counterpane and walked, again, to the window. It was almost dawn. That silent time when the creatures of the night have finished their nocturnal prowlings and scuttled off to their hide-aways to rest, and the creatures of the day have not yet stirred. A time of peace.

But not for her.

The door opened, then closed.

Elizabeth didn't turn. She didn't need to. Her heart, her senses, every fiber of her being told her it was Justin. She could feel him. She listened to his footsteps cross the room and the creak of the chair as it took his weight. She waited. He didn't speak.

Elizabeth's heart ached. She leaned against the casing and let the warm summer night air flow over her as her thoughts chased themselves around and around in her mind seeking a solution to her impossible situation. She thought about being branded an adulteress and murderer.

About going to jail. That thought had once terrified her; now, she felt nothing. She was too weary. Too benumbed by exhaustion. Jail would be better than this debilitating, humiliating, *agonizing* experience of living with a man that hated her. A man she loved.

Birds began to sing softly, their first gentle twitterings turning into full-throated songs as the first rosy streaks of a new day spread themselves in ever widening splendor across the brightening sky. There was no answering song in Elizabeth's heart. There was only the leaden weight of hopeless despair. She glanced over her shoulder at Justin. He was asleep. His head rested against the wing of the chair, his features relaxed in slumber. She sank to her knees, rested her folded hands on the sill, and lifted her dry, burning eyes to the rose-colored sky.

"Father God, I have tried my best to do what is right— but everything has turned out all wrong. I'm weary. I have no strength left—and no answer." Tears of exhaustion and helplessness slid down Elizabeth's cheeks and made dark spots of dampness on her lavender gown. "I don't know what to do, Father, and so I yield myself to Thee. Do whatever seems good to Thee, but, Father, please—whatever happens to me—make Justin, and Sarah and little Mary, happy. Amen."

For several minutes Elizabeth knelt beneath the window with her head resting on her folded hands. The gentle morning breeze caressed her hair. It was so tempting to sink into the oblivion of sleep, but there was something she had to do. She forced her eyes open, lifted her hand to brush back the wayward curls on her forehead, then rose to her feet and walked toward the door. Her movements were heavy and cumbersome. She moved so sluggishly there might already be fetters about her ankles.

She stepped into the hall and headed for the bridal chamber, stumbling in her weariness, trying with her fumbling fingers to undo the bodice of her gown. A good wash would take away some of the exhaustion, and then she would visit Sarah and Mary. Her throat constricted. These few stolen minutes might be the last opportunity she would ever have to see them.

Chapter Twenty-Seven

✤

There was no sound from within. The children were still asleep. Elizabeth swallowed her disappointment, opened the door to the nursery and stepped into the playroom. She couldn't wait for them to awaken—she would have to be satisfied with a last look and a goodbye kiss. She moved silently to Sarah's bedroom, tiptoed to her bed and knelt down to study the toddler, memorizing the way she looked so that she could carry the picture in her heart and mind forever. Her heart swelled. She pressed her lips together to hold back the sobs rising in her throat and reached out to touch a wisp of brown hair that lay like silk thread on the pillow.

Sarah stirred. She blinked her round, brown eyes once, twice, then focused them sleepily on Elizabeth. "Mama?"

"Yes, darling." Elizabeth rose to kiss the toddler's soft, warm cheek.

"Mama!" Sarah threw the rag doll she was clutching to the floor and flung her arms around Elizabeth's neck, hugging tightly. Knifelike pain slashed through Elizabeth's chest, lacerating her heart. How could she bear to be parted from this child? She lifted the sleep-warmed toddler into her arms, kissed her hair and buried her face in the sweet-smelling softness to hide her tears.

"I phought you went away with the bad mans, Mama!" Sarah sobbed the words and tightened her grip around Elizabeth's neck. "I phought you went away like my ofver mama, and got deaded!"

"Sarah!" Elizabeth sank down on the edge of the bed, tightened her arms about Sarah's small, trembling body and rocked back and forth shattered by a new pain—the pain of a mother that could not protect her child from hurt. What would Sarah think when she was jailed? How would it affect her when she went away and didn't return? *Oh, God, give me wisdom to help her!*

"Sarah? Sarah, darling—listen to Mama." Elizabeth stroked the toddler's hair and rocked her until she quieted. "You must not be frightened if...if I have to go away. Sometimes people do. Sometimes something happens and they...they have to leave. Even if they don't want to. Like your mama." Elizabeth ignored the pain that was ripping her apart and searched for a way to make the toddler understand. "Your mama got sick, Sarah. Very, very sick. And when that happens—sometimes people die. They—they go away. And though I'm not ill, I—"

Sarah released her grip on Elizabeth's neck and sat up straight and tall on her lap to face her. She lifted her little pointed chin in an astonishingly accurate imitation of Elizabeth's own gesture and shook her head from side to side. Her small little mouth was set in a determined line. "Mama went away with the bad mans. And then she got deaded."

Elizabeth stared at the toddler. "Sarah, what—"

"Well! So you *are* awake, Miss Sarah. I thought I heard you."

"Nanny, Mama's here!" Sarah twisted about on Elizabeth's lap and beamed happily up at her nurse. "She waketed me up."

"So I see. Didn't I tell you last night your mama would be coming back soon? All that fussing and carrying on over nothing." Anna Hammerfield walked over to the bed and gently tapped the end of Sarah's tiny nose. "A waste of time—that's what it was—a waste of time." She shifted her gaze to Elizabeth and smiled. "Good morning, madam." She crossed to the window and pulled back the curtains to let the early morning sun stream in. "It's going to be a lovely day."

Her warmth was a soothing salve to Elizabeth's bruised soul. At least she would know—wherever she was—that the children had a good nanny caring for them. "Good morning, Mrs. Hammerfield. I—"

"Can we go phwing, Nanny?" Sarah gave Elizabeth a quick hug and slid off her lap to run and look out the window.

"I might consider it…if you go tell your mama you're sorry for interrupting her." The nurse winked at Elizabeth. "A child with poor manners needn't expect any favors from me."

Sarah stared at her nurse, then turned and ran to Elizabeth. "I'm sorry for 'ruptin' you, Mama." She dropped a polite curtsy, placed her small hands on Elizabeth's knees and peered up at her. "Want to come phwing wiff me?"

"Oh, Sarah..." Elizabeth's heart broke. She brushed her finger lovingly down the child's soft, silky cheek, fighting for composure. "I'd love to come swing with you, darling, but I—I can't. I— Aunt Abigail is not feeling well, and I must sit with her."

The little girl's face clouded. "Will she get deaded, Mama?"

Elizabeth stared at the solemn little face. "I don't know, Sarah. I hope not." She took the child's small hands in hers. "But if she does, we mustn't be sad for her, for she will go to heaven to live with Jesus. And when we go to heaven we will see her again."

Sarah studied Elizabeth's face, thinking that over. Finally, she nodded. "All wight, Mama." Her voice was solemn. "I won't be sad. I'll go phwing."

"Aunt Abigail would like that, darling." Elizabeth pulled the child close for another moment, then she cleared the huskiness from her voice and smiled brightly for Sarah's sake. "Now, you get washed up and ready for breakfast, while I go peek in on Mary. I want to see her for a moment before I return to Aunt Abigail."

"All wight, Mama." Sarah skipped over to her nanny, then turned and looked back at Elizabeth. "Will you come wead me a stowy today, Mama?"

"I'll try, Sarah. But I can't promise." Elizabeth blinked away the tears that burned her eyes. "Anna, if I'm unable to return—"

"I'll explain to Sarah, madam."

"Thank you." Elizabeth turned away from the nurse's

kind, but curious gaze and started for the baby's room. She didn't want Sarah to see her cry and tears were threatening to overflow at any moment.

"Will the bad mans come again, Mama?"

Elizabeth froze. Sudden, sickening terror gripped her. She hadn't thought— So much had happened, so quickly, she hadn't even considered the possibility of Reginald's returning. Where was he? *Would* he come after her again? Would he carry out his threats to kill Justin and Sarah because she had run away from him? *Where was Reginald Burton-Smythe?* The words seared into her brain like redhot coals. She turned and opened her mouth to answer Sarah, but no sound came. She couldn't speak.

Anna Hammerfield glanced at her, then leaned down and lifted her charge into her arms. "Such a one you are for asking silly questions, Miss Sarah. If there *was* a bad man— and mind you I'm not saying there was—" she carried the little girl across the room and sat her on a stool next to the washstand "—it wouldn't matter. Your papa is home now." She lifted warm water from the hearth, poured it into the large basin and began to wash the toddler's face. "And your papa will not let any bad man in his house." She put a suspenseful tone in her voice, hunched her shoulders and peered around the room. "And if one should *sneak* in—" Sarah's eyes widened and she squirmed on the stool "—then Mr. Buffy will *bite his ears off!*" Anna Hammerfield laughed and plucked at Sarah's ears with the warm, wet cloth.

Sarah squealed, and giggled and drew her shoulders up to protect her ears. Mister Buffy, responding to his name, jumped from his basket in the corner and ran in circles around the stool, barking and jumping up to lick Sarah's toes.

Elizabeth threw the nanny a look of gratitude and rushed from the room.

"Jeanne!"

The old woman's head craned around at Elizabeth's urgent whisper. She frowned when Elizabeth crooked her finger and beckoned her to the door, then set aside the petticoat she was mending, rose to her feet and moved slowly across the room on her stiff, arthritic legs.

"Yes, mum?"

Elizabeth motioned her closer to the partially opened door. "I don't want to disturb Miss Abigail, but I must speak with Mr. Randolph. Please ask him to come out into the hallway."

"Mr. Justin isn't here, miss. He went to the library to—" She stared agape as Elizabeth whirled about and ran toward the staircase. "Such goings on!" Jeanne pursed her dry, wrinkled lips in disapproval, shook her head and closed the door.

Elizabeth's legs trembled with exhaustion as she hurried down the stairs. At the bottom she leaned against the newel post for support and paused to catch her breath. "Please, Lord...make Justin...listen...to me." It was all the prayer she had breath for. She placed her hand over the stitch in her side, pushed away from the post and rushed across the entrance hall. Her heart pounded as she neared the library—the thought of Justin's hatred and disgust unnerved her. She stopped beside the open door, tucked her wayward curls behind her ears, fixed her thoughts firmly on Sarah and Mary and stepped into the room. She could face his scorn for them. He was searching through the books that lined the shelves on the far wall. Her steps faltered at sight of him.

"Justin?"

He spun about. Fear leaped into his eyes. "Abigail?" He dropped the book he held and rushed toward the door.

"No! No, Justin. It's not Abigail. I'm sorry. I should have thought—"

He lifted his hand to stop Elizabeth's apology, then raked it through his hair as he blew his breath out in a long sigh. "Thank God! I can't seem to make myself accept the fact that I might lose her." For a moment their gazes met, then Justin turned away. He picked up the book he had dropped and slid it back into place on the shelf, found the volume of poetry he wanted for Abigail and turned to leave.

Elizabeth moved to the center of the doorway.

His brows knit together. "Was there something you wanted?"

Elizabeth blanched at his tone but stood her ground, forcing herself to meet his contemptuous gaze. "Yes. I want to speak with you."

Justin's face tightened. "I don't care to hear anything you have to say, Elizabeth. Go back upstairs to Abigail."

She drew her breath in sharply. His cold, autocratic dismissal bringing an anger surging up in her she didn't know she possessed. She had had enough. She pulled the door closed and fastened her gaze on his. "No." Surprise at her defiance spread across his face. Elizabeth lifted her chin. "I've come to find out where Reginald is, Justin. What, if anything, has happened to him. And I'll not leave until you tell me."

Justin's body stiffened. The muscle along his jaw jumped. "You dare ask *me* about your lover? Under the circumstan—"

"You have misjudged the circumstances! And me. However, I have come to neither explain, nor defend myself, since you have made it abundantly clear that you wish no explanation." Elizabeth drew a deep breath to calm herself, then rushed on. He looked ready to throw her bodily from the room.

"In spite of what you think of me, Justin. In spite of what you *believe* to be true. I am asking you to tell me what you know of Reginald's whereabouts. Not for my sake—" she hurled the words at him as he drew breath to respond "—for Sarah's. She is in *danger!*" Elizabeth's voice broke and hot tears stung the back of her eyes but she kept her gaze fastened on his as she waited for his answer.

Justin swept his gaze over her face. Her lips trembled. She lifted her chin. His face tightened. "All right, Elizabeth—for Sarah's sake." He motioned her forward. "Come away from the door, I'll not have the servants eavesdropping. They've grist enough for their gossip mill."

Elizabeth almost fell to the floor with relief. *He would listen! He would know how to keep Sarah safe!* Her legs trembled as she moved forward as Justin had asked. She blinked back tears of thankfulness, stopped in the center of the room to grip the back of a chair for support and looked up at him.

He turned away. "All right, Elizabeth—explain yourself.

Exactly how is Sarah in danger? And what does Burton-Smythe's whereabouts have to do with it?"

Justin's voice was like ice, but Elizabeth was so grateful he was willing to listen to her she didn't care. "He threatened to harm her." Her voice shook so badly she had to stop for a moment. The look in his eyes as he turned back to face her didn't help. "He threatened to kidnap her or—or worse." She couldn't look at his face. She dropped her gaze to her hands, they looked small, white and ineffective against the back of the chair. She pulled air into her lungs—she had to say it. "He also threatened to have you killed." Her voice was a mere whisper.

Justin went rigid. "And why should he do such a thing?"

"To make me go with him."

Dead silence followed her whispered words. Elizabeth forced herself to look up at him. Her knees went weak. She had never seen such cold contempt in anyone's eyes. She dug her fingers into the back of the chair as pain slashed through her.

"He was obviously successful." Justin ignored her gasp, placed the volume of poetry on the table beside him and walked to the fireplace. He leaned back against the mantel and folded his arms across his chest. "If this story is true, why didn't you call for help?"

"Of whom?" Elizabeth took refuge from the pain in anger. "You were out of town and Owen is an old man. He could not have stopped Reginald. And I did not want to see him harmed trying to do so!" She swallowed a sudden lump in her throat. "It would not have helped anyway. Reginald said if I didn't go with him he would return again and again until his vengeance was complete. And then he would take me."

"I see." Justin's voice was thick with sarcasm. "If I understand you correctly, you are saying you were forced to go with Burton-Smythe to protect my family, my staff and myself. Is that it?"

"Yes." Elizabeth's heart tore in two. He didn't believe her.

"Admirable of you I'm sure." Justin gave her a thin, cold smile and crossed one ankle over the other in a pose of complete relaxation. "Why didn't you leave a message?"

Her message! She darted a glance at the Bible on the rosewood table. *Thank heaven he hadn't found it—it would be unbearable!* Elizabeth looked back at him. Her mouth went dry. "There was no opportunity. He never left me alone." For the first time she was not being completely honest with him—and she could tell he knew it. The knowledge of her duplicity was in his eyes. She looked away.

"I see." Justin's voice was absolutely glacial. "A most ingenious story, Elizabeth. One that absolves you of all duplicity, or guilt, in either running off with your lover or plotting my demise. It also furnishes you with the perfect excuse for coming in here and asking me for your lover's whereabouts. You are a very clever woman, Elizabeth— whatever else you might be."

She lifted her head and stared at him, stunned by the way he had twisted her words into something utterly opposite of the truth—and then the shock gave way to outrage at his incredible arrogance. She straightened to her full height and fastened her gaze on his cold, cold eyes. "I have answered your questions, Justin. Now I ask one of you. Are you so anxious to be right in your judgment of my character you would blind yourself to the truth—even if it means harm to your daughter?" She neither expected, nor waited, for an answer. She gathered her long skirts into her hands and walked toward the door.

"Elizabeth?"

She halted, then turned and met his furious gaze.

"Have you been in touch with Burton-Smythe since you have been in this house?"

Her heart filled with hope. Had she shaken his certainty of her guilt?

"No, I have not."

"Then how did he know where to find you?"

She could almost hear the jaws of the trap he had set for her snapping closed. Elizabeth stared at him while her foolish hope died—he would never believe her. Still, for Sarah's sake...for his sake...she had to continue to try. She took a deep breath. "He told me he overheard a conversation at your sister Laina's birthday celebration in which you mentioned my name and the fact that we were married in March. It was enough to bring him searching for me."

Justin's face went slack with surprise. He stared at her a moment, then lowered his brows in a deep scowl. "Either you're telling the truth, Elizabeth—or you're the most damnably clever liar I've ever met! What do you mean 'it was enough'? Why would Burton-Smythe come searching for you?"

His continued skepticism broke the last of Elizabeth's control. She snapped out the answer. "Because we were betrothed and I ran away!"

"*Betrothed!*"

The word was a surprised, outraged roar.

Elizabeth, suddenly realizing what she had blurted out in her anger, gave a startled gasp, whirled around and rushed for the door. She was brought up short by Justin's firm grasp on her arm. He spun her about to face him.

"Where do you think you're going?"

"T-to sit with Abigail—"

His eyes narrowed.

Elizabeth shivered.

Abruptly, he released her arm. "Go sit down, Elizabeth."

She had never seen him so angry—not even when he had accused her of plotting his murder. She walked back to the chair and perched gingerly on the edge of the seat, poised for rapid flight should it prove necessary. Summoning her courage she looked up at him. He was standing in front of the door, his face a perfect picture of controlled fury.

"This has gone far enough. You are not leaving this room until I have the truth, Elizabeth. *All* of it." His voice was quiet. Deadly quiet. "You may begin by telling me about your lover."

"*Do not call him that!*" Exhaustion, worry, fear and frustration all combined to push Elizabeth over the edge. She jumped to her feet and stamped her foot on the floor. "Reginald is *not* my lover. I *loathe* him!"

Justin lifted one dark, well-formed eyebrow in disbelief.

She wanted to rip it from his face.

"You were betrothed to a man you loathe?"

"Yes!"

"I think you had better explain."

He had gone back to his cool, disbelieving tone. Elizabeth glared at him. The man was absolutely maddening! "Very well." With a toss of her head she threw caution to the winds. What difference could the truth make? He hated her anyway. She pulled herself to her full height. "My father is Ezra Landis Frazier." *That* caught him by surprise—*both* of his dark-brown eyebrows had shot skyward.

"Of Frazier and Stoneham in New York?"

His voice was incredulous.

"Yes." Elizabeth felt a moment's satisfaction at his shock—and then a crushing disappointment. How ironic it would be if he gave credence to her story because of her father's position. She had thought better of him. Too agitated to sit, she walked around to the back of the chair and turned to face him. She felt safer with a solid piece of furniture between them.

"Obviously, you know of my father. And if you do, then you know that he is a wealthy man. However, he is not satisfied with his present riches. For some time now he has desired a particularly valuable waterfront property located beside his present warehouse. That property is owned by Reginald Burton-Smythe."

Justin crossed his arms over his broad chest, fastened a cynical gaze on her, and leaned back against the door to listen.

She clenched her hands. She wanted to shake him. Anger at his attitude drove her into her story. "Father offered, time and again, to purchase the property, but Reginald refused. Father became obsessed. He hatched plot after plot, devised scheme after scheme to acquire that waterfront acreage—all to no avail." She drew a deep breath and looked full into Justin's eyes. "And then one night Father brought Reginald home and introduced him to me."

Elizabeth faltered. Her anger dissolved in the flood of painful memories her words released. She looked down at the chair, then back up at Justin. Telling him was going to be harder than she thought.

"Go on."

His eyes were narrowed. He was watching her closely. Elizabeth looked away. Her face suddenly felt stiff and unnatural. She stared down at her hands to avoid Justin's suspicious gaze. "Reginald became a frequent guest at our house...and then my suitor, though I begged Father to refuse his request to court me. I— There was something about him..." Her throat convulsed and her stomach began to churn. Elizabeth swallowed hard, moistened her dry lips with the tip of her tongue and lifted her gaze to Justin's face. "On my eighteenth birthday, he asked for my hand in marriage. I refused."

Justin frowned. There was something in her eyes...

Elizabeth looked away. "Father was incensed, of course. He ordered me to marry Reginald and I told him I wouldn't. I...couldn't." She swallowed again and placed her hand over her roiling stomach. "The following evening, Father summoned me to his study. When I entered the room I found Reginald waiting there for me. He, again, asked for my hand, and when I refused, he—he said I would have no choice." Elizabeth shuddered. She wrapped her arms around her waist in an unconscious gesture of protection and her voice dropped to a whisper. "He said he would soil me so that no decent man would have me."

Justin sucked his breath in sharply. The sound drew Elizabeth's gaze. His stomach contracted. She looked as if she was about to shatter. Suddenly nothing mattered but that she be all right. He pushed away from the door and started toward her. She looked down at her hands. "Elizabeth, you needn't—"

"He asked me again to marry him—I refused. He struck me...."

Justin stopped. She was trembling violently and staring into the distance and her voice had taken on a flat, faraway quality that frightened him. He was afraid to go to her— afraid his touch would make her swoon. Uncertain of what to do, he stood and watched helplessly as she lifted her hand and touched her cheek—the one that had been bruised and swollen when they met. Something hot and ugly rose up inside him.

"His blow stunned me and I fell to the floor. When I came to, he was on top of me, tearing at my gown."

She looked up at him then, her eyes filled with fear and horror, and a rage such as he had never known filled Justin. It rose from his stomach into his chest and spread throughout his body. He curled his hands into fists wanting to smash, destroy, hurt something, as she had been hurt. "Elizabeth?" He choked out her name. She looked away.

"My uncle Charles called unexpectedly that night. And when he heard my screams he rushed into Father's study and pulled Reginald off me before—before—" She stopped and drew a deep, shuddering breath.

The relief was so intense, so unexpected, it made Justin weak. He sagged back against the door, surprised to find that he was trembling.

"If it hadn't been for my uncle Charles's unexpected visit, no one would have saved me." Elizabeth focused her gaze on him. "You see, *I* was the price Reginald had placed on the waterfront property and Father had agreed. Father had promised me to him."

The rage came again, black and ugly, the heat of it searing Justin's heart. "What of your mother? Surely your mother tried to help. Surely your mother did not agree?"

Elizabeth swept her lashes down to hide her eyes. "Mother said it would be easier for me if I did not resist Reginald. She said that all men are alike—and that money can make anything bearable."

"Dear heaven, Elizabeth!" Justin's anger exploded. "What sort of people—?" He bit off the rest as her gaze swept back up to his face.

"My parents locked me in my room and ordered the servants to stay away. Father even took my shoes and boots." Elizabeth's lips quivered, tears sprang into her eyes. "They meant to keep me imprisoned until the wedding. They didn't know about the key." Her chin lifted a notch and when she continued her voice was stronger. "It was Miss

Essie's key. She hid it in the hollow base of my pewter candlestick when my parents dismissed her. 'Just in case you should ever need it,' she told me—" Elizabeth's voice broke on a sob. She turned away to hide her tears from him. "I had forgotten about the key. It was when I started to pray that I suddenly remembered it. It gave me hope." She wiped away the tears and turned back to face him—her eyes were unnaturally bright.

"I made a bag out of an old gown, hid it in my wardrobe and waited for morning. When Father left to call on Reginald to make the final arrangements for our wedding, I got the key, unlocked the door, and walked away." She drew a deep breath and expelled it in a long, shaky sigh.

"I was searching for a way out of town when I came to the Haversham Coach House that evening and Judge Braden approached me with your offer. At first I didn't understand—I thought Reginald had set the law on me. But then I realized some man had arranged to buy a wife...and, of course, I accepted." She paused and dropped her gaze to the chair. With one long finger she began to trace the pattern of the tapestry fabric. "I knew that was wrong of me, of course, but I was desperate. All I could think of was that I would be safe from them all. And I was—" Her finger stilled. She went deathly pale. "U-un-t-til y-yester-d-day."

Elizabeth clamped her jaws tightly together to stop her suddenly chattering teeth. She began to shiver uncontrollably. Her eyes widened with fear and the shock of delayed reaction. She lifted her gaze to Justin's face and opened her mouth to ask him for help, but no sound came. She couldn't speak. She couldn't breathe. In panic she lifted her hand toward him—and then the darkness came.

"Elizabeth!"

Justin leaped forward and caught her in his arms as her knees buckled and she slid down the back of the chair toward the floor.

Chapter Twenty-Eight

❖

Elizabeth felt wonderful. Secure in a sense of well-being she had never known. She curved her lips in a small, contented half smile and a soft sigh of pleasure escaped from between their rose-colored fullness as she turned to snuggle more deeply under the covers. Abruptly, the strong warmth that had encased her hand was gone—and along with it the sense of well-being. She came instantly awake. She snapped her eyes open and jerked to a sitting position, then, just as quickly, threw herself back down on the pillows and tugged the covers up under her chin. *Justin!* Her cheeks warmed. She had been dreaming about him. He had been holding her hand.

"Hello."

The smile that accompanied the softly spoken word brought fresh heat into Elizabeth's cheeks. Had she talked aloud in her sleep? Perhaps spoken his name or—or worse? She closed her eyes in an agony of embarrassment and when she opened them again, he was still smiling. She looked away. She glanced across the room to the darkness outside the window and then dropped her gaze to the lounge beside it. It was covered with a rumpled blanket and a bed pillow lay at its head. She frowned. Why was someone sleeping on her chaise? For that matter, why was Justin sitting beside her bed? Her sleep-befuddled mind started to clear, and, suddenly uneasy, she looked back at him.

"Is something wrong? Am I ill?"

"You don't remember?"

"Nooo..." Elizabeth's stomach began to churn.

"You swooned." Justin's voice was gentle. "In the library, while we were talking."

"I *swooned?*" Elizabeth stared up at him. "But I'm not afrai— I mean, I— Oh." Memory came rushing back and she jerked upright. "Abigail!"

"Abigail is fine." He grinned. "More than fine actually. She is trying to run the entire household from her bed."

"*Sarah?*" Sudden panic gripped Elizabeth. "Is Sarah—?"

Justin lifted a hand to halt her rush of words. "Everyone is fine—and safe. And they will stay safe. It's you I'm concerned about." His voice was warm. "How are you feeling?"

"Me?" Elizabeth's voice squeaked. "I'm all right." She watched Justin warily. He had been very angry with her. Why was he being so pleasant? "A little confused perhaps."

He nodded. "Dr. Allen said you might be."

"Dr. Allen?"

"Yes. I had him look in on you when he visited Abigail. I hope you don't mind?"

"No, I don't—" Elizabeth stopped and stared at him. "When he came to visit Abigail? How long have I been here?"

Justin pulled his gold watch from his pocket and glanced at it. "Sixteen hours."

"Sixteen hours!"

He nodded affirmation, then quickly offered reassurance. "It's no cause for concern. Dr. Allen assures me such an occurrence is not unusual in cases of extreme stress and anxiety."

"Extreme— Oh." Her stomach knotted. With a deliberate effort Elizabeth pushed the dark memories away, and hoped, fervently, that he would not pursue their discussion of Reginald and all that had happened to her. To avoid his gaze she glanced back over at the lounge.

"Has Trudy been sleeping here?"

Justin shook his head. "No. I have. The groom's room was not close enough. I wanted to be here if you needed me."

Elizabeth jerked her gaze to his face.

He smiled. "Nightmares and such." He nodded toward the bedside table. "There is a tray with biscuits, cheese and fruit if you are hungry. Or, if you would prefer, I could ring and have some hot tea or broth prepared."

"No, thank you." Elizabeth's stomach was churning with nerves. "Perhaps a little water."

She leaned back against the headboard, gripped the coverlet securely under her chin and watched Justin as he rose and poured water into a glass. What was his real reason for spending the night in her room? And why was he staying with her now that she was awake? The troubling thought made her stomach heave. She cast about for something to distract and calm her. She looked down at Justin's hands, at his long, strong fingers, at the few crisp, dark hairs that curled across their backs. It seemed impossible that only a few weeks ago the sight of his hands had so frightened her she had swooned, and now she wanted nothing more than to press her cheek against them. Her face burned at the thought and she carefully avoided touching his hand when he held the glass out to her.

"Thank you."

Justin nodded and fastened his intense blue gaze upon her. "You're flushed." He lifted his hand toward her forehead, then quickly dropped it back down to his side. "Have you a fever?"

Elizabeth's cheeks grew warmer. She shook her head and took a sip of the cool liquid in the glass, unable to speak, unable even to swallow. It felt as if her heart was in her throat. She forced the liquid down and handed the glass back to him, withdrawing her hand quickly when his fingers brushed against hers. Small circles of heat from his fingertips burned her flesh. Awed by the strange feeling, she laid her hand on her lap and stared down at it as if it belonged to someone else.

"Elizabeth?"

She didn't dare look up at him. She was afraid of what he would read in her eyes. She stared at her hand. "Yes?"

"We need to talk, Elizabeth."

Her breath caught painfully in her throat. So he was going to pursue their conversation about Reginald—or perhaps he had decided to tell her what her fate was to be. Her heart pounded. She swallowed hard, glanced up at him and nodded.

Justin sucked in his breath as their gazes met. How he longed to take her in his arms and hold her until that fear left her eyes! He spun on his heel and walked away from the bed putting distance between himself and temptation. "Do you feel strong enough to talk?" His voice was brusque. There was a pause, during which he heard nothing but the heavy thudding of his own heart. He closed his eyes and clenched his hands in frustration. *Please, God, give me strength.*

"Yes. I'm strong enough."

Her voice sounded small and frightened. Justin clamped his teeth together so tightly the muscle in his jaw jumped. How could he ever break through her fear of him? Especially after last night. *Oh, God, don't make me eat of the fruit of my foolishness! Have mercy on me. For all our sakes.* He took a deep breath and turned around to face her.

"I'm tired of this charade, Elizabeth." He was amazed that his voice sounded calm and cool when his every nerve was taut with tension. "I know that I'm the one that instigated it. But I can no longer endure it. It simply cannot continue."

Elizabeth blanched. So there it was. He hadn't believed her and now her worst fear was coming true. He was going to put her out—rid himself of her and the trouble she caused him once and for all. Pain slashed through her, stealing her breath. She stiffened her back and lifted her gaze to his denying pain the victory. At least she could leave with her pride intact. "As you wish." Her lips trembled in spite of her best efforts to control them.

Justin frowned. She was scared to death! He shouldn't have blurted out the truth like that. He stalked over to the door of her dressing room, wrenched it open and emerged a moment later carrying the blue silk dressing gown he had given her. He tossed it onto the bed. "Put that on, Elizabeth." Self-disgust made his voice gruff. "We can't discuss this matter with you hiding behind the covers." He turned his back and went to look out the window to give her privacy.

Elizabeth slid from the bed and lifted the dressing gown into her shaking hands. She slipped her arms into the sleeves and pulled the sash about her tiny waist, fumbling to tie it in place as her vision blurred. She swallowed back a sob, blinked her eyes and drew a deep breath of air into her lungs. She didn't dare let the tears come—not now. She knew once they started they would go on forever.

Justin...Sarah...Mary... To never see them again! To never hear them laugh, or— Pain slashed through her again. Elizabeth gasped and reached out to grasp the carved post at the corner of the bed for support. Somehow, some way, she must get through these next few minutes without Justin learning the truth. She fixed her mind on that thought and lifted her gaze to him. For a long moment she stood memorizing the way he looked with the candlelight gleaming on his dark hair and highlighting his broad shoulders. He lifted a hand and combed it through his hair as she watched, and her chest tightened so painfully at the familiar gesture she almost cried out. At last, she straightened her back, squared her shoulders and lifted her chin.

At least no one could take away her memories. She would carry them in her heart no matter where she might go. Even if it was jail. The thought terrified her anew, but she gathered her courage. There was no point in prolonging the agony.

"I'm ready now."

Justin turned around. The dark-blue silk dressing gown draped softly over Elizabeth's slender body. Tension pulsed through him. He started forward, then stopped and clasped his hands behind his back to keep from reaching for her. "I owe you an apology, Elizabeth." The words came out more abruptly than he had intended. He frowned. "More than an apology actually. I owe you an explanation." He watched surprise leap into her beautiful eyes, followed by an expression of wariness that made his heart sink. She didn't trust him. Not that she had any reason to—not after the way he had treated her.

"You asked me a question yesterday, Elizabeth." He softened his voice and locked his gaze on hers. "You asked me if I was so anxious to be right in my judgment of your character that I would blind myself to the truth. The answer is yes. I've been doing exactly that since the day we met. And I've been wrong...I've been a fool." His eyes made a silent plea for her understanding. "I've no excuse for that, Elizabeth. There is no excuse for that. But there is a reason. I'd like to explain by telling you my story. Will you listen?"

Elizabeth stared at him, too astonished by his change in attitude and demeanor toward her to even answer. Had he believed her after all? Her knees gave way and she plopped down on the edge of the bed, her mind whirling. What did this mean? Would he let her stay? She opened her mouth to ask, then closed it. If he said no her hope would be gone.

"I'll take your silence for assent." Justin's voice trembled. He pivoted away from her and gripped the window frame so hard his hands cramped. "I've told you a little about my past, Elizabeth—but there's much you do not know." He tried to relax but found it impossible. These next few minutes were too important—he *had* to make her understand. He expelled his held breath and plunged into his story.

"When I was a young, callow and carefree youth, Rebecca Sterns was the belle of Philadelphia. Every young swain in town was running after her—including me." He grimaced at the memory. "When she seemed to prefer my company to the others, I worked up enough courage to ask for her hand in marriage. To my amazement, her father approved and Rebecca accepted." Justin lowered his hands to his sides and leaned one broad shoulder against the window casing to stare out into the night.

"Our families gave the usual parties and balls honoring us of course, but then, only a few weeks before the wedding was to take place, the bottom suddenly fell out of my father's shipping business. The details aren't important. It's enough to know that we traced the problem to his factor in London. We discovered he had been systematically stealing my father's profits for years. Anyway, the whole thing had come to a head and the business itself was about to collapse. My father made plans to leave for England at once to set things aright. Unfortunately, the whole episode proved too much for him. He had a seizure which incapacitated him."

Elizabeth made a soft sound of sympathy. Justin glanced over his shoulder and smiled at her. "Thank you for caring." He drew a not too steady breath and turned back to stare out the window. It was easier to concentrate on his story that way.

"Rebecca was most understanding, of course. When I explained the situation to her she agreed I should go to London in my father's stead. She pledged her undying love and fidelity and promised that she and her family would carry on with the wedding preparations and we would marry the very week I returned. So, with my heart full, and my hopes high, I took ship for London. The crossing was uneventful. When I arrived, I hurriedly secured a new factor, arranged to pay off the debts accrued by the old one, smoothed ruffled feathers where necessary and took the first available ship for home—the *Barbara*. On the way we were caught in the hurricane I told you about, with its accompanying complications, but, eventually, we made port."

Justin straightened. His voice hardened. "Philadelphia had never looked more beautiful to me. Eager to see my promised bride I rushed straight to the Sterns's home. It was then I discovered everything Rebecca had told me was a lie. She had decided my inheritance was in jeopardy and she could do better financially. So, after seeing me off to London, she turned her attention and her charms on an elderly count who was visiting Philadelphia at the time of my departure. While I was in London working to secure our future, Rebecca was busy being courted by the widowed, somewhat infirm count. His title, vast English estates, and very large purse made him more attractive to Rebecca than a young man struggling to maintain a family shipping business that was in danger of failing. She married him. They sailed for England the week before my return. I never saw her again."

"And just as well!"

"You're right of course—though I didn't feel that way at the time. I felt hurt, betrayed and angry." Justin's voice was full of tension. He turned from the window to face Elizabeth and his heart leaped with hope. She was on her feet, her hands were clenched and her lovely blue eyes were flashing fire. She was the very picture of indignation. Surely, she would not be so angry on his behalf if she did not care for him at least a little! He turned away to hide the smile he could not stop, lowered his head, clasped his hands behind his back and began to pace as he picked up the thread of his story.

"My father had never recovered fully from the seizure, Laina was already married to Stanford Brighton and living in New York, so I—having been soured on romantic relationships by my experience with Rebecca—threw all of my energy into rebuilding the shipping line, or what was left of it." The loneliness he had felt then crept into Justin's voice. He stopped in front of the fireplace, lifted a piece of sculpture off the mantel and turned it over and over in his hands as he continued.

"I worked hard, put in long hours and took a few risks.

When father died, and the war came, I took a few more. I was fortunate. Eventually I paid off the debts and profits began to accumulate. I made a few new investments and bought new, faster ships to add to the line. Everything I touched prospered. But I didn't have a home—at least, not the kind I wanted."

He put the sculpture back, folded his arms across his broad chest, leaned back against the mantel and swept the room with his gaze. "So, I had this house built—complete with bridal chamber and a fanlight above the front door that shouted to the world that I had hope again. Hope for a family...a home...love. And then I met Margaret." Justin shoved away from the mantel and pulled his gaze back to fasten on Elizabeth's.

"She swooned at my feet in the middle of Chestnut Street. That was our introduction. From the very first it seemed I had found all I had ever wanted. She was attractive, sweet, loving, helpless...." He drew a deep breath and focused his gaze on the opposite wall. "When she told me her husband had been killed—that she had a small child and was carrying another, she seemed so pathetically brave and noble I asked her to be my wife."

Elizabeth felt the color drain from her face. She stepped to the chair Justin had been sitting in and stood behind it with her hands clutching the back rail. She did not want to hear about Justin's love for his first wife. She tried her best to shut out his voice by concentrating on the intricate stitches of the beautifully woven fabric covering the seat.

"Because of the situation there was no wedding trip, of course." Justin glanced at Elizabeth's pale, tense face and allowed himself another tiny measure of hope. "I brought Margaret home to these rooms—and out of consideration for her delicate condition remained in mine."

Elizabeth winced. "Justin, please—"

"I'm almost finished, Elizabeth." He turned and gripped the mantel with both hands. "I gave Margaret whatever she desired, whatever she asked for—jewelry, clothes, money." He paused. The muscle along his jaw twitched with remembered anger. He pushed himself away and walked over to stare out the window again. "We went on that way until Mary's birth. A few weeks after that stressful event, I made a business trip to New York. I had expected to be gone several days but I finished my business early, and, eager to be with my new family, I hurried home. Margaret was gone when I arrived. Her lover—Sarah and Mary's father—had escaped jail and come for her."

He heard Elizabeth's startled gasp and turned around to look at her. She was staring at him with a mixture of shock, disbelief and horror. "How terrible for you!" Her eyes widened. "And how...how uncanny. No wonder you thought that I—"

Justin nodded. The relief made him feel light-headed. She understood! Or at least she recognized the similarities. It was a start.

"What did you do?"

Her voice was a mere whisper.

"I went after them." He lifted his hand and rubbed at the tense muscles in the back of his neck. "Margaret knew where I kept money, jewelry and other valuables. They took it all and used my carriage to make their escape. The only thing they left behind was their children." He heard the bitterness creeping into his voice but made no effort to hide it. He had carried it inside for too long—it was time to be rid of it.

"Eventually, I found them on a little traveled path outside of town. They had missed a curve and gone over an embankment." His mind filled with the remembered carnage of the scene—the maimed horse he had to destroy, the broken body of his wife's lover pinned beneath the wrecked carriage with a shard of glass from the broken lamp protruding from his throat, and Margaret herself lying hurt and unconscious in the dirt and blood.

"Her lover died instantly. His neck was...broken." Justin pushed open the casement and took a deep breath of the soft, night air. "Margaret was alive but badly hurt. I brought her back here, to this room, and sent for the doctor. There was nothing he could do. It was only a matter of time."

Mama went away with the bad mans, and then got deaded. Sarah had been right. Elizabeth's eyes filled with tears for the betrayed man and the frightened, abandoned child.

"Margaret regained consciousness just before she died." Justin drew a ragged breath and turned back to look at Elizabeth. "It was then she told me what a fool I was. How easy it had been for her to trick me into believing she loved me—that all along she had only wanted a place of comfort to stay in until her lover came for her. A place to leave their children. She laughed at me—ridiculed what she called my noble, romantic love. With her last breath she killed the man I was before I met her. She died mocking me and I vowed I would never trust, never *love*, another woman as long as I lived. I was sick of lies...sick of duplicity...and sick of greed."

The bitterness poured out of Justin along with his words. For the first time he saw how sad a person Margaret had been and forgave her. The burden of anger he had carried for so long disappeared—he was free. He turned, took another deep breath of the soft, evening air, pulled the window closed and faced Elizabeth again.

"Of course, it wasn't long before I realized I needed someone to run my home and care for the children Margaret had left behind. I also needed someone to serve as a barrier to all the scheming women that wanted my money and didn't care what they had to do to get it. I needed a relationship that was safe."

"The marriage of convenience."

"Yes. The marriage of convenience. My *safe* relationship." Justin's heart pounded as he moved forward until he was inches from the chair that stood between them. "That's why you entered into the agreement isn't it, Elizabeth? So that you would be safe."

She dropped her gaze to her hands. "Yes."

"And because you didn't believe in love? Isn't that what you told me that day in the library?" His deep voice trembled as he laid out the truth between them. "Didn't you say you didn't believe in love between a man and woman— between a husband and wife?"

Sorrow and grief for all they would never have in life closed her throat. She nodded.

"And do you still believe that, Elizabeth?"

His voice...there was something... Elizabeth lifted her head. There, resting on Justin's upturned palm, was her grandmother's brooch. The strength left her body. She dug her fingers into the back of the chair for support. She had hoped—

"I know how much you enjoy reading my grandmother's Bible, Elizabeth, so I went to the library to bring it upstairs for you. I found the brooch tucked between the pages of the book of Ruth." His hand shook. "You were in the library when Burton-Smythe came, weren't you?"

Her heart pounded. She couldn't face him. She closed her eyes and nodded.

"And you left the brooch as a message to me."

So he *had* understood. Tears squeezed from under Elizabeth's lashes. She was to have nothing left—not even her pride. She wiped the tears away and straightened her shoulders. "Yes. Reginald was watching me so closely I had no opportunity to speak to anyone, or to write a note." She reached out and touched the betraying brooch with a trembling finger. "This was the only message I could leave you. I wasn't certain you would remember the story of it and understand, but...I had to try. I—I couldn't bear the thought that—that you would never know that—that—" A sob caught in her throat. She buried her face in her hands.

Joy, swift and powerful, flooded Justin's soul. He dropped the brooch into his waistcoat pocket, pulled out the emerald-and-gold ring she had returned to him and gently lowered her left hand from her face. It trembled as he pressed his lips to it. "I've a confession to make, Elizabeth...I love you." Her head jerked up and he took her astounded gaze captive with his own. "I've fought it with everything I had in me, but I've loved you from the beginning—and I want to love you forever." His hand shook as he slid the ring on her finger, turned her hand over, kissed her palm, then trailed his lips across the soft mound at the base of her thumb and pressed their heat to her narrow wrist. "I don't want a safe marriage of convenience, Elizabeth—I want you in my arms." His voice was ragged with desire. Justin cleared his throat, released her hand and stepped back before he lost control.

"I know you are frightened of me—of...of intimate love, Elizabeth. And I understand your fear, now. I understand, and I promise I will do my very best to be patient in my love for you. But, oh, I need you so, Elizabeth!" He held his breath. "Will you do me the honor of being my wife?"

For one frightful moment, Elizabeth thought she was going to die from her happiness. Her heart raced. Her pulse thudded. Her lungs forgot how to breathe—and then the tears came and the pressure in her chest released. She blinked the tears away and gave Justin a smile that completely destroyed his hard-won self-control. "Yes—oh, yes, Justin! I love you. I love you so much! And you don't have to be patient with me. Not now...not ever! I'm not afraid of your love."

The blue silk dressing gown whispered softly as Elizabeth Shannon Randolph moved around the chair and stepped joyfully into the safe, loving circle of her husband's strong, welcoming arms.

Epilogue

✧

"It's all clear, sir." Owen smiled. "The lady of the house is upstairs preparing for the party."

Justin grinned, stepped through the door the butler pulled open for him and swung the large package he was hiding behind himself around to the front. He grasped it firmly in both hands, headed for the staircase and took the steps two at a time. The upstairs hall was empty. He hurried to the bridal chamber, pressed his ear against the door and listened.

Silence.

Justin smiled and quietly opened the door far enough to peek in. There was no one in sight. He pushed the door wide, stepped into their bedroom and nodded with satisfaction at the muted voices that came from Elizabeth's dressing room. Judging from the chatter they would be busy for quite a while. He closed the door, tiptoed to the fireplace, leaned the package against the wall and reached up to remove the picture that hung above the mantel.

"Is the pwesent for me, Papa?"

Justin almost dropped the picture he held in his hands. He spun about and immediately spotted Sarah sitting on the floor beside their bed. Elizabeth's open jewelry box was on her lap and she was looking up at him with an expectant smile on her face. Mr. Buffy sat beside her, as always. His great size dwarfed the child. He cocked his head to one side and looked at Justin.

Justin grinned and laid his finger across his lips cautioning Sarah to silence. He walked quietly across the room, propped the picture he held against the bed and squatted down in front of her. "The present is a surprise for Mama."

Sarah giggled at his exaggerated whisper.

Justin winked and reached into his pocket. "I brought *this* for you." He pulled out a licorice whip.

The toddler smiled. "Thank you, Papa." She bit off an end and held it out to Mr. Buffy who sniffed it, licked it, then lay down and crossed one huge paw over the other to make a resting place for his muzzle. Sarah popped the piece of licorice into her mouth.

Justin's dark-brown eyebrows lifted in surprise. Elizabeth must not know *that* was going on. He looked down at his small daughter and chuckled inwardly. She was absolutely dripping with jewelry! He reached out and touched the strand of pearls that dangled down from the pink bow on top of her head over one bright, shining brown eye. "You look very elegant, Miss Sarah. But I'm a little surprised to see you in such finery. What are you doing?"

The little girl pulled the licorice stick from her mouth leaving a dark circle around her lips. "I'm dwessing for Mama's party."

"Ah! I see. And does Mama know about this?"

Sarah shook her head. The chewed licorice made a black mark on her soft, rosy cheek as she placed a tiny finger against her lips. "It's a secret."

"Hmm. Well, this is a problem." Justin frowned and rubbed his chin thoughtfully. "I didn't know you would be attending our party tonight. I planned a surprise party for you and Mister Buffy upstairs, with cookies and cake—and a bone." He sighed and watched Sarah out of the corner of his eye as he rose to his feet. "I'll have to tell Cook not to bother. That you will be joining us for dinner and Mr. Buffy will eat in the kitchen as usual."

Sarah popped the last of the licorice into her mouth and scrambled to her feet. Jewelry dropped everywhere. She grabbed hold of Justin's long fingers with her sticky little hand and tugged. "I'll go to my party wiff Mithter Buffy, Papa."

Justin grinned. He removed two necklaces from around the little girl's neck and dropped them into the jewelry box. "I thought you might, Sarah." He laughed and scooped his daughter up into his arms. She placed one little hand on either side of his face and leaned back to look at him.

"Can I have bwown cake, Papa?"

"Indeed you may."

"Oh, goody! I like bwown cake." Sarah threw her arms around Justin's neck and planted a sticky kiss on his cheek.

Justin returned the favor. He rained kisses upon Sarah's face and neck while she giggled and ducked her head trying to protect her ticklish spots from the sudden attack. Spurred on by her laughter, Justin made a growling sound deep in his throat and burrowed his chin into her shoulder. Sarah giggled and squealed and kicked her dangling legs trying to wriggle free of the exquisite torture. The dog barked sharply and began to run in circles around Justin's legs.

"So *this* is where you've gotten to!"

Anna Hammerfield burst through the door from Elizabeth's dressing room and stopped dead in her tracks when she spotted Justin. Her rosy cheeks turned a bright scarlet. "I'm sorry, sir. I didn't know you were—" She stopped and stared in amusement as Justin and Sarah, in perfect imitation of her father, lifted their fingers to their lips and hissed, "Shhh!"

She nodded and pulled the door behind her closed. Her eyes widened in dismay when she turned back and spotted the jewelry on the floor. She scowled in mock severity and advanced into the room shaking her pudgy finger at the big, black dog that now sat at Justin's feet watching her. "I told you to watch Miss Sarah, Mister Buffy! And look at what she's been up to!"

Mr. Buffy pricked his ears, cocked his head to one side and thumped his long, thick tail against the floor.

"Don't you go wagging your tail at me, you big, black brute! I'm immune to your charms." Anna Hammerfield laughed, patted the dog on the shoulder and held out her plump arms for her charge. "I'm sorry, sir. I brought Miss Sarah down to watch her mama get ready for tonight's festivities and she slipped away from me in the hubbub."

"No harm done." Justin smiled down at the short, matronly woman and transferred his daughter to her arms. "Though this one needs a good wash."

The nurse glanced at Sarah's face.

"Licorice again, sir?"

Justin grinned. "Don't tell her mother."

"Not a word, sir." The nurse chuckled and looked down at the child in her arms. "And what do you mean by slipping away from me and coming in here to play with your mama's jewelry, Miss Sarah?"

"I was dwessing for Mama's party."

"Dressing for—oh. Oh!" The nurse's gaze shot to Justin.

"She's decided she would rather have her own party upstairs with Mr. Buffy in attendance." Justin's voice was solemn, but he closed one eye in a conspiratorial wink.

Sarah gave a vigorous nod and clasped her nurse's face in her small hands. "I get bwown cake, Nanny! And cookies!"

"Oh you do, do you?" The nurse laughed at the child's excitement. "Well, in that case, we had better go and get you cleaned up, miss." She set her charge down on the floor and took her by the hand. "You can't go to a party with licorice smeared on your face, you know. It's simply not the thing." She looked up at Justin, and shook her head in mock disapproval. "Brown cake and cookies, indeed! It's out-and-out bribery. That's what it is. Bribery!"

Justin grinned, shrugged his broad shoulders and spread his hands wide in silent admission of the crime.

Anna Hammerfield laughed and walked to the door with Sarah skipping along happily at her side. "There'll be no cake for you after this episode, Mr. Buffy." She held the door open for Sarah and the big black dog who padded softly after his small mistress. "You get a dry, old bone."

Mr. Buffy wagged his tail and exited the room.

Justin grinned and knelt to pick up the jewelry on the floor as the door closed behind the small entourage. What a change in Sarah. In *all* of them. They were a real family now. He lifted his gaze to the package he had left leaning against the fireplace, dropped the jewelry he held into the box and walked across the room. His strong, nimble fingers made short work of the knotted string and crisp brown paper that covered it.

"Oh, you do look lovely, mum!"

"Thank you, Trudy."

Elizabeth smiled and turned slowly in front of the mirror admiring her new gown of watered silk taffeta. "I do believe Madame Duval has outdone herself this time. I'm sure Justin will be pleased." She lifted her hand and gently touched the blossoms Trudy had placed in her hair. How frightened she had been that first time when she discovered Trudy had filched the flowers from the table arrangement! She laughed softly and dismissed her maid. She wanted a few moments alone to savor her happiness. She did another pirouette out of pure joy, then, catching a glimpse of herself in the mirror, suddenly turned and walked to the connecting bedroom door. There was one thing more she needed. Tonight, of all nights, she must wear her grandmother's brooch.

Elizabeth opened the door and stepped into the bedroom. Her heart gave a little skip of excitement at the sight of her tall, handsome husband standing in the center of the room. A warm rush of love brought tears to her eyes. She lifted the skirt of her new gown in her, suddenly, trembling hands and hurried toward him. She couldn't wait another minute!

Justin pivoted with a guilty start and hurried toward her.

"I didn't know you had returned, Justin." Elizabeth smiled up at him. "You should have sent word. Was your errand successful?"

"Very." He opened his arms. Elizabeth stepped inside their welcoming circle, sighed softly and laid her head against her husband's chest listening contentedly to the beat of the heart that loved her. It was all still a wonder to her. She smiled when his hand gently touched her chin, and eagerly lifted her mouth to meet his. Justin's arms slid around her waist and drew her closer. Elizabeth clung to him. Tears of thankfulness dampened her lashes.

"I love you, Elizabeth." Justin's voice was husky. The scent of his cologne mingled with the fragrance of the flowers that were crushed beneath his cheek as he laid his head against her hair.

"I love you, Justin." Elizabeth hid her face against his broad chest, as always, a little shy at the depth of their response to each other. They stood that way for a moment, each savoring the feel of the other in their arms, and then Elizabeth lifted her head. She smiled and touched his cheek. "Happy Anniversary, darling. Do you like your gift?"

"My gift?" Justin frowned and looked down into her beautiful dark-blue eyes. "What gift?"

Elizabeth smiled, a smile Justin had never seen before.

"The one you're holding in your hands."

He looked down to his hands that circled her tiny waist, then shot his gaze back up to Elizabeth's face. "A baby?"

She nodded and laughed at the stunned look on his face.

"Are you certain?"

"Yes."

She gasped and clutched at Justin's shoulders as he let out a whoop of joy and lifted her into the air. "A baby!" He whirled her around and around, laughing with delight. "We're going to have a *baby*, Elizabeth!" Suddenly, he crushed her to him, then just as quickly relaxed his grip. "Did I hurt you?"

"No." She laughed down at him. "I'm fine."

Justin lowered her gently to the floor, drew her into his arms and held her close. He was trembling.

"Justin?" His name was a soft whisper against the fabric of his shirt.

"Yes?"

"I'm glad you're pleased."

He tightened his arms around her. "I could ask for nothing more, Elizabeth—save that you be all right."

It was the first time Elizabeth had ever heard Justin sound afraid. She leaned her head back and looked up at him. "I've told you, sir, I am neither weak nor sickly." She curved her lips in a saucy smile. "But this time—I *am* with child."

It had the desired result. Justin threw his head back and laughed until tears filled his eyes. He looked down and their gazes met. "Oh, Elizabeth—" their warm breath mingled as he brushed his lips ever so lightly against hers "—what a long way we have come."

She parted her lips and answered his hunger.

When Justin finally lifted his head they were both trembling. "If this continues, madam, we will be very late meeting our guests."

Elizabeth's cheeks flamed.

Justin laughed. "You're a delectable wench, Elizabeth. And your blushes delight me still." He kissed the top of her golden curls and smiled down at her. "Though it cannot compare to yours...would you like to see your gift?"

"Now? Before the party?"

He nodded.

"Yes!" Elizabeth laughed and patted his waistcoat pocket. "Where is it?"

Justin grinned, lifted his hands to her shoulders and gently turned her around.

"There."

Elizabeth's gaze followed the direction of his pointing finger and her laughter died. "Oh, Justin..." She stepped out from beneath her husband's hands and moved to stand looking up at the new painting that hung above the mantel. Her eyes misted as she gazed up at the shaft of sunlight that slanted down through the trees of a forest to highlight two beautiful red roses growing out of a pile of ashes and charred ruins in the foreground of the painting. Tears slid down her cheeks. She lifted her hand and gently touched the roses. "You painted this for me?"

Justin stepped forward, wrapped his arms around his wife and lowered his head to rest his cheek against her soft, golden curls. "I wanted to give you something that would tell you how much I love you—how thankful I am for you." He pulled her closer into his embrace and smiled when she rested her head back against him. "I wanted to give you something that would remind us both, every day for the rest of our lives, that miracles do happen. That God loves us. And that He truly does give *beauty for ashes*."

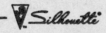

SPECIAL EDITION™

Welcome to Danbury Way— where nothing is as it seems...

Megan Schumacher has managed to maintain a low profile on Danbury Way by keeping the huge success of her graphics business a secret. But when a new client turns out to be a neighbor's sexy ex-husband, rumors of their developing romance quickly start to swirl.

THE RELUCTANT CINDERELLA

by CHRISTINE RIMMER

Available July 2006

Don't miss the first book from the Talk of the Neighborhood miniseries.

The Marian priestesses were destroyed long ago,
but their daughters live on. The time has come
for the heiresses to learn of their legacy, to unite
the pieces of a powerful mosaic and bring light to
a secret their ancestors died to protect.

The Madonna Key

Follow their quests each month.

Lost Calling by Evelyn Vaughn,
July 2006

Haunted Echoes by Cindy Dees,
August 2006

Dark Revelations by Lorna Tedder,
September 2006

Shadow Lines by Carol Stephenson,
October 2006

Hidden Sanctuary by Sharron McClellan,
November 2006

Veiled Legacy by Jenna Mills,
December 2006

Seventh Key by Evelyn Vaughn,
January 2007

REQUEST YOUR FREE BOOKS!

2 FREE INSPIRATIONAL NOVELS
PLUS A
FREE
MYSTERY GIFT

Love Inspired

YES! Please send me 2 FREE Love Inspired® novels and my FREE mystery gift. After receiving them, if I don't wish to receive any more books, I can return the shipping statement marked "cancel." If I don't cancel, I will receive 4 brand-new novels every month and be billed just $3.99 per book in the U.S., or $4.74 per book in Canada, plus 25¢ shipping and handling per book and applicable taxes, if any*. That's a savings of over 20% off the cover price! I understand that accepting the 2 free books and gift places me under no obligation to buy anything. I can always return a shipment and cancel at any time. Even if I never buy another book from Steeple Hill, the two free books and gift are mine to keep forever.

113 IDN D74R 313 IDN D743

Name	(PLEASE PRINT)	
Address		Apt.
City	State/Prov.	Zip/Postal Code

Signature (if under 18, a parent or guardian must sign)

Order online at www.LoveInspiredBooks.com

Or mail to Steeple Hill Reader Service™:

IN U.S.A.	IN CANADA
3010 Walden Ave.	P.O. Box 609
P.O. Box 1867	Fort Erie, Ontario
Buffalo, NY 14240-1867	L2A 5X3

Not valid to current Love Inspired subscribers.

Want to try two free books from another series?

Call 1-800-873-8635 or visit www.morefreebooks.com

* Terms and prices subject to change without notice. NY residents add applicable sales tax. Canadian residents will be charged applicable provincial taxes and GST. This offer is limited to one order per household. All orders subject to approval. Credit or debit balances in a customer's account(s) may be offset by any other outstanding balance owed by or to the customer.

LIREG05

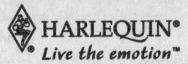

Life.
It could happen to her!

Never Happened just about sums up
Alexis Jackson's life. Independent and
successful, Alexis has concentrated on
building her own business, leaving no
time for love. Now at forty, Alexis
discovers that she still has a few things
to learn about life—that the life unlived
is the one that "Never happened"
and it's her time to make a change....

Never Happened
by Debra Webb

**Hidden in the secrets of antiquity,
lies the unimagined truth...**

Introducing

a brand-new line filled with mystery
and suspense, action and adventure,
and a fascinating look into history.

And it all begins with DESTINY.

In a sealed crypt in
France, where the
terrifying legend of
the beast of Gevaudan
begins to unravel,
Annja Creed discovers
a stunning artifact
that will seal her destiny.

*Available every other
month starting
July 2006, wherever
you buy books.*

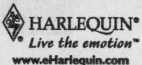